TEA TIME
by Dorothy Howell

TEA TIME

DOROTHY HOWELL

JOVE BOOKS, NEW YORK

TEA TIME

A Jove Book / published by arrangement with
the author

PRINTING HISTORY
Jove edition / September 1995

ISBN: 0-515-11721-8

A JOVE BOOK®
Jove Books are published by The Berkley Publishing Group,
200 Madison Avenue, New York, New York 10016.
JOVE and the "J" design are trademarks
belonging to Jove Publications, Inc.

PRINTED IN THE UNITED STATES OF AMERICA

10 9 8 7 6 5 4 3 2 1

To David, Judy and Stacy—
for your love, understanding and patience.

Also,
To my eighth grade English teacher
who encouraged my first attempt
at creative writing—
Thanks Mr. Donovan,
wherever you are.

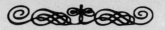

Chapter One

Nevada, 1885

Sin, wickedness, and wanton displays of immorality. Appalling!

Allison Tremaine leaned forward on the buggy seat and stared wide-eyed at the streets of Brighton. What had happened in the time she'd been away?

"I can hardly believe it." She tapped the driver's shoulder. "Cecil, what is going on in this town?"

"What's that, Miss Allison?"

Another thing that had changed since her last visit was that Cecil, her aunt's driver, had aged immeasurably. Stoop-shouldered and hard of hearing, he moved like a turtle in an early frost.

"I said, what has happened to Brighton?" Allison shouted the words at the back of his head.

He lifted one shoulder. "It's changed a mite."

"A mite, indeed. Why, I've never imagined such a sight."

Allison inched back on the seat, shoulders square, chin high, hands folded primly in her lap as they proceeded down Main Street away from the train station. She saw several vacant storefronts along with many of the old businesses and shops she remembered. Taylor's General Store and Melody's Sweet Shop were still there, as well as some new places. But set among them were saloons. More saloons than she'd seen in her life. Allison counted off six of them from where she sat.

And all open for business, though it was barely noon. The plinking and plunking of piano music spilled into the streets along with raucous laughter and the clink of glasses. Men in dusty clothes with guns strapped to their thighs crowded the boardwalks.

Allison tapped Cecil's shoulder again. "Aunt Lydia must be beside herself over what's happened to her town."

"I wouldn't know about that. She don't get into town much anymore." He shook his head slowly. "Fact is, I don't rightly recall the last time Miss Lydia left the house."

Allison's stomach knotted. She'd feared as much.

Gunfire sounded and Allison jumped. Heart pounding, she whirled around searching the crowd. Everyone continued on their way as though nothing had happened.

"Isn't there a sheriff in this town anymore?"

"Don't know, Miss Allison. I don't get into town much either."

In the distance a woman screamed and that too went unnoticed. By everyone but Allison. She cringed and clutched her reticule closer and wished Cecil would hurry the horses.

They continued on and Allison became aware that she was receiving as many curious stares as she was giving. The back of her buggy was crowded with trunks and she was dressed in traveling clothes, a pale gray dress with a froth of pink at her throat and a matching coat. A small hat sat among her dark curls and beside her on the leather seat was a delicate parasol. The ensemble was the height of fashion in New York where she'd purchased it. An eye-catcher here in Brighton as well, it seemed. But this type of attention gave her cause for alarm.

A man in patched trousers and a long, scraggly beard stopped on the boardwalk and openly ogled at her. He elbowed the man beside him, then let out a low whistle and called, "Welcome to Brighton, sister!" Both men howled with laughter.

Stunned, Allison jerked her chin around. How dare he address her in such a fashion. Did no one in this town have manners?

Another voice joined the chorus of welcomes that suddenly sprang from the men standing on the boardwalks. And her fright and indignation turned to anger.

"As soon as I get settled at Aunt Lydia's, I intend to have a good long talk with the sheriff," Allison shouted to Cecil. "The streets aren't safe for decent people."

Just ahead, the swinging doors of the Pleasure Palace Saloon flew open and two men fell headlong into the street in front of the buggy. The horses shied to the right and the buggy lurched sideways sending Allison sprawling across the seat. She grabbed her parasol just before it slipped over the side. Cecil reined in the team.

A small crowd filed out of the Pleasure Palace watching the two men in battered hats and ragged clothes roll around in the street, cursing, grunting, and exchanging punches. The fracas blocked the horses, leaving Allison an unwilling audience as well. This was too much!

Allison jumped from the buggy clutching her parasol. "Who is responsible for this?" she demanded.

The men on the boardwalk turned to her with curious stares. No one spoke.

That angered her further. "I demand to know who is responsible for this!"

They looked at each other and a mumble went through the crowd. They all gazed at Allison again.

"Who is—"

The saloon doors swung open and a man strode out. He stood nearly a head taller than the rest of the crowd, with broad, square shoulders. He wore dark trousers, a crisp white shirt closed at the throat with a string tie, and a brocade vest. His black hair was combed carefully in place.

This was the man she sought. The swagger in his step and the angle of his square jaw told Allison he was the one in charge. The crowd parted as he stepped onto the boardwalk.

Allison's stomach coiled. "Are you the proprietor of this establishment?"

His gaze ran the length of her, in slow, easy measure. "I am," he replied. "Cade Jessup's the name. And who might you be?"

She flushed at his bold gaze and drew herself up to her greatest height. "I am Allison Augusta Tremaine. And, Mr. Jessup, I'll thank you to get these two hoodlums out of my way." She jabbed her parasol toward the men blocking her buggy.

A grin crossed his lips. "Well, Miss Allison Augusta Tremaine, what exactly would you like me to do?"

His amusement angered her. "It's a disgrace that decent citizens cannot pass through a public thoroughfare unmolested. I insist you remove them at once."

The crowd on the boardwalk turned to Cade.

"I can't do that, Miss Tremaine. I had them kicked out in the street and I'm sure not taking them back inside and have them bust up my place."

Allison's back stiffened. "You are responsible for their unseemly display of public drunkenness. Have you not a shred of conscience? Or at the very least, civic pride enough to keep this sort of behavior contained?"

Cade shook his head. "I've got no beef with the two of them. As long as they keep it out of my place, I'm happy."

"Happy! You're happy?" Allison tightened her hold on the parasol. "I find your conduct in this matter greatly wanting, Mr. Jessup, and your character questionable. With businessmen like you in Brighton it's abundantly clear why the town has decayed into a quagmire of sin and immorality."

The playful grin disappeared from his face. "Now hold on—"

"And since you refuse to take responsibility for your actions, I'll see to it myself." Jaw set, parasol in hand, Allison marched to the front of the buggy. The people gathered around Cade gaped as Allison approached the two men fighting in the street.

"You two! Stop that! Stop that at once!" Allison shouted at the men as they struggled on the ground. The fight continued and the watching crowd chuckled. Her cheeks flushed.

A flash of white teeth showed as Cade laughed with the others. "Maybe if you said pretty please?" he suggested.

Her temper exploded. Allison whacked the men with her parasol as they rolled on the ground. "You two are a disgrace to the entire town. Get up!"

She pummeled them until they stopped fighting and looked up at her, dumbfounded.

"I said get up!" She struck them again. "You two are an embarrassment to the good people of this town."

The crowd edged closer, staring in disbelief.

The two men cowered, holding up their arms to protect themselves against Allison's relentless, though weak, blows.

"Get off the streets immediately."

Rupert Frazier, the bigger of the two men, scowled up at her. "Just hold on there one damn minute. . . ."

Cade stepped off the boardwalk. Rupert was known for brawling and was not one to take orders—especially from a woman.

"That's enough now. Break it up." Cade reached for the parasol.

Allison whirled around and swatted him across the chest with it. "You had your chance, Mr. Jessup, but your callous disregard for decency has revealed your true character. Stand aside!"

Allison turned back to the two men sitting in the street. She poked Rupert with the tip of her parasol. "Remove yourself from this public thoroughfare and take your disreputable associate with you."

Rupert's brows drew together and he looked at Otis Collins on the ground beside him. "What did she say?"

He scratched his chin. "Dang if I know."

In a quick motion Cade pulled the parasol from Allison's hand. She gasped and reached for it, but he held it high over his head.

"Come on back inside, boys. Have a drink. It's on the house," Cade told them.

The two clamored to their feet and headed toward the saloon without so much as a look back at Allison.

Her eyes narrowed. "I cannot believe you are rewarding this type of behavior."

He planted his fists on his hips. "I don't know where

you're from, Miss Tremaine, but we do things different here in Brighton."

She gave him her iciest stare. "That, Mr. Jessup, is abundantly clear."

His gaze turned cold. "And you'd do well to remember it."

They glared at each other for a long moment. Finally Allison pulled her parasol from his hand.

"I assure you, Mr. Jessup, you have not heard the last of this." Allison climbed into the buggy seat. "Let's go, Cecil."

Allison felt the gaze of everyone on the boardwalk upon her until Cecil finally jangled the reins and the buggy lurched forward. She didn't have to look behind her to know the coldest glare was from Mr. Cade Jessup.

Cade mumbled a curse under his breath and went back into the Pleasure Palace, the men on the boardwalk at his heels.

"What you reckon she's going to do, boss?"

He threw a glance at the slender young man beside him. "Nothing, Billy. She'll do nothing."

Billy, the piano man, shook his head as did the men crowded around. "I don't know, boss, she looked mighty worked up to me." His New Orleans accent thickened with every word he spoke.

"What can one woman do by herself?" He patted Billy on the shoulder. "Play us a tune."

He frowned. "Do I have to?"

"Tell Vance to pour a round of drinks on the house. That should keep them from throwing things at you for a while."

A cheer went up and the men headed toward the bar, the incident on the street forgotten.

Cade ran his fingers through the hair at his temple. He didn't need any trouble from the uppity Miss Tremaine. He knew her kind all too well. He'd come to Brighton to escape them. And besides, he had enough problems to contend with already.

The saloon was nearly empty, as expected for so early in the day. It was a wide room with windows across the front and a swinging door. The bar located at the far end of the room was backed by an etched mirror sent all the way from Philadelphia. Shelves of liquor bottles and glasses lined the wall. To the left was the door that led to the kitchen and to the right stood the cause of so much of Cade's worries.

The half-finished stage was starting to keep him up at night. There'd been problems with the carpentry crew, complaints by the girls upstairs at the early morning hammering and sawing, delays in the shipment of fabric he expected from St. Louis, and a question about who in town he'd get to actually sew the curtains he needed. And there'd been no response from New York on the most prized shipment, the one item he absolutely couldn't do without.

Cade rubbed his chin and crossed the room, heading for the kitchen. Vance, the bartender, waited for him at the end of the bar. Like Billy and the girls, he'd been with Cade since the Pleasure Palace opened nearly a year ago. Close to forty, barrel-chested with a heavy mustache, Vance missed nothing that went on in the saloon.

He nodded toward the corner. "Satch Wilkens again."

Across the room Cade saw the familiar fixture slumped over the table, a bottle clutched in his hand. He shook his head. "Better get him home. Send Billy with him."

Vance polished a heavy mug with the linen towel he held. "Last time, Mrs. Wilkens ran Billy off with the shotgun. Said she'd shoot him if he brought Satch home like that again."

Cade pulled the watch from his vest pocket and flipped it open. "All right, I'll take him home. Give Billy a hand and get him on his horse. And tell Billy that new sheet music came in the express package yesterday. It's up in my office. I want him practicing while I'm gone."

Vance's expression darkened. "In that case, I'll take Satch home myself."

Cade chuckled. "He'll get better."

"He hasn't gotten one whit better in the last six months. It's a damn miracle he hasn't been strung up by now."

Cade nodded. The two songs Billy could play had a tendency to grind on everyone's nerves after a while. "Just tell him to practice."

Vance shrugged and walked away.

In the kitchen, Cade took his hat, double ulster, and gun belt from the peg beside the cook stove. The sky looked gray and he didn't want to get caught unprepared in a storm.

The breeze had picked up some time ago and now dark clouds threatened overhead. Allison rubbed her upper arms briskly as the buggy bounced along the rutted roadway. The Nevada landscape that spread out on each side of her was beautiful, hills gray with sagebrush, juniper and pines on the basin ranges, the great Sierra Nevada in the distance, its aspen, fir, pine, and spruce capped with the last remnants of winter's mantle. Beautiful, just as she remembered. At least this part of Brighton hadn't changed, Allison thought with relief.

But what else was different, she wondered. What would she find when she reached Aunt Lydia's home? The cheerful letters Allison had always received from her aunt had turned dark and remorseful in the past few months, then had stopped altogether. She'd tried everything—even sent telegrams—but hadn't heard from her. Finally, despite the protests from her family, Allison had made up her mind to come see what had happened for herself.

She shifted on the buggy seat and a shiver ran up her spine, partly from the cool wind, partly from recollections of Brighton. Maybe Nigel had been right.

Allison looked down at the garnet and diamond ring on her left hand. Nigel. He knew by now she was gone.

Splintering wood sounded like a crack of thunder shattering Allison's thoughts. The buggy tilted to the left and she grabbed the seat to keep from falling.

"Whoa!" Cecil pulled back the reins and slid across the leather seat. "My word, my word. . . ."

"What is it? What happened?" Allison's heart pounded.

"My word. . . ." Cecil peered over the side of the buggy. "Wheel's busted. Busted real bad, Miss Allison."

She ventured closer to the side and looked down. The spokes of the left front wheel were shattered, leaving the buggy resting on the hub. There was no way they could repair it, and no way the horses could pull the buggy in this condition.

Allison slid down the seat and carefully eased herself from the buggy. Cecil did the same, at a much slower pace. Together they stood on the roadside looking at the wheel, then at each other.

"I'm real sorry, Miss Allison." He dragged his hat from his head and pressed it to his chest. "Real sorry."

She gazed down the roadway in both directions. They'd passed no one since leaving town and hadn't seen a farmhouse in several miles.

"Do you suppose someone will come along soon?" Allison asked.

"Maybe." Cecil looked up at the sky. "Course with the storm coming on, most people will be indoors. Looks like a big one."

A big one, to say the least, Allison thought as she turned her gaze skyward. "Aunt Lydia will surely send someone to town when they realize we're overdue."

Cecil shrugged. "Maybe so. But that train don't run on schedule too often. Most likely they won't think nothing of it 'less we're not back by dark."

Dark? That was hours away. Heaven knows what could happen to them in the meantime.

"I'll go for help," Allison decided.

"That wouldn't be right, Miss Allison." Cecil pulled on his hat again. "I'll go. You just sit right here while I walk to Miss Lydia's. It won't take no time."

Allison nearly gasped aloud. The way Cecil walked she could be out here for days. "No, no. I'm going."

"But what about the storm? You can't be caught out in the rain like that."

She picked up her parasol from the ground and tucked it under her arm. "I'll be fine."

He gestured toward her trunks that had spilled out onto the roadway. "And all your nice things? What's gonna happen to them?"

"That's why you're staying to watch over them. I'll be there in no time and send a wagon back for you and the trunks."

Allison drew in a determined breath and started walking
before Cecil could think of any more protests or offer to
come with her and slow her pace to a crawl.

"It's a long way, Miss Allison," Cecil called. "Do you
remember how to get there?"

"Of course," she shouted back over her shoulder. "It's
just beyond the next bend in the road."

"But—"

Allison hurried on, confident her aunt's home was only a
few steps away. And the fact that she hadn't been there
since she was sixteen—and that was eight years ago—gave
her no cause for concern. She was sure it was just around
the bend.

But it wasn't. It wasn't even around the next one, or the
one after that. Slightly breathless, Allison stopped and
looked up and down the road hoping to spot a landmark
she remembered. Nothing look familiar.

The rain began a few moments later, a light drizzle that
dampened her clothing, but not her spirits. Allison looked
skyward and raised her parasol. No reason to worry, she
thought, it may only be a shower and pass quickly.

In the next moment lightning lit the horizon and the sky
opened. A heavy, driving rain pelted the earth. Her parasol,
which had suffered some damage this morning, was feeble
protection from the rain. The wind tore at it, ripping the
fabric, leaving it flapping in the breeze. The road quickly
became a path of puddles and mud. Allison picked her way
along, trying to avoid the worst of it. She sank down to her
ankles, the hem of her dress acting as an anchor slowing her
further.

The rain turned heavier and she could barely see a few
hundred feet off the road as she searched for a farmhouse, a barn, shelter of any kind. She began to shiver.
Good gracious, she thought suddenly, what if Nigel, her
fiancé, saw her now. He'd be furious at finding her in this
condition.

But at least he'd be gentleman enough to help, she realized. At that moment, Nigel seemed very dear to her.

Down the road a man on horseback came into view. Allison blinked away the raindrops and squinted. Thank goodness, someone who could help her.

Through the driving rain the man drew nearer and Allison's breath caught. She recognized him immediately. Her stomach knotted. This certainly wasn't Nigel.

And after their meeting in town this morning, she knew he was no gentleman either.

Chapter
Two

Allison stopped as Cade Jessup drew nearer. Mud seeped over the tops of her shoes and raindrops poured through the tear in her parasol. Her hat sat askew amid her drooping curls. She was soaked to the skin.

"Afternoon, Miss Tremaine." Cade touched the brim of his black Stetson and rode past without giving her a second look.

Allison's mouth flew open. "Wa—wait! What are you doing?"

He turned the horse and rested one arm on the saddle horn looking down at her. Rainwater spilled off the brim of his hat. He looked warm and dry inside the double ulster he wore. "Just doing like any responsible citizen should. I'm keeping this public thoroughfare open for decent folks to pass through unmolested."

Allison gaped, too stunned to speak.

He gestured grandly to the empty, desolate road. "Proceed, Miss Tremaine."

Color drained from her cheeks. "But—"

"My civic conscience won't allow me to do otherwise. Good day." He headed the horse down the road again.

"Stop!" Allison splashed down the roadway after him. "Don't go!"

He reined in the horse and waited until she caught up to

him. "Was there some other matter of a civic nature you felt a need to talk about, Miss Tremaine?"

She pushed a strand of wet hair from her face. "You can't just leave me out here like this."

"I can't?" He stroked his chin. "And why not? It shouldn't be too much of a surprise for a man of my questionable character."

Allison's chin went up a notch. So that was it. He was retaliating against her harsh words in town. Nothing the man had done so far had changed her earlier opinion of him, but at the moment he was her only hope.

She squared her shoulders and took a deep breath. "Perhaps I was a bit hasty in my judgment this morning."

Her gaze locked with his and she was startled by the blueness of his eyes. Deep, dark blue like the ocean at its greatest depths. Magnificent blue.

Allison looked away.

Cade straightened in the saddle. "What'd you do, beat your driver to a pulp with that lethal parasol of yours?"

"I certainly did not. The buggy's wheel broke and I'm on my way to Aunt Lydia's to get help. Do you know my Aunt Lydia? Lydia Allbright. Is her house much farther?"

He nodded in the direction he'd come. "Another couple of miles."

Allison's shoulders sagged. "Miles. . . ." She couldn't walk that far. Not in this rain and mud. She licked the raindrops from her lips. "I don't suppose you'd consider taking a message there for me?"

Cade stared down at her.

"I'll pay you."

His jaw tightened and his back stiffened. "Where are you from, Miss Tremaine?"

Her heart began to pound. He had a dangerous look about him now. "New York City."

"Well, you're not in New York City anymore. You're in Brighton, Nevada, and in Brighton, Nevada, we don't accept money as payment from women stranded on deserted roads." His eyes narrowed. "We handle things differently."

Fear surged through Allison and she shrank back. Gripping the handle of her parasol, her gaze swept the road in both directions. Was there any place to run?

Cade swung down from his horse and was in front of her in two long steps. Allison shook her parasol at him. "I'm not afraid to use this."

He tore it from her fingers and tossed it aside, then closed his hands around her waist. She braced her hands against his chest, pushing with all her might.

"Stop!" His chest was hard as a wall and his hands were like iron around her waist. She had never felt such strength. "Why are you doing this?"

He released his grip and frowned down at her. "I'm putting you up on my horse. You're not likely to climb on by yourself dressed in a getup like that."

Allison stepped back, putting some distance between them. Her pulse raced. "I—I don't want to ride that horse."

A deep frown drew his brows together. "I'm sure as hell not leaving you out here in this weather. God knows who might come along next and have their way with you."

Bright crimson colored Allison's cheeks. "Just—just go tell my aunt where I am. I'll not ride that horse . . . with you. . . . It's not proper."

Cade mumbled a curse and opened his mouth to speak, but didn't. Instead he stepped forward and circled her waist with his hands, and swung her into the saddle.

Allison gasped and grabbed the saddle for support, both her feet dangling down the left side of the horse. "I told you—"

He pointed a finger up at her. "Shut up. Just shut your high-toned, uppity mouth. Believe me, lady, it's mighty tempting to leave you out here, but I'm not going to. So be quiet and do what I tell you to do."

Before Allison could respond, Cade climbed into the saddle behind her and lifted her onto his lap. The feel of his hard thighs burned through her dress, scorching her legs. He wrapped one arm around her, pinning her to his chest.

She pushed away from him. "This isn't proper."

He tightened his grip. "It may not be proper, but it's what we're going to do."

Cade pulled a poncho from his saddlebag and spread it over her. She shivered.

"My God, you're freezing." He opened the buttons of his ulster and pulled her against him.

She leaned away and looked up at him. "But I'll get you all wet."

He shook his head. "You've got a lot to learn about living in Brighton, Miss Tremaine."

Cade pulled her against his chest, keeping one arm securely around her, and adjusted the poncho to cover her head. He urged the horse forward.

He gave off the heat of a cookstove on Sunday afternoon. Everything Allison had learned from hundreds of hours in etiquette classes told her this was totally inappropriate behavior, but Cade was warm and the feel of his arms around her evoked a sense of security she'd never experienced. And he smelled good. A deep, clean masculine scent. The rhythm of the horse's gait soothed her and finally Allison relaxed, soaking up Cade's warmth and strength.

They reached her aunt's home and the horse slowed to a walk. Allison peeked from under the poncho. Only a light drizzle fell.

And there stood Aunt Lydia's house.

Allison sat upright. She hadn't been here in years, but it looked just as she remembered. A stately, white two-story home with a wide, wraparound porch and columns reaching to the slate roof. A carefully tended lawn and a split rail fence made it an oasis in the harsh prairie.

Allison smiled up at Cade. "I haven't been here since I was a young girl. I have the fondest memories of visiting this place."

She looked so pleased Cade couldn't help smiling too. "So, Miss Allbright is your aunt?"

"No, not really. She knew my mother and father in New York and I always called her my aunt, though there's no blood relation. She's very well traveled—the East, the Continent, the Orient. Aunt Lydia knows many people and we all call her Aunt. I'm not sure she's really anyone's aunt. She never married, you know."

Cade didn't know much about Lydia Allbright, except

that her father founded the town years ago and left his daughter enough money to live her life in grand style. From what he'd heard, that's exactly what she'd done. Now, she was known only as a recluse who rarely ventured out of her house.

As they continued up the drive, a man on horseback approached. He was draped in a poncho and wearing a tan slouch hat with a snakeskin band pulled low on his forehead. A Winchester rested across his lap.

"That's far enough. Just turn around and get back where you came from." His thick black mustache fell to his chin and wiggled when he spoke.

Cade pulled back on the reins. His hand dropped to the Colt Peacemaker at his side. "We're here to see Miss Allbright."

"She ain't seeing anybody." He waved the rifle. "Just get on out of here."

Allison pushed away the poncho and sat up straighter. "And who are you?"

Cade cringed. The woman was going to get him killed before the day was over.

The man's gaze was cold. "Name's Wes Palmer and I run this place. You got business here, you'd better spit it out right now."

Her nose crept an inch higher in the air. "I am Allison Augusta Tremaine. I've traveled from New York City to see my Aunt Lydia. She is expecting me. Now, kindly stand aside."

Palmer shook his head. "I don't know nothing about no visitor from New York City."

Allison tossed her head. "I hardly expect Aunt Lydia would keep the hired help apprised of her social calendar."

He scowled and raised the Winchester. "I'm only telling you one more time—"

Cade drew his Colt and leveled it at Palmer. "But I'm not listening to it another time."

Startled, Allison looked up at Cade. His deep blue eyes had turned to cold steel. Beneath her, she felt his body tense, and for an instant she was more afraid of Cade than Wes Palmer.

"Miss Allison! Miss Allison!"

The gleeful cries from the house broke the tension as Georgia, Aunt Lydia's housekeeper, waved her handkerchief and hurried across the front porch.

Allison smiled and waved back. "Georgia!"

The robust, gray-haired woman planted her hands on her ample hips. "It's all right, Mr. Palmer! It's Miss Lydia's niece!"

Palmer exchanged one last harsh look with Cade before lowering his rifle. He wheeled his horse around and rode away. Only then did Cade holster his Colt.

Allison wiggled from Cade's lap and he caught her arms and helped her down before she landed headlong in the mud.

"Georgia!" She ran up the walk and onto the porch taking Georgia's outstretched hands.

"My goodness, we have missed you so." Georgia's mouth dropped open. "Goodness' sake, child. What's happened to you?"

Allison pushed away her wet, tangled hair. "Cecil and I were on our way home when the buggy wheel broke. I started walking, thinking it was only a short way, then the rain started. If it hadn't been for Mr. Jessup—"

She whirled around, realizing she'd completely forgotten him. He sat on his horse, watching her intently with those deep blue eyes of his and looking incredibly handsome. That thought struck her as if it were another bolt of lightning.

Allison hurried back down the walk in the misting rain. "Mr. Jessup, please come inside. Have some tea and warm yourself by the fire."

He couldn't remember the last time he'd been offered tea, but it certainly hadn't been since his arrival in Brighton. And certainly it had never been offered by a woman who had insulted him to his face and nearly gotten him shot.

Cade shook his head. "No thanks. I've got to get back to town."

Suddenly she didn't want him to go. "Are you sure?"

No. He wasn't sure at all. She was quite a sight with her wet curls sagging and her hat cocked at an odd angle. Rain had soaked her clothing, molding them to her ample breasts and tiny waist. Her face was pale and dewy as droplets clung to her long, dark lashes and spattered against her creamy skin and generous lips. Her amber eyes—deep and rich as the finest aged bourbon—watched him, and unsettled him.

Or was it his own thoughts that unsettled him?

Cade shifted in the saddle. "I've got to be going."

She took a step closer. "Thank you."

He touched the brim of his hat and took up the reins.

"I suppose I'll see you in town. I'll be there tomorrow."

Cade frowned. "What for?" From the number of trunks he'd seen piled in the back of her buggy, the woman right now could clothe half the country.

"To see the sheriff, of course. And the mayor."

"What kind of business could you have with the sheriff and the mayor?"

His condescending tone struck a nerve. "I intend to discuss with them the disreputable state of Brighton."

He raised one eyebrow. "And just what is so disreputable about Brighton?"

"The saloons, I suspect. There must be dozens of them. They've ruined the entire town for decent citizens."

His jaw twitched. "The saloons are what saved this place from becoming a ghost town."

She blinked up at him. "I find that very hard to believe."

He pointed a finger at her. "Don't think you can come sashaying in here with your high-handed Eastern ways and change what's happening here in Brighton. You don't know anything about it."

"I know a great deal about it." Her back stiffened. "This was a lovely, decent town long before you and your abhorrent saloon arrived."

"It's none of your business."

"My aunt's father founded this town. That makes it my business."

Cade sat back in the saddle and laughed. "You may get your dander up and stir a little fuss, but you're not going to change anything in Brighton. Not a woman. A woman by herself."

He'd thrown the words at her in a challenge she couldn't resist. "We'll see about that."

He gave her a quick nod. "We sure as hell will."

Cade wheeled his horse around and rode off down the drive, kicking up mud and water as he went. Allison turned quickly and marched up the walkway, stirring up a wake of rainwater of her own.

Allison sat on the edge of the canopy bed sipping the last of her tea. She'd had a bath and was now snug and dry in her wrapper.

"Beautiful things, my dear. Beautiful!"

Georgia pulled another matching skirt, overskirt, and blouse from her trunk and held it up. Cecil had done a commendable job fitting her bags into the buggy to spare them from the rain, and most of her things had arrived at Aunt Lydia's, as had Cecil, safe and sound. Georgia was thoroughly enjoying putting them away.

"Reminds me of when your Aunt Lydia used to come back from her trips. She brought home the most beautiful gowns! She had quite the eye for fashion." Georgia hung the garment in the big redwood closet.

Allison eased off the bed. This was the room she always took when she visited, decorated with rosebud wallpaper, ornate cherry furniture, and Aunt Lydia's doll collection. It felt so right to be here again, yet her concern for her aunt still weighed heavily upon her.

"What's wrong with Aunt Lydia? You've known her for more years that I can remember and—"

"Indeed I have. Nearly all her life. I was but a teenage girl myself when her father—God rest his soul—hired me in as nanny for Miss Lydia." Georgia hugged the blue print overskirt to her bosom and smiled at the memory. "I've been at her side through the good years and the bad, the happiness and the heartbreak."

"Heartbreak?" Allison frowned. "I know she never married but—"

"Oh, it's nothing." Georgia turned away. "I'm a bit dramatic, I suppose. She was just a young girl—younger even than you. It was before her father made himself so wealthy and her young man wasn't willing to settle for a plain girl from a small town. Newly rich, he was. He wanted to see the sights of the big city with a grand lady on his arm. So, off he went."

Allison sank down on the bed again. "Aunt Lydia must have been devastated."

Georgia busied herself in the trunks once more. "Time's a great healer. She had a wonderful life without an ounce of regret. Just ask her—she'll tell you."

"I'd like to see Aunt Lydia now."

Georgia laid aside the pink gown. "If you'd like."

Allison crossed the room and a movement outside the window caught her eye. She looked down and realized it was Wes Palmer. He was on horseback, just outside the yard, staring up at her window. A chill swept up her spine.

Allison stepped back from the window. "How long has Wes Palmer worked here?"

"Oh, six months or so, I believe. Mr. Stallworth, your aunt's attorney in Brighton, hired him through one of those agencies or something."

"He pulled a gun on Cade and me when we rode up today."

Georgia gave her a reassuring smile. "He does a fine job of keeping the place safe, running off squatters, watching over the other hands."

"And who watches over Wes Palmer?"

She pursed her lips. "Well, no one I guess. Mr. Stallworth audits the books every now and again, but aside from that . . ."

Allison digested her words, then pushed them aside. "Let's go see Aunt Lydia."

She walked with Georgia down the familiar corridor to the biggest room at the corner of the house. Lydia lay in the four-poster bed, sleeping. Her white hair blended perfectly with the linen pillow beneath her head, and her skin, nearly the same hue, showed lines and wrinkles Allison did not remember. This wasn't the vibrant woman she'd known all her life. Allison had seen her only a year ago in New York. What had happened?

"She sleeps a good bit of the time." Georgia shook her

head, gazing down at the bed. "Hasn't been out of this room in months."

Allison's heart ached. "What does the doctor say?"

"Nothing. Claims he can't find anything wrong."

"Then we'll consult another doctor."

Georgia shrugged. "I've tried. I can't get her to go. Says there's no point."

"No point?" Her aunt had always been full of life, ready to take on a cause, speak her mind, head off on a moment's notice for a shopping trip to London. Though physically she was close to sixty, mentally she had always been a young woman. "What happened to make her feel this way?"

"I don't know. She stopped corresponding with her friends, stopped going out, stopped receiving callers." Georgia gestured to the stack of newspapers beside the bed. "Miss Lydia seldom reads her papers anymore. And you know how she enjoyed them."

Because of her extensive travel, Lydia received newspapers from the major cities in the East, as well as from abroad. She frequently saw articles concerning her many friends. She'd even seen the picture of Allison and Nigel on the society page and written Allison wanting all the details. Now, like everything else in the room, the stack of newspapers looked as though it hadn't been touched for months.

Allison glanced over the desk near her aunt's bed. Normally neat as a pin, it was cluttered with unopened envelopes—she saw two of her own letters among them—pages of other correspondence scattered about. Several newspapers were there as well, creased open as though Aunt Lydia still read them often. One was the grainy photograph of herself and Nigel, another was the wedding announcement of Madeline Fairchild, a young woman who traveled in their social set, and the other was a story of a riverboat accident.

Allison picked up the newspaper and glanced over the story—months old now—of an explosion and fire aboard the *Mississippi Lady* outside St. Louis, the detailed loss of life and missing persons. Allison cringed.

"Why is she reading of such tragedies?" She held the paper out.

Georgia shook her head. "It's a bad sign. Seems as though Miss Lydia has got no will to live."

Allison's heart sank. "No . . ."

"Come along, dearie. You're worn out and you need to rest." Georgia took the newspaper from her hand and guided her from the room.

Allison went willingly, bone-tired and mentally exhausted. In her room she said good night to Georgia and blew out the lantern on the bureau. A strange feeling of foreboding swept over her as she slipped out of her wrapper. Allison crept to the window.

Wes Palmer was still there. Watching.

"It was a ghost, I tell you. Plain and simple."

Rupert Frazier thumped his fist on the bar and took another drink. "Ask the preacher. He heard it too."

Beside him, Otis Collins shook his head. "I ain't never heard of no ghost being inside of a church."

"It's true," Rupert insisted. "Ain't that right, Cade?"

Cade leaned against the bar. He believed there were things that could haunt a man's life, but he didn't necessarily believe in ghosts.

"I don't know, boys. It's pretty hard to believe the ghost of Miss Marshall has come back and is playing the church piano at night."

"It's got to be her." Rupert wiped his mouth with the back of his hand. "It's pitch-black inside the church at night and she was the only one who could play that piano without looking at that paper full of them squiggly lines. Preacher Kent heard it too. He said so, over at Taylor's General Store this afternoon. Just ask 'ol Will Taylor. He'll tell you."

Nearly dark outside now, the saloon was crowded. Men stood at the bar and sat around the tables, talking, drinking, playing cards. Will Taylor, who ran the general store next door along with his wife Edith, was a regular, slipping over whenever he could escape his wife's disapproving glare.

"Hey, Will!" Cade waved him over.

Tall, slender, with a touch of gray at his temples, Will Taylor wound his way through the crowd. He wore a linen shirt with a coat and string tie, and looked the prosperous, respectable businessman that he was.

"Evening, Cade." Will cast a curious look at Rupert and Otis. They were a scroungy pair who eked a living out of a claim they mined up in the hills somewhere near town.

"I told Otis here about what the preacher said over to your store this afternoon." Rupert jerked his thumb toward his friend. "Only he don't believe me."

Otis belched and nodded.

"Go on. Tell him. Tell him what the preacher said about them strange happenings over to the church."

Will hung his thumbs in the pockets of his vest and looked thoughtful. "Preacher said he heard piano music coming from the church. And it was dark inside. Not a light anywhere."

Otis looked skeptical and leaned closer. "And Preacher said it was a ghost?"

Will cleared his throat. "Somebody said maybe it was Miss Marshall come back to play for us, since we've got no pianist now that she passed on. I don't rightly recall it being Preacher Kent who said it."

"I shoulda knowed it . . ." Otis gave Rupert a scathing look and walked away.

"I'm telling you it was the God's truth." Rupert took his mug and followed Otis through the crowd.

"I saw the little fracas outside your place this afternoon," Will said to Cade.

Cade shook his head. It seemed everyone had either seen or heard of his exchange with Miss Allison Augusta Tremaine. "Some city woman from back East."

"Lydia Allbright's niece, I heard." Will nodded his head. "Quite a little spitfire."

Annoyed, Cade shrugged off the comment and leaned back on the bar.

"Edith got all fired up about it and told Mabel Duncan what had happened when she came in the store. Then they both started in on it, giving me an earful about decency and how the streets aren't safe for a woman to walk alone." Will frowned. "This could be trouble, Cade. You've got to do something."

"Me?" Cade straightened.

"Yes, you. You're the one who started in with that Miss Tremaine. It happened right outside your place."

Cade waved away his concern. "Nothing is going to happen. It's just a bunch of women talking. It will blow over. What can women do, anyway?"

Will digested his words, then nodded. "I guess you're right."

"Of course I'm right. Tomorrow somebody will show up in town in a hat they all despise and they'll be talking about that. You know how women are."

"I do, I sure do." He nodded wisely.

Satisfied the subject was closed, Cade eased away. He was having enough trouble keeping the outspoken Miss Tremaine from his thoughts without everyone reminding him of her. He sought solitude in the kitchen.

Vance met him in the doorway. "I told him he could eat supper if he put away the supplies."

Vance threw a fit if anyone touched his supply room and it surprised Cade that he'd let anyone else lay a hand on it. But Vance hurried into the saloon before Cade could question him. He searched the darkened room, looking for the man Vance had made this exception for.

It was a boy. He was standing between the stove and cupboard, holding the plate to his mouth, raking the food in. The most pitiful-looking thing Cade had ever seen.

He was short, odd-shaped, with a head too small for his body and eyes that were too big for his head. It was hard to guess his age, eleven, maybe twelve. His hair was matted down. The clothes he wore were ragged and torn. His face and hands were crusted with dirt.

The boy watched Cade warily, his eyes darting to the back door as if determining his escape route, all the while shoving food into his mouth. He looked like a cornered animal. A starved, cornered animal.

Cade suddenly felt guilty that he was clean and dry and that his belly was full and always had been. That, as least, was one thing he could thank his father for.

Concerned the boy might bolt before finishing his food,

Cade stopped beside the table. "Did Vance show you where to put the supplies?"

His gaze swept the crates stacked beside the stockroom, then returned quickly to Cade. He nodded.

"You can sit down and eat your meal." He gestured toward the table.

The boy shrank back, frightened by the sudden movement. His eyes shone like beacons in the dim room, bright with fear and distrust.

Tempting as it was to question the boy about his circumstances, Cade felt compelled to allow him to eat undisturbed. He returned to the saloon.

Vance stood behind the bar now and Billy was plunking away at the piano; luckily the sound was nearly lost in the din of the crowd. Bad as Billy's playing was, Cade needed him. The Pleasure Palace was the biggest and the best saloon in town. Cade intended to keep it that way. And the plans he had would ensure it.

He took a turn through the room, talking as he went; he knew most every man in Brighton. He kept a constant eye out for trouble that might be brewing, a fistfight, an unhappy loser at the tables. The girls would be down soon. Things would heat up then.

He returned to the kitchen but found no sign of the boy. His plate sat on the sideboard, licked clean. Cade checked the storage room and saw that the supplies had been unloaded and stacked on the shelves. It disturbed Cade that the boy was out on the streets alone.

Cade raked his fingers through the hair at his temple. The ghost of Miss Marshall was pumping out hymns in the dead of night, a ragtag boy had materialized and disappeared just as quickly, and Miss Allison Augusta Tremaine thought she could single-handedly change the morals of the entire town.

Everything had been normal when he awoke this morning. What the hell was happening to Brighton?

Cade pulled at the tight muscles of his neck as the image of Allison flashed in his mind. What the hell was happening to him?

Chapter
Three

Too much solitude wasn't good for a man, but Cade liked his share of it. That's why he cherished these early morning hours before Vance, Billy, and the girls came down. He didn't need as much sleep as the others, as long as he got his six hours in uninterrupted.

He set his empty cup on the sideboard and pulled on his black Stetson. A plate of biscuits and gravy from the Red Eye Cafe was calling his name.

The morning sun shone bright on the horizon as Cade stepped onto the boardwalk at the rear of the saloon. Always quiet at this time of the day, with the other merchants along Main Street rousing, readying for the business day ahead, it was odd that he heard shouts. Down the alley Cade saw Dutch Myer, the owner of Brighton's tobacco shop, toss a large bundle out his back door onto the boardwalk.

"And stay out!" Myer stormed into his shop and slammed the door.

Arms and legs and a filthy head of hair took shape from the bundle and rolled over on the boardwalk. It was the boy, Cade realized, the one who'd been in his kitchen last night. The boy lay on his belly, face buried in his arms, his whole body shaking. He was crying.

Anger whipped through Cade. He'd never liked that bastard Myer to begin with. But he held his temper in check and walked over. Cade sat down on the nail keg outside Myer's back door and waited. Finally the boy raised his head and looked at him. Though Cade hadn't imagined it possible, he looked worse in the daylight.

The boy tried to scurry away, but Cade grabbed his foot. His boot came off in his hand. The boy dropped to the boardwalk once more, his gaze darting from his boot to Cade.

A sorry piece of footwear, the heel was run down to nothing and the soul was separated from the boot along the outer edge. Cade grabbed the boy's ankle and held the boot up to the bottom of his foot; it was three inches too long.

"How do you walk in these things?" He tossed the boot back to him.

The boy hurriedly pulled it on and scooted away—an arm's length away. He drew himself into a tight little ball. His big eyes watched Cade warily.

"Name's Cade Jessup. You stacked supplies and ate at my saloon last night. Remember?"

The boy nodded and wiped his eyes with the sleeve of his torn coat.

Cade gestured to the tobacco shop behind him. "I guess old man Myer wasn't looking for any extra help today."

He shook his head and looked away. For a moment Cade thought he might cry again.

Cade pulled his hat off, raked his fingers through his hair, and settled it into place once more. "What's your name, boy?"

"Tyler." His voice was soft and unsure. "Tyler James."

"How old are you?"

He sniffed. "Thirteen."

Cade was surprised. From his size, he'd guessed him younger. "Where're you from?"

He thought for a moment, then shrugged. "Nowhere."

"How about your folks? Where are they?"

He frowned. "My what?"

"Your folks. Your pa and your ma."

The boy blanched and turned away. "They're . . . dead."

Not dead long, Cade guessed. The pain was fresh in the

boy's eyes. From the look of him, some dirt farmer's kid left to fend for himself.

"Are you in trouble with the law?"

"I don't think so."

Cade rubbed his chin and sighed. He'd known since last night what needed to be done.

"Well, Tyler, I'm looking to hire an errand boy to work for me at the saloon. You interested in the job?"

His gaze came up slowly and met Cade's. "What?"

For a moment Cade wondered whether the boy couldn't hear right or just didn't understand. "I need an errand boy. Do you know what that means?"

The boy studied him thoughtfully. "I know what 'boy' means."

Some dirt farmer's uneducated boy, Cade decided. "If I need somebody to go to the express office or the train station, you go. You do chores for me, like sweeping the floor, mopping, helping in the kitchen. Things like that. Understand?"

He nodded.

"I'll pay you four-bits a week, plus room and board. That means you can live at the saloon and eat there too."

The boy's brown eyes grew larger. He sat up. "Food?"

"Yes, son. Food." Cade extended his hand. "Deal?"

Slowly Tyler reached out and they shook hands.

Cade rose to his feet. "First things first. Come on."

"Where?" Tyler scrambled to his feet and hurried after him. He dragged his sleeve across his nose.

"You'll see."

The boardwalk was busy now as shops and stores opened and began conducting business. Wagons, buggies, and horses made their way down the muddy streets. Cade led the way to the west end of town and stopped outside Bailey's Bathhouse.

"Have you been in one of these before?" He guessed that like most farm families, the boy bathed in a creek or washed in a pan by the stove on Saturday night.

Tyler studied the sign. "What is it?"

"You're about to find out."

Bailey, a wiry man in arm garters and an apron, peered at

them through tiny spectacles perched on the end of his thin nose. He paused over the towels he was folding and threw Tyler a questioning look. He wrinkled his nose. "Morning, Cade."

Cade dropped his hand on Tyler's shoulder as the boy's gaze roamed the premises. "Bailey, this is Tyler James. He's working for me now. He needs a bath."

"I should say so." He turned away and pointed down the hallway. "Just filled the tub for myself, but you take it. Please."

They entered a small room equipped with a brass tub, a bench stacked with towels, and a narrow, full-length mirror affixed to the wall. Steam rose from the tub.

Cade picked up a newspaper from Virginia City lying on the bench. Bailey liked to keep up on happenings around the state. "Get out of those clothes and climb in," Cade said as he looked over the front page.

Tyler undressed, dropping layer after layer of clothing onto the bench. Two coats. Sweaters that covered shirts and other sweaters, all lined with crumbled newspapers for extra warmth. Two pairs of trousers, all tattered and worn. His long johns and two pairs of socks were in no better condition.

He was rail-thin, with white pasty skin stretched over his ribs. He no longer looked so out of proportion as Cade had first thought, only skinny and frail. He turned to climb into the tub. The newspaper fell from Cade's hand. "What the hell happened to you?"

He grasped Tyler's shoulder and turned him toward the light from the tiny window near the ceiling. His bottom and legs were covered with large purple bruises.

"What happened to you?"

Tyler looked back over his shoulder. "I don't know."

Cade frowned. "You don't get beat like this and not know what happened. Who did this to you?"

Tyler shrugged.

His anger doubled. "Was it Dutch Myer at the tobacco shop?"

"No." Pain showed on Tyler's face. He looked away. "I don't know who it was."

Cade mumbled a curse and let go of Tyler's shoulder. He
patted his back gently. "Scrub yourself good, son."

Tyler eased into the water.

Cade dropped a bar of soap and the brush into the tub.
"Scrub everything. Twice."

He scooped up the boy's clothing and boots and headed
out the door.

"Wait!"

Tyler scrambled from the tub and raced after him, fling-
ing water as he went. Bailey's mouth dropped open as the
boy rushed by. He followed him into the street. "Hold on
there, young fella!"

A woman screamed and commotion broke out behind
Cade as he headed down the boardwalk. He turned and saw
Tyler running buck naked after him, and Allison Tremaine
staring wide-eyed at both of them.

"Christ. . . ."

Cade ran down the boardwalk, scooped up the boy, and
carried him back inside. He dumped him in the tub. Water
splashed over the sides as Tyler disappeared under the sur-
face, then came up quickly, coughing and wheezing.

"You're not out on the farm anymore. You can't go running around town bare-butt naked. Now stay in there and
wash. I'll be back later."

"You got no reason to steal my things and leave me in
here with nothing!"

"I'm not stealing your things!" Cade curbed his anger.
Life had been tough for the boy, he realized. He trusted no
one. And from the look of him, with good reason.

He softened his tone. "I'm taking them to the laundry. I'll
be back by the time you're done washing. I swear."

Cade strode from the room and closed the door firmly
behind him. Bailey's disapproving stare met him.

"Not good. Not good at all." He shook his head gravely.

"Sorry about the trouble." Cade shifted the bundle of
filthy clothes to the other arm.

"Not good for business. Not good."

Cade dug into his pocket and flipped him another nickel.
"It won't happen again."

Bailey shrugged as if he doubted it, but tucked the coin in his pocket and went back to his folding.

Allison stood on the boardwalk when Cade walked outside, her cheeks still crimson. She looked at him as though it seemed quite natural he would be party to a public display of nudity.

Cade touched the brim of his hat and smiled cordially. "Good morning, Miss Tremaine. Lovely day, wouldn't you say?"

Allison touched her handkerchief to her breast. "I'm not sure, Mr. Jessup. I seem to have lost my breath for a moment."

"Our Nevada mornings are breathtaking."

"I must agree, Mr. Jessup, that I've never seen the sights in New York that I have witnessed here today." Allison waved her handkerchief toward the bathhouse. "Was that some relative of yours?"

Lord, she looked pretty this morning, fresh and inviting as the sunrise. She had on a pink skirt and print overskirt and blouse, with a tiny hat placed just so, and dark ringlets trailing down the back of her head. She looked like a lady, the kind Cade hadn't seen in years.

"No," he told her. "And what brings you in to town so soon, Miss Tremaine?"

"I have some errands to run. My aunt's health is very poor and I intend to discuss it with the doctor."

He grinned. "Taking on the medical profession today, Miss Tremaine?"

Her chin went up a notch. "If need be."

He touched the brim of his hat. "I trust I'll be seeing you around town?"

"Most assuredly, Mr. Jessup." She smiled up at him. "You can count on it."

He watched her go, her bustle swaying with each tiny step. Cade never for a moment thought he'd seen the last of Allison Tremaine.

Hardly a moment's rest had come to her during the night and Allison had awakened early this morning with much on her mind. She'd tried to see her aunt again, but the woman only slept, unaware of her presence. Allison couldn't abide being in the house, not knowing the details of Aunt Lydia's condition, not doing something to learn of them. So as she walked down the boardwalk of Brighton, she kept an eye out for the office of Dr. Efrain Tanner that Cecil had described when he'd dropped her off this morning.

She located the doctor's office with no problem, but there was a sign hanging in the window advising patients that Dr. Tanner was out on a call and expected back by midafternoon. Allison sighed and looked around. It didn't matter. She had a long list of people she intended to see today.

The sheriff's office was a few doors down and Allison slipped inside, shuddering momentarily as she stepped through the threshold. The room was rather dim, with a desk and potbellied stove, and racks of rifles on the walls. Posters of wanted criminals hung beside the windows. A narrow hallway ran toward the back of the building and she guessed it led to the cells. Allison tightened her hold on her own resolve and closed the door.

Sheriff Mack Carson looked up from his paperwork, did a double take, and lurched to his feet. "Yes, ma'am?"

She approached the desk, feeling as out of place as she looked. "Good morning, Sheriff. My name is Miss Allison Augusta Tremaine and I wonder if I might have a moment of your time?"

"Sure thing, ma'am. Sit yourself down." He gestured toward the chair across from his desk but struck his coffee cup and spilled the dark liquid all over his reports. "Damnit. Oh, sorry, ma'am." He pulled his handkerchief from his hip pocket.

Allison perched on the edge of the chair and watched as he mopped up the mess he'd made. The sheriff was very tall, in his early thirties, with black hair and a strong chin. Like most of the men she'd seen in Brighton, he had a gun holstered on his hip.

The sheriff wrung his handkerchief over the trash can beside his desk and sat down. He wiped his hands on his shirt. "Well, Miss Tremaine, what can I do for you?"

Allison smiled sweetly. "I'm here visiting my aunt, Lydia Allbright. You might know her?"

A big grin broke over his face. "I didn't think you were from around here."

She batted her long lashes. "How very perceptive of you, Sheriff Carson. I can easily see why you are in a position of authority in Brighton."

He flushed and wiggled in his chair. "I've been sheriff here for now on to six months."

"My, but that's quite an accomplishment."

"Before that I was deputy sheriff down in Texas."

"You've certainly come a long way, Sheriff Carson." Allison dipped her head coyly. "And now you have the responsibility of insuring the safety of all the good people of Brighton. Is that right?"

He grinned proudly. "Yes, ma'am, it's all on my shoulders."

Allison looked directly at him. "Then, Sheriff Carson, perhaps you can explain to me why the streets are no longer safe for decent people to walk, why public drunkenness is accepted as commonplace, why the saloons have taken over the town, and why nothing is being done to stop this appalling degradation of morals?"

The smile fell from his face. "Huh?"

"Upon my arrival in Brighton yesterday, I was shocked to see that—"

"That was you." Sheriff Carson sat forward and pointed an accusing finger at her. A deep frown cut a groove in his forehead. "You're the one I heard about outside of Cade's saloon yesterday, aren't you?"

Apparently news of her encounter outside the Pleasure Palace had swept Brighton like wildfire. And the sheriff was looking at her as though she'd committed a capital offense. "Yes, I was—"

The sheriff rose quickly. "Well, ma'am, that's just the way things are in Brighton. Things are different out here."

Allison gazed up at him as he towered over her. "Am I to understand, Sheriff, that you intend to do nothing about the shameful state of affairs in town?"

He hung his thumbs in his gun belt. "I'm sworn to keep the peace, Miss Tremaine, and that's what I do. You're just going to have to get used to things the way they are."

"I sincerely doubt that will happen." Allison rose and walked to the door. "I'll be sure to mention your position to the mayor when I see him. Good day, Sheriff."

Allison stepped onto the boardwalk and closed the sheriff's door with a little more force than necessary. She'd expected he would have at least some concern over the condition of the town. Undaunted, Allison hurried down the street. She'd see the mayor. He would surely understand her position and do something about it.

But when Allison emerged from the mayor's office ten minutes later, she slammed his door with a great deal more force than necessary. Mayor Everette Hawkins had only half listened to her concerns, and had even suggested the saloons were a welcome industry in Brighton. A boon to the economy, he'd said. He'd made a halfhearted promise to look into the matter but Allison knew nothing would come of it.

Fueled by anger, Allison made her way down the boardwalk mindless of the shoppers she dodged and the curious stares that followed her. She found herself across the street from the Pleasure Palace. The most horrible piano music she'd ever heard poured out the open window, along with hammering and sawing and an occasional curse. Doubly annoyed, she ducked into the dressmaker's shop beside her.

Bolts of fabrics, spools of ribbons and threads, and baskets of buttons were displayed in a neat, orderly fashion. The shop was alive with colors and textures, a welcome relief from what she'd been through this morning.

The proprietor came through the curtain at the back of the store, an attractive blond woman about the same age as she. A genuine smile lit her face.

"Allison? Allison Tremaine?"

It took only a fraction of a second for Allison to match the face and voice with a memory of her previous visit to Brighton. She smiled. "Jenna? Jenna, is that really you?"

The two women squealed with delight and hugged.

"I'd heard you were in town. Oh, let me look at you."

"Jenna, you've no idea how wonderful it is to see a friendly face in this town."

Jenna's eyes widened. "I saw you outside the Pleasure

Palace yesterday. My goodness, I could hardly believe my eyes."

Allison waved away the thought. "I could hardly believe it myself. Now, tell me all about yourself, Jenna. What have you been up to? It looks as though you got your dream of having a dress shop."

Pride filled her eyes. "Thanks to Dan, my husband. He had faith in me and set me up in business."

"You're married? How wonderful."

The two women had been introduced by Aunt Lydia during Allison's last visit to Brighton some eight years ago. She'd known Allison would need someone her own age to associate with during her long six-month visit while her parents were having a second honeymoon in London. The girls had become fast friends, sharing secrets and making plans for their futures. They'd stayed in touch for a while after Allison left, but finally the letters had stopped as they both had become involved in their own very different lives.

Allison scanned the shop. "Where is your husband? I'd love to meet him."

Jenna's smile faded. "Dan was killed two years ago during a bank holdup. He was standing on the corner when a gunfight broke out."

It took a moment for the words to sink in. "How horrible for you."

Jenna nodded. "But I had my business. And Holly, of course." She smiled again. "You must meet her. Holly! Come here, honey!"

The curtain opened and a little girl with long blond braids ran out. Jenna scooped her up. "This is Holly. My daughter."

"Oh, Jenna, she's beautiful."

Her face was a fine porcelain, her eyes big and blue. The very image of her mother. She offered Allison a shy smile.

"She's five years old already, and growing up much too fast." Jenna gave her a squeeze and the little girl giggled. "We live here in the back of the shop and Holly helps me out. She's becoming quite a good seamstress."

The two of them looked so happy together that Allison

could feel the love they shared. "It seems as though you've done very well for yourself, Jenna, despite everything."

"Thank you." She placed Holly on the floor. "What about you? Have you married? Had children?"

"Well, no. . . ." Allison shifted uncomfortably. "But I am seeing someone . . . in a way."

"I hope you'll be as happy as Dan and I were."

Allison wondered if that could be possible.

Holly pulled on her mother's skirt. "Can I have a cookie, Mama?"

"Sure, honey. But just one." Jenna patted the child as she hurried from the shop. She turned to Allison again. "Let's go have—"

The bell over the door jangled, interrupting Jenna. She looked past Allison. "Good morning, Mrs. Taylor."

"Good morning, Jenna." She joined them and gave Allison a critical gaze. The woman was older, her dark hair drawn back in a severe bun. "And who might you be?"

"Mrs. Taylor, this is Allison Tremaine, Miss Allbright's niece visiting from New York. Edith Taylor owns the general store across the street."

Allison smiled. "Very nice to—"

Edith's eyes bulged and the corners of her mouth curled downward. "You! You were the one in the street outside the saloon yesterday."

If one more person told her the goings-on in Brighton were none of her business, Allison thought she might very well scream. She stood her ground. "Yes. I was."

Edith glared at her, then looked at Jenna and back to Allison again. "Good for you, I say. It's time somebody stood up and said something about what's happened to Brighton."

"Do you mean you agree?" Allison was stunned.

"Yes I do. Why, I told Mabel Duncan about what you did and she said the same. The streets aren't safe, thanks to those saloons and the riffraff they cater to. We get no relief —not even on the Sabbath."

"The saloons are open on Sunday?" Allison's eyes widened. "How did this happen? Brighton used to be such a nice town."

Edith pursed her lips. "It was Lydia Allbright that started it."

"Aunt Lydia?"

"Once she closed the Carriage Works there was no work. Most everybody moved on."

"Brighton nearly became a ghost town," Jenna added.

"Then that Cade Jessup came with his saloon—and put it right next door to my business—and soon the whole place was filled with ranch hands and miners and all sorts of men. So quite naturally, other saloons opened and all the town's businesses began to benefit. And here we are." Edith's expression grew more sour with each word.

Jenna nodded solemnly. "There's really not much we can do."

"But if all the decent people banded together and insisted the saloons curtail their activities, then the mayor and sheriff would have to do something," Allison insisted.

"Oh, pooh! Men!" Edith rolled her eyes. "They're not going to do anything because now the town is prosperous again."

Allison considered her words for a moment. "Then maybe the women should get together and do something."

Edith and Jenna looked at each other, then turned to Allison. "That just might work," Edith told her.

The bell jangled again and the women turned to see Cade Jessup saunter in.

Edith turned up her nose and ignored him. "Jenna, is my fabric in yet?"

"Yes, Mrs. Taylor. I unpacked it last night. Would you like to see it?"

Edith threw Cade a cold look. "No thank you. I'll come back later." She put her nose in the air and glided past him.

Cade smiled broadly and tipped his hat in an exaggerated gesture. "Good morning, Mrs. Taylor."

"Good morning." She forced the greeting through pinched lips and left the shop.

Cade turned to Allison and she felt his gaze burn through her. His smile became a faint smirk as he gestured to the bolts of fabric that surrounded them. "Finished so soon with the medical profession, Miss Tremaine? Taking on the textile industry now, or are you having the town re-outfitted in colors that are more to your taste?"

"Just ordering a new supply of parasols, Mr. Jessup. A lady never knows what she might encounter." Her brow rose to a delicate arch. "Or who."

Jenna stepped between them, breaking the tension. "What can I do for you today, Mr. Jessup?"

He turned to Jenna. "I need curtains sewn for the new stage I'm building. I want to offer the work to you."

"What type of fabric will I be working with?"

Cade frowned. "Red."

Jenna smiled. "Maybe you could send over a swatch and the measurements. I'll give you an estimate."

"I'm on a tight schedule. I need them on time, not a day late. Can you handle the job?"

"That shouldn't be a problem."

"Good day, ladies." Cade tipped his hat. He gave Allison a long, lazy glance and left the store.

Jenna studied her friend for a long moment. "Allison, is there something going on between you and Cade?"

Allison shook her head to clear her thoughts. "What? Good heavens, don't be silly. And you. You're not actually going to sew those curtains for him, are you?"

Jenna shrugged. "I need the work."

"But by doing that, you're encouraging the saloons and the problems they cause."

"Allison, I have Holly to think about. And besides, what good will it do if I turn the work down. He'll just take it to some other seamstress in town."

"Not if all the women band together," Allison said.

Jenna shook her head. "How could we do that?"

"There must be something we can do." Allison paced the floor restlessly, then stopped suddenly. "I know—a ladies' club."

"A what?"

"We'll start a ladies' club." Allison smiled as the idea bloomed in her mind. "They're all over London. It's a place where women go and discuss mutual problems, share ideas, have tea. A place to get away from husbands and families and problems."

"Like the men go to a saloon?"

"No, not at all like saloons," Allison insisted. "We'll focus our efforts on the betterment of Brighton. There are many women in business here, like you and Edith Taylor, who have a stake in the future of the town. And I'm sure most of the wives must feel the same too."

Jenna smiled. "Do you think we could do it? Could we make it work?"

"Of course." Allison tapped her finger against her cheek. "First, we'll need a place to meet."

"The shop right next door is empty." Jenna pointed through the east wall. "I'd thought of expanding and using the space. The Taylors own it and they've been saving it for me. But you can use it."

Allison's eyes widened. "Me?"

"Of course, you." Jenna laughed. "You have to run it. You're perfect."

Allison's stomach coiled into a knot. Yes, she could do it. She could bring the women of Brighton together. And together they could restore the town to its former decent, law-abiding self.

She looked out the front window and across the street at the Pleasure Palace. The ladies club would take on the town.

And they'd start with Cade Jessup.

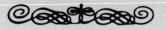

Chapter
Four

"Let's see, that's three shirts, two pairs of trousers, long johns, socks, and boots. Anything else?"

Cade contemplated the stack of new clothing on the counter. "Better throw in suspenders."

"Sure thing." Will Taylor fetched the suspenders from the shelf behind the counter and added the cost to the order pad. "Anything else?"

"No. That should do it."

From the corner of his eye Cade saw Edith Taylor watching him from behind the display of copper pots on the next aisle. She'd not let him out of her sight since he'd begun his shopping. He knew she was ready to pop a stay with curiosity, but was too stubborn to ask why he was buying an armload of boys' clothing. He had no intention of offering an explanation.

"How's business been?" Cade asked.

"Busy this morning," Will replied. He cast a quick glance at Edith, then leaned toward Cade and whispered, "Mrs. Wilkens was in earlier, asking for credit again."

Cade nodded solemnly. The woman had children to feed and a husband who drank away nearly every cent she laid her hands on.

Will shrugged and glanced at his wife again. "What could I do? I know I've got to turn a profit, just like the next man, but how could I say no?"

"I thought Satch would have pulled himself together by now."

Will shook his head. "Some things a man just can't get over."

The bell over the door jangled and Sheriff Mack Carson strode in. He tipped his hat to Edith and joined the men at the counter.

"Howdy, Sheriff, what brings you in this morning?" Will asked.

Mack pulled at the back of his neck. "Didn't get much sleep last night. I figure some fresh coffee ought to do the trick."

Cade frowned. "Trouble last night?" By the nature of his own business he was usually up during the wee hours when most folks were sleeping. He'd heard or seen nothing unusual during the night.

Mack braced both arms against the counter and yawned. "Miss Marshall's ghost again."

"At the church?"

"Yeah. Those damn fools Rupert and Otis came banging on my door in the middle of the night claiming they heard music coming from the church again."

Cade shook his head. "You didn't find anything, did you?"

"Course not." Mack straightened. "Those two fools see more in the bottom of a bottle than they'll ever see or hear down at the church." He looked down at the clothing on the counter. "Who's all this for?"

Cade reached for his leather wallet. "I hired a new errand boy."

"Yeah? Who's that?"

"His name's Tyler. He showed up on my doorstep asking for work," Cade explained. "Looked like he was down on his luck."

Mack nodded. "I saw that boy around town the last couple of days. Pretty skittish. I couldn't get close enough to ask him his name."

"He came by here the other night." Will glanced at Edith again and lowered his voice. "I gave him a plate of food out the back door."

The bell jangled again and Holly McCain ran into the store, her blond braids swinging.

"Don't run, Holly." Jenna followed her in, reaching for her hand. Behind her was Allison.

"Morning, ladies," Will called.

Both the women stopped and smiled.

Mack swept his hat from his head. "Morning, Mrs. Mc-Cain." His elbow upset a glass jar of licorice, spilling it across the counter. He mumbled a curse and righted the jar, placing it upright with a thud.

Jenna smiled sweetly. "Good morning, Sheriff."

Mack stood frozen in place, a silly smile plastered on his face, as Edith shepherded the two women to the back of the store.

Cade stood rooted on the spot as well, gazing at the pink bustle of Allison Tremaine as it bounced along.

"I don't like the looks of this," Will whispered.

Both men turned.

"What are you talking about?" Cade asked.

"Your Miss Tremaine in town again. This could mean something."

Cade turned and saw the three women huddled together beside the yard goods, talking in low voices.

"It doesn't mean anything."

Mack gazed back at the ladies. "She was in my office this morning."

Will's eyes widened. "See?"

Cade waved away his comment. "What did she want?"

He shrugged. "She started carrying on about the town being safer and how it was up to me to see to it."

Will's gaze drilled Cade. "See?"

Annoyed, Cade turned to Mack. "What did you tell her?"

He hung his thumbs in his gun belt. "I told her that's just the way things are in Brighton and that's all there is to it."

Satisfied, Cade nodded. "There. That's the end of the whole matter."

Mack grimaced. "Then she said she was going to go see the mayor."

Will's eyes bulged. "The mayor?"

"Christ. . . ." Cade swore another curse. "Look, it doesn't mean anything. Everette Hawkins isn't going to pay any attention to some city woman barging into his office, asking a lot of questions. He won't give her the time of day."

Will and Mack both gave him a dubious look. And Cade couldn't blame them, though he wouldn't admit it. Mayor Everette Hawkins wasn't exactly the most decisive man he'd ever known.

Cade looked back at the women again. They were still bunched together, whispering and occasionally glancing at the three of them . . . who were also bunched, whispering and glancing. He suddenly felt silly.

"What do I owe you, Will?"

Will turned to his order pad and tallied the figures with a stub of a pencil. "Four-fifty."

Cade laid his money on the counter and waited while Will wrapped the clothing in brown paper and tied it securely with waxed string.

"See you boys around." Cade tucked the package under his arm and headed for the door.

"Good day, ladies." He tipped his hat in exaggerated style. "Good day, Mrs. Taylor."

She threw him a contemptuous look and turned away. Cade knew Edith Taylor didn't like his saloon next door, and didn't like him personally. He always made it a point to shop in her store.

Cade walked to the bathhouse. Two men in filthy clothes waited outside and from within came the sound of off-key singing. Bailey's thick brows disappeared behind his lenses as Cade walked in.

"He's still in there, isn't he?"

Bailey rolled his eyes. "By some miracle, I'd say."

Tyler sat perched on a stack of towels balanced precariously on the wooden bench when Cade entered the room. His arms were wrapped around his drawn-up legs and his chin rested on his knees. His damp hair stuck out like a porcupine.

Cade closed the door. "Did you scrub yourself good?"

Tyler looked up and blinked. "What?"

"I hope you washed your ears so you can hear better."
He dropped the package on the bench. "Come over here."

Tyler climbed from the bench holding the towel around
him.

"Let's see." Cade took the boy's head and turned it
toward the light from the window. He tried to pull away but
Cade held him firmly.

"I'm not taking you back to my place with a scalp full of
head lice. Belle and the girls would have my hide. Hold still,
now."

Cade dug through Tyler's hair until he was satisfied no
insects were hiding there, then peered behind his ears. They
were clean—a little red, but clean. He looked down at the
boy's feet. They were well scrubbed also.

"Top and bottom look okay. What about everything in
between?" Tyler nodded and Cade pointed to the package
on the bench. "This is for you."

Tyler looked at it and frowned. "What is it?"

"Open it and find out."

He knelt down in front of the bench and pulled at the
string, drawing it into a tight knot. He fumbled with it awkwardly until finally Cade took out his pocketknife and cut it
open. Tyler folded back the paper, examining each piece.
He looked up at Cade. "Where are my things?"

"I took them to the laundry, but they couldn't clean
them." Cade didn't tell him Mabel Duncan had in fact refused to laundry them.

His brown eyes widened. He leapt to his feet. "My things
—" He patted his hips frantically. "Where are the things in
my—my—"

"Your pockets?" Cade drew a small cloth sack from inside his coat. "I've got them right here."

Tyler grabbed it. He pulled it open and peered inside.

Cade hadn't paid much attention to the contents of the
sack. A spent shell casing, a knife with a broken blade,
pieces of crumbled newspaper, a few other odds and ends.
As far as he was concerned their only value was what it had
cost him to get Mabel to put her hands in the pockets.

"Everything there?" Cade asked.

Tyler nodded and looked again at the stack of clothing. He shook his head slowly. "I have no money."

"Don't worry about it." Cade pulled a pair of long johns from the package and held them out. But Tyler didn't take them, he only watched Cade with guarded wariness.

Cade sank down onto the bench. "I can see that life's not been easy for you lately. Those bruises you've got tell me you learned the hard way not to trust anyone. But all I can offer you is my word that I want to help you."

Tyler studied him for a long moment until Cade rose. "Besides, I can't have you working for me looking like something the cat dragged in. If it will make you feel better I'll take the cost out of your pay. Now get your clothes on, boy. Let's go have some breakfast."

His eyes lit up. "Food?"

Cade chuckled. "Food."

Tyler dressed quickly and Cade helped him hook up his suspenders. Everything fit pretty well, a bit big, but Cade had figured on that; surely the boy would grow sooner or later. Remembering that Tyler had no comb, Cade gave him his and he slicked his light brown hair down; they'd have to stop by Lloyd's place today too.

Tyler ran his hands down his belly and sniffed his shirt sleeve. He looked up at Cade. A tiny smile tugged at his lips. "Smells good."

He took his shoulders and turned him toward the mirror on the wall. "Looks good too."

He glanced at his reflection, then turned away as if troubled by what he saw.

"Something wrong?"

Tyler shook his head but didn't look up at him.

"Let's go eat." Cade wrapped the rest of the new clothing in the brown paper and tied it securely.

They passed up the Red Eye Cafe, where Cade usually had breakfast, and went into the dining room at the Brighton Hotel. The food was good there, though the atmosphere was a little too stiff for Cade's taste. He preferred the Red Eye and the patrons who gathered there. But today the Brighton Hotel had something the cafe didn't offer—cushions on the chairs.

He and Tyler settled into a table by the front window and Cade ordered steak and eggs for them both. Sipping his coffee, he gazed across the street to Taylor's General Store. Was that Miss Tremaine's pink hat he saw through the window?

Annoyed with himself, Cade looked away.

Tyler didn't talk, and Cade could have used the conversation to keep his mind off other things, but they ate in silence. The boy's manners were much better than he'd demonstrated in the kitchen of the saloon the night before, and Cade was pleased to see that at least the boy's mama had taught him something.

"She's pretty."

Jarred from his thoughts Cade turned to the boy. He was gazing out the window and Cade realized that's exactly what he had been doing as well. He looked out and saw Allison leaving Taylor's General Store along with Jenna and her daughter. Cade frowned. Edith Taylor was with them also.

Cade shifted in his chair and determinedly focused his eyes on Tyler. "Yeah, she's that all right."

The boy swallowed the last of his milk, still peering out the window. "She's not from around here, is she?"

Despite himself, Cade's gaze strayed to the street again. "No, not by a long shot."

"New York, probably."

"How did you know that?"

Tyler picked up his biscuit and dragged it across his plate. "Her clothes."

Cade shrugged. "She sticks out in a crowd. She's here visiting her aunt."

The boy bit into his biscuit. "Her what?"

"Her aunt," he repeated. "I thought you washed your ears. Anyway, once her visit with Miss Allbright is over, she'll be on her way again."

Tyler sat up straighter in his chair, his eyes wide. "Who?"

"Lydia Allbright." Irritated by the amount of his time and thought Allison Tremaine seemed to be occupying, Cade suddenly felt anxious to go. "Let's go, boy. I've got things to do today."

"But—"

Cade rose from his chair and tossed coins on the table. Tyler stuffed the last of his biscuit in his mouth, grabbed his package, and hurried after him.

The streets were busy with people, wagons, and horses, and Cade found himself scanning the crowd for a pink hat, so he was more than a little annoyed when he finally arrived at the express office.

"Morning, Harry," Cade called to the man behind the counter.

Harry Finch peered across his ledger and rose from his desk. A tall, lanky man in his fifties, his bald spot shone like a beacon above his green visor. "Morning yourself, Cade. Running a bit behind schedule today?"

Cade shrugged. "I had some things to take care of."

"Why, I can almost set my watch by you, these last two weeks." He folded his long, thin arms over each other. "You're more reliable than the train."

Cade nodded. "I'm pretty anxious for that shipment to get here."

"Well, do tell." Harry rolled his eyes, then looked past Cade to Tyler lingering by the door. "And who is this?"

As senior agent of the express office, Harry made it his policy to know everyone in town—it was only natural, since he also made it his policy to know everything about everyone in town.

Cade introduced them and Tyler came forward and shook Harry's hand. "Tyler's working for me. Now, about my shipment?"

Harry rolled his eyes again and sighed heavily. "Like I've told you every day for the last two weeks, it's not here. When it gets here you'll know it because it's going to take two dozen men to deliver it to your place. Just wait until the streets empty out and come on over."

Harry's sense of humor grated on Cade's nerves more and more these last two weeks. He pulled his hat lower on his forehead. "Send them a telegram. Find out what the holdup is."

Harry drew in an exasperated breath. "If you want to spend your money, it's up to you. A thing like that is bound to take a while getting here, coming all the way from New

York City. It's not like it's something that gets shipped every day. You're just going to have to wait."

Waiting was grating on his nerves as much as Harry himself. Cade nodded. "All right, I'll give it a while longer."

"See you tomorrow," Harry called as Cade headed out of the office.

Agitated, Cade strode down the street. Everything was riding on that shipment getting here. If it didn't arrive on time, he faced ruin.

Cade suddenly realized Tyler wasn't beside him. He turned to see the boy, absorbed in the sights of the town, wander out into the path of a freight wagon. Cade's heart lurched. He grabbed Tyler's arm and yanked him back onto the boardwalk.

Relief, then anger filled him. "What's the matter with you? Haven't you got better sense than to walk out in front of a freight wagon?"

Tyler's big brown eyes grew even larger as the conveyance thundered past. He swallowed hard and looked up at Cade. "I don't know . . ."

In that instant Cade wasn't sure if Tyler was more afraid of the freight wagon or him. He didn't like the feeling.

Cade loosened his grip on Tyler's thin arm and softened his voice. "I guess you haven't been in a town too much. Just be careful from now on."

Tyler gave him a small nod and ducked his head.

"Cade! Cade! Wait up!"

He turned to see Everette Hawkins hurrying along the boardwalk toward him. Cade mumbled a curse under his breath.

"Cade, I've got to talk to you." The mayor stopped beside Cade and pulled a handkerchief from his hip pocket. The buttons of his coat strained as he huffed and puffed to catch his breath. He patted his perspiring forehead. "It's trouble. Trouble, I tell you. Big, big trouble."

A myriad of possibilities flashed through Cade's mind. He didn't need any more problems. "Christ, Everette, will you spit it out?"

He drew in a deep breath. "I was in my office this morning—my own office, I tell you—minding my own business when my door flew open and in came trouble."

"Jesus. . . ." Cade shook his head. "What happened?"

"What happened? I'll tell you what happened. This Miss Allison Augusta Tremaine sat her pretty little self down in my office and started making all sorts of demands." Everette mopped his forehead again.

Doubly annoyed now, Cade asked, "What did she want?"

"She was asking questions. All sorts of questions. And wanting to know things. And claiming the town wasn't safe anymore for decent people." Everette pressed the handkerchief to his upper lip. "I don't need this kind of trouble. The election is coming up next year. You've got to do something, Cade."

"Me!"

"Yes, you. Everyone knows you provoked her outside your saloon—you're the one who started all of this."

"Now hold on just one damn minute. I didn't start anything—"

Everette's eyes narrowed. "You know her kind, Cade. You're from the East too. You know how to deal with this sort of woman."

Cade pulled off his hat and plowed his fingers through his hair. He'd had his fill of this kind of woman. He'd come west to escape them—them and the whole structured lifestyle of the East.

"Besides," the mayor went on, "folks in town look up to you. Your Pleasure Palace is what got us going again. The other saloon owners will follow your lead. You've got to stop this thing before it gets out of hand."

"It's not going to get out of hand, Everette. She's here visiting her aunt and she'll be gone in a week or two. These city women are all tea parties, etiquette classes, and fancy dresses. Believe me, I know. She's going to raise a little fuss, then be gone. It's not worth worrying about."

The mayor shook his head. "I don't know. I've never seen a woman get so worked up before. A Texas twister, she was, a real Texas twister. And that can cause a lot of trouble. Big trouble."

Cade couldn't disagree with that description of Allison

Tremaine. He patted the mayor's shoulder. "There's nothing she can do, Everette. She's just one woman—and a city woman at that. She'll be gone and this whole thing will be forgotten in no time."

"I hope you're right." Everette mopped his forehead again. "I hope you're right."

Cade sighed heavily as the mayor walked away. He knew he was right. He'd bet the Pleasure Palace on it.

Chapter
Five

Edith Taylor turned the key in the lock and pushed the front door open. "Bear in mind the place has been empty for a while. It will need a good cleaning."

"Of course." Allison gave Jenna a confident nod. Beside her, Holly fidgeted.

Allison led the way through the threshold of the shop next door to Jenna's and stopped in the center of the room. Her smile faded.

Cobwebs crowded every corner and the floor was carpeted with a thick layer of dust. Muted light filtered through the streaked windows that flanked the door. Several crates and barrels were piled by the wall.

"It was a dry goods store before," Jenna offered. "The folks moved back East, I believe— No, Holly, don't touch anything."

Holly jumped across the floor as if on an invisible hopscotch board.

Edith dropped the key in her pocket. "They couldn't make a go of it. Nevada isn't for everyone."

Allison felt the eyes of both ladies on her and she was sure they were wondering if Nevada would be too much for her as well.

She squared her shoulders. "What's behind the curtain?"

"The living quarters. Come look."

Edith pushed aside the ragged curtain that separated the

two rooms and Allison followed her in. A large cookstove squatted in the corner near the door that led to the alley. A window let in enough light to illuminate the dust and dirt that covered everything.

"Over here is the bedroom."

Allison followed Edith into the room off the kitchen. It was small, but adequate for Allison's needs.

Jenna peeked into the room. "I guess it's not exactly what you're used to."

No, it wasn't. Allison's family was quite wealthy and she had funds of her own, thanks to her doting grandmother. But dust and dirt were not her concern now. Not at all.

Images of her Aunt Lydia and the time she'd spent here as a young girl filled her mind. She treasured those memories, a span of months in her young life that had left an indelible impression. Allison wanted them back. She wanted Brighton back.

"This place will be spotless in no time," Allison declared. "Brighton's ladies' club will be open before you know it."

Edith looked at her, a deep crease cut into her brow. "Are you sure?"

Edith had been enthusiastic about the idea of a ladies' club when she and Jenna had presented it to her in her store. If it was to succeed, Allison would need Edith's support.

Allison stood a little straighter. "Yes. Quite certain. I care a great deal for this town. And besides, I can hardly leave my aunt with her health so poor."

The corners of Edith's mouth turned downward. "There's no one back in New York you have to get home to? Family?"

She'd write to her parents immediately. "They will understand completely."

Edith leaned closer. "Someone else? Someone . . . special?"

Allison's stomach tightened. She twisted the ring on her finger. "No one."

"Good." Edith's pinched lips drew a little tighter. She dropped the key in Allison's hand. "I'll be back tomorrow to collect the rent."

The three women left the store with Holly darting ahead. Allison locked the door securely behind her. They said good-bye to Edith and went inside Jenna's shop.

Jenna settled Holly on a high stool at her worktable and took the seat next to her.

"Where are you going to get the furniture to fill the club?" Jenna asked as she sat down and picked up her sewing.

Allison took a pad and small pencil from her reticule and began to write. "From Aunt Lydia's house. She has tons of things there that will work perfectly."

"Won't she mind?"

She thought of her aunt lying lifelessly in bed. "Actually, I'd be relieved if she would put up a fuss."

Jenna nodded sympathetically. "She's doing poorly?"

"Yes. But I hope that opening the ladies' club may help snap her out of it." Allison sat down on a stool across from Jenna and jotted notes on the pad. "First of all, I'm going to need your services, Jenna."

"What did you have in mind?"

Allison tilted her head. "Mauve, I think. And lace. Lots of lace so the place looks very feminine."

Jenna nodded. "Sounds perfect."

Allison began writing again. "I'll need curtains and table-cloths, for starters. Can you begin right away?"

Jenna looked at the other orders waiting. "I have several orders ahead of you. But I can shuffle them around, if need be."

"I can give you a hand too." Allison sighed with pleasure. "And I've got a fantastic idea to announce our opening."

The kitchen was crowded when Cade came through the back door of the saloon and dropped his hat on the peg beside the storeroom. Vance stood at the cookstove expertly tending the pots and pans, the air rich with the smell of bacon frying.

Billy looked up from the bread he was slicing at the side-board. "Hey, boss, you heard the news?"

"Don't say it." Belle waved away Billy's words with her long, carefully manicured hand. Seated at the table, legs resting on the chair beside her, she gave him a scathing look. "It's blasphemy, Billy. Don't you start talking that nonsense again."

"It's true—every word of it." Billy gestured with the knife in one hand and a hunk of bread in the other. "Tell her, Clare."

Clare, younger than Belle by a suspected decade, eased beside Vance at the cookstove and poured herself another cup of coffee. She pushed her dark hair over her shoulder. "Some say it's a miracle, Belle."

"It's demons, I tell you, demons." Belle brushed her red hair aside and rubbed her feet. "You ought not be talking about it."

"Yeah, I heard. Miss Marshall was at the church again." Cade dismissed their chatter and reached behind him to pull Tyler into the room. "Meet Tyler. He's working here now."

Everybody fell silent and stared for a moment. Belle shifted uncomfortably and pulled her turquoise wrapper closed over her ample bosoms. Clare tightened the sash on hers.

Tyler clutched the package tight against his chest. "Hello." His voice was soft and unsure.

Billy wiped his hand on his apron. "Glad to have you with us, Tyler."

He responded with a tentative smile and a handshake.

Belle pulled at her wrapper again, gave Cade a questioning look, and smiled. "Welcome, young fella."

Vance offered a quick nod and Clare smiled.

Cade rubbed his hands together. "Tyler, bring in a load of wood from outside, will you?"

"Wood?"

"Yes, wood. For the stove. It's stacked by the door."

Tyler nodded and headed outside.

Four sets of questioning eyes bored into him. Cade took a cup from the cupboard and poured himself coffee. "He's the kid who showed up here last night asking for work."

Vance frowned. "That's him? He cleaned up good."

Cade pulled back a chair and sat down across from Belle.

"His parents died not too long ago and he's got no place to live. I hired him to run errands and help around here."

"Where's he from?" Clare sauntered to the sideboard and helped herself to a slice of bread.

Cade shrugged. "Says he moved around a lot. Some dirt farmer's kid, I suspect."

"What's he doing in Brighton?" Billy asked.

"I don't know." Cade sipped his coffee. "But somebody beat him half to death as a welcoming gift. He's got bruises all over him."

"Bastard . . ." Belle hissed the word, grimaced, and rubbed her feet again.

Cade glanced back over his shoulder. "I don't think the boy's too bright."

"Well, hell, that won't bother us any." Clare popped a crust of bread in her mouth. "We're used to Billy here, aren't we?"

Everybody laughed, bringing a blush to Billy's cheeks.

Cade looked around the room, then across the table at Belle. "Where's Sonny?"

She shrugged. "Upstairs sleeping."

Cade shook his head and downed the rest of his coffee.

He'd hired Sonny a few weeks ago, against his better judgment. Belle and Clare had been dancing in the saloon for him since the Pleasure Palace had opened and he'd needed a third girl since Maggie had run off and married a cowhand from the Dillon Ranch a month ago. Sonny had come along when he'd needed someone. All the girls' routines were planned for three. Sonny was young—only seventeen—but there'd been something about her he didn't trust. He'd hired her because he was desperate, hoping she'd fit in. So far, she hadn't.

"Eating with us, boss?" Billy took a stack of plates from the shelf above the sideboard.

Cade rubbed his belly. "No. I've got things to do."

Tyler came into the room juggling his package of new clothes and several pieces of wood. He stopped in the doorway.

"Put it in the wood box," Cade told him.

Tyler only stood there.

Cade rose from his chair and pointed. "The wood box by the stove."

Tyler scurried to the box, lifted the lid, and dropped the wood inside.

"Grab the broom from the storage room and sweep up in the bar." Cade looked at Billy. "Show him what to do, will you?"

"Sure, boss."

Cade headed up the steps, then turned back. "Vance, give the boy a piece of the curtain fabric and have him run it over to Jenna McCain's place. Looks like she'll do the sewing I need."

Vance nodded and scraped the eggs from the pan.

Cade started up the stairs again but turned around. He pointed at Tyler. "You be careful crossing the street. Understand?"

Tyler nodded quickly and Cade climbed the stairs to his bedroom.

Situated at the front of the building the room was comfortable, big enough to accommodate the brass bed, bureau, and armoire, and afford him a view of Main Street from his desk by the window.

The chair creaked as he settled into it and swiveled around to look at the street below. Cade locked his hands behind his head and leaned back. Brighton had changed since he'd arrived. He'd been a big part of turning the place around. Sometimes he wished he could share his accomplishments with—

Cade pushed the thought from his mind and turned back to his desk. Better to let sleeping dogs lie, he decided. Cade took out his ledger and began to work.

The bell over the door jangled drawing Allison's attention from the hem she was stitching. Though she wasn't nearly as good with a needle as Jenna, her stitches were passable. She smiled at the young boy standing in the doorway.

"Come in. Can I help you?"

His eyes roamed the bolts of colorful fabric, the baskets

of buttons and threads, then settled on Allison. "I'm suppose to bring this to Mrs. McCain."

Allison put aside the calico dress and slid from the stool. He seemed uncomfortable in the shop, but most men did. She didn't realize it started at such a young age.

"Mrs. McCain went to Taylor's to buy a spool of thread. I'm watching the shop. What do you have for her?"

He closed the door and took a swatch of red fabric from the pocket of his loose-fitting trousers. "Cade sent me over with this."

Allison's back stiffened. "Cade Jessup? From across the street?"

He held out the swatch. "Yes, ma'am."

"Whatever are you doing in that abhorrent establishment?"

His eyes widened. "What?"

Allison drew in a quick breath. "You work there, don't you?"

"Yes, ma'am."

Allison's stomach knotted. He was hardly more than a child, a thin, half-starved child at that, in need of a good haircut. Was there nothing Cade Jessup wouldn't stoop to?

"What's your name?" Allison asked gently.

"Tyler."

"And how long have you been in Mr. Jessup's employ?"

He lifted one shoulder. "What?"

Her eyes narrowed. "Does he pay you?"

"No, ma'am. Not yet. But—"

"This is an outrage." Allison took the swatch of fabric from Tyler and placed it on the worktable. The boy was shorter than her own five and a half feet and dreadfully thin. "And by the looks of you he never feeds you either. Do you want something to eat?"

He nodded eagerly. "Yes, ma'am."

"Come along. But quietly, please, Holly is napping."

Allison led the way to the kitchen at the back of the shop. She was sure Jenna wouldn't mind her giving out a piece of the apple pie cooling on the sideboard—she'd do it herself, if she were here.

Taking a knife from the drawer, she cut the pie and

placed the slice on a plate. "Have you worked for Mr. Jessup very long, Tyler?"

"No, I haven't been in this town very long." Tyler accepted the plate and cut into it hungrily.

She gestured toward the table. "Sit down, Tyler."

He eyed the chairs. "No, thank you."

"I'm new in town also," Allison said. "I'm visiting my aunt."

The boy stopped suddenly and swallowed. "You're the lady from New York."

"Yes. How did you know?" She didn't realize her reputation had spread throughout the entire town already.

"Cade said so." Tyler took another bite. "You're Aunt Lydia's niece."

Allison's temper raised a notch. "Cade—Mr. Jessup—was discussing me?"

Tyler nodded. "We saw you. He said you were pretty."

"Pretty?" Her temper flared. How dare he discuss her as though she were some common floozie on the street?

"Is she here with you?" He scraped his fork across the plate.

"What's that?" His question about Aunt Lydia drove away a measure of her anger. She took his empty plate. "No. She's quite ill, I'm afraid."

"Do you mean she's sick?"

"Yes, very sick."

Color drained from his face. "She's going to be all right, isn't she?"

"I'm not sure, Tyler. She hasn't been out of bed in months, I understand. I've got to talk to the doctor. That's one of the reasons I'm staying in Brighton." She gave him a smile. "Would you like another slice?"

An expression of confusion crossed his face and his brows drew together in lines of worry. He rubbed his forehead.

"Tyler, are you feeling all right?" Allison asked gently.

He looked up at her. "I—"

The bell over the door jangled once more, drawing Allison's attention. It was probably Jenna returning from Taylor's, but it could be a customer.

"I'll be right back."

Allison slipped through the curtain into the shop. Cade Jessup stood beside the worktable. He looked as surprised at seeing her as she felt at seeing him.

"Mr. Jessup." The words came out in a tight, pinched voice.

He tipped his hat but didn't venture closer. "Afternoon, Miss Tremaine."

A long, tense moment passed before Cade spoke again. "I've come to see Mrs. McCain."

"She's not here just now." Her chin went up a notch. "But one of your . . . employees . . . is. Tyler?"

The curtain opened and Tyler walked into the shop. He looked past Allison to Cade.

"I brought that thing over like you asked," he explained hurriedly.

Cade nodded. "That's fine. Why don't you go on back and give Vance a hand in the kitchen."

Tyler gave Allison only a glance before hurrying out of the shop.

"And be careful crossing the street," Cade called as the door closed.

Another long moment passed while Cade and Allison stared at each other. Again, Cade spoke first.

"I needed to give the curtain measurements to Mrs. McCain." He pulled a piece of paper from his vest pocket.

Allison rounded the worktable and accepted it as though it were the most vile item she'd ever touched. She laid it aside. "I'll see that she gets it, though I'm not certain how quickly she can get the job done now."

He frowned. "Why not?"

"She's accepted a rather large order."

His eyes narrowed. "From who?"

She squared her shoulders. "From myself."

Anger spread across his face. "Anything you need can wait. I need my curtains."

"You can't just come in here ordering people around," Allison told him. "There are no children employed here whom you can bully."

He planted his fists on his lean hips. "What are you talking about?"

She pointed toward the street. "I'm speaking of that child who was just in here. A child—working in a saloon."

"You don't know what you're talking about, lady."

"I think it's quite obvious."

He stepped closer. "What you think and what is true are two different things."

"Do you deny that boy is employed in your saloon?"

"No, I don't deny it for a second." His temper rose.

"Further proof," Allison concluded, "of the moral decay this town has suffered."

"This isn't the East. You can't bring all your ideals and grand notions here and expect them to work."

"And you can't expect to leave them all behind," she told him. "This is still a civilized society."

"This isn't the East!"

"And you can't pretend decency doesn't exist simply because you choose to profit from others' indiscretions!" Allison faced him squarely. "Why, the very name of your saloon is—"

He edged nearer. "Is what?"

Allison's cheeks flushed. She backed up a step. "It's . . . vulgar."

"Vulgar?" A slow smile spread across his face. "Do you think having pleasure in a man's life is vulgar?"

Heat rose from the very pit of her stomach and spread through her. She backed into the worktable. "I think that displaying it in public is vulgar."

He leaned closer, placing one hand on the edge of the table, blocking her in. "So it's all right for a man to have his pleasure, just not so anybody can know about it?"

His body was only inches away and the desire to press herself against him nearly overwhelmed her. She remembered the hard lines of his chest she'd felt when she'd ridden on his horse with him in the rain, and the feel of his muscled thighs against her. The heat he gave off was as compelling as her own internal fire.

Allison lifted her face to his. She smelled his deep, masculine scent, drawing it in, savoring it. And suddenly his eyes were no longer taunting, his expression no longer teasing. His lips closed over hers, caressing her mouth gently.

He moved softly, with great tenderness, plying her until she responded and her lips parted. His tongue touched hers, politely, with great care so as not to rush. She met his caress, unable not to.

Then suddenly he pulled away. Their gazes met and held, both stunned by what had just happened. Cade turned on his heels and left the shop. Allison had to grasp the edge of the worktable to keep from falling.

What in the hell was the matter with him? What in the hell had he done?

Cade tossed his trousers across the desk chair and yanked down the quilt. He'd berated himself over and over since this afternoon and now here it was after midnight and he still didn't know what had come over him.

He slid into bed and dropped his arm over his forehead. He'd kissed her. He'd kissed the uppity, high-toned Miss Allison Augusta Tremaine. Right there in broad daylight. In the middle of the dress shop. What the hell was he thinking?

He'd thought of little else all evening. He'd found that the woman had been in his thoughts almost constantly. He'd even caught himself watching the street until he saw her leave town with that old driver of her aunt's. Cade flopped over in the bed. What the hell had he been thinking?

He'd not been thinking at all, he decided as he stared into the darkness of his room. He'd just acted on some instinct that had possessed him inexplicably. That was all it was, just instinct.

Cade jabbed his fist into his pillow and forced his eyes shut.

Screams broke into his sleep. Cade jumped from the bed, shoved into his trousers, and grabbed his Peacemaker from the desk drawer. He wasn't sure how long he'd been asleep.

Belle and Clare peered out of their room when he charged into the hall.

"What in the world?" Belle's eyes were saucers in the dim light.

"Get back inside."

Vance came from his room dressed in a long nightshirt, and Billy stumbled out in his long johns.

"What's up, boss?"

The screams grew louder. Cade hurried down the passageway searching for their source. He stopped outside the small room at the end of the hall. It had been a storage room until this afternoon when he'd had Billy and Tyler clean it out and make it into a bedroom.

Cade opened the door. The lantern beside the bed burned low. Tyler was tangled in the covers, in the throes of a horrible nightmare, screaming.

"No! No! Don't! Please . . . don't!"

Cade dropped his gun on the bedside table and shook the boy's shoulders. The nightmare's grip was strong and he had to shake him again to rouse him from sleep. Still, he didn't wake completely.

Belle came into the room as Clare, Vance, and Billy peered in from the hallway. "What's wrong with him?"

"Just a bad dream." Cade rolled him onto his belly and pulled the quilt off the bed.

"Must have been one hell of a dream."

He looked pale and drawn in the lamplight, and even thinner in his ill-fitting long johns, but he slept still, the nightmare seemingly gone.

Cade straightened the quilt and spread it over him. "My guess is that we can thank whoever gave him that beating for causing this."

Belle nodded. "Poor little fella. I'd like to get my hands on the coward who did it."

"Let's try to get some sleep." Cade picked up his gun from the table and followed Belle into the hall. They exchange a look acknowledging Sonny's absence, but neither mentioned it.

Billy yawned and ambled back to his room; Vance scratched his head and disappeared.

"Sleep well," Belle said as she slipped into the room she shared with Clare.

Cade nodded. But between Tyler's nightmares and intrusive thoughts of Allison, he doubted he'd get any sleep at all.

Chapter
Six

Silence hung heavy in the big, empty house with only the ticking of the clock in the parlor to keep her company. Allison sat at the head of the dining-room table, her breakfast plate pushed aside, forcing her thoughts on the writing tablet before her. She tried desperately to complete the list of things she must accomplish today, but other images kept intruding.

The kiss. No one had ever kissed her before, not like Cade Jessup had kissed her. Certainly—especially—not Nigel. It was improper. Indecent. It was . . . wonderful.

The thought stunned her and Allison jumped in her chair. Good gracious, whatever was the matter with her? She snatched up the tablet before her.

"Georgia!" She didn't bother with the bell.

The housekeeper's cheerful face appeared through the adjoining door. "Yes, Miss Allison?"

"Where is Wes Palmer?" The words came out harshly.

It didn't appear to faze Georgia. "He's coming. I just saw him out the back window."

"Good." Allison consulted her list. "Did you get together the other things I asked for?"

"Yes, indeed. All packed up and ready to go." Georgia took the empty breakfast plate from the table. "And I have to say, the whole idea is so exciting. Imagine, a ladies' club right here in Brighton."

"Keep it to yourself for now, Georgia. I don't want word
getting out until we open."

She nodded. "Miss Lydia will be so pleased."

"I hope you're right." Allison turned back to her list and
Georgia left her alone.

The door to the kitchen opened a moment later and Wes
Palmer walked in. He was dressed as he had been the first
day Allison had seen him when he and Cade had nearly
come to blows, in a hat with the snakeskin band and a gun
on his hip. His mustache drooped past his mouth.

"You want something?"

He didn't remove his hat, but stood by the door, his
thumbs hung in his gun belt. His tone told her he resented
the intrusion on his day.

"Gather several men and bring a wagon around. I need
these items moved into town." Allison took a sheet of paper
from the tablet and laid it out on the table.

With a loose, deliberate step he crossed the room and
picked up the list. "What for?"

Her back stiffened. "Because I asked you to."

His eyes narrowed. "I've been watching over this place
for a long time and—"

"And now you don't have to do it anymore. Not while I'm
here." Allison gave him her coldest look, the one she per-
fected in New York dealing with insolent servants and dis-
obedient children.

He crammed the paper into his pocket and turned to
leave.

"And one more thing, Mr. Palmer. I'd like the ranch
books delivered here to the house."

Palmer's eyes narrowed. "You want what?"

"By the end of the day, if you please. That will be all."
She turned back to her writing, her silence dismissing him.

Allison didn't look up again until she heard the door
close. A chill swept up her spine. Wes Palmer struck a chord
in her she'd never felt before. It prompted her to add another item to her list of things to do in town today. She left
the room and hurried upstairs.

Aunt Lydia had been awake when she'd come home last
night and Allison had spent a few minutes with her. She'd

been excited to see her and they'd talked a bit before the older woman had fallen asleep again. Allison was heartened by the moment. She hoped that this morning would prove better.

She slipped inside her aunt's bedroom and pushed back the heavy drapes. Morning sunlight filled the room rousing Aunt Lydia from the depths of her covers.

"Good morning." Allison forced cheer into her voice and took a seat on the chair at her bedside.

She blinked and squinted. "Oh, my, Allison, you're really here? I thought it was only a dream."

"No, Aunt Lydia, I'm here." She took her aunt's thin, veined hand. "How are you feeling today?"

She shook her head and laid back on the pillow. "Oh, I don't know. . . ."

Allison squeezed her hand. "Do you remember what we talked about last night? The ladies' club I'm starting in Brighton. I'm so anxious for you to come in and see it."

Lydia turned her head away and gazed off as if seeing something no one else could. "Maybe someday, dear." She extracted her hand from Allison's. "But you go ahead. Take whatever you want from the house. It really doesn't matter. Nothing really matters, you know."

"But, Aunt Lydia, of course it matters," Allison insisted. "Don't you remember the clubs we visited in London? What a wonderful time we had? How the ladies there were—"

Emotion rose in her throat. Allison bit down on her lip. Aunt Lydia had fallen asleep again.

She'd finally gone by Dr. Tanner's office in town yesterday and questioned him at length about her aunt's health. He only said that he could find nothing wrong with her physically. She'd simply lost the will to participate in life. And there was no medicine for that.

Allison hadn't wanted to believe the old doctor, but seeing Aunt Lydia now was a convincing argument. She forced down her emotions and left the room.

In her own bedroom, determination hardened within her. More than ever, she knew she had to remain in Brighton.

She couldn't leave, not with the disheartening state of Aunt
Lydia's health.

Allison pulled open her bureau drawer and looked down
at the garnet and diamond ring on her finger. Aunt Lydia
needed her. Brighton needed her. And New York?

Nigel came into her thoughts. He'd make the perfect husband. They'd make the perfect match. Everyone had said it,
over and over again. They would be the link joining two
powerful, prominent families. Allison had heard it said so
many times, in fact, that she'd believed it too. But now that
she was in Brighton, everything looked different.

Allison bit down on her lip and dropped the ring into the
drawer. She was staying to help her aunt. Wasn't she?

She closed the drawer.

Grumpy from a lack of sleep, Cade settled himself into
the barber chair and closed his eyes. He'd decided to treat
himself to a shave this morning. Maybe it would improve
his mood. Tyler had awakened early. When Cade asked him
about the nightmare, he'd said he didn't remember it. He'd
brought him along with him this morning to Lloyd's Barbershop for a much needed haircut.

Lloyd soaped his face and raked the razor down Cade's
cheek. Approaching fifty, his thin mustache was peppered
with white, as was his carefully combed hair. He jerked his
chin in Tyler's direction. "Another newcomer, huh?"

"Two in two days, by golly that's something." Witt
Thomas threw in his opinion from his usual seat on the
bench by the door.

"Morning, boys." Bailey stepped through the door ad-
justing his spectacles.

Lloyd nodded. "We were just talking about our latest
newcomer. Have you seen her? Quite a sight."

Witt whistled low. "A fine-looking woman, that one."

"Have you seen Miss Tremaine?" Lloyd asked Cade.

Held in place by the razor at his throat, Cade only murmured, "Yes, we've met."

"That's right, she was the one out in front of your saloon." Lloyd looked at Witt. "Gave ol' Rupert and Otis
what-for."

"Wish I'd seen it." Witt scratched his chin.

"You might get to," Bailey said, "seeing as how she's staying on in Brighton."

Witt slapped his knees. "Hot damn!"

"What?" Cade jumped up. The razor nicked his chin. "Jesus, Lloyd. . . ."

A speck of blood oozed from the cut. Lloyd reached for a towel. "What are you so jumpy for? Land's sake, Cade, I could have killed you."

He pushed away the towel. "What do you mean she's staying? She's only here visiting her aunt."

Bailey shook his head. "Naw, she's staying. Rented her a shop right here on Main Street."

"A shop?" Cade looked at Lloyd for confirmation.

He nodded and touched the towel to Cade's chin. "I heard it myself just this morning. Will Taylor rented—"

"Will Taylor?"

"—rented her a place right next to that McCain woman's dress shop." Lloyd nodded. His brows drew together. "Why, that's right across the street from your place, isn't it?"

"Damn right it is." Cade grabbed the towel from Lloyd and wiped the shaving soap from his chin. "Give the boy a haircut. I'll be back later."

Cade strode from the barbershop without a backward glance.

Allison tossed the bucket full of dirty water out the back door and returned to the pump in the kitchen. She drew in a deep breath and refilled the bucket. Since her arrival at the shop this morning she'd knocked down all the cobwebs, swept and scrubbed the floor in the main part of the shop. Wes Palmer had shown up—late—with the furniture and placed it in the middle of the floor before leaving as quickly as he'd come.

Allison took the bucket from the sink and carried it into the bedroom. The shop was cool, the silence adding to the stillness of the air. Noises from the street drifted in. She'd clean the back rooms, then arrange the furniture, she decided.

Broom in hand, she began to sweep, humming softly to herself. The sound of the back door flying open startled her. She grasped the broom handle, her senses on full alert. This morning she'd gotten some curious stares through the window, but no one had ventured in to ask what she was doing. Now, someone was in her kitchen.

Her heart pounded in her chest as she crept to the door of the bedroom, gripping the broom handle. She peeped into the kitchen just as a man charged into the room. Allison screamed and swung the broom, landing a blow squarely across his chest.

"What the—?" Cade yanked the broom from her hands. His gaze bored into her like hot daggers. "What's the matter with you?"

Stunned, Allison jumped back. She pressed her fingertips to her lips. "Oh! I didn't know who it was."

Cade rubbed his chest and gave her a sour look. "Parasol, broom—give you anything with a handle on it, lady, and you're just plain dangerous."

Her jaw tightened. "If you hadn't come barging in, frightening me half to death, I certainly would not have needed to defend myself."

Cade propped the broom against the wall. "Defending yourself? Is that what you call it?"

"Yes, and—" Her eyes widened. "Oh, dear. I hurt you. You're bleeding."

He touched his fingers to his chin. The nick Lloyd had given him was oozing still. "It's nothing."

"It certainly is. Come into the light."

Allison took his wrist and pulled him into the kitchen. He grudgingly went along and stood by the sink where she indicated.

"I didn't mean to hurt you." Allison pulled an eyelet handkerchief trimmed with pink from her pocket and stretched up to reach his chin. She pressed it against the cut.

He pulled back. "It's nothing."

"Hold still," she insisted and moved with him. "These things shouldn't be taken lightly."

The soft, feminine scent of her wafted up, titillating

Cade's nose. God, she smelled good. He hadn't smelled anything that good in Brighton. She stood close, so close his body begged to lean forward the mere inch or two it would take to touch her. Cade closed his hand over the pump to steady himself.

Allison looked up, past her own hands, past the delicate handkerchief to Cade's eyes. They were watching her intently. For a moment she was lost in their blueness, lost in the spell he cast over her.

His fingers closed over hers. They were warm and strong. She sensed the power in them. He took the handkerchief from her.

She spoke in a soft whisper. "The bleeding has stopped."

That's because it had all rushed somewhere else, Cade thought. He cleared his throat and shoved the handkerchief in his pocket.

Annoyed with himself, Cade swung his arm across the room. "What are you doing here, anyway?"

His harsh tone drove the melancholy from her thoughts. "I'm cleaning."

"I can see that."

His gaze swept her from head to toe. She wore a simple calico dress and apron, with a scarf wrapped around her hair. But even in that outfit, Miss Allison Augusta Tremaine still looked out of place in Brighton.

"What for?" he asked.

"Because it's dirty." Allison gave him an indulgent smile. "Now, if you'll excuse me, I have a great deal to do." She turned on her toes and disappeared into the bedroom again.

Cade followed her. "I want to know what's going on here."

"And why is that?" She reached for the broom.

Cade grabbed it first. "I'll hold on to this, if you don't mind."

Allison sighed heavily and crossed her arms. She clamped her mouth shut and stared at him blankly.

He pointed a finger at her. "I know you rented this place from Will Taylor, so don't try to deny it. But you're wasting your time here. You don't know anything about running a business in Brighton."

"You needn't worry. I certainly have no plans to open a saloon, so they'll be no more competition for you and your . . . Pleasure Palace." She wrinkled her nose, the words distasteful on her tongue.

His eyes narrowed. "You'll never make a go of it. I know about Eastern women—all tea parties and luncheons and manners classes. It's a hard life here."

She planted her hands on her hips. "For your information, Mr. Jessup, I did not spend every waking moment of my entire life in meaningless pursuits. I have my teaching certificate and have taught in several schools in New York."

"A teacher?" His gaze swept her, as if seeing her in a different light now. His eyebrows crept upward. "Teaching what? Manners? How far to stick up your pinkie at tea time? How to catch a rich husband?"

Anger colored her cheeks. "Arithmetic. English. Reading. As I said, I am a credentialed teacher."

He swung his arm around the room. "So, is that what you're doing here? Opening a school? I hate to tell you, honey, but Brighton already has a school."

"One school, and how many saloons?"

His expression darkened. "Don't start with that nonsense about saloons again. Now, tell me what you're doing here."

She met his gaze steadily. "I can assure you this, Mr. Jessup, once this place opens, you'll wish it were merely another saloon."

"Is that some sort of threat?"

"It's a promise."

He nodded slowly. "We'll see who goes out of business first."

A confident smile spread over her face. "Yes, we will."

"My pleasure." Cade threw the word at her, remembering that she considered it vulgar. Shock showed on her face. He turned and left.

"I saw her, boss. I saw her walk past the window." Billy craned his neck looking over the top of the swinging doors.

He turned to Cade standing by the bar. "But I still can't tell what all's going on over there."

Behind the bar, Vance shook his head slowly as he polished a glass. "Beats me."

"Maybe it's nothing," Will Taylor offered.

It was early afternoon now and the saloon was nearly empty. Joe Capp and his crew of carpenters were busy hammering and sawing. Cade glared at Will standing beside him at the bar. "This is all your doing, renting the store to her."

Will's eyes widened. "It wasn't me. It was Edith. And it was over and done with before I knew what happened."

Billy walked back to the bar. "Didn't she tell you nothing about what Miss Tremaine was doing?"

"Not a word." Will sipped his beer.

"Afternoon, boys."

The swinging doors opened and Sheriff Mack Carson sauntered in. He eased up to the bar between Cade and Will. "What's going on?"

Billy pointed out the window at the end of the bar. "That Miss Tremaine has set up business here in Brighton. Right next door to Mrs. McCain's place."

Mack peered out the window, then looked at Cade. "I thought you said she was only staying for a few weeks."

Will drained his glass. "Cade, you've got to do something about it."

He nodded slowly. "Got any ideas?"

"Who? Me? Sorry, got to get back to the store." Will disappeared out the door.

"Give me a beer, Vance." Mack rested his elbow on the bar and gazed out the window for a long moment. He sighed heavily.

Cade peered out the window and saw Jenna McCain sweeping the boardwalk in front of her store. He looked at Mack. "You ought to go over and talk to the woman."

Vance placed the mug on the bar and went back to polishing the glasses.

"I can't do that," Mack insisted.

"Why not?"

"Because every time I get around a woman I get all tongue-tied and end up knocking something over." Mack reached for the mug, misjudged the distance, and sent it spilling across the bar. "Damn. . . . See what I mean?"

Vance righted the glass and wiped up the beer. "Harry Finch is courting her."

Mack straightened. "Harry Finch? From the express office?"

Vance nodded and placed another beer on the bar. "I saw him over at her place a few days ago. Took her out for supper at the hotel, I heard."

Cade leaned on the bar. "You'd better think about making your move."

Mack gazed out the window again. "But her husband's barely gone."

"Two years, Mack. You can't expect a good-looking young woman like her to stay unattached forever."

Mack's shoulders sagged. "But Harry Finch? He's an old man. What could she see in him?"

"Senior express agent." Vance nodded wisely. "It's a secure job. Women like that sort of thing. And she's got that little girl to think about."

Mack smiled. "Yeah, that little Holly is an angel. Looks just like her mama."

Cade patted him on the shoulder. Mack had been smitten with Jenna McCain since he'd arrived in Brighton; it was painfully obvious. "I wouldn't want to see you lose out to the likes of Harry Finch."

Mack downed the beer. "I'll see you later."

Cade watched out the window to see if Mack crossed the street to Jenna's place. He walked the other way instead.

"I've got book work to do." Cade went into the kitchen. Belle was in her wrapper, her feet soaking in a tub. Tyler stood at the sink washing dishes. Though his sleeves were rolled up, they were soaked, as were his shirt and the apron he wore. Water puddled on the floor at his feet.

The boy had demonstrated little ability at any job Cade had given him. It had taken him hours to sweep the bar because he didn't know to put the chairs atop the tables first, and even then he'd stirred up a good-sized dust storm. Cade had to show him the proper way to stack wood in his arms to fill the wood box, and he didn't know a pot from a frying pan. Cade hesitated to send him on errands for fear he'd wander in front of a freight wagon again. He seemed to lack plain, down-to-earth common sense.

But the boy tried hard. Simpleminded though he seemed to be, he worked diligently at whatever instructions Cade gave him. It didn't bother Cade anymore that he often had to explain things several times to him.

"Cade, we'll get to practicing in a bit." Belle raised one foot from the tub and flexed her toes. She frowned and lowered it into the water again.

"That's fine." Cade started up the steps, then turned back. "Tyler, come on up when you get finished."

"Yes, sir." Tyler turned and the glass he was washing slipped from his hand. It shattered on the floor.

Tyler gasped. He looked down at the broken glass, then up at Cade. Color drained from his face. "I'm sorry."

Frantic, he dropped to his knees and raked the shards together with his hands. He glanced up at Cade again. "I'm sorry. I'll be more careful. I promise I will. Please don't make me leave—I'll pay for the glass."

"Hold on there." Cade came down the stairs. "You're going to cut yourself. Use the—"

Tyler screamed and rocked back on his heels. "My finger! I cut my finger!"

Cade knelt beside Tyler. "Let me see."

Tyler clutched his wrist with the other hand, watching in horror as blood pooled at the end of his finger. "It's bleeding! My finger!"

Cade rose, wrapped his arm around Tyler's chest, and carried him to the sink. Belle hurried over and worked the pump.

Pinning Tyler between himself and the counter, Cade pried his hand open and held it under the water. The blood washed away, revealing a tiny cut.

"It's nothing, Tyler. It's not serious." Cade pulled a handkerchief from his pocket and pressed it against the wound. "Calm down. It's all right."

The kitchen door opened and Vance and Billy came in.

"What's all the commotion?" Billy asked.

Belle looked back over her shoulder. "Tyler cut himself on a glass. But it's okay, nothing serious."

"You all right, buddy?" Billy asked as he and Vance approached.

Tyler sniffed and nodded.

"Get the broom, Billy," Vance said. "Let's get this cleaned up."

"No," Cade told them. "Wait for Tyler and show him how to do it."

After a moment, Cade removed the handkerchief and dropped it in the sink. The bleeding had stopped. He turned Tyler to face him.

"See? Your finger will be fine."

Tyler looked at it, then curled his fingers inward and hugged his hand to his chest. He sniffed again.

Cade laid his hand on the boy's shoulder. "Now listen to me. You have a place here with us for as long as you want. I'm not going to make you leave just because you break a glass—or two glasses or three glasses. Do you understand?"

Tyler wiped his eyes with the back of his hand and nodded.

"Go get the broom and help clean up the glass." Cade patted the boy's shoulder as he hurried away.

Belle and Cade exchanged a troubled look.

"That boy is as emotional as a woman." Belle lifted the handkerchief from the sink and pumped water over it. "And pretty enough to be one too. I wish I had those eyes of his."

"He's been through a lot—much more than he's telling, I suspect."

She wrung water from the handkerchief. "I don't mind saying I've wondered a time or two where he came from."

Cade shrugged. "I don't want to push him. He seems sort of fragile. I need to take him down to Miss Warwick at the schoolhouse and get him in class, but I don't think he's ready. Whatever happened to him has left its mark. He'll tell us about it when he wants us to know."

"You might start by setting the example," Belle suggested.

"What are you talking about?"

She held up the white eyelet, pink-trimmed handkerchief. "You want to tell me where this came from?"

Cade shifted uncomfortably. It was Allison's handkerchief he'd stuffed in his pocket this morning.

"Let's see. Initials AAT. Now, I wonder who that could be?" Belle looked pointedly at him. It was obvious she already knew the answer.

Cade pulled the wet handkerchief from her hand and stalked out the back door. Heat radiated through him at the memory of Allison and their confrontation this morning. He closed his fist around the handkerchief. Now he'd have to return it to her.

No, maybe he wouldn't, he thought. Cade gazed off down the alley to the far end of town. Maybe he'd go to Phoebe's instead. He hadn't been there in a while. With the problems of the stage, the overdue shipment, the curtains, and the extravagant expenses hanging over his head, he hadn't taken time for himself.

The women at Phoebe's knew how to take care of a man. They knew what to do. They didn't argue, or annoy, or anger him. And not once had any one of them hit him with a broom.

Cade headed down the boardwalk. They weren't delicate or refined, either. The thought surfaced in his mind. None of them had porcelain skin or deep amber eyes like Allison. None were innocent. None blushed at his kiss, as Allison had.

Cade stopped and looked down at the handkerchief in his hand. Maybe he'd go to Phoebe's tomorrow. He ran his thumb over the delicate embroidered initials. Tomorrow . . . maybe.

Chapter
Seven

Allison slipped into the back entrance of her club and turned the key in the lock. She didn't want another unexpected intruder frightening her half to death. In her bedroom, she placed her aunt's ledger books and will in the bottom drawer of the bureau and covered them with an extra quilt. Her visit to her aunt's attorney this morning had yielded the things she'd needed, but was unsettling just the same.

Rory Stallworth had seemed on edge when she'd arrived, seated behind his desk in his office above the Brighton Grain Company. His shirt was wrinkled and the elbows of his jacket threadbare; Allison thought she smelled liquor on his breath.

She shoved the bottom drawer closed, the attorney's innuendo ringing in her head. He'd refused to turn over Aunt Lydia's papers, saying she had recently mentioned cutting someone from her will. He'd had the gall to suggest it might be Allison. She'd threatened to turn the whole matter over to her New York attorneys and Mr. Stallworth had suddenly become cooperative.

Allison considered doing just that, as she changed into the calico dress Jenna had loaned her to do her cleaning in, when she heard a tapping at the back door. She grabbed her head scarf and went into the kitchen. Jenna's smiling face was at the tiny window in the door.

"I've got your things done. I stayed up late last night getting them finished." Arms loaded, Jenna came inside followed by Holly.

Allison smiled down at the child. "Good morning, dear. My, but don't you look pretty."

Holly grinned shyly. "I helped Mama."

"You are a wonderful seamstress, Holly." She took the child's hand. "Let's go have a look."

In the bedroom Jenna spread the mauve curtains and tablecloths out on the bed. This was the only room Allison had finished yesterday, and now covered with a pale pink down coverlet, the brass bed looked inviting.

"They're perfect," Allison declared.

"Let's put up the curtains."

"Can you spare the time?" Allison knew Jenna had put several other orders on hold to do her own.

"Sure. Besides, I want to see how everything is turning out. You wouldn't believe the number of people who've come by the shop wanting to know what you're doing over here."

"You didn't tell them, did you?"

"Of course not."

Allison smiled. "The club will have more of an impact if its purpose is announced at our opening."

"Let's get going." Jenna picked up a set of curtains. "Come along, Holly."

The two women worked together in the main room hanging the curtains, discussing the furniture arrangement and plans for the grand opening. The morning grew warmer so they raised the two front windows and opened the door. The lace sheers and mauve curtains billowed in the gentle breeze.

Jenna looked at the settee, tables, chairs, rugs, and packing crates piled together in the center of the room. "This is going to be quite a chore."

Allison nodded. The pieces were quite heavy. "Well, it may take a while, but we can do it."

Jenna smiled. "I have a hammer next door. I'll run get it so we can open those crates. Holly, come along."

The child didn't answer. Jenna turned in a circle. "Holly! Holly, where are you?"

"She's probably playing in the back." Allison hurriedly checked the bedroom and kitchen, noting the back door was still securely locked. There was no sign of Holly. She returned to the front. "She's not there."

"Where could she—" Jenna turned and her gaze fell to rest on the opened front door. In the street, the stagecoach rumbled by. "Holly!"

Allison raced after her onto the boardwalk. Traffic was heavy on the street, a dozen shops stood open. Alleyways and staircases led to unknown places. A hundred spots for a child to hide. People were everywhere. Scruffy miners and dusty cowboys. Strangers. A hundred people she didn't know. Allison's heart pounded.

"I'll check this way, you go next door. Maybe she just went home."

Jenna nodded and hurried toward her shop.

Allison went the opposite direction frantically searching the crowd, praying, hoping. At the corner she turned down the alley. It was empty, not even a wagon or horse. Allison ran back to Main Street. Maybe she should get help. Maybe she should—

A head full of blond hair caught her eye. Allison's heart lurched. It was Holly, safe and secure in the strong arms of Sheriff Mack Carson, and he was heading her way.

"Jenna!" Allison shouted down the street. She was coming out of her dress shop. "Holly's here. She's all right."

Mack's heavy boots thudded on the boardwalk behind Allison. She turned. Relief flooded her. "Oh, Holly, we were so worried."

"I found her peeping into Melody's Sweet Shop. I knew she was too little to be out by herself." Mack tickled Holly's chin. She laughed, bringing a smile to his face. "But you're in a hurry to grow up, aren't you, honey."

Jenna ran up to them. Tears splashed onto her cheeks. "Oh, thank God."

Instinctively Mack put his arm around her shoulder. "It's okay, Mrs. McCain. Holly is fine."

Sobs choked her words. "I didn't know where she was. I turned and she was gone, and—"

Mack pulled her closer, holding her securely in one arm, Holly in the other. "Nothing bad happened."

Jenna threaded her hand through Holly's golden curls. "I should have watched her more closely. It's my fault. She could have—"

"It's nobody's fault." Mack patted her shoulder. "Kids will be kids."

"What kind of mother am I to let her just wander away like that? What if—"

"Now, don't talk that way. You're a fine mama. Everybody in town can see that."

Jenna hiccuped and gazed up at him. Her cheeks were wet with tears.

Mack pulled a handkerchief from his pocket. "You've got a lot on you, what with having no husband, working your own business—and doing a fine job at it—and raising a child by yourself. You can't keep on everything every second of the day."

Jenna dabbed her eyes with the handkerchief. "But—"

"Stop talking that way, Jenna." Mack's tone grew serious. "You're a fine woman, raising a fine child. Don't be so hard on yourself."

She sniffed and managed a smile. "Thank you."

Mack looked down at Holly in his arms. She was playing with the badge pinned to his vest. He lifted her chin. "As for you, young lady, don't go wandering off without your mama again. You could get hurt. Understand?"

Holly giggled and snuggled her head against Mack's neck. He looked at Jenna. "Does that mean she understands?"

"I think so." She grinned and took Holly from him. "I can't thank you enough."

Without Holly in his arms he shifted awkwardly. "Glad I could help."

Jenna hugged Holly close and turned to leave.

"Oh, wait." Mack pulled a peppermint stick from his pocket. "This is for Holly. She had her eye on it over at Melody's."

Jenna took it from his hand. "You shouldn't have."

A lopsided smile crossed his face and he shrugged. "Little girls ought to be spoiled."

"Thank you," Jenna said softly.

"Thank you, Sheriff," Allison called as they walked away. Mack nodded and watched them go.

"I think I'll take Holly home, if you don't mind," Jenna said when they reached the shop.

"That would be a good idea." She glanced back down the street. "Sheriff Carson seems like a nice man."

Jenna craned her neck to watch him walk away. "Yes, very nice."

"He certainly has a way with Holly," Allison said. "An interesting combination, a lawman good with children."

"Yes, very interesting. . . ." She seemed lost in thought for a moment before speaking again. "Sorry I can't help with the furniture."

"Don't give it another thought." She gave Jenna and Holly a hug.

Allison went inside and closed the door. The pile of furniture and crates looked ominous now, with no one to help. She took a deep breath and grasped the nearest wing-backed chair.

Half an hour later, Allison collapsed onto the settee. Aunt Lydia's furniture was beautiful—it was also tremendously heavy. She looked around the room. Little had been accomplished and she was already exhausted. For a moment she considered hiring a crew to handle the job. She shivered at the thought. Men were so temperamental when it came to arranging furniture.

A knock sounded at the front door and through the window Allison saw a young face. She smiled. "Come in, Tyler."

He glanced back over his shoulder and came quietly into the door. "Is it all right if I came over?" he asked shyly and closed the door.

"Of course." Allison waved her hand over the room. "Sit down, wherever you can find room."

Tyler settled on the edge of a chair across from her and his gaze swept the room. "What are you doing?"

"Attempting to arrange furniture." She blew out a heavy breath. "But it's much more difficult than I imagined."

He nodded. "Why do you have so much furniture?"

Allison sat up straighter. "Did someone send you over here to spy on me?"

"Spy?"

"To see what I'm doing, find out what's going on over here."

He shook his head as if the whole concept was completely foreign to him. "No. Many people are wondering, though."

"Really?"

"They've been in the saloon all day, asking questions."

Inwardly Allison beamed. She wanted her grand opening to create a stir.

"I came over to see if Aunt Lydia was better yet?"

She shook her head and rose from the settee. "No, not at all. I'm beginning to wonder about that doctor, though. I think he could be doing more."

"More what?"

She sighed heavily. "I don't know—something."

Allison pressed her hand to the small of her back and looked around the room. Where to start next, she wondered.

Tyler rose from the chair. "Can I help you?"

He was as small as she, and probably no stronger. But she wasn't about to turn down an extra pair of hands. "Thank you, Tyler, I'd appreciate it."

Between the two of them they pushed back the furniture and rolled out the rectangular oriental rug that had once graced one of Aunt Lydia's spare bedrooms. It was a floral design, woven in pinks, muted reds, and ivory.

Allison stood back surveying its placement in the center of the room. "That should do it. Tyler, would you run next door to Jenna's and ask if we can borrow a hammer."

"Hammer . . ." Tyler repeated the word quietly and left her alone.

Allison crossed her arms and tapped her fingertip to her lip, contemplating the placement of the settee and chairs. She wanted several groupings as well as isolated areas for

any woman who simply wanted to have a few minutes to
herself. The china hutch should go on the back wall with the
tea cart.

When the door opened a moment later she was surprised
to hear heavy footsteps. Allison whirled as Cade walked in
behind Tyler.

He pulled his Stetson from his head and nodded. "Afternoon."

Compared to the boy beside him, Cade looked tall and
sturdy. Dependable. Rugged. Handsome. Allison mentally
shook herself. Handsome? Yes, she thought. Very handsome.

When she didn't respond he pressed on. "I was looking
for Tyler and saw him over here."

"Was I keeping him from his work?"

"I just need him to run an errand." Cade looked down at
Tyler beside him. "Go over to the express office and ask
Harry if he knows anything about my shipment yet. The
express office. Do you remember where that is?"

Tyler nodded. He started out the door, then handed Cade
the tool he'd fetched from Jenna's. "Hammer."

Cade nodded. "Yes, I know."

"Bye." Tyler waved to Allison and hurried out the door.

"And be careful crossing the street," Cade called after
him.

An awkward moment passed while Cade fumbled with
his hat and the hammer. "I was coming over anyway to
return this," he finally said and pulled her handkerchief
from his pocket.

She crossed the room and accepted it from him. Their
fingers brushed, sending warm waves up Allison's arm.
"Thank you. I'd forgotten all about it."

"I had it laundered," Cade told her.

Allison spread it open. "Yes, I can see. Thank you."

He nodded. "Well . . . you're welcome. I appreciate the
use of it."

"You're welcome too."

Another long moment passed where they just stared at
each other.

"Would you like to sit down?" Allison chastised herself for forgetting her manners.

Cade looked around the room. A deep frown creased his brow. "What are you doing with all this furniture in here?"

"It's for my business," she said simply.

He shook his head. "I can tell you right now nobody in Brighton is going to buy this kind of furniture."

"I'm not opening a furniture store."

"Oh." His gaze swept the room again. "It looks like a great big parlor."

"I suppose that's a fair assessment." Allison nodded. "Or it will be when I get everything arranged."

He frowned again. "You're not planning to move all this furniture yourself, are you?"

"I had help," she said. "Until you sent him to the express office."

"Tyler was helping you? I didn't know."

"It's all right. I can manage on my own." She nodded confidently.

"You've got no business moving these heavy things. You might hurt yourself."

Allison grasped the back of a cane-bottomed chair. "No need to concern yourself."

He crossed the room and tossed the hammer and his hat on the settee. "Don't do that. I'll give you a hand."

"It's not necessary." She lifted the chair.

Cade laid his hands on it as well. "I said I'll do it."

She pulled it toward her. "There's no need."

"Give it to me." He yanked it from her hands forcibly. "I said I'll do it, damnit."

"Fine!"

They glared at each other.

"Where do you want it?"

Allison drew in a deep breath. "In the corner."

He crossed the room and dropped the chair by the wall.

"Angle it a bit more toward the center of the room, would you?"

Cade rolled his eyes but complied. "What else?"

She pointed. "The settee goes on that wall."

He lifted the heavy piece of furniture over the rug and placed it against the wall.

"A little more to the right, please."

He scooted it down.

"Another inch or so." She waved her hand.

Cade moved it again.

Allison contemplated the settee for a moment. "One more."

"How much difference can one more inch make?" he asked sourly.

"Never mind. I knew this wouldn't work. Just get out of my way." In a flurry, Allison brushed past him and grasped the end of the settee.

"Get your hands off that thing before you hurt yourself. I said I'd move it."

"I'll do it myself."

"Like hell you will."

He grabbed her wrists and pulled them from the settee. Caught off balance, Allison spun around and fell back against the wall, her wrists pinned beside her head by the force of Cade's hands.

They stood inches apart, his face hovering near hers, their gazes locked. Heat bound them together. Cade lowered his mouth and covered her lips with a hungry kiss. She responded, tilting her head back, giving him access. Passion grew between them, consuming them.

Cade pulled away. His breath heavy, he gazed at her. Her eyes were bright with longing, her lips wet with his kiss. He released her hands.

"My God, woman . . ."

He leaned down to kiss her again but the front door swung open. Cade whirled around as Tyler came inside. He stepped in front of Allison, shielding her.

"Mr. Finch wasn't there. A man named Ben said your shipment still isn't here. Is that all right?"

If the boy had seen them kissing, he gave no indication of it. Cade relaxed his stance. "Ben works when Harry is off. That's fine . . . thanks."

Allison stepped from behind Cade, color full in her

cheeks. Her hands trembled as she patted the back of her hair. "I think the furniture can wait until another day."

"No, I'll help you with it," Cade said softly.

Tension was high between them, thick enough to feel.

"Do you want me to go back to the saloon?" Tyler asked.

"No!" Cade and Allison both yelled in unison. By unspoken agreement, they knew it was unwise for them to be left alone together.

Allison cleared her throat and hurried across the room to him. She put her hand on his shoulder. "I mean, we can always use another set of hands."

"Get over here, boy. Help me move this settee," Cade ordered.

They worked feverishly, moving furniture, opening crates, hanging pictures, placing lamps, making certain Tyler was between the two of them at all times. The job was completed quickly and with a minimum of chatter.

Allison looked around the room, satisfied with the way it had turned out. "Thank you both, very much."

Tyler grinned. "You're welcome." He turned to Cade. "I'm supposed to help Vance with supper."

"Wait! I'll walk over with you."

Cade hurried to the door. Tyler was already on his way down the boardwalk. "Don't cross the street until I get there!"

Allison handed him his Stetson. They gazed at each other, neither speaking.

"Thank you for your help," she finally said.

Cade just nodded.

She looked past him to Tyler waiting patiently on the boardwalk. "He seems like a good boy."

"He showed up on my doorstep, ragged, filthy, and half starved. Lost his parents not long ago. I took him in, gave him a job."

She hadn't expected such kindness from Cade Jessup and a new emotion ribboned through her already churning stomach.

Cade shook his head. "He seems kind of frail, though. I guess he never got out in the world much. To tell you the truth, I haven't found one thing he's any good at. Can't fetch wood, can't sweep, can't wash a dish without flooding the place. Joe Capp asked him to fetch a couple of tools for him and the boy didn't know one from the other. I guess his family must have been dirt poor."

"Dirt poor? Perhaps." Allison's delicate brows rose. "Or perhaps very wealthy."

Chapter
Eight

The delicate china teacups rattled as Allison placed the service on the small table in front of the settee and poured.

"Aunt Lydia and I found this tea set in a quaint little shop in London. I've always been especially fond of the pattern." She passed the tiny cups to the ladies seated around her.

Morning sun filtered through the spotless windows and the lace curtains. Allison had arrived early to prepare for this first meeting with the ladies she needed to help launch the ladies' club.

"It's a lovely pattern," Jenna remarked.

Edith Taylor's mouth turned down as she gazed at the tea service. "London, hum?"

Mabel emptied her cup in two gulps and set it aside. She ran the laundry in town and did most of the work herself. Her arms were firm and strong from years of scrubbing and lifting heavy baskets. "So, what's this club of yours gonna be about?"

"A haven exclusively for women, where we can congregate to share problems and ideas." Allison set her cup aside. "Our primary goal, as I see it, is to make Brighton the safe, respectable town it once was."

"Amen to that." Mabel shifted her wide girth on the settee. "A woman can hardly walk the streets by herself these days."

"Exactly," Jenna agreed. She looked back at Holly playing with her doll in the corner. "It's not just ourselves we
have to think of, but our daughters."

"We can become a force to be reckoned with in this town
and see to it some changes are made," Allison added.

"Them damn saloons and their riffraff have got a stran-
glehold on things." Mabel shook her head in disgust. "But if
we drive them away, what's going to draw trade into Brighton?"

Edith's lips drew together in a tight pucker. "If Lydia
Allbright hadn't closed the Carriage Works we wouldn't be
in this mess."

"I am checking into that," Allison pointed out quickly.
"And as far as driving the saloons out of town, certainly
that's not possible—at least not anytime soon. But we can
have some influence on their hours of operation."

"Open on Sundays—it's a disgrace," Mabel declared.

All the women nodded their agreement.

Allison drew in a deep breath. "On that note, I would
like to propose that we take steps to have the saloons closed
on Sundays. Any disagreement to that?"

Edith shook her head. "I'm for it, but I don't know how
much good it will do."

"It's a place to start. Once our club gains members, we
will become more influential. For now, we'll focus our efforts on bringing more cultural and family-oriented events
to Brighton." Allison rose and stood behind her chair. "I
feel we should begin by sponsoring a community dance.
We'll have booths and music and use the opportunity to
recruit other women. What do you think?"

Jenna smiled. "I can't remember the last time we had a
dance in Brighton."

Mabel nodded. "It could work."

"Where will we have it?" Edith asked.

"I'm working on that," Allison admitted.

"And when?" Mabel wanted to know.

"A week from Saturday. That will give us enough time to
make the arrangements." Allison sat down once more. "I'll
have Georgia bake cakes and pies and make some of her
punch. She's very excited about the whole thing."

"I'll wash out my tubs and boil some corn," Mabel said.

Jenna leaned forward. "Edith, you make the best fried chicken in town."

A proud smile stretched over her face. "Well, thank you, Jenna dear."

"I can whip up some rag dolls to sell," Jenna offered.

Allison fished a small pencil and paper from her skirt pocket and jotted down notes. "I'll find a place for the dance and have some handbills printed up. We'll need music too. Any suggestions?"

Mabel shook her head. "Since Miss Marshall passed on we haven't even got music for church services."

"What about the Rafferty brothers?" Jenna suggested.

"They've got a small spread not far from here," Edith explained to Allison. "Banjo, fiddle, and guitar."

"It's a downright shame none of them boys can play piano," Mabel said.

"Why don't they play for the church service?" Allison asked. "I realize it isn't piano music, but I would think it would suffice until a new pianist could be found."

Mabel sucked her gums. "Ol' Jonas Rafferty—that's their pa—isn't exactly on speaking terms with the Lord since his wife passed away."

Edith sighed heavily, ending the matter. "I'll have Will drive me out to their place and make the arrangements."

Allison looked up from her writing. "Talk to the other women in town. Encourage them to come by and to contribute what they can. All proceeds will go into our treasury."

Jenna set her teacup aside. "It sounds like everything is settled."

Mabel pushed herself up from the settee. "I got to get back to work. We'll talk it up and see what happens."

The ladies left. Allison and Jenna waited at the door while Holly gathered her doll, named Aunt Mattie, and her blanket.

The morning sun was warm, the streets busy. Allison looked on it with a growing sense of pride. "If we can get enough support from the women in town, I think we'll have a good chance at making this a success."

"We'll have to talk to as many of the women as possible."

Allison nodded. "I believe they're as anxious for change as we are." Her gaze wandered to the opposite side of the street and the sight caused her eyebrows to bob. "Oh, my. Who are they?"

Jenna turned and gasped. She whirled back around quickly. "That's Phoebe and some of her girls," she whispered.

"Who?" Allison rose on her tiptoes to see over Jenna's shoulder.

"No! Don't stare." She leaned closer. "Phoebe runs the . . . house of ill-repute on the edge of town."

"You mean they're—whores?"

"Shhh!"

"Oh, my. . . ."

Allison couldn't resist staring. The three women were dressed in the finest gowns, the latest fashions, equal to what she'd seen in New York. And strutting along as if they knew they were attracting stares . . . and enjoying it.

"Those clothes are beautiful," Allison said. "How did they get them?"

"Any woman could afford them if nearly every man in the territory chipped in."

"Well, yes, I suppose you're right. Who is that woman behind them?"

Jenna chanced a look at the plainly dressed young woman following along behind. "I don't know her name, but I've seen her a few times. She cooks or cleans or something for Phoebe. She can't come out alone. Everyone in town scorns the sight of any of Phoebe's girls."

"Really?" Concern creased Allison's brow as she watched the young woman—clearly feeling out of place—disappear down the street with the others.

Jenna lifted Holly into her arms. "We've got to go. Holly and I have rag dolls to stitch. When will you be staying the nights here?"

Allison glanced behind her. The ladies' club was cozy and inviting, but didn't feel like home yet. "I'm not sure."

"Let me know. I'll keep an eye out for you."

"Thanks." Allison waved as they disappeared into the dress shop, then went back into the club.

It did look cozy and inviting, Allison told herself as she looked over the room. It had turned out much like she'd envisioned. But for the life of her she couldn't look at the settee without thinking of yesterday and Cade Jessup. Heat swelled within her each time she recalled his kiss.

"Gracious. . . ." Forcing the thought from her head, Allison lifted the tea tray and carried it into the kitchen. Her time would be better spent in more productive endeavors, she told herself. She left it on the sideboard and entered her bedroom.

From the bottom drawer of her bureau Allison removed the envelope containing Aunt Lydia's will. It had occurred to her during last night's fitful sleep that if she knew who her aunt planned to cut out of her will, it might provide some clue as to why she'd given up on everything.

Settled on the edge of the bed, she leafed through the thick document. As she suspected, her aunt had left bequeaths to many people. So many, in fact, that Allison didn't know who they all were. But it was only a temporary setback, she realized. There was one person who would know everyone named in the will, Aunt Lydia's long-time and very close friend—Allison's own mother.

Allison took stationery from her small writing desk beside the bed. She still needed to explain her reasons for staying in Brighton. And a few other things, as well.

"Aren't they ever going to get done?"

Belle rolled her eyes toward the carpenter crew working on the stage. "I swear I'm hearing hammers beating in my dreams at night."

Beside her at the table, Cade rubbed his eyes with the heels of his hands. "I'd be happy to hear anything but that boy screaming every night."

Since his arrival, Tyler's screams had awakened Cade every night and brought him running down the hall to jar the boy from the hellish nightmare. Yet when asked about them, Tyler only said he didn't remember any of it.

Belle waved away his concern. "Shoot, I don't pay it any

mind now. Why don't you just leave him alone. He'll get over it sooner or later."

"I can't do that." Cade gripped the coffee mug on the table in front of him. "I remember having nightmares when I was a kid."

"Your pa came and woke you, didn't he?"

He cut his gaze to meet hers, then back again to the coffee.

Belle reached across the table and touched his hand. "You know, Cade, this thing between you and your pa has gone on for a long time now. Maybe you should—"

He withdrew his hand. "No."

Belle pushed back her chair. "I know why the two of you couldn't get along—I know and you never told me a word about it. You're as stubborn as he is. I'd stake my legs on it."

Cade frowned and turned away.

Belle softened her tone. "He's getting old, Cade. Time is passing. You ought to—"

"I've got work to do." His chair scraped along the floor as he rose.

"Whether you like it or not, Cade, your pa means something to you. He's the one who taught you how to be kind and patient with that boy, to take him in and give him a chance."

Cade dropped his cup on the table and left the kitchen without another word.

Billy's piano practice and Joe Capp's carpenter crew competed for who could be the most nerve-racking, Cade thought as he stepped into the barroom. Vance polished glasses and served drinks to the few morning customers. Mack Carson leaned against the bar.

"You're in early." Cade settled against the bar beside the sheriff.

Mack eyed the mug of beer in front of him. "I had a peculiar visitor at the jail first thing this morning."

"Yeah? Who's that?"

"A Pinkerton man."

Billy stopped playing and whirled around on the piano stool. Joe Capp and the carpenters looked up.

"A Pinkerton man?" Vance edged closer.

"What did he want?" Cade asked.

"Couldn't say. Some private matter, nothing criminal. He just wanted to let me know he was in town." Mack hitched up his gun belt. "Professional courtesy."

Billy hurried to the bar. "A Pinkerton man in Brighton? That's never happened before. What ya'll reckon it's all about, boss?"

"He didn't give you any clue?" Vance asked.

Mack shook his head. "Just said he was investigating a matter for a party back East."

They all turned to Cade. He straightened. "What are you looking at me for?"

"Well, you are from back there, boss."

Vance stroked his chin thoughtfully. "Maybe your pa finally decided to hunt you down. Maybe he—"

"It's got nothing to do with me." That was the second time his father had come up this morning. Cade pushed the thought from his mind.

Billy shrugged. "Then who could it be?"

"One person comes to mind," Mack said.

Cade nodded as he realized who the sheriff meant. "Brighton's newest businesswoman."

Billy's eyes widened. "Miss Tremaine? Do ya'll think so?"

"Who else in town would warrant an investigator from the Pinkerton Agency? I can't think of another soul."

Mack nodded in agreement. "That's how I figure it."

"But who all would want to track down Miss Tremaine?" Billy asked.

Cade stroked his chin. Who, indeed?

Did Brighton have a law against loitering? Allison searched the street on both sides. No sign of Sheriff Carson. Thank goodness, she thought and breathed a sigh of relief.

She wasn't sure how long she'd been milling around outside the shops on Main Street but the sun dipped toward the horizon now. Traffic on the street had thinned and stores would close soon. The infernal racket from inside the Pleasure Palace still spilled out through the open windows.

She wished the men would finish up for the day. She felt people staring and was sure they wondered why a decent woman like herself was hanging around outside a saloon—the brawdiest saloon in town, at that.

Allison gazed at the hats in the window of the shop next door for the tenth time. Darn that Cade Jessup, she thought. He probably knew somehow that she wanted to talk to Joe Capp and was keeping the crew working late on purpose.

"Miss Tremaine?"

Allison gasped and spun around.

"Sorry, I didn't mean to startle you."

"Oh, no, you didn't." Allison offered a smile to the preacher standing before her.

He pulled off his wide-brimmed black hat. "I'm Reverend Charles Kent. A pleasure to meet you, ma'am."

Reverend Kent was in his late thirties, slightly taller than herself, with even, attractive features. Allison smiled in earnest. "I'm very pleased to make your acquaintance, Reverend."

"I hope you'll forgive me for approaching you on the street like this, but I hadn't been able to catch you at your shop and I wanted to welcome you to Brighton."

"That's very kind of you." She glanced past him at the entrance to the Pleasure Palace. There was no sign of Joe Capp yet.

"I'd like to invite you to attend services on Sunday." Reverend Kent smiled apologetically. "We're without a pianist just now, but our choir is carrying on well."

"One can't walk twenty feet in this town without hearing piano music coming from any number of saloons. Can't you find someone who can play for you?"

"Most of the men who play for the saloons know only a few songs from memory and they're hardly appropriate for church. Besides, I don't think the congregation would be pleased with having that sort occupying Miss Marshall's spot on the bench." Reverend Kent shifted his hat to the other hand. "Which brings us to you, Miss Tremaine. I'd heard of your background and it was suggested that you may have some musical training you'd be willing to share with us."

Absently she stole a glance at the saloon entrance. "I do play a bit."

Reverend Kent beamed. "Wonderful!"

"But I'm hardly considered accomplished," she rushed to point out. After four years of lessons she'd finally given up. She could play the notes, her teacher had told her, but she could never make the music.

"That's fine—much more than anyone else in town can claim."

"But, Reverend, I'm sure your congregation deserves more—"

"That's more than good enough for us, Miss Tremaine. So how about it? Could you help us out? It would mean a lot to the folks here in town."

"Well. . . ." She had so much to do now, with the ladies' club starting and her aunt to attend to.

"You've seen the church, I'm sure. Right on the edge of town. It's on your way to Miss Allbright's."

"Yes, I have, but . . ." Allison stopped. "The white clapboard church on the edge of town? With the trees and that lovely wide yard?"

He smiled proudly. "Yes, that's it."

Allison tapped her finger against her chin as an idea took full form. "Tell me, Reverend, how do you feel about the number of saloons here in Brighton. Aren't you appalled?"

"Yes, the deacons and I have had many a solemn talk on the matter."

Allison changed the subject again. "Well, Reverend, I'd be pleased to help out with the music."

"Thank you, Miss Tremaine. Choir practice is Friday night after supper." He put on his hat. "And if the church can be of service to you in any way, please let me know."

"I'll do just that, Reverend." It was a promise she was sure she'd keep.

Down the boardwalk the swinging doors opened and several men carrying toolboxes walked out. They stood there for a moment, talking. Allison excused herself and hurried over.

"Mr. Capp? Mr. Capp?"

The man rounded on her, bringing her up short. A mountain of a man, tall, with thick arms and chest, he squinted down at her through small eyes.

"Yeah?"

Not an ounce of tolerance shone in his voice or expression. Allison squared her shoulders. "I am Allison—"

"Yeah, I know who you are, lady. What do you want?"

"I was told you're the finest carpenter in Brighton and I want to offer you work. Are you interested?" Her words came out in a rush.

He glared at her as if sizing her up. "What kind of work?"

Obviously not the type for idle chatter, she got right to the point. "I need a dance floor and about ten booths built by next Saturday."

"Where at?"

A little smile tugged at her lips. "Do you know the white clapboard church on the edge of town? The one with that lovely wide yard?"

"Course I know."

"There. By next Saturday. Can you handle the job?"

Joe glanced inside the Pleasure Palace, then back at her as if weighing the decision. He shrugged and finally said, "Yeah, I reckon I can."

"Excellent. Now, here's what I need—"

The swinging doors flew open and banged against the wall. Cade strode out. "What's going on here?"

Thoroughly pleased with herself, Allison smiled. "Just conducting a little business. Mr. Capp is building something for me."

"What?" Cade spoke to Joe as if Allison weren't even present.

"I don't know that it's any of your concern," Allison told him. "But next Saturday night I'm—"

He ignored her. "You're supposed to be working on my stage, Joe. I need that thing finished."

Joe winced. "What she wants won't take no time, Cade. I'll have that stage of yours done up in plenty of time."

"We have a deal." Anger tinged his words.

"Yeah, well . . ." Joe scratched his beard. "I guess you're right, Cade. Sorry, ma'am, you'll have to find someone else to build your dance floor."

Allison's stomach coiled. No! She wasn't going to find anyone else. She wasn't going to let Cade get away with this. She curbed her anger. "I'll pay you double."

Joe squinted down at her, then over at Cade.

"I've been in town a long time, Joe. I've given you work before. I've sent a lot of business your way too."

Joe nodded. "Yeah, you have. I guess—"

"Triple."

Cade glared at her with an intensity that would warp iron. He pointed a finger at her. "You can't come in here throwing money around, thinking you can buy everything in sight."

Allison drew herself up straighter. "Mr. Capp is a businessman and this is a business transaction. Nothing more."

"Business! You don't know a damn thing about running a business!"

Anger coiled so deep within her. "I know enough about business, Mr. Jessup, to hire the best carpenter in town and beat out the competition for his services."

Faces appeared over the door and out the windows of the Pleasure Palace. Cade and Allison glared at each other for a long moment, then turned to Joe.

He vacillated between the two. Finally he spoke to Cade. "Sorry, Cade, but I've got a wife and kids to feed." He turned to Allison. "I'll be by your place tomorrow. You can show me what you want."

"Thank you, Mr. Capp." She watched with smug delight as he walked away.

Cade stepped closer. "What are you up to?" His voice sounded low and menacing.

She lifted one shoulder casually. "Just following your suggestion."

His eyes narrowed. "What are you talking about?"

"I've formed a ladies' club. Ladies for the Advancement of Cultural Events. L-A-C-E." She leaned closer, anger coloring her cheeks. "It was you who said a woman—a woman alone—couldn't change this town. I'm not alone anymore."

He bent down until his nose was even with hers. "We'll see how much in this town gets changed—ladies' club or not."

"With pleasure." Allison hissed the words at him and left in a flurry of skirts and petticoats.

Chapter
Nine

"Praise the Lord, it's good to hear music in this church again." Reverend Kent smiled broadly and pulled the door closed. "I felt the spirit of the Lord within me tonight."

They walked down the church steps together. It was her first practice with the choir and Allison had been a little nervous. She hadn't touched a keyboard in a very long time. But after a few false starts and a minimum of clinkers, her notes had blended well with the eight-member choir.

"Very nice practice this evening, Mrs. Taylor," the reverend said as they stopped at the bottom of the steps.

Edith glanced back at him. "Yes, Reverend. It's about time the deacons got us a pianist."

He snapped his fingers and turned to Allison. "That reminds me. I spoke with the deacons about our conversation of yesterday, Miss Tremaine, and we've decided that having your ladies' club dance here at church would be agreeable to everybody—and beneficial for the town too."

The dark evening couldn't hide the radiance of Allison's smile. "Reverend, we certainly appreciate your support."

They said good night to Reverend Kent and crossed the church yard to meet Will Taylor, waiting to walk them home.

Edith talked continually as they passed darkened stores and shops through town, giving Allison an earful about each and every choir member. They zigzagged through the streets, crossing to avoid one saloon, then doubling back to avoid another. Friday was a big night for Brighton's biggest industry. As they passed the Steer's Horns, Allison thought she saw Wes Palmer among the crowd at the bar. But it was only a glance through a dirty window and she couldn't be sure. Still, it gave her a chill.

As they approached the Pleasure Palace, they crossed again. A steady stream of men poured inside, while laughter and shouts poured out. Through the brightly lit windows men could be seen elbow-to-elbow at the bar, seated at and around gaming tables. A haze of cigar smoke gave the room a bluish cast. A rendition of "O Susannah" plodded along.

Edith glared at the Pleasure Palace. "There's that boy inside the saloon, big as life, working for Cade Jessup. Something ought to be done."

"Now, now, Edith." Will patted her shoulder. "Cade's just giving the boy a job to help him out."

Edith jerked her chin around. "Humph! That Cade Jessup thinks he can do anything in this town."

They stopped in front of the ladies' club. "Thank you for walking me home," Allison said.

"Don't mention it," Will told her. "It's—"

Edith gasped and pointed to the front door. "What's that?"

A bowie knife was driven into the door. Beneath it was a scrap of paper.

Will pulled it free and held it up to the light. "It says, 'Go home or else.' "

A chill slithered up Allison's spine. "Oh, dear. . . ."

"I'll go get the sheriff," Will offered.

Edith grabbed his arm. "Where will you find him? He's always off in one of these saloons warding off all kinds of trouble. Decent people can't get help when they need it."

Will patted her hand. "I won't be gone long. I promise." He eased away, leaving them alone.

Allison clasped her hands together to still their quivering. "I guess someone in Brighton doesn't like the idea of a ladies' club."

Since she'd blurted out the news to Cade in front of the Pleasure Palace two days ago, word had swept through town like a runaway freight train. She hadn't meant to tell him, but he'd made her so angry she couldn't hold it in. Since then, several women had come by the club to inquire and many more had peeped through the windows, so it had turned out for the best, she'd decided.

An eternity passed while the women waited in silence and finally Will appeared with the sheriff. He had a Colt Peacemaker strapped to each hip and in his hand was a sawed-off double-barreled shotgun—his street sweeper. The sight made Allison tremble worse.

"Evening, ladies." Mack tipped his hat. "Will told me what you found. Any idea of who did it?"

Allison bit down on her lip. "No, Sheriff."

"I'll ask around, find out if anybody saw anything."

"This is an outrage," Edith declared. "No one is safe in this town anymore."

"I don't take kindly to any citizen in my town being threatened, Mrs. Taylor. I'll find out who's behind this."

Edith tossed her head as if she doubted it. "Allison, you're staying the night with us. It isn't safe for you here."

Tempted as she was to say yes, Allison couldn't bring herself to speak the words. If she left now, if she let them run her off, she'd never have the nerve to stay there again.

"Might not be a bad idea," Mack said. "At least until I can check into this thing."

"No," Allison said. She drew in a deep breath. "No. That would be exactly what whoever did this would want. I'm staying here tonight."

Mack nodded. "I'll go inside with you."

Allison followed him through the club while he lit the lanterns and checked behind every door, every chair, and under the bed. Nothing was out of place. He rattled the back door twice, ensuring it was securely locked. On the boardwalk again Allison thanked him and the Taylors.

"And, Sheriff, could you keep this as quiet as possible?" Allison asked. "I don't want word to get out. It might keep the ladies away."

"I'll do what I can."

Allison closed herself up in the club and locked the door.

She waved to them through the window, then pulled the curtains closed.

An eerie silence permeated the club that Allison hadn't notice last night, her first night here. The noise from the Pleasure Palace seemed distant. The club felt isolated.

She checked the locks again, then closed herself up in the bedroom and changed into her night rail. Fear grew inside her as she blew out the lantern at her bedside and huddled beneath the coverlet.

Allison lay awake, staring at the darkness, listening to every step on the boardwalk outside her window. She heard hoofs pounding on the dirt street and the creak of an occasional wagon wheel. Shouts, laughter, and piano music blended together. They'd seemed exciting last night, the sounds of her new home.

When the morning sun filtered through the edges of the window the next morning, Allison was still awake.

Cade closed his ledger book and sat back in his chair. He pulled at his neck and relaxed a moment as the breeze blew in through the open window across from his desk. Things were tight. Tighter than they'd ever been. Tighter than he liked them. Time was running out too. The shipment still wasn't in and the curtains weren't ready either. And the stage—

"Damn. . . ."

Cade rose from his chair and braced his arms against the window casing. His gaze strayed across Main Street to the headquarters of the Ladies for the Advancement of Cultural Events. His gut churned. A stream of ladies had come and gone from the club all day, but he hadn't seen Allison once. She was holed up inside, pouring tea and plotting something. He was sure of it.

Cade muttered an oath and turned away. Time was short. Only a few weeks remained, and if he didn't get that stage finished, the curtains up, and the shipment delivered, he'd be ruined financially and professionally.

Cade strode across the room. He had no intention of going back home to his father penniless and broken. He was pulling off this plan come hell or high water—or Allison Tremaine.

The afternoon crowd in the barroom was a good one, a buildup to tonight's Saturday crowd, the biggest night for the saloons in town. Cade surveyed the room from the end of the bar where Billy poured drinks.

"Everything going smooth?"

Billy nodded to the corner table where Satch Wilkens sat slumped in a chair, holding a bottle against his chest. "I'm keeping my eye on him."

Cade nodded, satisfied Billy could handle Satch if trouble broke out. Lately, though, Satch did little more than drink himself unconscious.

"Looks like that Pinkerton agent is paying us a little visit." Billy nodded to the table across the room.

The man wasn't hard to pick out, dressed in a green plaid vest and a bowler. Cade had seen him on the street a few times since Mack had said he was in town.

"Wonder what all he wants, boss?" Billy's eyes widened.

He'd wondered the same. Pinkerton agents weren't cheap and they didn't come all the way to Nevada without good reason. Whoever he was trailing had to be important, important to somebody rich and powerful.

Billy leaned closer. "Maybe you ought to go talk to him, boss. Maybe you can find out what he's doing here."

At that moment the swinging door burst open and Rupert Frazier and Otis Collins pushed their way inside, each jockeying to get in ahead of the other. Rupert shoved Otis aside, hitched up his baggy trousers, and led the way to the table where the agent sat. "You that there Pinkerton man?"

He put down his beer and regarded them a moment before answering. "Yes. Manning is my name."

Otis elbowed Rupert aside. "We hear'd you were in town and we come to testify to what all we know."

He gestured to the chairs across from him. "Have a seat, boys."

They fought for a moment for the seat next to the agent before Rupert yanked the chair away and plopped into it, sending a puff of dust up around him.

Manning sipped from his mug. "How is it you boys know what I'm in town for?"

Otis snorted. "It's just about as plain as that big ol' nose on Rupert's face."

"Yeah. I don't know how come nobody in town's figured it out but me and Otis here," Rupert told him.

Otis leaned forward. "We hear'd it first, with our own two ears—twice. Nobody else has done hear'd it twice but me and Rupert here."

"And what is it you two have heard?"

"We hear'd Miss Marshall playing down to the church." Manning's brows drew together. "Miss Marshall?"

"Her ghost," Rupert corrected.

The agent sat back. "Are you boys thinking you've got a ghost haunting your church?"

Otis wiped his mouth on his shirtsleeve. "It's got to be her de-vine spirit—she never played that good when she was alive."

Rupert glared at him. "What do you know about piano music, anyway."

"Piano?" The agent sat forward again. "Someone's playing the church piano?"

"At night. And it's pitch-black inside—"

Otis butted in. "Everybody knows can't no real person play the piano without looking at what they're doing."

"Miss Marshall played good and all, but she never played songs like this while she was alive," Rupert told him.

Manning leaned his arm on the table. "Plays pretty good, huh?"

Rupert nodded. "Like the hand of God reached down and touched that old piano."

"The hand of God . . ." Manning stroked his chin. "When did you last hear this?"

They looked at each other. "A couple of nights ago, I reckon," Otis said. "You're going down there, aren't you?"

He lifted his mug and took a sip. "I might go check into it."

Otis elbowed Rupert. "See? I told you that's what he's in town fer. I told you, didn't I?"

"You gonna tell everybody back there at your Pinkerton

place that it was me and Otis who put you on to this, ain't you? Right?" Rupert's head bobbed excitedly.

Manning dug into his pocket and dropped coins onto the table. "You'll get the credit you deserve, boys."

"See? I told you so," Otis said to Rupert.

Rupert scowled at him. "Why don't you just shut up."

"Why don't you?"

Rupert grabbed his shirtfront. "Maybe I'll make you."

"Maybe I'll make you right back." Otis drew back his fist.

"All right, you two. That's enough." Cade stepped between them. "What are you boys arguing about now?"

"We just tol' this here Pinkerton man about—"

Otis stopped and looked across the table. Manning was gone. He turned to Rupert. "Where'd he go?"

He gazed around the room. "Beats me."

"We tol' him about Miss Marshall playing down at the church," Rupert said.

Cade's eyes widened. "You told him that?"

"Uh-huh." Otis nodded proudly. "We was the first. And he said we'd get the credit we deserve."

"Yes, I'll just bet you boys will." Cade imagined the Pinkerton agent had gotten a good laugh out of their ghost story; a lot of people in town already had.

Otis rose, his argument with Rupert forgotten. "We got to get on over to the livery. We got some dealings going on with Beau over there. Old Ruth needs tendin' to. That 'ol mule may stink like the dickens, but she's a good 'un."

Rupert and Otis ambled out of the saloon. Cade followed them to the door. Across the street he saw Allison standing on the boardwalk outside her ladies' club, chatting with two women who had small children in their arms. She was wearing a vibrant green dress that made her shine like an emerald in a setting of plain brown stones.

The Pinkerton agent was on the boardwalk too, he realized, watching the gathering at the ladies' club also. Something about the agent worried Cade. He couldn't explain it, but he didn't like the man.

Cade saw him walk past the club and tip his hat to Allison and the ladies. It rankled him that the agent seemed to linger there an instant more than necessary.

Cade stepped out onto the boardwalk ready to cross the street when he saw the Pinkerton man walk away. His gaze followed him down the street. And into the express office.

Exhausted, Allison stepped out of Jenna's back door into the crisp night air. She tightened her grip on the bundle of rag dolls in her arms. "I'll take these home and put them with the other things. You did a beautiful job on them, Jenna. Have you considered making doll clothes for a living?"

Jenna laughed. "You're delirious from sewing all evening. There's not enough need for doll clothes in Brighton to keep me in business for five minutes."

"Maybe not in Brighton," she mused.

"Oh, by the way, did Maude Wilkens come by to see you today?"

"No, I didn't see her."

"Oh, dear. I was afraid of that." Jenna stepped out onto the boardwalk. Holly slept in her room off the kitchen. She lowered her voice. "I saw Maude outside Taylor's this morning. Poor thing, it's been so hard on her since her husband took a turn."

Allison tightened her grip on the dolls, afraid one would slip from the stack. "What happened?"

"Satch was the foreman at the Carriage Works. When it closed down he lost his job, of course. It's been hard on them since." Jenna shook her head. "I suggested to Maude that she come to the club. I thought it might do her some good to be with other women, maybe take her mind off her problems for a while. She doesn't get into town very often."

A pang of guilt stabbed Allison. The closing of the Carriage Works kept haunting her.

"Next time you see her, let me know. I'd like to meet her."

"I will." Jenna waved. "Good night."

"See you in church tomorrow." Allison walked the short distance to her own back door. The alley behind the shops was empty and dark and Allison fumbled for her key, juggling the dolls and digging in her pocket before she was able to let herself inside the club. She kicked the door closed and made her way to her bedroom by memory. She dropped the dolls on the bed and lit the lantern on the bed table.

The sulfur stung her nose as the flame danced to life. Sounds from the Pleasure Palace drifted in, though the window was shut tight. It seemed louder than usual tonight.

Allison pulled back the shade and gazed across the street. She caught a glimpse of women in red costumes with feathers in their hair, dancing among the men, high-kicking to an erratic version of "O Susannah." Each kick was accompanied to a new round of hoots and catcalls.

Allison changed into her nightrail and took down her hair. Her dark tresses fell nearly to her waist. Too tired to braid them for the night, she slid under the coverlet and blew out the lantern. The now familiar sounds of Brighton lulled her to sleep quickly.

A moment later Allison came full awake. Her eyes searched the darkness as if she could see the disturbance that roused her. Footsteps, slow and methodical, sounded on the boardwalk. But not from out front, she realized, from the alley.

Allison's heart slammed against her ribs as the doorknob rattled, then creaked as it gave way. She sat up in bed and clamped her hand across her mouth to keep from screaming.

She'd forgotten to lock the back door.

Chapter
Ten

How long had it been? A minute? Ten minutes? An hour?
Staring wide-eyed into the darkness, heart pounding, Allison sat up in bed, unsure of how much time had passed
since she'd heard the creaking of the hinges on her back
door. Her heart lurched again as she heard heavy boots
walk across her kitchen.

Allison flung back the coverlet and crept silently to the
window. She hesitated for a moment, unsure of which was
the lesser of the two evils: running barefoot through the
streets of Brighton on a Saturday night, her night rail and
hair blowing in the breeze, or waiting helplessly in her room
for whatever fate might befall her.

She made her choice quickly. Allison grabbed the window and pushed up with all her might. It didn't move. She
pushed again, harder this time, but with no better results.

The footsteps drew closer, thudding on the wooden floor
as they approached her bedroom door. Panic seized her.
She turned in a circle, searching the darkness for any type
of weapon. Where was her parasol?

The door to her bedroom swung open slowly, the hinges
squeaking. She grabbed the book from the bedside table
and dove behind the upholstered chair in the corner of the
room. Allison drew herself up in a tiny knot, clutching the
book. She fought to control her labored breath and said a
silent prayer that her pounding heart couldn't be heard.

The footsteps drew nearer. Allison peeped around the chair and saw the silhouette of a man crossing the room toward her. He was easily seven feet tall with shoulders wide enough to scrape the door casings. For a moment he only stood there, his gaze searching the room. Then he turned her way and walked forward. Had he seen her? Had he heard her?

He came toward her, steadily. And in that split second, she made her decision. She wouldn't just cower in a corner and let this intruder do what he chose. No, she'd fight him, with every ounce of her strength.

The element of surprise on her side, Allison judged the distance to the door. If she could distract him for just a second, she could make a break for it. She tightened her grip on the book, sprang to her feet, and hurled the volume at him with all her strength. A bloodcurdling scream tore from her throat.

His gun cleared its holster in the same instant the book struck his chest. It bounced off, hit the window, and sent the shade flying upward. Light from the street gleamed off the gun barrel pointed straight at her. Allison screamed again.

"Allison?"

She sucked in a quick breath. "Cade?"

"Jesus Christ. . . . What did you hit me with this time?" He rubbed his chest and holstered the gun.

"Cade? Cade!"

Allison flew from behind the chair and wrapped her arms around him. "Cade, there's somebody in here. I heard them. Someone came in through the back door."

"Nobody's in here."

"Yes there is." She hiccuped to hold back the tears. "I forgot to lock the door. Someone came in."

In the faint light he looked down at her. Her eyes were shining with sheer terror. He closed his arms around her. "It's all right. You're safe now."

"No," she insisted. "I heard footsteps."

Thick dark hair curled softly around her face and brushed against his hands. It felt like silk.

Cade cleared his throat. "That was me you heard. Jenna came over and got me when she couldn't find the sheriff.

She saw somebody sneaking around in the alley. I saw your door open so I came in to check."

She shook her head. "He came in before you got here."

She was in her night rail. The realization hit Cade like a frying pan whacked across his head. His body reacted swiftly and urgently.

He shifted, trying to put some distance between them. She clung to him tightly. "It, ah, it was only, ah, me you heard."

Her breasts, unbound, pressed against his chest, full and soft. Her thighs rubbed against his. His body responded with an overwhelming urgency. Cade wanted to press himself against her and know completely the secrets that were hers alone. Desire welled deep within him.

She looked up at him and a tear trickled down her cheek. "Please believe me."

He felt like such a cad. She was terrified and crying and here he stood only thinking of passion.

Cade sighed heavily. "All right, I'll go check around again and prove there's nobody here."

"No!" She pulled him tight against her again. "Don't leave me alone."

His knees threatened to give out.

"Okay. You come with me. I'll show you nobody's here."

Allison pushed him away. "Are you insane? I'm not going out there."

In that instant, her fright, her helplessness, were gone. Angry, Cade threw out his arms. "Then what the hell do you want me to do?"

She burst into tears. "I don't know!"

Cade waved his arms around feeling like an idiot while she sobbed into her hands. Finally he grasped her shoulders and pulled her against his chest.

"It's all right." He patted her back gently.

"Somebody really was here." She cried into his chest.

"I believe you. But it's okay now."

Allison looked up at him, her cheeks wet with tears. "Really? You believe me?"

"Well, no, not really," he admitted. "But you believe it and the important thing is that you're safe now."

She raised her face to his. "Thank you."

Oh, God, he couldn't hold back another second. Cade dipped his head and covered her lips with his, kneading them together gently. She tasted salty from her tears. He deepened the kiss until her tears were gone, until the taste was gone, until he'd driven away every trace of her fear. He felt her relax against him. She sighed contentedly and tilted her head back giving him access.

Cade dug his hand into the thickness of her hair, and the other he slid down her spine to the small of her back. She felt delicate, fragile, like the most exquisite china doll he'd ever imagined. But she was soft and warm, her flesh pliant. All woman.

She made him feel all male, driven by urges too powerful to resist. Cade pressed himself against her, his desire obvious. Her delicate flesh yielded.

Allison gasped and broke off their kiss. He thought she would slap him—he wished she would. Like a drowning man he was sinking into a pool of desire he couldn't pull free from. But she didn't slap him. In the pale light her gaze held steady with his. He saw no fear, no anger, no indignation. Mirrored in her eyes was his own desire.

Cade released her and fell back a step. As if acutely aware of the distance between them, Allison crossed her arms in front of herself and turned away.

"Jenna's waiting out back." His voice was thick.

She only nodded.

He wanted to touch her again but found the strength to overcome the desire. Cade coiled his hands into fists and left.

The room seemed suddenly cool. Allison slipped into her wrapper and followed Cade out the door. He was on the boardwalk near Jenna's shop, standing in the shadows. Jenna was in the doorway. She was still dressed, double-barreled shotgun tucked under one arm.

"Are you all right?" Jenna gave her a hug. "You poor dear, you're trembling."

Her mouth fell open. "You have a gun?"

"Of course."

Allison was stunned. "Do you know how to shoot it?"

"Certainly," Jenna said, as if it were the most natural thing in the world. "Are you all right?"

"I'll be fine." She forced a small smile and drew in a deep breath.

"Did anything out of the ordinary happen inside?" Jenna asked Cade.

He shifted uncomfortably and looked at Allison. Her gaze came up quickly to meet his. For an instant they stared at each other, then looked away.

"No." Cade coughed. "No, everything inside was just the way it ought to be."

"I was so frightened when I saw that man lurking around out here," Jenna said. "Thank you for coming over."

"I sent Billy to find Mack before I came over here. He'll keep an eye on the place tonight. But I don't expect whoever you saw will be back. Probably just some drunk cowboy looking for his horse. You two get on back inside and lock up."

Jenna gave Allison another hug and went back inside her shop.

Allison lingered for a moment. "Thank you," she finally said. "I'm in your debt. Again."

He touched the brim of his Stetson. "We'll talk about it some other time."

Quietly she slipped inside and made very sure this time she locked the door behind her.

Cade headed back around the dress shop toward the Pleasure Palace. He was on fire. For a moment he considered throwing himself into the horse trough in front of the saloon. He stood there, gazing at the darkened ladies' club and listening to the laughter and music coming from the Pleasure Palace.

"Hell. . . ." Cade turned and walked toward Phoebe's place.

It was after two in the morning and the streets were still busy. Noise from the other saloons in town greeted Cade as he walked determinedly down the boardwalk. He needed this. He'd earned it, he told himself.

A man hurrying down a flight of steps to his left nearly collided with him. Cade stopped short but the man pressed on without a word. Anger flew through Cade, another emotion in his churning gut. From the light of the Steer's Horn, the man looked familiar. Slough hat, a heavy mustache.

Recognition registered in his mind and Cade wished he could take back the last few seconds when he let the man pass unheeded. It was Wes Palmer. Their confrontation outside Lydia Allbright's place was still fresh in his mind. That was one man he'd like to bust square in the face. Palmer hurried on his way, shoulders hunched, without a look back.

Cade glanced up the stairs and saw a light on in the office. It was late for Rory Stallworth to be working. He wondered what business the likes of Wes Palmer could have with Brighton's one and only attorney.

Annoyed, he walked on to Phoebe's place at the edge of town. Several horses were tied to the hitching post and lantern light shone in nearly every window of the big, two-story frame house. It was crowded. He'd have to wait.

And he was in no mood to wait for anything. Cade stood at the edge of the yard listening to murmured voices and the shrill laughter of the girls inside. No one here would look up at him with big doe eyes when they realized his condition. And no one would gasp and pull away.

The image of Allison floated through his mind. No one here would make his heart swell or cloud his thoughts either. Only Allison had done that.

"Damnit." Cade picked up a stone from the yard and hurled it into the darkness. Then he turned and walked back to town.

Allison smiled at the choir members as they filed past, then tucked her sheet music inside the piano bench and followed them outside. At the foot of the church steps several members of the congregation stopped to compliment her piano playing and welcome her to the church. She put on her best New York smile and answered all their questions.

Gradually the congregation went on their way, standing in small groups in the churchyard to talk and catch up on the latest news and gossip. Jenna joined Allison.

"We're fortunate Reverend Kent announced the ladies' club dance from the pulpit this morning," she whispered. "We'll have a big turnout. I just know it."

Allison smiled. "An endorsement from the reverend and the deacons is just what we needed."

"So many people were asking about the dance." Jenna spoke to Allison but kept an eye on Holly as she played with the other children. She was showing off the new pink dress her doll, Aunt Mattie, was wearing that matched her own dress exactly.

"I have a few more ideas to spread the news," Allison said. She raised on her toes and gazed over the churchyard. "I want to let Mabel and Edith know we're having a meeting tomorrow morning. Do you see them anywhere?"

Jenna turned in a circle. "No, I don't—" She whipped back around and ducked her head. "Oh, dear."

"What's wrong?"

"No, don't look," she whispered urgently. "It's Harry Finch. I think he's coming this way. I don't want to talk to him."

"Why?"

"Because." Jenna stole a glance behind her.

Holly appeared beside them hopping up and down and pointing. "Look, Mama, it's the candy sheriff!"

Holly ran across the churchyard and wrapped herself around the leg of Sheriff Carson as he stood talking with a group of men. He was wearing a white shirt closed with a string tie and a leather vest. Mack smiled down at her and lifted her into his arms. Holly kissed him on the cheek, then smashed Aunt Mattie against his face in what was supposed to be a kiss. Mack laughed and carried her back to where Jenna and Allison stood.

Jenna smiled. "She's been calling you the candy sheriff since you gave her the peppermint stick the other day."

"I hope word of that doesn't get around," Mack joked. "It might ruin my reputation."

Holly shoved her doll in front of his face and pulled up her dress. "See Aunt Mattie? She's got new pantalettes, with lace at the bottom, like Mama's."

Mack's gaze collided with Jenna's. His face turned beet-red. She gasped and blushed. Allison broke out laughing. After a moment they joined in.

"I'm so sorry," Jenna said through her laughter as she took Holly from his arms.

Mack gulped and ran his finger around his shirt collar.

"Good morning, ladies, Sheriff."

Harry Finch stepped into their circle. He looked quite the dandy, wearing a fine jacket and beaver hat. He touched the brim and smiled. Jenna and Allison cut off their laughter. Mack cleared his throat and straightened.

Allison regained her composure first. "Good morning, Mr. Finch."

"How are you ladies this fine morning?" He addressed them both but looked only at Jenna.

"Quite well, thank you, Mr. Finch." Jenna busied herself straightening Holly's dress.

"I'd like to come call on you this afternoon, Mrs. Mc-Cain." He glanced up at Mack. "Provided you have no other plans, of course."

Her eyes came up sharply, then glanced at Mack. He stood there, still as a statue.

"Very well, Mr. Finch." Jenna took Holly's hand. "I've got to be going now."

Harry swept his hat from his head, his bald spot shining in the morning sun. "Allow me the honor of walking you home."

Once more, she looked at Mack. He did nothing. Jenna squared her shoulders. "Certainly."

Holly jumped up and down and pulled on her mother's skirt. "But, Mama, I want—"

"Hush now, child." Harry pointed a stern finger at her. "Little girls should be seen and not heard."

The three of them walked away leaving Allison and Mack standing together in the churchyard. After a moment Allison excused herself. When she looked back, Mack stood alone, watching Jenna, Holly, and Harry Finch walk toward town.

Chapter
Eleven

With the dance less than a week away, many things still needed to be completed. Allison sighed and consulted her list.

"Decorations," she announced. "Do we have a volunteer for decorations?"

The ladies seated around the club looked at one another. She held her breath hoping she wouldn't have to appoint a volunteer. To her relief, a hand slowly rose.

"I'd like to volunteer." Mrs. Wade quickly looked at the other women. "If no one else wants to, that is."

Esther Wade's husband ran Brighton's newspaper. She was an attractive woman and, judging from her clothing, had an eye for color. Allison was grateful Mabel Duncan hadn't volunteered.

"Thank you, Mrs. Wade." Allison looked at the twelve other women seated in the club. "All those interested in assisting Esther, please see her after our meeting."

The club had buzzed with activity all morning as ladies dropped by, some wanting to help, others merely curious. Reverend Kent's announcement at church on Sunday had created a great deal of interest in the dance as well as the ladies' club.

Most of the women were wives of shop owners in Brighton. It was hard for those living in the surrounding ranches, farms, and mining camps to get into town during the week.

There were all ages, young mothers to grandmothers. In the corner of the club three little girls played noisily, arguing over who would get to hold Aunt Mattie. Allison scrawled a note to herself at the bottom of her notepad.

"My pots are all ready." Mabel slurped her tea and shoved a muffin into her mouth.

"Very good." Allison looked at her list. "Melody? Penelope? How about your booths?"

Melody ran the sweet shop just down the street and years of sampling her own confections had taken its toll. She nodded that all was well and reached for another sweet cake.

Penelope Sage owned the Red Eye Cafe. It was her first time at the club. She shifted uneasily on the settee. "I thought I'd make corn bread with honey and some muffins. Does that sound all right? I've never had a booth before."

Allison noted her choices on the notepad. "It sounds perfect."

"Why not throw in some pickles and boiled eggs?" Mabel made the suggestion around a mouthful of cake. "Everybody likes them."

Allison suspected it was Mabel who like them most. Nevertheless, she nodded her approval and noted the addition to Penelope's booth.

"Any luck on the musicians yet, Edith?"

She sat forward on the edge of the settee and placed her teacup aside. "I'll have Will take me out to the Rafferty place in plenty of time."

"Good." Allison touched the tip of her pencil to her chin. "Well, I guess that just about does it. I know Jenna has the rag doll booth under control and Mary Grable is going to handle the apple bobbing game for the children."

"What about the dance floor?" Jenna asked.

"I'll check with Joe Capp this afternoon." Allison laid her notepad aside. "Unless there's anything else, this meeting is adjourned."

The ladies finished their tea and cakes and chatted another moment before leaving the club. Allison walked them to the door, thanked them for coming and for all their help.

She blew out a heavy breath and closed the door behind them.

Allison took off her apron; a great deal still needed to be accomplished today.

In her bedroom she pinned her deep blue hat among her curls and picked up her reticule from the bureau. She was careful to lock both front and back doors when she left.

Today, fewer people were on the streets and Allison enjoyed the relative calm as she made her way down the boardwalk toward the west end of town. All was quiet at the schoolhouse as well as she stepped inside the tidy building across from the church. The students sat bent over their desks. Their teacher, Miss Rebecca Warwick, walked slowly through the room looking over each young shoulder, appraising their work. She noticed Allison standing just outside the door and left the room.

"May I help you?"

An attractive woman in her early thirties with light brown hair and large amber eyes, Rebecca wore a simple dark skirt and white blouse, as a schoolmarm should. A restraint enveloped her, a wariness. Allison introduced herself.

"You're Lydia Allbright's niece, aren't you?"

Allison brightened. "Yes. Do you know my aunt?"

Rebecca shook her head. "I've heard of her, of course, but I've never met her."

"I'm sorry to interrupt your class, but I was hoping to trouble you for some assistance. I've opened the ladies' club in town. Have you heard of it?"

"Yes."

"Many of the ladies in the club have children. I hoped you may have some picture books to help keep them occupied."

"The books aren't mine to give away. The town council keeps a close eye on the supplies I use here at the school."

"I would imagine the town council keeps a close eye on everything at the school," Allison said gently.

She suddenly understood Rebecca Warwick's restraint and reserve. She'd been a teacher herself. Teachers were expected to be beyond reproach, their conduct without question. Even a hint of impropriety—no matter how minor—could end a career. And once that happened, finding another teaching post was nearly impossible.

Rebecca smiled. "Yes, you're right about that."

"I'm a teacher myself. I understand."

"Really?" She smiled in earnest.

At least something about her life hadn't made it through the rumor mill, Allison thought. "Would you like to come by the ladies' club?"

Rebecca shook her head quickly. "No. I'd better not."

The verdict wasn't in yet on her club, Allison realized. Rebecca Warwick couldn't commit to being a party to it until she was absolutely sure it wouldn't endanger her job.

"I'll ask the town council about the books."

"Thank you. Let them know I intend to make a donation to the school for their use."

Rebecca glanced inside the classroom. "I have to get back to my students."

Allison left, her heart suddenly weighted down. The Rebecca Warwicks of Brighton needed companionship and friendship. Her ladies' club must succeed.

Cade took his own sweet time browsing through the merchandise in Taylor's General Store. From the corner of his eye he saw Edith behind the counter. True to form, she watched him like a hawk, her dislike for him etched in the severe lines of her face.

The bell over the door jangled and Allison walked in. Cade's belly tightened. Annoying Edith suddenly became the furthest thing from his mind.

He touched the brim of his Stetson. "Good morning."

She seemed startled to see him and slightly breathless.

"Good morning," she answered.

"No more late-night callers, I hope."

Her lashes fluttered and he knew they were both recalling the same thing.

"No, I've been quite alone, thank you."

He'd like to put an end to that. "Mack said he'd keep a closer eye on your place."

"That was kind of you to arrange."

Lordy, could he ever look at her again and not remember

her silky hair loose about her shoulders, the feel of her soft breasts tight against him, the taste of her lips on his? Cade mentally shook himself. He'd better learn to, before he disgraced himself right here in the middle of Taylor's General Store. And wouldn't that give Edith something to flap about.

"Hello, Miss Allison." Tyler appeared at her side. "How is Aunt Lydia? Is she better yet?"

Allison smiled, touched by Tyler's concern for her dear aunt, when everyone else in town had seemingly forgotten her. "No better. But no worse either. I went to see her after church on Sunday. I hope she can come to the dance this week."

Tyler's gaze dropped to the floor and he turned away.

"What can I get for you, Cade?" Will finished with his customer at the counter.

"Let me see what Vance has on his list." Cade walked to the counter. "Tyler, what do we need?"

The boy pulled the list from his pocket and studied it a moment. "I don't know."

"What do you mean you don't know?" Edith's eyes narrowed. "You can read, can't you?"

A look of complete incomprehension so familiar to Cade crossed the boy's face. Cade took the list from him.

The corners of Edith's mouth turned down in disgust as though she didn't really expect any better from him. "A boy as old as you and can't even read. Humph!" She put her nose in the air and huffed across the store to help Allison.

Cade bought the coffee and salt Vance had asked for and left the store with Tyler carrying the supplies. He kept a close eye on the boy in case he stumbled or dropped them.

As of yet, he hadn't found anything Tyler could do well. He still hadn't displayed a natural ability at anything. At times, Cade wondered what would ever become of him. He wondered, too, how he'd gotten along this far in the world. The boy must have had a patient, understanding father, was all Cade could figure.

A wellspring of memories suddenly flooded Cade's mind and this time they were too strong to push aside. His own father taking him fishing, wrestling around in the parlor despite his mother's protests, holding him on his lap when he was very small, and tucking him into bed each night. His father brought the fondest of memories.

And then it had all changed. Overnight, almost. In its place was the arguing, bickering, and disagreements that eventually led to name calling, finger pointing, and insults. Finally, nothing remained between them, and Cade had left. Bitter memories atop the sweet ones.

Cade dropped his hand on Tyler's shoulder when they stopped outside the Pleasure Palace. "Take the supplies in to Vance. I'm going for a shave."

"I'll get on my chores," he promised.

Cade squeezed his shoulder and headed down the boardwalk.

Allison lit the lantern against the growing darkness and settled it amid the ledger books spread out on her kitchen table. The facts and figures of Aunt Lydia's personal and business finances lay before her in Rory Stallworth's careful hand. The affairs of the ranch were documented in Wes Palmer's bold pencil strokes. It was all there. The problem was, Allison didn't know what to look for.

The figures all added up correctly; she'd verified that first. The expenditures shown in the debit column seemed justified. The reported income appeared reasonable, though she had little to compare it to. How would she know if it all made sense?

Allison pushed the ledger aside and took out Aunt Lydia's will. She read it again, noting the generous bequeath she'd left for Georgia and a few people in Brighton including Rebecca Warwick, which surprised her. Most of the estate had gone to her friends—those she considered her family—in New York, Boston, and around the world.

But who had she decided to cut out of her will, Allison wondered. Rory Stallworth had told her Aunt Lydia was planning to change something. Allison had written to her own mother, asking for her help with the matter. She hoped to hear back from her very soon. She honestly felt the answer to that question would shed light on everything else.

Allison closed the ledger, resigning herself to the fact

that she'd need help to decipher the true meaning of the figures. The chair scraped along the floor as she stood.

Another sound broke the silence of her kitchen. Allison's breath caught. Footsteps echoed from outside her back door.

Fear surged through her. Was it the same man who'd left the threatening note on her front door a few nights ago?

She didn't intend to wait around and question him herself. Allison tiptoed silently toward the front door.

A knock sounded at the back door. Soft first, then more demanding.

"Miss Tremaine? Miss Tremaine, open up. It's me, Sheriff Carson."

Allison's knees nearly gave out as she made her way to the door and opened it. The sheriff smiled and touched the brim of his hat.

"Evening, Miss Tremaine."

She felt almost giddy with relief. "Sheriff, I'm so glad it's you."

He gave her a quick nod. "Just wanted you to know I'm keeping an extra eye on the place from now on."

"Thank you, Sheriff. I appreciate it very much."

"I'm still checking into the problems you've had of late. But nothing's turned up yet."

He stood there for a long moment, then pulled his hat from his head and passed it between his hands. He cleared his throat and shifted his weight from one foot to the other.

"I was wondering . . ." He looked at his Stetson, then up at Allison. "Well, I was wondering if maybe you know where Mrs. McCain is tonight."

"Oh, dear. . . ." The frightened, hopeful expression on his face touched Allison's heart. She hated to be the one to tell him. "Jenna is having supper at the hotel. She's with . . . Harry Finch."

Mack fell back a step and pulled on his Stetson. "I'm keeping an eye on your place. I just wanted you to know. Good night."

Allison's heart ached as she watched him disappear around the corner. She locked the door and gathered up the ledgers and papers and stuffed them in the bottom drawer of her bureau. She took down her hair and plaited it into a long, single braid down the middle of her back, and dressed in her night rail. In her bed she lay awake for a very long time, listening to the sounds on the street before finally falling to sleep.

A gunshot woke her hours later. Allison sat upright in bed, clutching the quilt to her chin. Her whole body shook.

Then suddenly she was mad at herself and tired of being afraid all the time. Allison jumped out of bed. She would not spend another moment in this place trembling with fear.

She pulled off her night rail and dressed in only her pantalettes, chemise, and petticoats beneath the simple calico dress she kept to clean in. She crammed her feet into slippers and threw a shawl around her shoulders.

After tonight, she'd never be afraid again.

The kitchen was empty when Cade walked in from the barroom, the sound of the piano and the din of the crowd following him. He hadn't seen Tyler in a while and he wondered if he'd gone up to bed already. The boy usually stayed up until closing and went upstairs when everybody else did. It was after two in the morning. Where else could he be?

Cade turned to climb the stairs, then saw Tyler come through the back door. "Where have you been, boy?"

He gasped when he saw Cade and his big eyes grew bigger.

"You're supposed to be helping Vance with the glasses. Where have you been?" His tone was stern.

"I was . . . I was at the outhouse."

Cade's brows drew together. "You've been at the outhouse all this time? Are you sick?"

"No."

Cade plastered his big hand across the boy's forehead. "You're not feverish. Go give Vance a hand with the glasses."

"There's a lady outside."

"A what?"

"A lady," Tyler repeated. "I'm not sure, but I think it's Miss Allison. It kind of looks like her."

Allison Tremaine was lurking outside his saloon at two in the morning? What was that woman up to now?

He patted Tyler's shoulder. "Get out there and help Vance. We'll be closing up soon."

Cade strode out the back door. Noise from the barroom faded in the stillness of the deserted alley.

"Pssst!"

His gaze probed the darkness. "Who's there?"

"Pssst! Over here."

He could recognize that voice in his sleep. "Allison?"

"Shhhh! Don't be so loud!" Like Rebecca Warwick, there were places Allison couldn't be seen either. She stepped from the shadow. "Come over here."

"What the devil are you doing out here at this time of night?" And with your hair down? And no corset on? Cade's mouth went dry.

She grabbed his arm and dragged him into the shadow with her. "I need you."

His stomach bottomed out. "Huh?"

Allison glanced around the alley making sure no one else was around and stepped back against the wall of the Pleasure Palace. "I was lying in bed thinking, and suddenly you came to mind. I had to see you immediately. It couldn't wait. Have you ever felt that way?"

"Oh, God, yes."

Allison touched her hand to her throat. "I can't fight this any longer. I can't live this way."

"Me either, honey." He braced one arm on the wall near her head.

She looked up at him in the dim light and saw the intensity in his expression. Good, he was paying attention. "It's rather personal and you're the only person I can turn to. I don't really know anyone else well enough to ask."

The scent of her drew him closer. "Whatever you want."

"Good." Allison heaved a sigh of relief. "I'm tired of being afraid in this town all the time. I can't stand sleeping alone and wondering if someone will break into the club again. After the other night when you were there I realized what it would take to make me feel safe. And I'm willing to do it. If you're willing to help, of course."

Heat spread low across his belly. "Are you asking me what I think you're asking me?"

"Yes." Allison took a deep breath. "Cade, I want you to get me a gun."

Chapter
Twelve

"This is serious, Cade. You've got to do something."

Cade yanked the towel from Lloyd's hand and wiped the last of the shaving lather from his chin. He should have known better than to come back to Lloyd's again. Surrounding him were four angry faces—and that made him angry as well.

He flung the towel to the floor. Lloyd jumped back out of the way. "Just what the hell do you expect me to do?"

Drew Cabbot, owner of the Steer's Horn, stepped forward. "You started this mess."

"And you said it weren't nothing to worry about," added Buck Mock, owner of the Sud's Bucket.

Jack Short pushed his spectacles up on his nose. "I'm looking at shutting my place down for the night."

"And it's Saturday!" Hank Minor waved his arms wildly.

Cade pushed himself out of the barber chair. "I know what day it is."

"The Miner's Gold has never been closed on a Saturday," Hank said.

Jack nodded. "Neither has my place. And the Crystal Pistol has been here almost as long as any of you."

"What are you going to do, Cade?"

Drew asked the question, but they all stared up at him wanting to know the answer. Cade paced back and forth

between the barber chair and the sideboard where Lloyd
kept his hair tonics, scissors, and combs.

He turned to face them. "It's only a dance."

Witt Thomas, seated as always on the bench by the door,
sucked his gums. "And they said Sherman was only a general."

"Them Lace Ladies have been buzzing around all week
long, stirring up a fuss everywhere," Buck said.

"Everybody's been talking about this dance the whole
blasted week," Jack added. "The whole town is on its ear."

Drew nodded. "Folks are pouring in from all over."

"And not none of them is coming to the saloons!" Hank
flung out both arms again. "This could ruin us. Ruin us!"

"We're not going to be ruined!" Cade planted his fists on
his hips. "I swear, you men wouldn't know a good business
opportunity if it bit you in the butt."

They all looked at one another, then at Cade. Drew's
brows pulled together. "What are you talking about?"

"Sure, most everybody will be at the dance tonight, but
it's drawing people in town that haven't been here before.
Those people will see what Brighton has to offer and they'll
come back." Cade nodded. "In fact, we ought to thank the
Lace Ladies for bringing in new blood."

Hank scratched his head. "Yeah, maybe you're right."

"Of course I'm right." Cade waved them toward the
door. "Now get on back to your saloons and figure a way to
make this thing work in your favor. That's what I'm doing."

Mumbling and muttering, the four men left. Cade sighed
heavily and shook his head.

Still clutching the towel in the corner of the room, Lloyd
inched forward. "What are you planning, Cade?"

A smile crossed his face. "Come on out to the dance
tonight. You'll see."

"Does that Miss Tremaine know about it?"

His smile grew bigger. "And ruin the surprise? Not on
your life."

Witt slapped his knee. "Hot damn!"

Brighton had been busy all day with the usual Saturday
shoppers, but the streets were still busy, Cade noted as he
made his way through the crowd. It was late. The sun

dipped toward the horizon but folks were staying on in town, waiting for the dance to start. Shops remained open to accommodate them. It seemed the Lace Ladies and their dance would prove good for the businesses, especially his own. He'd been hard at work on his plan all week.

He entered the Pleasure Palace through the swinging doors. The barroom was crowded with a lot of strangers in town for the evening, waiting for the dance to start. He smiled again. He'd have them back again for sure.

"Hey, boss!" Billy came from behind the bar, leaving Vance to pour whiskey to the cowboys waiting at the other end. "It's all set, just like you said."

He'd put Billy in charge of the project, confident he could carry out his instructions. "Are the banners up? Signs all painted?"

Billy nodded proudly. "Yes, sir. Everything's tucked away safe and sound inside the livery stable."

"What about the girls?"

"Getting dressed now."

"Good. Did Tyler get the handbills? Where's that boy?" He looked around the saloon. "Tyler!"

The kitchen door swung open and Tyler backed into the room carrying a tray full of glasses. Vance's eyes bugged out and he rushed over to relieve the boy of his delicate burden. Tyler hurried over to Cade.

"Did you pick up those handbills like I told you?"

He nodded quickly. "Yes, sir."

"Was everything printed right on them?"

The blank, lost look Cade had seen so many times before crossed Tyler's face. He had no idea what Cade was asking.

Billy spoke up. "I checked them, boss. They're just like you wanted."

Cade nodded slowly and rubbed his hands together. "Good. Sounds like we're in for one hell of a night. Vance?" He walked to the end of the bar and Vance joined him. Billy and Tyler followed. "Sorry you can't be in on this, but I need somebody here to look after things."

Vance nodded. "No sense in shutting down. We'll get some business in. But I wish I could be there to see the look on the faces of Miss Tremaine and those Lace Ladies when you pull up in that wagon."

Cade smiled. "I'm looking forward to that myself."

"Come on, buddy, let's get those handbills down to the livery." Billy tugged at Tyler's shirtsleeve and they left.

The swinging doors opened and Mack Carson came into the saloon. He looked tired when he stepped up to the bar.

"What's wrong, Sheriff?" Vance drew a beer and sat it on the bar in front of him.

Mack pulled off his hat and wiped his brow with his shirtsleeve. "Every yahoo in the territory is in town today waiting to cause some kind of trouble. I ought to lock up every damn one of them."

"All of them wanting to go to the dance tonight." Cade slapped him on the shoulder. "You ought to go yourself, take a turn around the floor with Jenna McCain."

Mack shrugged and gulped his beer.

Vance leaned on the bar. "I think Harry Finch has already got that same idea."

Mack's eyes narrowed. "What are you talking about?"

"I saw him over at Mrs. McCain's this morning."

"Damn. . . ."

"Old Harry's not letting any grass grow under his feet," Vance said.

Mack stared straight ahead for a long moment, then gulped down the last of his beer. He slammed the glass down on the bar. "I'll see you boys later."

"Where are you going?" Cade asked.

Mack hitched up his gun belt. "I'm going to find me some reason to throw Finch in jail before sundown."

Allison stood like the eye of a storm in the center of the ladies' club, calm and in control while chaos reigned around her. She clutched her list in one hand and checked off each item completed, referring to every reminder she'd noted for herself all week long. Time was short. The dance would start soon and all the provisions had to be moved down to the church.

"Mabel? Where's Mabel?" Allison scanned the room full

of women. She saw her and waved her over. Allison consulted her list. "Is your booth ready?"

Mabel tugged at her bodice. "The water's boiling and the
corn's cooking. It'll be ready for eating by the time it's ready
to get eaten."

Allison checked the item off her list. "Melody? Are you
here?" She spied Esther Wade helping Edith with the trays
of fried chicken. "Esther!"

The woman made her way through the crowd. "Oh! This
is all so exciting!"

"I wanted to compliment you on your decorations. The
booths are beautifully done," Allison told her.

She beamed. "I had so much fun."

Finally everything was moved out of the ladies' club and
on its way to the churchyard. Allison did a quick look
around to make sure nothing had been missed. In her bedroom she checked her appearance one final time in the
mirror and decided the lavender dress she'd picked for the
evening had been a good selection. The bodice was low,
accentuating her bosom and tiny waist. She pulled her
shawl from the drawer of the bureau and left the club.

As Allison approached the churchyard, she smiled. The
dance floor and booths Joe Capp and his crew built had
turned out perfectly. He'd whitewashed them and Esther
Wade on the decorating committee had hung mauve banners, white lace, and ribbons on everything. Beneath the
oaks of the churchyard, the lanterns were lit and the atmosphere was festive. A number of horses, wagons, and buggies were already parked on the other side of the church.
The Rafferty brothers were on the bandstand tuning up.

Allison strolled past the booths placed around the dance
floor. Georgia served punch and a slab of chocolate cake to
a young couple. She'd spent the last two days cooking non-
stop and had prepared every imaginable cake. Mabel had
her corn on the cob going and Edith's fried chicken booth
was already selling. Penelope Sage, who ran the Red Eye
Cafe, was selling pickles, boiled eggs, corn bread, and muffins dripping with butter and honey. Jenna's rag dolls decorated her booth and already drew the attention of several
little girls. Beside her, Mary Grable who ran the Sunday

school had three young boys bobbing for apples in a wood tub of water. A line had already formed at Melody's candy booth.

Allison looked on with pride at what the ladies of Brighton had put together. The booths would donate a portion of their profits to the ladies' club and with that money they would begin their fight against the saloons in earnest.

Allison drew in a deep breath. Everything was in place. Now all they needed was more people to arrive.

That didn't take long. Within the hour, the dance floor was filled and people crowded every booth. The three Rafferty brothers played lively tunes. Laughter rose above the music as the younger children played games in the churchyard. Allison smiled in delight as she looked on from the edge of the dance floor.

Jenna stepped up beside her. Another lady from the club had taken over her rag doll booth. Allison had worked out a schedule that allowed everyone free time to enjoy the dance.

"Everything turned out so well." Jenna gazed at the dance floor. "We haven't had a gathering like this in such a long time."

Mostly married folk with children were there. Good, hardworking people who got precious little time to enjoy themselves. The dance had drawn younger people too, of course, the girls on one side of the dance floor and the boys on the other, making eyes at each other.

Jenna laughed gently. "I remember when Dan asked me to dance the first time. That night, when he held me in his arms, I knew I wanted him to hold me forever."

Allison sighed inwardly. She'd never felt that way before, and she'd certainly danced more than her share of dances. Maybe the right man just hadn't turned her around the floor yet, she thought.

"Do you miss Dan?" Allison asked gently.

"I suppose I'll always miss him a little." She drew in a deep breath and smiled. "Especially at dances."

The Rafferty brothers finished their rendition of "Camp Town Ladies" and strains of "O Susannah" faded in. Surprised, the crowd turned. A wagon loaded with a piano and

three dancing girls lumbered across the churchyard and
stopped a short distance from the dance floor. It was rigged
with a string of lanterns swaying on ropes strung from poles,
and a red and white banner proclaiming the Pleasure Palace
Saloon.

The song played on and the girls wearing scanty red and
black lace costumes high-kicked their way from one end of
the wagon to the other. Hoots and catcalls rose from the
churchyard as everyone gathered around. The song ended
and Cade Jessup jumped up onto the wagon.

"Ladies and gentlemen, gather around and hear the biggest news to hit Brighton in years!" He waved his hands
drawing everyone closer. "That's it, just step right up. Be
the first to hear the news and spread the good word."

Allison's mouth fell open.

"What's he doing?" Jenna asked.

"I don't know, but I intend to find out." Allison marched
into the crowd surrounding the wagon.

The gathering fell silent, waiting and watching Cade.

"It is my distinct honor and privilege to invite each and
every one of you to the Pleasure Palace Saloon to hear one
of the stage's most sought after performers. A singer whose
presence has graced the footboards of America's greatest
theaters—New York, Philadelphia, Boston, Cincinnati. Not
to mention command performances before the crowned
heads of Europe. A woman who has sung for kings and
queens on every continent."

Cade paused for a moment. The crowd drew closer,
hanging on every word.

"Ladies and gentlemen, two weeks from tonight, on the
newly built stage of the Pleasure Palace Saloon, it will be
my privilege to present to you, in her first concert tour west
of the Mississippi, none other than the great songstress
Miss Vivian Devaine!"

A gasp went up from the crowd followed by a roar of
applause. Billy jumped up from the piano bench and held a
placard of Miss Devaine high over his head. A cheer rose
from the gathering.

As it died down, Cade held up his hands for silence. "So
spread the word and make your plans now to be at the

Pleasure Palace. And in special recognition to the Ladies for the Advancement of Cultural Events, anybody showing up with one of these handbills will get a free drink!"

A cheer went up again. Cade motioned to Tyler who climbed onto the wagon and began passing out the hand-bills. The crowd rushed the wagon, grabbing them as quickly as he could hand them out.

"Oh!" Allison stamped her foot. That man! That irritating man! She'd give anything to have her parasol with her tonight.

Instead she pushed her way through the crowd to the bandstand. The Rafferty boys were on their feet watching along with everyone else.

"Play!" They all stared at her. "Play something. Now!"

Quickly they struck up a lively song. The crowd, charged by Cade's announcement, surged onto the dance floor again.

Allison fought her way toward the wagon, ready to give Cade Jessup a piece of her mind, when Jenna cut her off.

"Don't make a scene now. That's what he wants." She pulled Allison to the edge of the dance floor where the music could cover their conversation. A moment later Edith and Mabel joined them and they bent their heads together talking quietly.

Cade watched the scene from across the churchyard and chuckled to himself. Billy jumped down from the wagon.

"I guess we got the word out, huh, boss?"

He nodded, a slow, satisfied smile on his face. "I'd say we did, Billy." He gestured to the wagon. "Why don't you get that thing put up for the night and come on back and join in the dancing."

"Sure thing, boss."

Cade waved to Belle, Clare, and Sonny. "Nice work, girls. Thanks."

They all smiled, except for Sonny. She studied her nails and ignored the compliment.

Billy tugged Tyler's shirtsleeve as he walked by. "Come on, let's get going."

"No," Cade interrupted. "Tyler stays. Come over here, boy." He'd had him at the livery stable with him once when he'd gone down to check on his horse and pay Beau his monthly boarding bill. Tyler hadn't known one end of the tack from the other and had nearly gotten himself trampled to boot. He'd spent an hour trying to teach the boy to saddle a horse.

Billy drove the wagon away, the girls in the back smiling and waving to the crowd.

Mack made his way through the crowd and slapped Cade on the back. "You old dog, you. Vivian Devaine! My God! How'd you do it?"

A proud smile crossed his face. "It took some talking, but it's in the bag."

"So that's what all that construction is about. You need that fancy stage for Miss Devaine to sing."

Cade nodded. "And it's only the beginning, Mack. Before I'm done, I'll have every singer, piano player, and guitar picker you ever heard of begging to appear at the Pleasure Palace."

Mack grinned. "Is that right?"

"Want some advice, Mack? Buy yourself some property. Values will be going sky-high," Cade predicted.

Cade, Mack, and Tyler walked toward the dance floor. On the opposite side, Allison and the ladies were still huddled together.

"Looks like your announcement didn't set too well with the Lace Ladies," Mack said.

Cade rubbed his chin. "No, I didn't expect it would."

They watched until the gathering finally broke up and the ladies went back to their booths. Allison and Jenna moved to the edge of the dance floor.

Cade scanned the crowd. "I don't see Harry Finch here tonight."

Mack nodded slowly. "Finch had to be on duty tonight."

"On duty? Ben always works nights."

"Not tonight. Ben got himself thrown in jail this afternoon."

Cade looked over at his friend. "On what charge?"

Mack hitched up his gun belt. "I'll think of something by tomorrow morning."

The Rafferty brothers struck up a rendition of "I Dream

of Jeannie," slowing the dancers. Mack elbowed Cade in the ribs. "Would you look at that?"

Cade followed his line of vision and saw Tyler walk up to Allison. She smiled and offered her hand as they stepped onto the dance floor.

And the boy could dance. Cade looked on in shock as Tyler waltzed her around the floor with more grace and ease than anyone he'd seen in his life. He led her fluidly through the other couples, sweeping her along perfectly to the gentle rhythm of the music. Everyone else noticed, as well. Heads turned. People whispered. Some even pointed. Cade shook his head. The boy couldn't do anything else, but he could dance.

When the song ended, Cade and Mack both grabbed him as he left the floor.

"Where'd you learn to dance like that?" Cade asked.

"My mama made me learn." Tyler looked up at Cade. "Miss Allison is pretty. She smells real good, up close."

Mack sighted Jenna in the crowd and drew in a deep breath. "If you'll excuse me. . . ."

Cade patted Tyler on the shoulder. "Stay out of trouble now." He moved through the gathering in search of Allison.

"Evening, Miss Tremaine." He tipped his hat when he found her beside the pickle booth. "Would you care to dance?"

Allison whirled around. She didn't display the look he'd seen when Tyler had asked the same question. Not by a long shot.

"I'd rather dance with a skunk—a rabid, tick-infested skunk—than the likes of you, Cade Jessup."

She was a spitfire. The urge to kiss her nearly overwhelmed him.

Instead he smiled. "Is that what the well-bred ladies of New York City are saying this season, Miss Tremaine?"

Anger swelled her breasts upward in her gown. "What would you know about well-bred ladies?"

Cade glanced around at the stares they were getting. "I know they don't like making a scene."

Allison curbed her anger. No, she didn't want to make a scene, but she intended to give Cade Jessup an earful. It was scandalous to go off with him, so she did the only thing she could. A sardonic smile twisted her lips. "In that case, Mr. Jessup, I'd love to dance with you."

On the dance floor, Cade swept her into his arms and led her in a slow waltz through the other couples. Tyler was right, he realized. Allison's unique feminine fragrance drifted over him. Her hand felt delicate and soft. The small of her back was fragile as he closed his fingers over her flesh. And the view was knee-weakening. Not only were her porcelain skin, her wide amber eyes, and generous lips enticing, but from this angle the swell of her breasts was displayed for him alone.

"Your actions tonight were despicable." Her tone was cold, her body rigid.

He was rigid too, but not from anger. Cade gazed down at her. "Business is business."

"I can't believe you brought those half-naked dancers here to this family gathering. And on the churchyard too."

"I thought you were looking for new members tonight." A grin tugged at his lips. "Don't tell me my girls aren't good enough for your ladies' club."

Her chin went up a notch. "I didn't say that."

"You ought to invite them to join," he teased. "As long as there are women like them in town, saloons will never go out of business. Men like looking at a pretty woman."

Allison felt his gaze caress her. The tone of his voice dropped to a rich timber and sent a chill up her spine. She hardened her feelings. "You had no right breaking into this dance with your self-serving announcement about your saloon."

The song hadn't ended, but Cade stopped dancing. The blue of his eyes turned to steel. "Hear this now, Allison, once and for all. This isn't a game to me. I'm not running a saloon because I'm bored, or because it seems like fun, or because I don't have anything else pressing at the moment. It's my livelihood. It keeps me and a lot of other people fed and clothed. And nothing, not you, not your ladies' club, not your grand ideals and notions, is going to stop me. Do you understand that? Nothing."

Cade released her and walked away. The ferocity of his

words stunned Allison. She gathered her skirt and left the floor. Edith's disapproving gaze caught her eye as she passed the doll booth.

"That Cade Jessup—he thinks he owns this town." Edith's lips pursed. "Did you see him put that boy up on the wagon with those—those floozies?"

Allison leaned against the booth. "Yes, Edith, I saw."

"It's a disgrace. Why, the boy can't even read! And Cade has him up in front of the whole town giving out handbills for free liquor. The boy doesn't even know what he's involved in." Edith spied Cade across the churchyard and her eyes narrowed. "I've put up with his saloon next to my business, drunks, loud music 'til all hours, those women. But this is too much. Cade Jessup has gone too far this time."

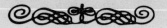

Chapter
Thirteen

Allison and Jenna sat alone in the ladies' club, the shades drawn to discourage visitors or curious sightseers. Church services were over and they'd had lunch together before putting Holly down for her nap in Allison's bedroom. Sunday was the only day the ladies' club was closed.

Jenna curled her feet under her on the settee. "So, all and all, I'd say the dance was a success."

"Well, there was that one scandal." A sly grin spread over Allison's face and she looked pointedly at Jenna. "A certain widow was seen dancing the night away with a certain sheriff."

Color rose in her cheeks, then she giggled.

"Mack is a very nice man," Allison observed.

"Well . . . yes."

"And handsome too. Holly is quite taken with him," Allison pointed out.

Jenna smiled. "He seems quite taken with her, as well."

They were silent for a long moment before Allison spoke again. "Was it my imagination, or were you dodging Harry Finch after church this morning?"

"I was in a hurry. That's all."

Allison leaned closer. "Is that the only reason?"

Jenna squeezed her eyes shut for a moment and sighed heavily. "I think Harry might ask me to marry him."

Allison's eyes widened. "How do you feel about him?"

"He's a widow, very stable and comfortably well off. And pleasant enough, I suppose."

"But what about Mack?"

Jenna shook her head. "I have my future to think of and, more importantly, Holly's future."

"Do you love Harry?" Allison asked softly.

Jenna turned away. "I married once for love. I don't know if I can allow myself that luxury again."

Allison sat back and fell silent. Neither spoke for a long moment.

"It's just not that simple," Jenna finally said. "Decisions like this never are."

Allison gazed at her left hand where the diamond and garnet ring used to be. No. Decisions were never simple.

Cade straightened when he saw Billy walk through the swinging doors and cross to the bar. Something was wrong.

"Boss, the sheriff sent word for ya'll to come over to the jail." He glanced at Tyler behind the bar. "Said to bring him along too."

"What's up?"

"I don't know," Billy said. "But Edith Taylor is over there with him."

Murder shone in the woman's eyes when Cade and Tyler entered the jail a few minutes later.

"What's this all about, Mack?"

The sheriff rose from behind his desk. "Mrs. Taylor has registered an official complaint about the boy. Since he's got no family we know of, and he's so young, she says he ought to be sent away to the orphans' asylum over in Virginia City."

The words hit Cade like a punch in the gut. "What are you talking about?"

Tyler tugged on Cade's shirtsleeve. "What's wrong?"

Edith glared up at Cade from her seat in front of the sheriff's desk. "He's becoming a menace to the entire town."

Anger grew inside Cade. "He works for me and he does a good job. He's caused no trouble. I'll vouch for him."

"And what kind of recommendation is that, from a saloon owner." Edith spat the words.

"I don't understand." Tyler's eyes were wide with fear. He pulled on Cade's sleeve again. "What does that word mean?"

"Mrs. Taylor here wants you sent to an orphanage. It's a place where children with no parents live and—"

"No!"

Tyler made a break for the door. Cade looped his arm around the boy's waist and pulled him off the floor.

"Hold still, now." Cade held him firmly.

"No!" Tyler struggled to get away. "I won't go there. I won't!"

"Be still." Cade gave him a little shake. "Nobody's going anywhere yet." Tyler calmed and Cade set him on the floor; he kept a hand on his elbow just in case.

"See what I mean?" Edith pointed at the boy. "See how he's turning out? And who can blame him, considering how he's living."

Mack shook his head. "I can't say that I blame him, Mrs. Taylor. I've been to that orphan asylum before and it's not the kind of place most people would want to live."

"And living in a saloon is better?" Edith's brow arched haughtily. "Up 'til all hours of the night, living among those heathen women, whiskey everywhere you turn. What kind of life is that? Why, the boy can't even read!"

Mack pulled at the tight muscles of his neck. "Fact is, I've got no jurisdiction over kids and orphan asylums and the like. We'll have to wait 'til the circuit judge comes around next time and let him decide."

"How soon will that be?" Cade asked.

"Another four to five weeks."

Edith's lips pinched together. "Are you going to allow this boy to live in a saloon and not even get an education?"

He scratched his head and looked at Cade. "If the boy can't read he ought to be in school." He turned to Tyler. "What about it, boy? Can you read and write?"

Tyler frowned. "Do you mean English?"

"Well, what do you think we study in school in America?" Edith snapped. She pursed her mouth in disgust.

"All right," Cade said. "I'll see to it he learns to read and write."

"Will that suit you, Mrs. Taylor?" the sheriff asked.

She tossed her head, making it clear it did not suit her in the least. "As long as the boy gets an education I'll wait for the judge to come and decide what to do with him. But," she added quickly, "if I see him running loose on the streets, or causing trouble, I'll contact the judge myself."

Mack threw up his hand. "All right. That settles it."

"For now." Edith rose and threw one final scathing look at Cade before she left the sheriff's office.

"I don't understand," Tyler said softly.

"It's not so bad." Cade draped his arms around Tyler's shoulder and gave him a little squeeze. "Starting tomorrow morning, you're going to learn to read and write."

"English?" His big brown eyes looked troubled.

Cade chuckled. "Yes, English."

"You'll like Miss Warwick," Mack told him. "She's a real nice lady."

"I never saw her before," Tyler said.

"No," Cade agreed. "You won't ever see Miss Warwick anywhere near the Pleasure Palace."

But two days later she showed up at Cade's back door, a shawl over her head, clutching her satchel. The afternoon breeze flirted with loose strands of her light brown hair. She'd been the schoolmarm in Brighton for a few years now, hired on from Virginia City. There'd been some sort of scandal surrounding her family, though Cade had never known the details. The old geezers on the town council had hired her anyway and she'd always been the epitome of propriety.

Cade didn't know whether to invite her inside to get her out of the public eye or to tell her to leave before some old busybody saw her.

"I won't take a minute of your time, Mr. Jessup." Rebecca glanced nervously up and down the alley. "I was worried about Tyler. Is he sick?"

Suspicion knotted in his belly. "Why do you ask?"

Rebecca pulled the shawl closer around her. "He left

without a word after the first recess yesterday, and he didn't come to school at all today. Is something wrong?"

Cade planted his fists on his hips. "I intend to find out."

"I only had a few minutes to work with him before he left, but he really should be in school. He can't read or write at all."

"I'll take care of it," Cade assured her.

"Thank you." Rebecca looked around, then hurried away.

Cade stepped back and closed the door. Anger built inside him. Tyler had lied to him. The boy had not said a word about a problem when he'd come home yesterday, and had given no indication he'd left halfway through the school day. He had, though, given every indication this morning that he was going to school, with his books and lunch pail in hand. He hadn't been seen since.

Cade pulled at the tight muscles of his neck. He wouldn't tolerate being lied to.

Up in his bedroom Cade worked on his ledgers until he heard the slow, thudding footsteps on the stairs. He looked up as Tyler came into the room juggling the broom and dustpan. The boy looked tired and haggard, with dark circles under his eyes. He'd gotten Cade up twice during the night, screaming and crying in his sleep; it was the first time he'd had the nightmare in weeks. Some of Cade's anger dissipated. Maybe more was going on than he realized.

Cade reared back in his chair. "How was school today?"

The dustpan slipped from Tyler's hand and clattered to the floor. He stopped quickly. "I don't know."

"What does that mean, you don't know?" His tone was harsh purposely.

Tyler jumped. "I don't know. I've got to sweep now."

"That can wait." Cade rose and rounded the desk. He took the broom from him and propped it against the wall. "Miss Warwick came by this afternoon."

The little color left in Tyler's face drained away.

"She said you hadn't been coming to school. I want to know why."

He swallowed hard. "I don't know."

Cade leaned closer. "That's not an answer, boy. Tell me why you lied to me."

Tyler turned away. "I—I—couldn't stay." Emotion choked his voice.

The boy was drawn tight as a bow and ready to pop, Cade realized. He softened his tone. "Did something bad happen at school?"

He shook his head.

"Did the kids make fun of you?"

"No."

"Were the bigger boys picking on you?"

"What does that mean?" He looked back over his shoulder. Tears welled in his eyes.

"Were they teasing you, hitting you, making fun of you?"

He shook his head quickly.

Cade blew out a heavy breath. "I can stand here all day guessing, son, but the sooner you tell me what's wrong, the sooner we can fix it."

"I can't go back. I just can't."

Cade threw up both hands. "Well I know it can't be Miss Warwick. She's about the nicest—"

Tyler covered his ears with his palms. "Don't talk about her."

Stunned, Cade stepped closer. "What did she do to you?"

Tyler shook his head frantically and turned away. "Please . . . don't. . . ."

"We're getting to the bottom of this right now." He grabbed Tyler's wrist. "Let's go down to the school and talk to Miss Warwick."

"No!" Tyler jerked his arm away. He stumbled backward and fell against the wall, banging his head. His lips curled down and a pent-up tear rolled from his eyes. He touched his palm to his head.

"Let me see," Cade said softly and reached for him.

Tyler jumped away. "No! I can't go to school! I can't see her again! Ever!"

Cade pointed a finger at him. "You tell me right now what that woman did to you."

"Nothing! She—she—" He hiccuped, trying desperately to hold in the tears.

"She what?"

"She looks like my mama!" Great racking sobs shook him and he fell against Cade and buried his face in his shirt. He locked both arms around his waist.

Cade wrapped him in a tight embrace. His own heart swelled with compassion for the boy. The teacher looked like his mama. His dead mama.

Tyler turned his tear-streaked face up to him. "I can't go back. Please don't make me go."

Cade studied him. Was there a resemblance to Rebecca Warwick? Or was it just his imagination? He seldom got close enough to the woman to see her well. Something about the eyes, maybe. Big brown eyes with long lashes. And the chin? He wasn't sure.

Cade patted him gently. "You won't have to go back."

"But Mrs. Taylor said—"

"You let me worry about Edith Taylor."

He sniffed. "She said I'd have to go to school."

"She said you'd have to learn to read and write," Cade pointed out.

"Is there another school here?"

"No." Cade drew in a deep breath and let it out slowly. "No, there's no other school. But there is another teacher."

Cade held the boy tight against him and gazed out the window at the meeting place of the Ladies for the Advancement of Cultural Events across the street. Inwardly he cringed, knowing there was no other way out of this predicament.

He was going to have to ask a favor of Miss Allison Augusta Tremaine.

"Flattery, I tell you, use flattery. It works every time." Vance delivered the advice with an emphatic nod.

"No, boss. Give her flowers," Billy advised.

"He's got a point," Vance agreed. "See, first you give her the flowers, then you butter her up. Tell her how pretty she is, and stuff like that."

Cade shook his head reluctantly. Getting back in any woman's good graces wasn't easy. Getting back in Allison Tremaine's good graces would be next to impossible.

He'd told Vance and Billy about his predicament with Tyler and Miss Warwick; they didn't envy him having to ask Allison Tremaine for help with tutoring, especially after what he'd pulled at her dance last week. But he wasn't sure flattery or gifts would sway Allison. She'd been wooed by some of the handsomest, wealthiest men in the state of New York, he was sure.

"If that doesn't work, go for pity," Vance advised.

Billy's head bodded. "Yeah, boss, make her feel sorry for you."

His back stiffened. "I don't need her pity."

Vance hit his swell of pride with a cold statement. "Maybe you don't. But Tyler does."

Cade couldn't argue with that. He'd finally gotten the boy calmed down after swearing to take care of the problem. Tyler had looked at him, and for the first time since he'd been at the Pleasure Palace, Cade had seen the tiniest hint of trust in his eyes. He doubted the boy had trusted anybody in a very long time. Cade couldn't let him down. Besides, he wasn't about to let Edith Taylor have her way and send him to that orphanage.

He'd given Tyler a shot of whiskey and he'd fallen asleep on Cade's bed. Now, with this abundance of well-intentioned advice from Vance and Billy, he was off to make good on his promise.

Cade tugged on his vest. "Look, I'm just going across the street and ask her flat out. Simple as that."

Vance and Billy exchanged a dubious look as he left the saloon.

Cade rapped on the back door of the ladies' club and after a moment Allison appeared. As always, the sight of her caused his belly to knot. But she hardly felt the same, he realized, by the look on her face. He wished he'd taken Billy up on his flower idea.

"Afternoon." He touched the brim of his hat cordially.

Allison stepped forward and looked up and down the alley. "What? No dancing girls? No free drinks? Oh, I know, you're saving them for church services this Sunday."

Cade shuffled his feet; he supposed he deserved her sarcasm. "Actually, I've come to ask a favor."

Allison rolled her eyes. "A favor? Such as, when I asked you to buy me a gun the other night? That kind of favor?"

"No," he said crossly. "In this kind of favor, nobody runs the risk of getting killed."

He'd flatly refused to buy her a gun when she'd asked him about it outside the Pleasure Palace, and it seemed he was no more inclined to do so now. Allison folded her arms under her breasts. "I have to admire your fortitude, after all you've done, coming over here like this. What do you want?"

"Edith Taylor has got it in her head to send Tyler to the orphans' asylum."

Allison stepped onto the boardwalk. "She was quite upset after the dance, but I didn't think she'd go this far. What can I do to help?"

Cade pushed his hat back on his head. "She's willing to wait for the judge to get here next month to decide, as long as he goes to school. But Tyler won't go to school. He says the teacher looks like his mama who just died."

"Oh, dear. Poor thing." Allison shook her head. "He says Rebecca Warwick looks like his mother? How odd."

"Why's that?"

She shrugged. "Miss Warwick keeps turning up in strange circumstances, that's all. My aunt was instrumental in securing her teaching post here in Brighton and is one of the few people in the town she left money to in her will. But Miss Warwick claims never to have met her." She looked up at Cade. "That's odd, don't you think?"

"Maybe." He braced his arm against the door casing above her head. "Do you think she looks like Tyler?"

"A family resemblance?" Allison considered it for a moment. "I'd never thought of it before. Lots of people look alike, in some way. What did Tyler say about it?"

"Nothing. The boy's mouth is closed tighter than a new hatband."

"I don't suppose Rebecca gave any indication she and Tyler are related?"

"Never mentioned a word about it, though it looks like she would, given his circumstances." Cade shook his head.

"Maybe this has something to do with Miss Warwick's family in Virginia City. There's some old scandal there, I hear."

Allison touched the tip of her finger to her chin. "And Tyler has never told you where he's from?"

"I didn't want to push him. Seems like he's been through a lot and I wanted him to feel good about staying with me. Did your aunt ever say anything about Miss Warwick or why she was named in her will?"

Allison sighed. "Aunt Lydia isn't saying any more than Tyler."

"Well, as I see it, only two people know the answer to this little mystery and neither one is talking. That leaves us with the problem at hand."

"Edith and her orphanage threat." Allison looked up at him. "How do I fit in to all of this?"

Cade straightened and shifted his weight from one foot to the other. "You're the only other teacher in Brighton. I was hoping you could tutor him."

"Of course."

Cade cleared his throat. "Well, thank you. I'll send him over in the morning."

They were quiet for a long moment while both gazed into each other's eyes. Finally Cade backed up a step. "Let me know if you have any trouble with the boy."

"I don't think he'll be a problem."

"Me either." Cade stepped closer. He couldn't stand it. In spite of himself, Cade leaned down and kissed her lips. She accommodated him by stretching up on her tiptoes and arching her head back.

Cade broke off the kiss, mumbled, and left, unaware of the eyes that watched from the shadows across the alley.

The uppity niece from New York and the saloon owner? A short bitter laugh blended with the sounds of the midday. One more fact to file away. One more fact to pass on.

Wes Palmer watched until Allison had gone back inside and Cade had disappeared across the street. It might be useful, he thought, to know such details. Useful, when the time came.

Chapter Fourteen

"I know we've only a few days before the meeting, but that will work in our favor. If we rally support quickly, then face the town council with the momentum of the citizens behind us, we can win."

Allison faced the roomful of ladies, all listening with rapt attention. The turnout for today's ladies' club meeting was excellent. And every woman in town would be needed to pull off what she had planned.

Allison continued. "We know what we're proposing is the right thing for the good people of Brighton. We can make the streets safe once again for women and children. We can make this the family town it once was. And closing the saloons on Sundays will be our first step."

The ladies responded with a round of applause and determined expressions on their faces.

"I think that with all of us working together, we can make this happen," Jenna predicted.

Esther Wade rose from her chair. "Those men on the council will have to sit up and take notice."

Mabel Duncan crammed another cake into her mouth. "I say we push for it!"

"It's about time we returned decency to Brighton!" Edith declared.

Another round of applause broke from the ladies.

"Those designated to circulate the petitions, please do so

immediately," Allison instructed. "Speak to as many people as you can. We need support from everyone."

The ladies rose and made their way toward the door. Allison parted the curtain at the rear of the shop and spoke to the children there. "Come along, it's time to go."

Reluctantly they put aside their toys. The children enjoyed coming to the club as much as their mothers. Allison had furnished one corner of her kitchen with a tiny table and chairs that Joe Capp had made, along with brightly colored building blocks, doll babies with clothes Jenna had sewn, and picture books Rebecca Warwick had sent over.

"Don't forget," Allison called. "We'll all gather at the town council meeting. Bring everyone you can find."

The ladies all nodded in agreement as they left.

Allison leaned against the door frame. The afternoon breeze was cool and strong; it ruffled her skirt and tugged at the wisps of her dark hair curling at her ears. Across the street, she noticed Cade standing outside the Pleasure Palace. He looked as though he'd been there for a while, and she wondered if he was waiting until the ladies left. She'd expected him to come over all day; this morning was Tyler's first tutoring session.

As Allison looked on, Phoebe and her entourage sauntered down the boardwalk and stopped in front of the Pleasure Palace. The woman was outfitted in pink today, her dress tight-fitted and cut low in the bodice. The fashionable kick pleat displayed a scandalous amount of ankle. She spoke with Cade for a moment, then he chuckled and Phoebe ran her finger down the front of his shirt. He stopped laughing. Allison whirled away and closed the door behind her.

Men were always attracted to whores. Allison's mother had told her that since she could remember. But no man married one. Right now, with her stomach knotted and her temper boiling, it seemed a small consolation to Allison.

She busied herself gathering the tea service and carried it into the kitchen, refusing to dwell on why it bothered her that Cade knew the town whore well enough to allow her to touch him in public. She pumped water into the pot and set it on the cookstove to warm, then straightened the children's play area in the corner.

A knock sounded on the back door sending an unexplained flash of anger through Allison. It was probably Cade, come to discuss Tyler. She pulled open the back door, only to find a small woman on the boardwalk. Her dress was plain and baggy, a bonnet long out of fashion covered her cornstalk hair.

"Get out," the woman hissed.

Stunned, Allison fell back a step.

The woman looked up and down the alley. "Get out while you still can."

Allison recovered marginally from her shock. She'd seen this woman somewhere before. "Who are you?"

The woman pointed a finger at her. Her hands were red and dry, her nails broken. "Go back where you belong—before it's too late."

The woman gathered her long skirt and hurried away.

"Come back!" Allison followed her through the alley, but the woman didn't stop. She disappeared in the crowd on the street.

A chill ran down Allison's spine. A note warning her to leave town had been pinned to her door with a knife. And now this. A direct threat from a woman she couldn't place.

Across the street, Phoebe and the other ladies had sauntered past the Pleasure Palace, headed toward Taylor's General Store. Allison shook her head to clear her thoughts. The woman was one of Phoebe's girls, she realized. But not one of the whores, according to Jenna. The scrub girl.

Anger hardened in Allison's stomach. She was tired of being threatened, tired of being afraid. This wouldn't go unchallenged.

She turned to the alley once more but caught sight of Cade. He jogged across the street and stepped up onto the boardwalk beside her. The breeze blew his dark hair across his forehead. An aura of warmth enveloped her as he stepped closer.

"Who is that girl who just ran out of the alley? Phoebe's

. . . employee." Since he knew Phoebe, he surely knew her girls.

Cade frowned. "How do you know about Phoebe?"

"I might ask you the same, but I don't really have time for a discussion of your morals, Mr. Jessup." Or the lack of them, she wanted to add.

He gazed down the street, then back at Allison. "Polly. Why do you want to know?"

That he knew her name so readily annoyed Allison, but she tossed her head, disinclined to share her feelings or the woman's threat with Cade. "I was thinking of inviting her to join the ladies' club."

He laughed. "Yeah, that will be the day."

Her chin went up a notch. "And why do you think the notion is so preposterous?"

"If it weren't for women like that in town, me and every other saloon would be out of business." Cade looked pointedly at her. "And there'd be no need for your ladies' club either."

Interesting, Allison thought. She filed the fact away, unwilling to debate the social virtue of whores and saloons while standing on a public street.

"I wanted to find out how Tyler did this morning. I know he's simpleminded, but were you able to get anywhere with him?"

Allison resisted the urge to tell him that, once again, he was wrong about something. "Actually, he's very intelligent."

His eyes widened. "Tyler?"

"Come along. I've got a pot on the stove." Allison walked back down the alley, leaving Cade to follow.

"Yes, I think he's very smart. He's just had no formal schooling." Allison closed the back door behind Cade.

"But the boy can't do anything."

"Physical abilities are not always an indication of intelligence, as you know." She reached for the pot of water she'd left to warm on the stove.

Cade picked it up first. "Where do you want this?"

Allison pointed to the dishpan beside the sink and Cade poured the water in.

"He thinks the alphabet starts with the letter C, which is quite odd. I've never encountered that before." Allison took her apron from the peg beside the back door and tied it around her waist. "But he can write with either hand equally well. Right or left, it doesn't matter."

"So he can write some?"

"A little. He can make the letters, but can't spell anything." Allison set the teacups in the dishpan and began to wash. "He's very good at arithmetic."

Cade picked up a linen towel from the sideboard and sidled up next to her. He began drying the delicate Haviland tea service.

"He doesn't know the formal process of arithmetic, but he can add and subtract, and even do division, in his head."

"Without writing it down?"

Allison nodded and passed him another teacup. "I don't understand it either, but somehow he knows the answers."

Cade shrugged. "I guess the boy knows more than I gave him credit for."

They were silent for a moment, with only the swishing of the dishwater and the squeak of linen against china to keep them company.

Allison glanced down at the cup Cade had placed aside. "You seem to know your way around the kitchen."

He chuckled. "When I was a kid this was my punishment. My pa would send me into the kitchen and have me wash dishes."

Allison smiled. "You don't seem to have an adversion to it now."

"Nope." He smiled. "Fact is, I kind of liked it. The kitchen was warm. It always smelled good. My ma would come in and have Cook make me something special after I was finished—quietly, of course, so my pa wouldn't find out."

"Where is your family now?" Allison passed him a saucer.

"Still in Connecticut. My pa's business is there." Cade nodded. "He made a handsome profit too."

"And your mother?" Allison asked.

He chuckled again and looked down at her. "Probably a

lot like your ma, giving parties, working with charities and the church, worrying about getting her daughters married off to the right man."

Allison shuddered. "Well, I hope your mother has better luck than mine."

"Last I heard, three down, two to go."

"You don't stay in touch with your family?" She handed him the last saucer.

"No."

His short answer and silence told Allison the subject was off-limits, but she didn't stop. "Five sisters? Your father must have been pleased to have you in the house."

His hands stilled on the saucer. "He was . . . for a while."

A painful memory, Allison could see, and she was willing to let it go, but Cade spoke again.

"I worked with him at the factory, learning everything there was to know about running a business from the time I could walk. I loved it too. I thought my pa was the smartest, richest man in the world. He took me everywhere with him. I was proud to have him for my pa." Cade gazed out the window over the sink, seeing nothing of the alley that was there. "Then he got sick, real sick. He was paralyzed on one side. The doctors said he'd never recover. I ran that business myself for years. I did everything just like he'd taught me. And the business grew—I did even better than he. Then he recovered, at least enough to get around and talk."

Allison bit on her bottom lip, fearful she already knew the answer to her question. "Was he pleased with what you'd done with the business?"

"Nothing pleased him." Cade shook his head and turned back to drying the saucer. "He became a hateful, bitter old man. Too sick to run the company himself, but unwilling to let me do it. He yelled and complained, called me names, humiliated me in public, undid everything I did, until no one knew who was running the company."

Allison took the saucer from his hand. "And so you left?"

"I couldn't take it anymore." Cade tossed the towel aside and pulled at the tight muscles in his neck. "My oldest sister's husband agreed to look after things. We already had enough money to keep the family living in style."

"It must have been hard to leave," Allison said softly. "It must be hard to stay away."

"Not as hard as going back would be." Cade wiped his hands on the front of his shirt.

"So your father wasn't the only thing about Connecticut that didn't sit well with you?" Allison folded the towels and placed them aside.

"That's the God's truth." Cade dumped the pan of water down the sink. "Every high-toned dowager in town sizing you up, looking you over for husband material. You couldn't talk to a woman without rumors flying, and Lord help you if you showed any affection. Keeping a woman out after dark was grounds for a wedding announcement."

"Eastern society is rigid," Allison agreed as she loaded the clean tea service onto the tray.

"I've had enough women batting their lashes at me to last a lifetime." Cade laughed bitterly, remembering the daughters of prominent families who pursued him, too delicate to touch, who'd likely have swooned if he'd actually kissed them. "I didn't want to be part of it anymore. No more balancing tiny teacups on my knee at parties, no more piano recitals, no more women with custard for brains."

"So you came West?" Allison reached for the tea tray.

Cade picked it up first and gave her a quick nod. "Yep. About two years ago. And I haven't regretted it once."

"I'm sure all the custard-headed women have regretted it." Allison smiled up at him. "I come from that same society, remember."

Cade followed her into the club trying to picture her fawning, giggling, and batting her lashes at eligible bachelors. Somehow, the image wouldn't form.

He set the tray down on the china hutch. "You must have given your mother a fit."

She only smiled and placed the tea service in the hutch, her hands as delicate as the thin china cups themselves. The hands of an Eastern woman, Cade thought, pampered and cared for her entire life. Hands that he hadn't seen in years. Hands that he longed to hold.

A long silence passed between them, and they were both comfortable with it, feeling no need to fill their time together with meaningless chatter.

When the tea service was finally put away, Allison smiled up at him, not unaware of the ease she found in his company. "Thank you."

"No need. I kind of enjoyed it. Reminded me of home, the good parts I recall." Cade shrugged. "Besides, I owe you for seeing to Tyler's studies."

As many times as Cade had come to her rescue, Allison felt he owed her nothing. "I'm happy to do it. Teaching reminds me of home too."

He wondered what other memories of home she held, but hadn't shared. "I ought to pay you something for your time."

"No, it's—" Allison stopped. "Well, maybe there is one small thing you could do for me."

"Name it."

"Come this way."

Allison hurried into her bedroom and took the ledgers from the bottom drawer of her bureau. She presented them to Cade.

"I got these from my aunt's attorney and ranch foreman. I'm concerned about her financial security now that she's not well enough to see to it herself."

Slowly Cade accepted the books. "Are you thinking something's not right?"

"I don't know. I've looked over them, but I'm not sure of what to look for. I don't know how to tell if someone is cheating."

His expression soured. "And I would?"

Color rose in her cheeks. "Oh, no. I didn't mean that. But you're more knowledgeable in business than I, and I thought you . . ." Her words trailed off as his expression grew more grim.

He tucked the ledgers under his arm. "I'll see what I can find."

"Thank you." It seemed she was always thanking him for something. Allison followed him to the back door and waved as he left. He didn't even look back.

*   *   *

Cool morning air tugged at Allison's skirt as she hurried through the nearly deserted streets. She seldom visited this end of town, except to come to the express office or Mr. Stallworth's place above the grain store. She passed those businesses, as well as the livery stable and the train station, and crossed the railroad tracks to the house at the very edge of town, a white, two-story clapboard home, with pink shutters and window boxes. Allison's steps slowed. She'd never seen a whorehouse before.

The tiny yard was well tended and the porch clean, she noted as she climbed the steps and lifted the ornate knocker on the front door. Finally, the door opened a crack and a woman peered out. Her hair hung loose about her shoulders, a wrapper draped her shoulders, not quite closed in front.

Allison willed herself not to blush. She drew herself up taller. "I'm here to see Phoebe."

The young woman opened the door farther and looked Allison up and down with critical eyes. "Phoebe's not looking for no more girls."

Color rushed across Allison's face. "I'm not here seeking employment. There is a matter I wish to discuss."

"Well, come on in, if you want to. Phoebe's not up yet. Nobody's up at this ungodly hour." She yawned and pulled the door open.

Allison stepped into the foyer. "Perhaps you could wake her for me? I really need to speak to her."

The girl sighed heavily. "All right, I'll see. Sit yourself down, if you want to."

She disappeared down the hallway, leaving Allison standing alone. In a whorehouse. Allison cringed. What would her mother say if she knew?

Allison stepped into the parlor. The heavy, emerald-green drapes were drawn, blocking out the morning sun. From what she could see, the room was decorated in heavy, ornate furnishings, a bit garish—much like Phoebe herself —but expensive. Which was also probably true of Phoebe, Allison thought.

Her gaze ventured to the stairway and the rooms above.

Curiosity ran wild for a moment as she wondered what all went on up there. She knew the basics, of course, but she'd experienced no more than a kiss. Anything else wouldn't have been proper and could have ruined the reputation that her mother—then herself—had so carefully guarded. And for a brief moment, she envied the women who could do as they pleased, with no thought of the consequences.

The swish of silk preceded Phoebe into the parlor. Swathed in a deep purple wrapper, her long blond hair curled into a hasty knot atop her head. Even in the dim light Allison saw that her appearance was nothing like the elegance she exhibited while in town. Unadorned by rouge and expensive clothing, Phoebe could have been a shopkeeper or someone's aunt. She face was slightly puffy and she appeared older than Allison had first imagined.

"Excuse my appearance." Phoebe patted the back of her hair. "But we keep late hours here and don't get too many early morning callers."

Allison felt herself flush and was glad for the dim light. "I'm sorry to disturb you. I'm Allison—"

"I know who you are." Phoebe eyed her cautiously. "And I take it you know who I am too."

Allison nodded, not unsurprised by the cool reception, but uncomfortable with it just the same. "Yes, I know."

"Then you also know what I am." Phoebe took a cheroot from the silver case on the table beside the settee. She lit it and slowly blew out the smoke, her gaze never leaving Allison.

The display was for her benefit, Allison knew. She refused to be put off by it. "The manner in which you choose to support yourself is not the purpose for my visit. I was rather hoping we could join forces."

Phoebe froze, the cheroot halfway to her mouth. She considered Allison for a long moment, then dropped the butt in the spittoon beside the settee. "All right. Let's talk. Have some coffee with me. Polly!"

A moment later the petite woman who'd threatened Allison at her back door yesterday came into the room. She looked smaller in the darkened room, her clothes fitting no better than when she'd last seen her.

"Bring us some coffee, dear," Phoebe said to her. "And open the drapes, will you?"

Silently Polly crossed the room and pulled back the heavy fabric covering the window. Early morning sunlight spilled into the room causing them all to blink. Recognition registered in Polly's eyes when her curious gaze swept the early morning visitor and saw that it was Allison. Fear shone in her face as she ducked her head and hurried away.

"Sit down." Phoebe gestured toward the settee and settled herself in the chair opposite it. "I understand you're here visiting your aunt. From New York, I believe."

Allison perched on the settee, mildly surprised that the woman knew so much about her. Then, she realized, this place was a hub of gossip, much as Taylor's General Store and the barbershop. "My aunt's not well, I'm afraid," Allison told her, though she was sure Phoebe knew that as well.

"Too bad. Miss Lydia was quite a lady, so I heard."

Polly carried a coffee service into the room and placed it on the table in front of the settee. It was expensive and Phoebe poured with the expertise of an Eastern dowager Cade had complained of the night before.

Phoebe sipped her coffee and set her cup aside. "Well, let's get down to business."

Allison placed her cup on the table. "You're probably aware of the ladies' club I've started here in Brighton. Many of the women in town believe, as do I, that Brighton is no longer safe, and that is due, in part, to the saloons and their activities. We intend to address the town council and ask them to require the saloons to close on Sundays."

Phoebe's jaw sagged open, then she threw back her head and laughed. She pressed her palm to her ample bosoms and laughed until tears rolled down her cheeks.

Stunned, Allison just sat there.

"I'm sorry." Phoebe dabbed at the corners of her eyes. "Cade told me you were going to kick this old town in the ass, but I didn't know you'd go this far."

A jolt like lightning struck Allison at the mention of Cade's name. He had discussed her? With the town whore?

Phoebe sniffed and tugged her wrapper together. "Pretty

gutsy show, if you ask me. Especially for an Eastern woman."

Allison relaxed when she realized Phoebe meant it as a compliment. She smiled. "I'm pleased to hear you approve. Does this mean I can count on your help?"

She wiped her eyes a final time. "What did you have in mind?"

"I'm circulating a petition asking for signatures supporting the ladies' club proposal. Will you sign it?"

Phoebe looked dubious. "Why should I get involved with the ladies in your club. I've got no beef with the saloons."

"I've seen you and your . . . employees . . . in town. You never walk alone. There's a reason for that." Allison leaned forward. "But I was thinking of it as more a business issue than a social one. You are, after all, a business-woman."

Phoebe sat up straighter. "What are you driving at?"

"It occurred to me that if the saloons were closed on Sundays, the men would have to go somewhere else." Allison looked at Phoebe. "Where do you suppose they would go?"

Phoebe shrugged. "Well, the married ones would most likely be home with their families."

"And the single ones?"

Understanding dawned in Phoebe's eyes and she smiled. "With the saloons closed, I guess they'd come here."

Allison nodded. "That's the way I see it too."

Phoebe chuckled and sat back. "You're wasting yourself with that ladies' club, honey. You ought to open a business of your own."

She smiled at the compliment but said nothing.

"Well, I wish I could help you, but I just can't." Phoebe shook her head reluctantly. "You see, my business here depends on the goodwill of others. Much as I'd like to see Brighton change, I can't risk making my customers mad by signing your petition."

Allison rose. She'd known it was unlikely Phoebe would help her, but worth the risk of coming here. After all, if the town council saw Phoebe's name on the petition and realized that even Brighton's soiled doves were afraid to walk the streets alone, maybe it would help sway the council in her favor.

"Sorry, honey." Phoebe rose, tugging her wrapper closer around her. "But let me know if there's anything else I can do for you."

"Thank you. I'll keep that in mind." Allison walked to the front door.

"Wait." Phoebe blocked her path. "It's getting late now and people will be out. Maybe you'd rather go the back way. There's a path that leads behind Beau's livery near the grain store."

Allison nodded, grateful—and a bit surprised—by Phoebe's offer. She slipped quietly down the hallway and into the kitchen. By contrast, the room was bright and sunny, and neat as a pin. Polly was there alone, sweeping. Her anger at the woman's threats came back to her.

"Why did you come to my club yesterday?"

Polly whirled around, clutching the broom in her hands. She gasped when she saw Allison.

"What did you mean, that I should get out while I still can?" For a moment Allison thought Polly would run.

"It was good advice. You ought to take it," Polly whispered. "You don't belong here. This place will eat you alive."

Allison refused to let herself be intimidated. "How?"

Polly laughed bitterly. "I used to live back East, just like you. Oh, I wasn't rich as you, but I was a schoolteacher from a respectable family. Then I read a newspaper announcement for teachers wanted in the West for mining camps. It sounded so exciting I sold everything I had to pay for my passage. And when I got to that camp, do you know what I found they really needed? There wasn't one child in that camp and only two other women. They were nobody's wives, that's for sure. They'd been tricked into coming west, just like me." Polly clutched the broom handle until her knuckles turned white. "I was lucky to get out of that place with my life."

"That's horrible." Visions of what the woman must have endured filled Allison with revulsion. "Why don't you go back home?"

"Oh, I will," Polly told her. "Soon as I can get enough money together."

She knew the woman couldn't be making much working here. "Why don't you take a teaching post? The pay would be much more."

"Like anyone would give me a decent job now, after living at that mine and working here." Polly jerked her chin and laughed bitterly. "But they gave that Rebecca Warwick a job, and her with a common slut for a mother."

The slur on Brighton's teacher stunned Allison. "What do you know about Miss Warwick?"

"Like it's a big secret?" Polly spat the words. "Her mother was nothing but a tramp who spread herself for some rich boy who wouldn't marry her. Then she raised that Rebecca, brazen as you please, as if there was nothing wrong with what she'd done. If it hadn't been for that aunt of yours, she'd never have gotten a decent job anywhere."

"She must not have known," Allison told her. "Aunt Lydia couldn't have been aware of Rebecca's past."

"She knew. Lydia Allbright was bedding down with the same boy as Rebecca's ma."

The accusation hit Allison like a slap in the face. "How do you know this? That must have been thirty years ago."

Polly jerked her chin toward the upstairs. "Nothing happens in Brighton that doesn't get whispered across a pillow sooner or later."

Allison lurched for the back door and stepped out onto the porch, gulping in fresh air. Aunt Lydia and Rebecca Warwick's mother both involved with the same boy? Thirty years ago? And both left behind, one to raise an illegitimate child alone.

At the bottom of the steps, Allison turned to see Polly standing in the doorway. The years, the hardships, had made her tough.

"See? You don't belong here."

"You don't either." Allison lifted her chin. Maybe it wasn't too late to help Polly. "The ladies' club is offering passage back East to any woman wanting it."

Polly's breath caught. "Since when?"

Since right now, Allison decided. The ladies' club trea-

sury held nearly nothing, but Allison had funds of her own.
"Do you want to go or not?"

"Of course." A flicker of hope gleamed in her eyes.

"Then come to the ladies' club when you're ready to
leave," Allison told her. "And spread the word. If you know
anyone else in your circumstances, have them come see
me."

A genuine smile spread over her face. "Yes, yes, I know
several others. I'll tell them."

Allison turned away and headed down the path back to
town. She didn't look back, even as Polly called her thanks.

Tyler grabbed his reader from the empty chair by the
window and gulped down the last of his milk. Across from
him, Cade talked to a man at the next table about something Tyler didn't understand. But he didn't care. Cade let
him come to breakfast with him at the Red Eye Cafe almost
every morning and let him eat as much as he wanted. He
liked Cade. Cade took care of him. Cade didn't make him
feel stupid for not understanding all the words.

Tyler rose from his chair and wiped his mouth on the red
checkered napkin. Cade stopped his conversation and
looked up at him.

"You mind Miss Allison today."

He dropped his napkin on the empty plate and nodded,
though he wasn't sure what that meant. "Yes, sir."

Cade turned back to his conversation and Tyler left the
cafe, book in hand. He hurried down the boardwalk trying
to think of a way to explain to Miss Allison that he had tried
to read the lesson she'd given him yesterday, but hadn't
gotten very far. She was a nice lady. He didn't want her to
be mad at him.

Tyler went down the alley between the dress shop and the
ladies' club and turned onto the back alley. To his surprise,
a man stood looking in Miss Allison's windows. Fear took
hold of him, fear born from the last six months of his life,
the fear of everything and everybody. Tyler froze in place.

The man grabbed the doorknob and shook it hard, then
cursed and pressed his face against the glass again. Another
string of foul words tumbled from his lips. Tyler didn't know

what they meant, exactly, but he'd heard the men in the saloon use them when they were mad or losing at cards.

Then the man turned his way. He wore a slouch hat with a snakeskin hatband, and his thick mustache drooped past his chin. Absolute terror gripped Tyler like an iron fist. The man recognized him at the same instant.

Tyler dropped his reader and turned to run, but the man grabbed his shirt and yanked him around. The fabric ripped as he pulled him off his feet. Instinctively, Tyler curled his hands behind him to protect them.

"So, it's you, huh, still hanging around?"

Tyler strained against the man, but he was bigger, stronger. He knew he couldn't fight him off. He hadn't been able to the last time, either.

"I thought I'd taught you a good lesson already, boy, but I guess one beating's not enough for you."

Breath laced with whiskey and tobacco smelled foul. He turned his head away, but the man grabbed a handful of his hair. Tyler yelped.

"Shut up, boy! You want me to get that strap and light into you again?" Cold, hard eyes bored into him. The man shook Tyler again. "Answer me, boy!"

"No. . . ." Tyler eked out the word, his throat tight with fear.

"You listen, boy, and you listen good." He pulled harder on Tyler's hair. "You never saw me here. Got that?"

The man shook him once more and Tyler nodded. "Yes."

He leered cruelly at him. "I know where you live now, boy. I'll come get you at night. You keep your mouth shut. Swear it. Swear it!"

"I swear!"

The man pushed him to the boardwalk. He hit hard, but scrambled to his feet and ran. He ran as fast as he could, dodging shoppers on the boardwalk. His only thought was to get to the Red Eye Cafe and Cade. Cade would take care of him.

Tyler skidded to a halt outside the Brighton Bank and looped his arm around the support column. Across the street he could see Cade through the window of the cafe, still sitting at the table. He looked back over his shoulder, but there was no sign that the man had pursued him.

His chest heaving, Tyler stood there shaking. He wanted to tell Cade. He wanted to tell him everything. But he couldn't. If he made trouble, the sheriff might get involved. They would start asking questions, making inquiries about his parents, his past.

Tyler gulped in quick breaths. He couldn't tell Cade. He couldn't tell anyone.

Because if anyone ever found out who he was and what he'd done, he wouldn't find a safe place to hide on the continent.

Chapter Fifteen

The stifling heat of so many bodies pressed in so small a space had everyone on edge. And the topic left to discuss did nothing to alleviate the problem.

Perched on the edge of a straight-backed chair—one of the few lucky enough to have a chair—Allison kept her chin up, her hands folded primly in her lap. Beside her, Edith Taylor and Mabel Duncan fanned themselves, and behind her, crowded into the mayor's office, were the rest of the Ladies for the Advancement of Cultural Events.

On the other side of the room stood the saloon owners, a much smaller group, other businessmen, and curious on-lookers. Some still wore their shop aprons, others stood with arms folded, all with stoic expressions on their faces. The one man suspiciously missing, Allison noted, was Cade Jessup. She wondered where he was and why he wasn't here. But the meeting was far from over, and it made Allison nervous not knowing what he may have up his sleeve.

Between the two factions, seated around the mayor's desk, was the mayor himself, Everette Hawkins, and the four members of the town council. The meeting had already dragged on endlessly, as the council reviewed proposals requiring individual businesses to maintain the hitching posts and water troughs nearest them, hire a full-time deputy, replace the boardwalk near Grabel's Dry Goods Store damaged in the winter rains, and give a fresh coat of paint to Brighton's schoolhouse.

Rebecca Warwick had fidgeted throughout the proceedings, then thanked the council profusely when the proposal passed, and hurried away. No doubt, Allison thought, she hadn't wanted to appear aligned with the ladies' club on the controversial matter pending before the council.

Just as Allison thought someone might actually swoon from the heat, Mayor Hawkins cleared his throat and shuffled the stack of papers before him.

"Well, let's see now, let's see. I believe we have one more matter to hear." He glanced nervously around the room as if he sincerely hoped someone would pop up and take the proposal off the calendar.

Allison's stomach tightened as she glanced at the faces of the council members. Harry Finch, seated to the mayor's right, was a businessman, but a family man also with grown children, and likely to vote with the ladies' club, she figured. Albert Wade, a deacon and editor of the newspaper with a wife and five daughters, could be swayed also. Will Taylor might just be afraid enough of his wife to vote for the proposal, Allison thought, leaving only Dutch Myer as the uncertain factor; the mayor, Allison was sure, would go with the majority vote.

Mayor Hawkins patted his perspiring head with a handkerchief and glanced at the other council members. They all shifted in their chairs.

"Well, what we have here is a proposal from Miss Tremaine and the Ladies for the Advancement of Cultural Events." The mayor mopped his forehead again. "And what they're asking is for the saloons to be closed on Sundays."

A murmur went through the crowd. Necks craned and bodies shuffled to get a better view.

"Miss Tremaine? Would you like to address the council on this matter?" He frowned as if praying she'd simply say no and stay in her chair.

"Thank you, Mr. Mayor." Allison rose, the petitions, now damp and wrinkled, clutched in her hand. She'd practiced her speech all night.

"Mayor Hawkins and members of the town council, the ladies of Brighton are making this proposal out of a desire to make our town a safer, more decent place to live. As I'm sure you are all aware, women and children cannot walk the streets alone." Allison looked pointedly at Harry Finch and Albert Wade, the family members of the council. "We feel this lack of safety has been brought about by an unsavory element drawn to our town by the saloons. To curtail this type of activity, we are proposing the saloons be closed on the Sabbath."

Mayor Hawkins cleared his throat again and glanced nervously at the other members of the council. "Well now, Miss Tremaine, this is a big issue. There's a lot of people to consider, you know."

Allison placed on the mayor's desk the sheafs of paper bearing the names of those in Brighton who had signed the petitions. "As you can see, Mayor Hawkins, many, many people in town share our concerns and support our proposal."

The council members passed the petitions between them. Eyebrows rose. Harry and Albert mumbled to each other.

Allison pressed on. "The good family men of this town are afraid. Afraid for their wives. Afraid for their daughters. The good Christian men of this town are appalled by the saloons, with their liquor and their gambling, operating on the Lord's day. I say it's time to change things. Return Brighton to the decent, God-fearing town it once was. Bring dignity and respect back to our streets. Make us a proud, respectable town. And above all, let's make it a place where women don't have to be afraid."

The room buzzed as the mayor and the council members looked at each other. Pride swelled in Allison. She had them. It was all over their faces.

The crowd suddenly quieted and a path broke open from the door. Cade Jessup stepped into the room.

"If the women are afraid to go out, I say they ought to stay home where they belong."

A cheer rose from the saloon owners.

"That's for damn sure!" Jack Short declared.

"You tell 'em, Cade!" Drew Cabbot cheered.

"Quiet down, now, quiet down!" Mayor Hawkins rapped his knuckles on the desk. "Cade, you want to say something?"

"That I do, Mayor." Cade stepped to the front of the room, the width of the mayor's desk separating him from Allison. He looked cool and fresh, attired in his customary crisp white shirt, string tie, and brocade vest. His Stetson sat at a rakish angle in his dark hair.

"Everybody in this room—except for the newcomers in town"—he glanced pointedly at Allison—"knows that Brighton nearly went under. Have we forgotten already how we struggled? What it was like not to have food on our tables? How it felt wondering where the next customers to our businesses would come from?"

A murmur went through the crowd. Heads nodded.

"What if we close the saloons on Sunday to make the ladies happy?" Cade gestured toward the women in the room. "Who's to say that will be enough for them? What if they want us to close on Saturdays too? And then Fridays? Where will it end?"

Cade pointed to the crowd of men. "Beau, you own the livery stable. What if they decide they don't like the smell of your horses? What if they want you closed down? And, Joe, how about if they don't like the noise your hammering and sawing makes. How about if they want to shut you down too?"

"It's not the same!" Allison took a breath to control her anger. "The livery and the carpenter don't bring in the bad element that makes our streets unsafe for the women. The saloons do."

Cade turned back to the men. "It was our fathers who pushed west to settle this land. We fought the Indians, the weather, the disease to build what's here. I say a man deserves a drink when he wants one."

A cheer went up from the men.

"I say a man ought to have his pleasure"—Cade threw Allison a taunting look—"when he wants it."

Buck Mock shook his fist in the air. "Yeah!"

"And what self-respecting woman would be walking the streets alone, anyway!" Drew Cabbot shouted.

Shouts erupted from both sides of the room. Allison fumed silently as Cade threw her a smug look.

Mayor Hawkins pounded for silence. "Quiet down, now! Quiet down, all of you!"

The noise died down and the mayor spoke again. "Cade, you got anything else to say?"

Slowly, deliberately, his gaze raked the crowd, then settled on the mayor and the council members.

"It's up to you boys," he said. "You can keep the businesses operating, or you can drive away the customers so these ladies can have their tea parties."

The mayor mopped his forehead again and glanced nervously at Allison. He cleared his throat. "Well . . ."

Dutch Myer slapped his open palm down on the desktop. "I got a business to run. I say the proposal is hogwash."

Beside him, Harry Finch adjusted his spectacles. His gaze touched on Jenna for an instant. "A man's got to provide for his wife. I've got a big investment in Brighton. I can't afford to lose it. I say no to the proposal."

"We'll just have to find other ways to look after our women," Albert Wade offered. "I say no."

Everyone turned to Will Taylor. He glanced at his grim-faced wife and forced a weak smile. "The majority has it."

Mayor Hawkins surged to his feet. "That's it. Proposal defeated. Meeting adjourned."

The men and saloon owners cheered and slapped each other's backs as they left the mayor's office. Slump-shouldered and defeated, the women filed out of the room. Will Taylor hurried after Edith; she burrowed her way through the crowd, her nose in the air. The mayor and the town council members left the office too, all obviously relieved this difficult situation was over and done with. Allison and Cade stood alone. They glared at each other for a long moment.

The line of Cade's face hardened. "Nothing is going to stand in the way of my business. I've told you that before."

"It's not safe here for decent people," Allison snapped.

"Not safe? By whose standards?" he demanded. "New York standards? Your standards?"

Emotionally drained, hot and nearly exhausted, Allison held herself straight. "You may have won this battle, Mr. Jessup, but you won't win the war."

He touched the brim of his Stetson. "As always, Miss Tremaine, a . . . pleasure . . . doing battle with you."

Her hand itched to slap that smug grin off his face, but Allison turned sharply and left the mayor's office.

Outside, several ladies waited. It was a relief to hear their kind words for what she'd attempted, and their disgust at the saloon owners and the men of the town.

"We're not finished yet," Allison told them, though at the moment, she hardly felt up to it.

Jenna caught her arm and led her down the street. "How about a cool bath and a nice cup of tea?"

They walked together past the dress shop and down the side alley. "I'll get Holly and be right over," Jenna said. "Mrs. Sage is anxious to get home, I'm sure."

Allison nodded as Jenna disappeared into the dress shop, then headed toward the back entrance of the ladies' club. She stopped short. The door stood open.

Cautiously she peered inside. Allison's heart sank. Cabinets stood open, broken dishes littered the floor. She went inside, stepping over the remains of her broken chairs, and entered her bedroom. The mattress lay on the floor, bureau drawers stood open, her clothing scattered everywhere. She walked into the club room giving no thought to the possibility that whoever had ransacked the place might still be there. The china hutch lay smashed on the floor, the Haviland tea service shattered into a million pieces. The furniture lay overturned, pictures hung askew, delicate figurines and lamps smashed.

Allison sank onto the settee. She covered her face with her hands and cried.

"Sickening, just sickening."

The bits of broken china rattled as Edith dumped them into the waste bin. She brushed her hands on her apron. "And a sick mind, as well. Who would do such a thing?"

Allison pressed the hem of her apron to her cheek. "That seems to be the question of the day."

Around her, other ladies worked to restore order to the club. Word had spread through town quickly that the place had been ransacked during yesterday's town council meeting, and women had appeared throughout the morning, brooms, mops, and cleaning tools in hand. They'd all pulled together and quickly restored the club to order.

"The sheriff came by last night and took a look around." Jenna leaned on the broom. "He thinks it's someone trying to run Allison out of town."

"Well, I'm not leaving." Allison's chin went up.

Esther Wade ventured closer. "I don't know. Having a club here is nice, but not worth anybody getting hurt over."

"She's right." Penelope Sage came through the curtain from the kitchen. "This isn't the first time something has happened here. Some of the men in town just don't like the idea of us having a club."

"All the more reason to stay." Allison squared her shoulders.

Edith gave her an emphatic nod. "Good for you. Change doesn't come easy. You can't quit just because things get tough."

"Well, I guess that's about it." Allison brushed her hands together and looked around the room. "Thank you all for coming."

All had been done that could be done. Joe Capp had been by this morning and was salvaging as much of the furniture as possible. She'd have to make another trip to Aunt Lydia's to borrow the furnishings that couldn't be repaired.

The ladies offered her their support as they left the club. Jenna remained. She closed the door and turned to Allison. "I think we'd better have a talk."

Certain that Holly had heard that same tone in Jenna's voice, Allison sat down on the settee.

"This whole idea of a ladies' club started out as a commendable idea. But, Allison, this is serious. Someone could get hurt." Jenna sat down across from her. "And that someone could be you."

"Whoever is doing this is only trying to scare me."

"Well, aren't they?"

"Yes," Allison admitted. "I'm scared. A little."

"I think you should consider closing the ladies' club."

Allison's gaze came up quickly. "And do what? Stand by

while Brighton goes to the dogs? Watch as a lovely town
with respectable people is pushed aside by a minority of
ruffians? I won't run from this."

"You don't have to make this your fight," Jenna rea-
soned. "You have people waiting for you back in New
York."

"I don't want to go back to New York." Allison gasped as
the words tumbled out, stunned that she'd said them.

A long moment passed before Jenna spoke again.
"What's waiting in New York that you don't want to return
to?"

Allison twisted her fingers together, the finger where the
garnet and diamond ring should have been. "Nothing," she
said quickly. She cleared her throat and rose. "What I
meant is, I don't want to return to New York until things
are settled here. Aunt Lydia is quite ill. I can't leave her
now. And I want to do something for the town."

Jenna rose. Doubt of Allison's real intentions clouded
her face. "All right. But you'd better be extra careful from
now on."

"I will," Allison promised.

Jenna got Holly from the kitchen and they left by the
back way. Allison busied herself in the kitchen, though the
ladies who'd come to help had left it spotless. A knock
sounded at her front door, drawing her back into the club.
It was probably Mabel Duncan, she thought. After discover-
ing all her clothing strewn about the room, Allison couldn't
bear the thought of wearing them again after having been
fondled by whoever had broken in, so she'd taken everything to Mabel's laundry. She'd promised to bring it back
today.

Allison opened the door to find her aunt's attorney waiting on the boardwalk. "Mr. Stallworth, this is a surprise."

He pressed his hat to his chest. "Good day, Miss Tremaine. I hope I haven't come at a bad time."

Freshly shaven, hair plastered in place, Rory Stallworth
looked respectable. But his clothes were wrinkled, the collar of his shirt frayed. A sour odor hung over him.

"Of course not," Allison told him. But surely he knew he
couldn't have come at a worse time. The news of her break-

in was all over town since yesterday. She stepped back from the door. "Would you like to come in?"

He glanced curiously into the room, then shook his head. "No, thanks. I just stopped by to check on the ledgers I gave you. I was wondering if you'd found what you were looking for, or if I might assist you in any way?"

"Actually, I haven't had time to go over them thoroughly. I've been busy with other things."

"Yes. I'm sure you have." Stallworth gave her a thin smile. "I have a few minutes now. Why don't you get them out and we'll go over them together?"

"That's not possible."

His eyes narrowed. "Oh?"

A chill slithered up Allison's back. The attorney always set her nerves on end. "They're not here."

Stallworth smiled again. "They're at your aunt's, then. I'd be happy to meet there and go over them."

"I've left them with a friend," Allison said quickly. She clasped her hands behind her so he couldn't see them tremble.

"I see." His gaze roamed the length of her, then smiled. "Well, maybe we can get together another time."

"Maybe." Allison forced a smile. "Good day."

He put on his hat. "Good day."

Allison closed the door behind him and turned the lock.

"So, where the hell are they?"

Rory Stallworth reared back in his chair and took a long drink from the whiskey bottle. The sun had slipped behind the mountains leaving his office nearly dark. He liked it that way. He liked to sit in the dark and drink.

"I don't know, I told you." He took another long pull on the bottle and spoke to the man in the shadows across the room. "One of those Lace Ladies probably has them."

"No, she wouldn't give them to one of those ladies." Wes Palmer stroked his long mustache and stepped closer to the desk. "But I think I know who she'd trust with them."

"Damn fool woman nosing around in things that don't concern her." Stallworth wiped his sleeve across his mouth.

"She's been warned enough. Something's got to be done. And done fast."

"I'll handle it."

"Hire it done," Stallworth told him. "You can't afford to be involved. Do you know somebody dependable?"

Palmer uttered a bitter laugh. "Yeah. I know somebody who'll enjoy the hell out of convincing Miss Allison Tremaine that Brighton is too rough a town for her delicate little ass."

"Good." Stallworth took a long drink from the bottle and slumped lower in his chair. The door opened and closed softly. He settled back in the darkness and drank.

"I found this outside." Allison placed the reader on the table.

Tyler cringed and ducked his head. He'd dropped it when the man in the alley had grabbed him, and had forgotten all about it. He kept his head down, afraid to look up at Miss Allison standing over him in her kitchen.

"Did you lose it?"

She didn't sound mad, but he was still frightened. "I don't know."

"I believe you do know, Tyler." Allison sat down in the chair beside him.

Tyler shrugged. Her tone was stern, but not mean. She reminded him of Cade. And as when Cade spoke to him, Tyler felt compelled to tell the truth and try his best.

"I think I dropped it," he admitted.

Allison placed the reader in front of him and patted his arm gently. "Please be more careful in the future."

He looked across at her and his fear diminished. "I will," he promised.

Allison smiled. The boy was so tightly wrapped within himself it made her heart ache. He seemed to soak up the smallest kindness like a sponge, as if he were unaccustomed to such things. It made her want to hold him and make everything all better for him.

"Let's start with writing, shall we?" Allison placed a pencil and writing tablet before him.

Tyler picked it up and fumbled with the pencil for a moment.

Allison frowned. "We decided last time that you should write with your right hand. Remember?"

Tyler shrugged. "It doesn't matter. Either hand is the same."

"Didn't your teachers before want you to use your right hand?" The latest theory was that boys should be encouraged to be right-handed, making it easier for them to use the tools of their future chosen trades.

He shook his head. "I didn't go to school before."

She'd wanted to ask him that on their first visit, but like Cade couldn't bring herself to pry too deeply into his past. Cade had described the boy as frail, and now Allison understood why he felt that way.

Allison rested her arms on the table. "Didn't you miss your friends when they were in school?"

"No." Tyler fumbled with the pencil, switching it from one hand to the other. "I didn't have any friends."

"You must have had someone your age you played with. Neighbors, cousins, or someone."

"No, ma'am."

"Why not?"

"I don't know." Tyler looked up at her. "Do you want me to write those letters now?"

No, she wanted him to answer her questions. But it was none of her business and she was only being nosy, Allison realized. She nodded. "Yes. Write the alphabet."

Tyler picked up the pencil with his left hand and began to copy the letters from the book on the table.

Allison patted his other hand gently. "No, Tyler. This is your right hand."

"Oh." He passed the pencil to the other hand and began to copy.

While he worked, Allison attended to her own correspondence. She wrote regularly to her mother in New York as well as a few friends there. And cowardly as she felt, Allison was glad she could respond to their questions at her discretion, and didn't have to tackle them in person. She really had no answers to some of the things they wanted to know.

After nearly two hours of practicing the alphabet, struggling with reading, and explaining the necessity of writing the arithmetic problems down on paper, Allison was as ready for a break as Tyler.

"I think we've had enough for today." Allison rose from her chair. "Try to read as much as you can tonight. We'll review it tomorrow."

Tyler nodded. "Cade said that he wants me to read to him every day while he does his book work."

"Sounds like a very good idea." A little surprised, Allison fetched her hat and reticule from the bedroom.

"I'm going to take these letters to the express office." Allison pinned her hat in place. "Would you like to walk over with me?"

"Sure."

They walked through the quiet streets and found Harry Finch behind the counter at the express office.

"Good day to you, Miss Tremaine." He squinted at Tyler beside her. "Cade send you over here again, young fella?"

"No, sir."

He sighed heavily and crossed his thin arms in front of him. "Well, you can tell Cade Jessup again that his shipment still isn't here and if he keeps checking on it, it will never get here—just like waiting for a watched pot to boil."

Harry turned to Allison and rolled his eyes. "That man. Thinking he can rush something like this. And it coming all the way from back East."

Cade Jessup being the last person Allison wished to discuss, she changed the subject. "When will this go out?"

Harry took the letters she withdrew from her reticule and studied them. "On the afternoon train." He glanced over his shoulder at the cubbyholes above his desk. "Something came in for you this morning."

"Thank you, Mr. Finch." Allison took the envelope and stepped outside.

"Good day, Miss Tremaine," Harry shouted. "And give my best to Mrs. McCain when you see her."

Allison smiled and waved as Tyler closed the door.

"Miss Allison?" Tyler fell into step beside her on the boardwalk. "Is Mr. Finch a prissy old fart?"

She gasped. "Wherever did you hear that?"

"Cade says that's what Mr. Finch is. Is that his job?"

She nearly laughed aloud, for Cade's description couldn't be more accurate. But instead she replied in her best teaching voice. "No, Tyler. That isn't his job. And those aren't nice words. You shouldn't say them again."

Tyler nodded. "Oh. All right. Who did you get a letter from?"

"A friend of mine in New York. He owns a factory that makes toys."

Allison opened the letter and read it quickly, dodging the shoppers on the boardwalk. She smiled and held up a second sheaf of paper. "Tyler, this is such good news. I sent some of the doll dresses Jenna had made to a family friend. He wants to buy them. He's placed a large order."

Tyler studied the paper though he couldn't read a word written on it. "Will Miss Jenna be happy about that?"

"Well . . ." Allison's smile faded and she shoved the letter into her reticule. "She doesn't know about the business proposal I made on her behalf."

"Is she going to be mad at you?"

"No," Allison decided. "She'll be thrilled."

They walked down the boardwalk while Allison explained little girls' love for beautiful clothing to dress their dolls in. Tyler listened intently, though she wasn't sure he understood much of what she was saying.

Together they stepped off the boardwalk at the alley separating Myer's Tobacco Shop from Taylor's General Store.

"So you see," Allison continued, "if we have the women in Brighton doing piecework, they'll make money for themselves and Jenna will make a small profit as well. Now, if—"

A man stepped from the shadows. His fingers dug into the flesh of Allison's arm and yanked her into the alley. He slapped his hand across her mouth.

"Be nice and quiet and nobody will get hurt . . . much."

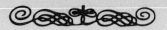

Chapter
Sixteen

Terror ripped through Allison as the man staring down at her smiled slowly and pushed her against the wall of the tobacco shop. She gasped for breath as his callused hand covered her mouth. He moved closer. A scream hung in her throat.

"You've been begging for a proper greeting to Brighton, sugar." He ran his finger down her cheek. "And I'm the man to give it to you."

A growth of dark beard covered his weathered face and unkempt hair showed from beneath his battered hat. Frantic, Allison's gaze swept the alley. She saw nothing. Nothing but cold eyes leering at her. Her heart slammed against her ribs, each beat pumping new fear through her.

His hand closed around her arm again, squeezing tightly. "Now, you and me are going back here behind this shed and get to know each other better. It's gonna take a while, darling, 'cause we're going to get to know each other real good."

Paralyzed with fear, Allison stiffened as he pulled her with him, his hand still covering her mouth. He leaned down and whispered in her ear. "Come on now, sugar, loosen up. You're going to like this."

His breath smelled foul against her face. She felt the strength of his chest and arms pressed to her back. Allison's head spun. She thought she might faint.

"Look now, sugar—"

"Hey!" Tyler approached, eyeing them. "What are you doing?"

Seeing him, Allison squirmed and bit at the man's hand. It tasted of dirt and sweat.

"Damnit." The man pulled his hand away, but tightened his grip on her arm. He shook her. "Don't make me have to slap you, honey, and ruin that pretty face of yours."

"Leave her alone." Tyler drew closer.

"Get on out of here, boy." His warning was low and guttural.

"Tyler!" Allison screamed.

He slapped his hand across her mouth again. "Shut up!" The man lunged forward and grabbed Tyler's shirtfront. He pulled him off his feet. "Get the hell out of here, boy. Nothing's going on in here you need to know anything about." He shoved him to the ground and dragged Allison toward the back of the alley.

Tyler hit hard. Stunned, he sat there for a moment, then lurched to his feet. He leapt onto the man's back and bit into his ear.

"Yeooww!" The man howled and pushed Allison away. He grabbed for Tyler, but the boy hung on tight. The man cursed and staggered across the alley, slamming Tyler against the wall. He lost his grip and fell to the ground.

"Damn you, you little bastard." He kicked him in the ribs.

A new kind of fear swelled within Allison. "Stop! Don't hurt him!" She pounded the man's back with her fists. Weak, useless blows that he didn't feel and only caused him to realize she was within arm's length.

He lunged for Allison but Tyler wrapped his arms around the man's foot. He stumbled to the ground, then came up cursing.

Allison looked on in horror as the man pulled Tyler up and drew back his hand. Terror filled her. She couldn't fight him, she couldn't stop him. Allison ran.

Down the back alley she raced. Only one man was strong enough, brave enough, and close enough to help. The back entrance stood open. She dashed inside.

"Cade!"

The bloodcurdling scream drove him from his chair at the kitchen table and sent his coffee cup flying. He whirled around.

"Christ. . . ." Sheer terror drew the lines of her face taut. He grasped her upper arms nearly pulling her off her feet. "What? What is it?"

She wanted to cry so badly that for an instant the words caught in her throat. She pointed. "Tyler . . . Myer's alley."

Cade ran out the door. Allison pressed her fingers to her lips and hurried after him. Knees wobbling, she stopped behind Taylor's store and peeped into the alley. Tyler lay on the ground, curled in a knot. Cade knelt beside him. She hurried toward them.

"How is—"

"Don't look." Cade turned and held up his hand, shielding her from the sight. Blood covered his palm. "Go get Doc Tanner. Now. Tell him to come to the saloon."

She ran all the way to the doctor's office with no thought except to do as Cade said. Dr. Tanner didn't question her. With one look at her face, he grabbed his bag.

Years of overindulgence at the supper table slowed their pace as the gray-whiskered doctor followed Allison to the back entrance of the Pleasure Palace. Voices in the upstairs hall drew them up the steps. Dr. Tanner pushed his way through the gathering and into the bedroom.

The door slammed shut in her face. Allison's heart raced. Fear consumed her. Fear for Tyler. Fear of what had nearly happened. She began to tremble, then realized she was surrounded by a crowd of people watching her intently.

A redheaded woman in a gapping wrapper stared at her, while another woman in a night rail eyed her cautiously. A man with a nightshirt stuffed into his trousers stood near her. Down the hall, a door opened and a young woman with soft blond hair swinging loose about her shoulders peeped out, then yawned and closed the door again. A younger man with trousers pulled over his long johns gave her a nervous smile and plastered down his sleep-tousled hair with a wide swipe of his palm. Allison swallowed hard. The hallway was dim and airless. She thought she might swoon.

The bedroom door whipped open and Cade strode out, his presence a force all its own. They surged forward. He held up his hands, ignoring their questions.

"Belle, get in here and give Doc a hand. Billy, get some fresh water. Clare, fetch those spare bandages from the supply room. And, Vance, get some extra lanterns in here."

Cade barked the orders and they sprang into action. His eyes settled on Allison standing alone in the hallway. He read the fear in her eyes, the fright that went beyond concern for the boy.

"Oh, God. . . ."

Cade grasped her arms and pulled her to the end of the hallway. His gaze swept the length of her and settled on the tightly drawn lines of her face. His brows pulled together. Now he was afraid too.

"What happened?"

She didn't want to talk; she didn't want to relive it by telling what had happened. But she knew Cade too well. He wouldn't let it go until he knew.

"Tyler and I were walking back from the express office and a man grabbed me and—"

The tears came. She couldn't stop them. They poured down her cheeks like a driving spring rain. Cade wrapped her in his arms and held her, nearly crushing her with his strength. And she soaked it up, every ounce, absorbing it hungrily until the tears finally stopped.

Cade pulled a handkerchief from his hip pocket and wiped her eyes. She sniffed and hiccuped and looked up at him. And while she felt better, the mantle of fear and dread still hung over him, the air between them heavy with the question he needed to ask.

"Did he . . ." His voice was gentle.

She shook her head quickly. "No. But I don't know what would have happened if Tyler hadn't been there."

His stance relaxed only marginally. "You're sure you're not hurt? Anywhere?"

Allison sniffed again and tried to laugh. "He squeezed my arm."

With exquisite gentleness, Cade ran his fingers over her arm, then bent and placed a kiss on the spot.

"He—he touched my cheek."

Cade brushed his knuckles across her cheek, then touched his lips to her delicate skin.

"His hand—" Allison shuddered. "He put his hand over my mouth."

His gaze captured hers and with the sheer force of his will, Allison felt herself relax. He rubbed his thumb across her lips, then kissed her. But not as he'd kissed her before. No fire. No passion. Only tenderness.

He released her from the kiss and gathered her against his chest once more. Allison clung to him, secure and contented. And no longer afraid.

Footsteps sounded on the stairs, then in the hall. Allison moved from his embrace. The bedroom door opened and Belle came into the corridor, joining the others.

Cade grasped Allison's elbow and placed her in the center of the gathering. "Allison, this is Vance, Billy, Belle, and Clare. Belle, take her downstairs."

He took the water pitcher from Billy and went into the bedroom.

They all turned to her, curious and uncomfortable. Finally, Belle draped an arm around her shoulders and gave her a squeeze.

"Come on down to the kitchen, honey. Let's have us some coffee. Billy, get a fire going. And, Vance, bust open that fresh sack of coffee."

The men hurried downstairs ahead of them. Clare patted Allison's hand. "Everything's going to be fine."

They gathered around the table while Vance and Billy put the coffee on. Mack Carson walked through the back door. Allison didn't know how he'd found out about the incident. Maybe the sight of Doc Tanner shuffling through town and her running with her dress hiked up past her ankles had been enough to alert everyone that something was wrong.

"Can you tell me what happened?" Mack stepped closer to the table. "I need to know as much as you can remember."

Allison cleared her throat. "We were walking back from the express office and a man grabbed me and pulled me into the alley."

Around the room, gazes collided. She knew what they suspected and shook her head quickly. "He didn't hurt me. Though, I'm sure he would have if Tyler hadn't been there."

"Tyler fought him off?" Vance asked.

"By golly, I didn't think the little fellow had it in him," Billy said.

"Did you recognize the man?" Mack asked. "Have you seen him before? I know you're upset, but I need to know."

Belle reached across the table and patted Allison's hand. "Just do the best you can, honey."

"I don't know who it was," Allison said. "I've never seen him before. He was dressed like a cowboy, I think."

"What's this town coming to?" Belle yanked the sash of her wrapper. "Maybe those Lace Ladies are right."

"Maybe so," Clare agreed.

Allison looked at Belle. "How is Tyler?"

She shuddered. "He looks bad. Real bad."

"I feel like this is all my fault."

Clare sat forward. "It's the fault of that bastard who attacked the two of you."

"I'll check into it," Mack promised. "Tell Cade I'll be back later."

Vance made coffee and they sat around the table together speculating on who might have done it, worrying about Tyler, and contemplating the state of Brighton. They behaved as if they were a family, Allison thought, and the warmth that flowed between them brought relief to her. She thought of Cade, who had gotten them all together and kept them together. He wasn't as removed from his real family in Connecticut as he pretended to be, she realized. He'd simply found a replacement for them. And somewhere deep inside her it was comforting to know that Cade needed family around him.

Dr. Tanner trudged down the staircase and into the kitchen. He adjusted his spectacles. "Nothing's broken. He needs rest for the next few days. Be sure he stays in bed."

Belle, Clare, Billy, and Vance all promised to take care of him.

Dr. Tanner's gaze settled on Allison. "Now, what about you, young lady?"

Allison rose from the chair. "I want to go see Tyler."

He shook his head. "No, he doesn't need any visitors, and you need some rest."

"But—"

"No buts." The doctor took a small bottle from his satchel. "This will make you sleep. I just left some for the boy. You need it too."

"I don't—"

"A drop or two will make you drowsy, more than that will put you to sleep." He gestured toward the door. "Let's go."

Something about the doctor's demeanor wouldn't allow her to disobey. Allison thanked everyone and left the saloon with Dr. Tanner.

"You go straight to bed," the doctor told her as they stopped in front of the ladies' club. "And take the laudanum."

Allison closed the bottle he'd given her in her fist. She'd seen a similar bottle at Aunt Lydia's home. "Have you ever prescribed this to my aunt?"

Dr. Tanner's bushy brows drew together as he considered the question. "No, just her housekeeper."

"Georgia? Why?"

"Said her rheumatism was bothering her."

Allison pressed her lips together. "Doctor, if a person were to take a drop or two of this each day, would it make them listless and sleepy all the time?"

"Sure. But why would anybody want to do that?"

"Why indeed. . . ." Allison thanked the doctor and went into the club.

Only a few hours ago she'd felt at home in the kitchen of the Pleasure Palace. Now, Allison hesitated at the back door. She shifted the tray she carried to her other hip and knocked.

Vance opened the door a moment later. He looked the part of a saloon keeper now, white shirt and vest replaced the nightshirt he'd stuffed into his trousers this morning. His hair was combed neatly into place and his apron sparkled.

"Miss Allison?" His brows bobbed. He glanced nervously up and down the alley.

"I brought soup for Tyler." She shifted the tray. "Is it all right if I come in?"

"Oh, well, I guess." Vance backed into the kitchen. "How, huh, how are you feeling?"

"Better." She'd had a bath and the long sleep the doctor had prescribed. "How is Tyler?"

"Cade's been up with him all day. He's resting."

"I want to go up and see him."

Vance glanced up the staircase. He cleared his throat. "I, uh, I don't know. . . ."

Allison looked him in the eye. "Do you realize what Tyler saved me from?"

"Yes, ma'am." Vance fidgeted with his apron.

"Then don't you think the least I can do is take him some soup?"

Vance ducked his head. "Yes, ma'am, I guess you can."

Allison climbed the steps to the second floor. Under the dire circumstances, standing on formality seemed of little concern. She'd felt that way when she'd dressed to come over. Her hair was caught back in a simple chignon and she wore a plain skirt and blouse.

The doors stood open. Muted light shone in the hallway suggesting the shades were drawn against the afternoon sun. She peeped inside and saw Cade seated in the rocker beside the bed. He saw her also and sprang from the chair.

The force of his presence coming through the doorway drove Allison backward down the hall. She gripped the tray with both hands.

"What are you doing here?" He glared down at her.

"I came to see about Tyler."

"You've got no business coming here." He spoke in a low, angry whisper.

This morning he'd been so kind and caring she'd thought of little else all day. Now Allison's back stiffened. "And why not?"

"Because a sickroom is no place for a high-toned Eastern woman."

"Oh!" Allison shoved the tray into Cade's belly. An involuntary *woff* slipped through his lips and he grabbed the tray with both hands. "I am sick to death of your constant slurs on my background. Do you know what I think, Cade Jessup? I think you're the one who can't turn loose of Eastern ways."

Allison advanced on Cade. He took a step backward. "You claim you want no part of your upbringing and nothing to do with the family you ran out on. Well, I say you're still holding on to them in your mind and heart, using your employees to fill your loneliness. You say you don't want an Eastern woman. But I don't see you courting a Western one. I don't see that you've snapped up a wife here in Brighton, one completely opposite of the women you claim you can't stand back East."

She'd backed him the length of the corridor and into the wall. Allison pointed a finger at him, only the tray separating his ashen face from her angry one.

"And I'll tell you one more thing, Mr. Saloon Owner. It's nothing but your own stubborn pride keeping you from the things you want. You're going to grow old, alone and miserable because you're so busy telling yourself you've got what you want here at this place that you're letting the things you really desire slip right through your fingers."

Allison tossed her head to shake off her anger and pulled the tray from his hands. "I'm going to see Tyler."

She turned on her heels and marched down the hall. Her anger vanished when she entered the bedroom.

Tyler lay still, his eyes closed. The big brass bed and the oversize nightshirt made him appear small and frail. A dark bruise shadowed his left eye. His bottom lip was cut; the corner of his mouth swollen.

Cade appeared at her side and took the tray. "He's been fading in and out all day. Doc says he's got a big knot on his head. Nothing's broken, but his ribs are all bruised."

Allison pressed her hand against Tyler's cheek. He snuggled against her. "I feel as though this were my fault."

Cade placed the tray on his desk and pushed his fingers through the hair at his temple. "No. It's not your fault."

"Dr. Tanner said he'd need to rest for several days." Allison gazed around the room. Cade's room, she realized. A masculine feel dominated, from the heavy furniture to the scent that permeated everything. She'd never been in a man's bedroom before. It was too personal here, as if she now knew something about Cade that no one else knew. Her stomach tingled.

Suddenly nervous, Allison gestured to the tray he'd placed on the desk. "I brought soup."

Cade flipped back the linen cloth and looked at the bowl of broth. "Did you get this from the hotel restaurant?"

"No." She crossed to the desk. "I made it myself."

Skepticism creased his brow. "You can cook?"

"I certainly can." She picked up the spoon and dipped it into the soup. "Taste."

A moment's hesitation dragged by before he relented and opened his mouth. She slid the spoon inside. His brows shot upward in surprise. "It's good."

"I know." Allison wiped the spoon on the linen towel and returned it to the tray. "I can cook stew, buttermilk biscuits, sweet potato pie . . ."

"Humm." Cade mumbled noncommittally.

"I can also make beef Stroganoff, chicken divan . . ."

Cade straightened, interested now. "You can really cook that yourself?"

Annoyed that he considered her so incapable, Allison said, "Yes, I can cook all the dishes enjoyed by rich Easterners with my own two high-toned Eastern hands."

He scowled at her and turned away, realizing he'd just confirmed the point she was trying to make when she'd berated him in the hallway.

Allison sat down in the rocker that had been drawn up to the bed. Cade had moved it, she realized, to keep watch over Tyler. He slept fitfully now, his head tossing on the pillow. He mumbled incoherently.

Cade moved to the bed. Allison sat forward. "What's wrong?"

"He has nightmares. Screams and cries in his sleep."

"What sort of nightmares?"

"Somebody trying to put him in something. I don't know, he never remembers the next morning—or claims he doesn't." Cade touched Tyler's shoulder and gave him a small shake.

But the nightmare already had him in its firm grip. Tyler moaned softly. "No . . . don't put me in there. . . ."

Cade shook him harder. As a child, Cade had his share of nightmares. They'd terrified him. "Tyler, wake up."

His head thrashed back and forth on the pillow. "Don't . . . please don't put me in there, Papa . . . please don't. Papa don't!" Tyler screamed.

A cold chill swept up Cade's back. "Tyler!"

His eyes opened wide with fright. He tried to rise, but Cade held him down. "Be still. Don't try to sit up."

Confused, he gazed at Cade, then Allison. His head fell back on the pillow.

She eased closer to the bed. "We were in the alley this morning, remember? A man attacked me and—"

"My hands!" Tyler struggled to free his hands from beneath the quilt pulled up to his chest. "My hands. . . ."

"They're fine," Cade said quickly. He turned back the quilt and lifted his hands. "See? Not a mark on them."

Tyler sighed and his head fell back on the pillow. He drifted off to sleep again.

Cade tucked him under the quilt again and turned away. Allison followed him. She wrapped her arms around her middle.

"That nightmare." Allison shivered. "Do you suppose his father—"

"I don't know." Cade turned to her, anger etched in the hard lines of his face. "I want to kill anybody who would hurt a kid."

They were quiet for a long moment. She hadn't expected to find those feelings in Cade. She touched his arm gently.

"You've been in here all day. Why don't you get some air?"

He shook his head. "No."

"I'll stay with Tyler." She patted his arm again. "It will do you good."

Cade pulled at his neck. "Yeah, maybe you're right."

He left but didn't stay away long. Allison looked up from the rocker beside the bed when Cade came into the room again.

"How is he? Any more nightmares?"

"No," Allison told him. "But he was talking in his sleep."

"What was he saying?"

"Something about his mother, I think." Allison looked up at Cade. "I can't be certain. He was speaking French."

The sun would rise in a couple of hours, Cade guessed as he stood in his darkened bedroom. He wasn't sure of the time just now. The saloon had closed and he'd heard Vance, Billy, and the girls come up long ago.

He gazed at Tyler sleeping soundly in his bed. A pitiful sight, he thought. A pitiful boy. Unable to read or write, do the simplest chore, or cross the street without nearly killing himself. Yet he spoke French in his sleep. Who was that boy, and where had he come from? Cade didn't know and at the moment it didn't matter. Somehow Tyler had wormed his way into a tiny corner of Cade's heart.

And today, he'd nearly lost him.

He gazed out the window and across the street. Despite the late hour, lantern light shone through Allison's bedroom shade. Fear, raw and unchecked, rose to clutch his heart. Good God, he'd nearly lost them both today.

He rested his forearm against the windowsill and wondered what she was doing over there so late at night. Plotting the ladies' club's next move? Or simply too afraid to sleep without the lantern burning. She'd asked him for a gun and he'd refused. Maybe today was partly his fault, Cade thought. Maybe Allison had been right about needing protection.

Cade rested his head against his forearm. Maybe she'd been right in accusing him of still holding on to his Eastern roots. No one in the whole town would have dared talk to him as Allison had today.

He was a sick man, he decided, thinking of the flush in her cheeks and the slight flare in her nostrils today when she'd given him a big piece of her mind. For when Allison got her dander up, so full of fire and vinegar, it left him nearly overwhelmed by the desire to lay claim to her on the spot.

He straightened and sighed heavily in the dark, silent room. Maybe, just maybe, Allison had been right about something else. The notion had nagged at him all day, dogged him relentlessly.

Cade took a final look at her bedroom window and turned to Tyler. Maybe the streets of Brighton really weren't safe for decent people.

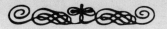

Chapter
Seventeen

She didn't expect anyone to be up yet, and so she was surprised to find the back door open. Allison walked inside. The kitchen of the Pleasure Palace was deserted. No coffee warmed on the stove, no breakfast preparations waited on the sideboard. She thought of leaving and coming back later, but she had a full day planned. Besides, she'd hardly slept all night worrying about Tyler. She had to see him this morning.

Quietly Allison climbed the stairs, her petticoats rustling. She peeped into Cade's room. Her breath caught.

He stood in front of the mirror on the bureau, shaving. He was also naked to the waist.

His trousers rode low on his hips, the sleeves of his long johns wrapped around him. The large expanse of his back rippled as he dragged the razor down his cheek and wiped it clean on the towel draped across his shoulder. Allison stood frozen in place, mesmerized by the bulging and flexing of his arms, and the intimacy of seeing him this way.

He turned sharply as though he'd sensed her gaping at him from the doorway. Their gazes collided. She saw the tight muscles of his belly clinch.

Heat surged upward through her, coloring her cheeks. Good heavens, what was she doing! Walking uninvited into a man's bedroom and ogling him as if he were a trinket on display in a shop window?

She dipped her gaze. "I'm sorry. . . ."

"No, wait. Don't go."

She looked up, and try as she might to focus on his soap-covered face, her gaze dropped to his chest. Dark hair covered him and arrowed in a line down the center of his belly into the open waistband of his trousers. A lady would be repulsed by the sight, she suddenly recalled her mother telling her, but Allison wasn't. Instead, she found it fascinating. And if that meant she wasn't a lady, at that moment Allison didn't care.

She stepped into the room, clutching her reticule while her heart raced. "How is Tyler?"

The perfunctory call she'd paid last night was all he'd expected from her. A well-bred lady didn't frequent the sickroom of anyone other than an immediate relative and certainly didn't frequent saloons. She'd surprised him. Again.

Cade gestured toward the bed with the razor. "Sleeping."

"More nightmares?" She walked to the foot of the bed.

"No." Cade turned back to the mirror. Her reflection was there along with his own, and he studied her as she looked at Tyler. She was dressed to the hilt, unlike last night. "You're not going out alone today, are you?"

"I have errands to run."

"That didn't answer my question."

She looked up and he'd turned her way, the razor drawn down his cheek. "Oh, really?"

That bullheaded, stubborn look had come over her. Cade pointed his razor at her. "Take some of your club friends with you. Don't be out by yourself."

Her brow arched. "Surely, Mr. Jessup, you're not suggesting the streets aren't safe?"

He knew her well enough now to know when to back off. She'd do the opposite, just for spite. "I'm saying you ought to be careful until Mack can find the man who attacked you yesterday."

"I'll keep that in mind." Allison left the room in a flurry of skirts and petticoats.

"Damn. . . ." Cade tossed the razor into the bowl on the

dresser and strode out of his room. He rapped on Billy's door until it finally opened.

"Yeah, boss?" He dug his knuckles into his eyes and yawned.

"How would you like to not play the piano tonight?"

"Sure!" Billy's eyes sprang open wide. "How?"

"Get your clothes on and get downstairs," he told him. "That damn stubborn woman is walking the streets by herself."

"Miss Tremaine?" Billy reached for his shirt thrown across the bottom of the bed. "She ought not be by herself, 'specially after what all happened yesterday."

"Follow her. Don't let her out of your sight. Understand?"

"Sure, boss."

"And don't let her know you're following her."

He shoved into his trousers. "Okay." Billy grabbed his boots and headed out the door.

Cade stopped him. "Take your gun, Billy."

He gave him a solemn nod. "I'll watch her good, boss."

Slowly Cade wiped the shave soap from his face as he watched Billy disappear down the staircase. Fear and anger knotted his gut, as it had since yesterday.

It wasn't enough that the woman had tried to put him out of business, tormented him with her bullheadedness, taunted him about his past. It wasn't enough that he worried about her safety.

Cade's shoulders sagged. Now he was in love with her too.

She wasn't going to take it anymore. She'd been threatened and attacked. She'd had her property destroyed. She'd very nearly been made the laughingstock of Brighton at the town council meeting. Well, no more.

Allison stomped down the boardwalk, filled with determination and rage. The mayor and his supposed council had made it clear they weren't going to change. And the saloon owners certainly weren't going to. The decent, law-abiding citizens who'd signed her petition had asked for help, but had gotten none. She was tired of waiting. Starting today, Allison was taking matters into her own hands.

Cade had given her the idea, and Allison intended to throw that in his face at her earliest opportunity. Lying awake most of the night, she'd relived the town council's defeat of the ladies' club's proposal. And along with that memory came recollections of suggestions Cade had made, albeit unknowingly, that would change the way saloons operated from now on.

Cade, she fumed silently. After all his high and mighty claims of how safe the streets were, he'd had the gall—the gall—to tell her not to go out alone today. Well, if he thought he could have it both ways, the man was in for a rude awakening.

She started with the Steer's Horn and roused the girls out of bed. They looked at her as if she were crazy at first, but by the time she left they were all gathered together, whispering. The Sud's Bucket was next on her list. Buck Mock gave her trouble at the door, but she shouted over his head to the girls huddled in the back. It was the same at the Miner's Gold, the Crystal Pistol, and every other saloon in town. Any woman wanting passage back East would have it, courtesy of the Ladies for the Advancement of Cultural Events. Cade had been right. The saloons would always be busy in Brighton as long as they were filled with pretty girls.

Next she stopped at the office of the Brighton *Gazette*. Albert Wade's brows bobbed when she ordered full-page ads to run over the next six weeks. If he questioned her intentions, he kept them to himself when she paid with cash.

Money spoke loudly to the merchants in Brighton. Another tidbit Cade had taught her. She'd make herself a financial force in Brighton, and the next time she addressed the town council, they would be mindful of her considerable impact on the town's economy, as well as the saloons'.

For hours Allison walked up and down Main Street, buying things she didn't need, ordering items that were of no use to her. Baskets for the poor, she told her merchants, though all they seemed to hear was the size of her order and all they saw was the color of her money.

Shortly after noon, Allison sat in the parlor of Phoebe's place, having tea. The older woman hadn't seemed particularly surprised at seeing her again.

Allison set her cup aside. "I came to tell you personally that my ladies' club is offering passage back East to any woman wanting it. That includes your . . . employees. I didn't want you to think I was sneaking around behind your back, stealing them away."

Dressed today in an elegant gown, Phoebe looked the part of a regal grande dame. "I appreciate that. But you know it won't matter. They'll always be women willing to do this kind of work. You take two, and three will show up on my doorstep."

"Perhaps. I only want to let those women who no longer want to do this work know that there is another way."

Phoebe eyed her and a slow smile spread over her face. "And if there are less of my girls in Brighton, maybe the town will be safer? Is that what you're thinking?"

Allison nodded. "Yes."

"Pretty good reasoning."

It had been Cade who'd given her the idea, though he hadn't realized it. She'd have to thank him for it.

"May I speak to your . . . employees?"

"No need." Phoebe shook her head. "I'll tell them myself."

Allison didn't doubt for an instant that Phoebe would keep her word. There was an earthy honesty about the woman, despite—or perhaps because of—her chosen profession.

"Have them come by the ladies' club, day or night."

Phoebe grinned. "Well, our nights are kind of busy around here."

Allison smiled and rose from her chair.

"You know, honey, I don't like being afraid on the streets any more than any other woman. You let me know if there's something more me and my girls can do for you."

"Thank you, Phoebe." She walked to the front door.

"Allison?"

She turned back. Phoebe rose. "Cade hasn't been down

here once since you came to town. I just thought you'd like to know."

Emotions too wild to name and too strong to contain swelled in Allison. She nodded and hurried away.

"I swear to God, boss, I didn't think one little lady could move so fast." Panting, Billy leaned on the bar and gulped down the mug of water Vance put before him.

"Where is she now?"

Midafternoon had brought out the heat of the sun and more than the usual crowd to the Pleasure Palace. They kept busy at the gaming tables while Cade, Vance, and Billy whispered at the corner of the bar.

Billy dragged his hand across his mouth. "She's at her place. I tell you, boss, she's been all over town today."

Cade's eyes narrowed. "What's she up to?"

"You're not going to believe what all she's doing." Billy's eyes rolled. Vance and Cade leaned closer, and he filled them in on Allison's escapades.

Cade and Vance jumped back.

"Damn . . ." Vance swore softly.

"What the hell is that woman thinking?" Cade struck the bar with his fist. "Whoever is behind the break-ins at her club and the attack yesterday is trying to run her out of town. When word gets around that she's paying passage for saloon girls to go back East, all hell's liable to break loose."

"You think the attack yesterday was planned? Somebody is really out to get Miss Tremaine?" Billy's eyes widened.

"Looks that way." Cade plowed his fingers through his hair. "Mack was by this morning and we talked it over. The note stuck to her door with a knife, the break-in, the place being ransacked. It all adds up."

Vance pulled at his mustache. "Then that would mean one of the saloon owners is behind it all."

"Could be." Cade nodded. "Saloons would have the most to lose if Allison and her Lace Ladies get their way."

"Has Mack got any ideas on who it might be?"

Cade shook his head. "He's checking around."

"Miss Tremaine was all over town, at the newspaper office, the livery, buying stuff and ordering stuff." Billy's eyes rounded. "She was even over at Phoebe's place."

"Phoebe's place!" Cade swore a vile curse and stormed out of the Pleasure Palace.

He beat his fist on the front door of the ladies' club until she opened it. She wore the same gown he'd seen her in this morning, but her hat was off. Wisps of hair curled about her face. A light dew of perspiration dotted her forehead.

"What in the hell do you think you're doing!" he bellowed.

Taken aback, she stiffened. "I'm trying to have a cup of tea!"

"You know what I mean!" Cade pushed his way inside and slammed the door. "Haven't you got enough trouble hanging over your head? Do you have to go out and invite more?"

Her jaw tightened and anger sparked in her deep brown eyes. "How dare you come in here and—"

"Haven't you got any better sense than to parade yourself around town—alone—trying to empty out the saloons?" he shouted down at her. "You're inviting more trouble on yourself. Can't you see that?"

"I'm doing what I believe in!" Allison's fists clenched at her sides.

"While you get yourself killed along the way!"

It took less time than she'd thought for word to spread through Brighton. "I tried going through the town council, I tried talking to the sheriff and the mayor, but it didn't work. Now I'm taking your lead, Mr. Jessup. Economics talks in this town. Thanks to you, I learned to speak the language. And I appreciate all your suggestions!"

Cade leaned down. "I didn't tell you to do any of this!"

She sprang upward on her tiptoes until her nose was even with his. "Wait until you see what I plan to do next!"

"Damnit, Allison!" Cade wrapped his arms around her and crushed her against him. His mouth covered hers with a demanding kiss. She leaned backward, pushing at his chest. Cade wound his hand through her hair and held her still.

Allison tore her lips from his. "Let go of me."

He held her tighter. His chest heaved. "I can't."

Her heart pounded wildly as she gazed into his eyes, dark with passion. His breath was hot and ragged against her face. "I hate you."

Driving heat consumed him. "Good."

Allison flung her arms around his neck and covered his lips with hers. Passion, hot and strong, drove them together with a blinding urgency.

"Promise me . . ." Cade kissed a wet trail down her cheek to the softness of her neck.

Allison laced her fingers through the hair at his nape. "Anything . . ."

"Stop this nonsense." He muzzled the sweet flesh behind her ear. "Forget the town and the saloons and this damn fool crusade of yours. Leave it be, before you get hurt."

Allison felt as though she'd been hit with a cold dose of reality. She pressed her hands to his face and pushed him away. "Are you willing to close your saloon on Sundays? Are you willing to ask the other saloon owners to do the same?"

She was like ice in his arms. His passion cooled. "I can't do that."

Allison wiggled from his arms and stepped back. Her knees wobbled. She drew in a deep breath. "But you want me to give up the cause I'm fighting for?"

"I don't want you to get hurt," he told her.

"It's not your place to worry."

"Like hell it isn't."

Allison squared her shoulders. "You've chosen your side of the issue. I don't see that we have anything else to discuss."

Cade swore a scathing oath and stormed out the door.

Vance and Billy watched out the window as Cade stalked back across the street and into the bar. Jaw set, he went straight into the kitchen. They exchanged a wary look and followed him.

"What happened, boss?"

"Damn fool woman. . . ." Cade crammed on his Stetson and took down his gun belt from the peg by the back door.

Vance ventured closer. "Where you going?"

"To do something that should have been done long ago."

He strapped the Colt low on his hips. "Be sure somebody stays with Tyler. I'll be back later."

"Boss, you want me to keep watching over Miss Tremaine?"

He rounded, his eyes blazing. "Hell if I care what happens to the woman! She's so damn hardheaded she deserves what she gets!"

Billy shrank back. "Yes, sir."

Cade swore again and kicked the door frame. He pointed at Billy. "Don't you let her out of your sight for a minute." He stormed out the door.

Most of her anger had been expended, thanks to Jenna's willing ear, so when Allison returned to the club after having an early supper with her friend and Holly, she felt better. She fixed a cup of tea and took her writing tablet into the club. After some fast talking, Jenna had been thrilled when Allison had told her about the orders for doll clothes she'd gotten from her friend's toy store in New York. She just needed to work out a few of the details to get Jenna's new business going.

A knock sounded, and since it didn't seem as if the door were about to be torn from its hinges, she doubted it was Cade. Allison found Maude Wilkens on the boardwalk.

"Am I too late?" The older woman wrung a handkerchief in her hands. She looked tired and drawn.

"Of course not. Come in." Allison stepped back.

Her gaze roamed the room and drifted to the floor. "Jenna McCain said it would be all right if I came over."

"I'm happy you came, Mrs. Wilkens. Please sit down."

"I don't want to be any bother." Maude perched on the edge of the settee.

Allison sat down across from her. She remembered Jenna mentioning how upset Maude Wilkens had been lately; things weren't going well with her husband, Satch.

"I don't know that it's right, me coming here. But I—I just don't know what else to do." Tears welled in her eyes.

Allison moved quickly to sit beside her. "What's wrong?"

She pressed the handkerchief to her lips. "It's just that—

It's my husband, Satch. He's a good man, and a good provider. At least, until the Carriage Works closed."

Allison cringed. Her aunt's closing of the town's main industry dogged her relentlessly.

"My Satch was the foreman." A proud smile crossed her face. "We moved here to Brighton because Satch got a job, and we bought a little piece of land outside of town. It was our dream. The kids were happy here and so were we. Then, the place closed down."

"Why didn't you move on like everyone else did?"

She shrugged. "We should have. But the kids liked it here and Satch thought he could farm enough to feed us. But Satch didn't know a thing about farming. He couldn't get nothing to grow. He tried, but nothing turned out for him. After a time, he just gave up. All he does now is drink. I don't see him, the kids don't see him. It just breaks my heart to know what he was, and see what he's become."

"Has he looked for work anywhere else?"

Maude shook her head. "We can't get enough money together to keep the kids fed, let alone send him looking for work. The eggs I sell to the Taylors just don't go far."

"What can I do to help?" Allison asked.

"Well, I heard over at the Taylor's store today that you were paying passage back East." She sniffed. "Now, I know the offer was for women only, but I was wondering if you could see your way clear to send my whole family?"

The Wilkens family wasn't the sort she intended to get rid of with her offer. "Is this what your husband wants?"

Maude twisted the handkerchief in her fingers. "I haven't told Satch about it yet. No sense in getting his hopes up for nothing, you understand. But, yes, I think he'd like it. He's got a brother back in Tennessee. I thought we'd go there. If you can help us out, that is."

The burdens Maude carried of children, home, and husband had worn her down. Each problem etched a new line in her once pretty face. "I'd pay you back," she said quickly. "I swear I would. Just as soon as we got on our feet."

"That's not necessary." Allison smiled. "I'd—that is, the ladies' club—would be happy to pay your passage."

"Oh, bless you, my dear." Maude squeezed Allison's

hands and smiled. "I'll go tell Satch. It's going to make all the difference to him. I just know it."

Maude thanked her all the way to the door.

Cade strode across the wide porch and banged the brass knocker against the door. He paced, adjusted his hat, and knocked again. Finally the door crept open and the soft, round face of the housekeeper peered at him.

Cade planted his fists on his hips. "I'm here to see Miss Allbright."

Georgia's brows shot up. "Miss Allbright isn't receiving guests."

"She is now."

Georgia gasped. "Oh, dear. Is something wrong? Is Miss Allison all right?"

"No," he barked. "She's about to get her fool self killed."

"Oh, dear." Georgia wrung her apron and stepped back from the door. "Oh, well then, I suppose you'd better come in. I'll go tell Miss Allbright you're here."

"I'll come up with you."

Georgia's eyes rounded. "Well, all right."

Her brisk footsteps sounded on the stairs followed by the thud of Cade's boots. She led the way down the hall to Lydia's bedroom door.

"I'll let her know you're here." Georgia disappeared behind the closed door.

Cade paced and mumbled a curse. Damn that stubborn woman, he fumed. He couldn't do anything with her. And he was scared to death for her safety now. Billy couldn't follow her around indefinitely. His only hope was that Allison would listen to her aunt. She'd crossed the continent to see the old woman. Maybe she'd have some influence over her hotheaded niece.

Georgia slipped into the hallway and closed the door again. She wrung her apron. "I'm sorry, Mr. Jessup. Miss Allbright says she's just not up to seeing you today."

His temper flared. "Why not?"

"She's not well," Georgia explained hastily. "The doctor says he can't find what's wrong with her. She's just lost her will to live—given up on everything."

Well, he hadn't given up on a damn thing. And he wasn't going to stand by and do nothing simply because the only person who could help him just didn't quite feel up to it.

Cade pushed past her and into Lydia Allbright's bedroom. The smell of sickness permeated the dark, shuttered room. He barely made out the shape of the woman propped up against a stack of pillows in the bed.

He crossed the room in two long strides. "Miss Allbright, my name's Cade Jessup and I've got to talk to you about your niece."

Lydia's head shifted on the pillow. She blinked rapidly. "What's that?" Her voice was reed-thin.

Georgia bustled to the bedside. "I told him, Miss Lydia. I told him you weren't up to a visit today."

"Well frankly, lady, I don't give a damn what you're feeling up to. That niece of yours is about to get herself killed and as I see it, you're the only one who can help. If you want to give up on life and lay there and die, that's your business. But before you go, you're going to do something to help Allison."

Lydia stared blankly at him, then pulled herself higher on the pillow. "Georgia, open the curtains a bit. I want to get a better look at this young man."

Georgia bustled to the window and pulled back the drapes. Light from the disappearing sun slanted into the room.

"Thank you, Georgia. That will be all." She waved her frail hand sending the housekeeper from the room.

Slowly, with time-worn deliberance, Lydia appraised Cade. Then, as if satisfied with what she saw, she folded her hands together. "Now then, Mr. Jessup, suppose you tell me just what my Allison is up to now."

Cade told her everything. The ladies' club she'd started, the threatening note, the break-in, the ransacking of the club, the saloon owners and businessmen she'd offended at the town council meeting, and finally the attack on her and her response to it. And the more he talked, the madder he got.

"She's going to get herself killed, and she's just too stubborn to listen to good sense."

Lydia listened intently. "Tell me one more thing, Mr. Jessup. How long have you been in love with my niece?"

The wind left Cade's lungs in a big huff. He pulled off his hat and plowed his fingers through his hair. "I don't know. . . . Since I met her, I guess."

"Does she love you?"

"She hates me."

The tiniest laugh slipped through Lydia's lips. "I'd say, Mr. Jessup, that if you've awakened any emotion in Allison at all, it could only be love."

Cade shook his head. "I tried talking some sense into her, but she's bound and determined to have her own way. I can't stand by and see something happen to her. She thinks the world of you, Miss Allbright, otherwise she'd never have traveled this far to see you."

Her forehead wrinkled as her brows drew together. "I'm certain that the need to visit with me was only part of her reason for leaving New York."

Cade shrugged, sure there was a double meaning in her comment. "You've got to talk to her. She'll listen to you."

Lydia lay quiet for a long moment, her eyes shut. Cade thought she'd drifted off, but then she looked up at him.

"I'll do what I can, Mr. Jessup. Keep a close watch over her in the meantime."

"I don't think she'll let me." Sooner or later Allison would realize Billy was following her, and he'd get an earful from her.

Lydia smiled. "You seem like a resourceful man. I'm sure you can think of a way to protect her. Good day, Mr. Jessup. On your way out, tell Georgia to come in, please. I'd like to get up and walk for a while."

Chapter
Eighteen

The Woolridge farm lay between Lydia Allbright's place and town, and it had taken only a few moments for Cade to make his purchase and be on his way. Now, with darkness closing in, he stood at Allison's back door carrying a picnic basket covered with a checkered tablecloth.

He knocked and finally the door opened; he'd wondered for a brief second whether she would let him in or not.

"Good evening." He tipped his hat. "Can I come in?"

After their last disagreement, she hadn't thought he'd show up on her doorstep. She didn't invite him in, only watched him shift back and forth. "What's that behind you? Are you hiding something?"

A little grin tugged at his lips. "You asked me for a gun. Remember?"

Allison peered around him. "Is that what you've got behind you?"

"You wanted protection, so that's what I've got for you." Cade held up the picnic basket.

It took on a life of its own, moving and swaying, the checkered tablecloth rising from the basket.

A big smile spread over his face. "Open it. Go on."

Cautiously Allison pushed back the cloth and the small, fuzzy head of a shepherd puppy popped up.

Her heart melted. "Oh, Cade, he's adorable." Allison

lifted the ball of fur from the basket and hugged it to her breast. The puppy whined and licked her chin. She laughed.

Seeing her smile lit Cade up like a full moon on a summer's night. "He's a loyal and watchful breed—best protection you can have. I know it's not a gun like you wanted, but this little fellow isn't going to get you thrown in jail for shooting an innocent bystander."

"He's precious, Cade. Thank you so much." Instinctively she rose on her tiptoes and placed a kiss on his cheek. "What should we name him? Oh, I know. Fluffy."

"Fluffy!" Cade gasped in horror.

"Yes, because he's so soft and furry and fluffy."

"You can't name a guard dog Fluffy," Cade told her. "Besides, I'd already picked out a name for him."

She looked up at him while the puppy licked her fingers. "What name do you like?"

"Butch."

"Butch!" Allison turned the puppy his way and held him up. "Look at that sweet face. Can you honestly say he looks like a Butch?"

Well, he couldn't argue with that logic. "Since you wanted a gun in the first place, why not call him Winchester."

She held up the puppy and studied his face. "I think you look like a Winchester."

Cade backed away from the door. "You two take care of each other."

"We will." Allison waved Winchester's paw at Cade. "Good night."

He waited until he heard the lock turn. Cade pushed his Stetson back on his forehead and strolled over to the Pleasure Palace. Convincing her to take the dog instead of a gun proved easier than he'd imagined. Of course, the idea of getting the puppy was brilliant, even if he'd thought of it himself. But maybe she was just coming around, he thought. Maybe she was starting to listen to him now.

The idea pleased him. Yes, maybe she was.

The following morning when Harry Finch appeared at the Pleasure Palace, Cade's heart jumped in his throat. His shipment was in. And not a minute too soon. But Harry asked to see Billy instead. The news wasn't good.

Billy swallowed hard and looked up from the telegram. "It's my aunt. You know, my Aunt Raina, who raised me. She's took terrible sick, boss. I've got to go home."

Cade patted his shoulder. "You go to your family, Billy. They need you."

Billy woke everyone and told them good-bye. Cade walked with him to the train station, his possessions stuffed into a single carpetbag, and waited with him until the last minute.

"Thanks for everything you done for me, boss."

Cade shook his outstretched hand. "You did a good job for me, Billy. You've been a good friend too. The place won't be the same without you."

Cade pressed a wad of folded money into his hand. Billy shook his head. "No, I can't take this. I know things are tight for you now, what with Miss Devaine coming and all."

"You deserve that and more." Cade patted his shoulder. "Take care of yourself and write to us."

The steam engine's whistle blew and black smoke belched from its stacks. Billy hurried onboard and found a seat near the front of the coach. He waved to Cade as the train lurched forward and it was then that he remembered something very important he should have told Cade last night. Things had gotten hectic in the saloon and he'd forgotten.

But it was too late now. The feeling that he'd somehow failed swept over Billy. He should have told Cade. Cade would want to know that yesterday, while following her through town, he'd seen Miss Tremaine buy herself a gun.

"It's here! It's here!"

Ben from the express office rushed into the Pleasure Palace waving his arms wildly. The afternoon crowd fell silent as he turned in a circle in the middle of the room.

"Where's Cade? It's finally here!"

Cade pushed open the kitchen door, banging it against the wall. He grabbed Ben by the shoulders. "Are you sure? This isn't just Harry Finch's idea of a joke, is it?"

His eyes bulged. "I swear, Cade, it's here. Harry is taking it off the freight car now."

Cade let out a whoop. "Come on, boys, let's go look!"

The saloon emptied out. The town had buzzed about it for months now, but Cade had been tight-lipped about the mysterious shipment.

A crowd gathered and grew larger as Cade supervised the arduous task of removing the huge crates from the freight car and loading them onto the freight wagon for transport to the Pleasure Palace. Rumors and speculation flew. Everyone ventured a guess at what it might be.

The procession made its way slowly through town, drawing the eye of every shopper, bystander, and storekeeper. Traffic stopped. People came out onto the boardwalk and stared. Cade stood tall and proud in the back of the wagon. They stopped outside the Pleasure Palace and the crowd gathered closer.

"Come on, Cade, tell us what it is!" A voice shouted from the back of the gathering. Others joined in.

Cade held up his hands for silence. "Gentlemen, I invite each and every one of you to come to the Pleasure Palace this Saturday night. You will witness history being made inside the walls of my own saloon! For not only will you delight to the singing of Miss Vivian Devaine . . ."

A cheer broke out. Men whistled and applauded.

". . . but you will hear for the very first time in the state of Nevada, all the way from New York City, Miss Devaine's accompaniment on a new Steinway grand piano!"

Upstairs in the bedroom window, Tyler gasped. He leaned out to get a better look, even though it made his ribs ache. The crowd cheered as Cade talked about this Saturday's performance. Across the street he saw Miss Allison come out onto the boardwalk with several other ladies from her club. She'd been over to see him every day and brought books to read to him. She'd sat with him for hours. She was always nice to him.

But she didn't look so nice right now, he thought. She looked angry. He saw Jenna come out of her dress shop; the two women bent their heads together and talked.

Tyler stepped back from the window, afraid that Cade

would see him. He wasn't supposed to be out of bed yet. But he felt all right. His lip was healing and the swelling was down; the bruise under his eye had turned to a greenish yellow now. He was tired of staying in bed. He wanted to get a better look at all the excitement downstairs.

Tyler slipped down the hallway and tiptoed past Belle's bedroom. The door stood slightly ajar. Clare stroked her long dark hair by the window, and Belle, beside her, held the broom. Their backs were to him as they, too, watched the commotion on the street below. In his own room he pulled off his nightshirt and dressed quickly, the motion causing his ribs to hurt a little more. He pulled on his boots and headed down the hall again just as a figure darted into Cade's bedroom.

Fear paralyzed Tyler. His chest tightened and his breath stopped. The man was back. He'd come after him just like he'd said he would. Tyler turned to run but Belle's door swung open and he collided with her.

"What in the world are you doing up and dressed, young man?" Belle asked.

Clare stepped into the hallway running the hairbrush through her dark mane. "Does Cade know you're up?"

All he could do was point. "Man. . . ."

They both read the terror in his face and looked toward Cade's bedroom.

"Who is it?" Belle demanded. "Who's in there?"

"Go get Cade," Tyler whispered desperately. "It's the man—"

Clare's eyes widened. "The man who beat you?"

Trembling, he nodded quickly. "Go get Cade."

Fire blazed in Belle's eyes. "Bastard!"

"Let's get him," Clare swore.

"No!" Tyler pleaded.

Belle ducked inside her room, grabbed the broom, and charged into Cade's bedroom with Clare on her heels. The man's back was to her as he rifled through Cade's desk. Belle screamed and rammed the handle of the broom into his side, then swung it around and bashed him in the back of the head. He stumbled, knocked the chair over, and fell to the floor. She beat him in the face with the straw end of the broom. He scrambled to his feet and Clare whacked him over the head with her hairbrush. Staggering, he knocked the lantern from the bureau. It shattered across the floor. He slipped and cut his hand on the broken glass.

"Think you can go around hitting women and children!" Belle whacked him again.

Clare hit him over the head. "Take that, you animal!"

Belle and Clare closed in on him, beating him about the head and shoulders while he struggled to rise. Finally he got to his feet. Holding up his arms for protection, he pushed his way between them and ran from the room. They pursued him, screaming and calling him every filthy name they knew. Unhampered with long skirts and petticoats, the man dashed down the stairs and out the back door before they got to the kitchen.

Cade and Vance burst through the door from the barroom. Cade grabbed Belle's arms as she headed toward the door.

"What's going on in here?"

"That bastard was up there! The one who beat up Tyler! He just went out the back way!"

Vance grabbed the shotgun from the supply room and headed out the door.

Clare brandished her hairbrush. "We drove him off though, Cade."

"We hurt him pretty bad too." Belle shook the broom.

"Jesus Christ!" Cade plowed both hands through his hair and looked up at them with fury in his eyes. "What's the matter with the two of you? Taking after a man like that with a broom and a hairbrush? What the hell is wrong with all the women in this town! Have every single one of you lost your mind!"

"Maybe we've just come to our senses!" Belle shouted.

"Yeah!" Clare told him. "Maybe we're just sick and tired of waiting for men to protect us when they have no intention of doing it!"

Cade forced his anger to cool. Never, in the whole time he'd known Belle and Clare, had he exchanged a cross word with them. He drew in a deep breath. "Are you all right?"

Miffed, Belle lifted her shoulder. "We're fine."

"What about Tyler?"

"I guess so," Belle said. "I don't know what happened to him in all the commotion."

Cade hurried up the stairs and finally found him crouched on the floor, squeezed into the small spot between the wall and the bureau in his tiny bedroom at the end of the hall. Knees drawn up to his chest, his arms circled them, trying to make himself as small as possible.

"Are you all right?"

Tyler didn't answer. The bruise under his eye looked darker against his colorless face.

"Come on out of there," Cade told him. He made no move to come out of his hiding place. "The man's gone, son. He can't hurt you now."

Cade held out his hand and finally Tyler took it. He winced as he rose to his feet.

"Belle said that was the man who beat you. Is that true?"

Tyler ducked his head. "I don't know."

Cade knew that response meant just the opposite. He laid his hand on the boy's shoulder. "Tell me the truth. Was that the man who attacked you and Allison?"

He looked up quickly and shook his head. "No. That was a different man."

"Then who was this one?"

He looked away again. "I don't know."

Cade studied the top of the boy's light brown head. If it wasn't the man involved with the attack on Allison, then it could be one other person. "He was the one who beat you when you first got to town. Right?"

Finally, Tyler nodded. "I don't know his name."

"Have you seen him before?"

The boy seemed to shrink smaller with each question. Cade wasn't sure if it was pure fear or something deeper.

"Yes." A long moment crept by before Tyler raised his face again to look at Cade. "I saw him once. He was looking through the windows at Miss Allison's ladies' club."

It had taken all the courage the boy could muster to tell Cade that. He was scared to death of the man, and with good reason.

Tyler swallowed hard. "He saw me looking at him and he

said he knew where I lived and he'd come after me again if I told. I didn't tell anybody—I didn't. Why did he come?"

Cade didn't know. Why would a man—whose name Tyler didn't even know—want to hurt him badly enough to break into the Pleasure Palace?

"Come on downstairs with me. I got my shipment in and I want you to see it." The boy really should be sent back to bed, but Cade didn't want to leave him alone up here. He intended to keep an eye on him.

They went down to the kitchen. Clare and Belle were seated at the table sipping coffee. They glared at him and looked the other way. Cade sent Tyler into the barroom and sat down across from the girls.

He drummed his fingers on the table. "I didn't mean to yell at you. I was afraid for you, that's all."

Belle and Clare looked at each other, then relaxed too.

"Well, I guess all's forgiven." Belle reached across the table and squeezed Cade's hand.

"Vance came back a little bit ago. Says he got away. But he went and told Mack," Clare said.

"Tyler says that wasn't the man who attacked him and Allison in the alley." Cade reared back in the chair. "It's the man who beat him when he first got to town. I guess if we knew who he was, at least one mystery would be solved."

"Well, hell," Clare said, "I know who that man was."

Cade's head snapped up.

"Everybody in town knows Wes Palmer," Belle told him. "Foreman of Miss Lydia Allbright's ranch."

Cade sat forward. Why would Wes Palmer beat Tyler? The man was a bastard and Cade clearly remembered how Palmer had threatened him with a gun the day he'd delivered Allison to her aunt's ranch. Maybe Tyler had stopped there for a handout, he thought. He wouldn't put it past Palmer to beat a child for no more reason than that.

But that left him with the question of why Palmer had threatened the boy when he'd caught him peeping in the ladies' club's windows. Why had he taken the chance to sneak into the Pleasure Palace to come after the boy again in broad daylight? Why was he after Tyler? What had the boy seen? What did he know about Palmer that he wanted kept quiet?

Hair on the back of Cade's neck stood up and his stomach clinched. Cade rose from the chair. "Get the boy and send him upstairs."

"But, Cade, your fancy new piano is finally here," Belle said. "Aren't you even going to see it unpacked?"

"I've got book work to do." He bounded up the stairs.

Evening shadows crossed his bedroom when Cade rose from his desk and stretched. He closed the ledgers in front of him but instead of tossing them in the desk drawer he locked them securely in the safe he'd had built into the floor of his closet when he'd bought the Pleasure Palace.

He was mad. Mad as hell. His first instinct was to take care of the situation himself. But instead he strapped on his gun and left the Pleasure Palace. Mack Carson sat behind his desk when Cade walked into the jail.

"Evening, Cade." Mack put down his pencil and pushed the reports aside. "What brings you over this late in the day?"

Cade stopped in front of his desk. "I know who threatened Allison Tremaine. I know who attacked her." He pulled his hat lower on his forehead. "And I know why."

A cheer went up from the crowd gathered below the platform as Cade stepped from the passenger car. The noon sun shone like a diamond in the clear blue sky, and Cade's smile was as brilliant.

"Ladies and gentlemen! It is my distinct honor and privilege to present to you, that world-renowned songstress, the lady with the golden voice, in her first ever performance in our great state—Miss Vivian Devaine!"

She stepped from the passenger car and accepted his hand, touched her fingertips to her lips and tossed a kiss into the gathering. A thunderous cheer rose from the crowd.

She moved with the regalness of a well-schooled artisan, accustomed to having her every action scrutinized. Her heart-shaped face offered a smile to the throng of cheering admirers. She waved, certain that her gaze swept the crowd right and left, back and front.

Tall and statuesque, Vivian Devaine wore an emerald gown that hugged her curves and perfectly matched the sparkling green of her eyes. A walking pleat showed a glimpse of tightly laced kid leather boots. Among her dark curls sat a hat with an emerald ostrich feather sweeping up to the left. She carried her matching parasol, touching its tip to the broad wooden beams of the railroad platform, accentuating the sway of her hips when she walked. The men gathered at her feet whistled and cheered.

Mayor Everette Hawkins bustled onto the platform. He tugged at his vest and lifted his hat to mop his forehead. Nervous and sweating, he contrasted Cade's smooth, easy grace as he stood on the other side of her.

"All right now, boys, hold it down, just hold it down." Everette mopped his forehead again. "On behalf of the good citizens of Brighton, it's my pleasure to officially welcome you to our town, Miss Devaine. We're just pleased as punch to have you here."

"I'm thrilled to be invited here." Her voice was husky, a slow, deep purr. She pointed a long finger at the men in the crowd. "And I want to see each and every one of you boys tomorrow night at the Pleasure Palace."

Vivian took Cade's arm and they stepped into the waiting buggy. Everette crowded his wide girth onto the same seat with them, and Cade drove the team to the door of the Brighton Hotel while Vivian and Everette waved to the men who followed on foot and stared from shops and businesses along the way. A wagon carrying Vivian's maid and pianist and a dozen trunks followed. She took a final bow and threw another kiss to the crowd before disappearing into the hotel.

Everette wiped his brow and heaved a sigh of relief. "That's a woman, I tell you. That's a woman."

Cade chuckled and slapped him on the shoulder. "Come on over to the Pleasure Palace tomorrow night, Everette. Get a look at her in action."

"Oh, I'll be there. Right on the front row!"

Cade waved and made his way through the crowd that

seemed unwilling to disperse. Men stopped him to offer their approval and assure him they'd be at the Pleasure Palace tomorrow night, come hell or high water.

Thoroughly pleased with himself, Cade made his way back to the saloon. He'd taken a big gamble in getting Vivian Devaine out here. The curtains, the piano, the stage, new costumes for the girls, and the supply of extra liquor had nearly bankrupted him. But now it was all paying off. Tomorrow night, Vivian Devaine would put the Pleasure Palace on the map. And that was only the beginning.

The Pleasure Palace didn't open at noon, as usual, that day. Shades drawn and doors closed, Vivian Devaine and her entourage slipped through the back way for rehearsal. Lilly, the petite, dark-haired maid smiled a shy hello and hurried after Vivian, fussing over her every movement. Bernard, the pianist, ignored Cade's outstretched hand and coughed behind his white linen handkerchief.

He rolled his eyes and shuddered. "I can't believe we're actually in this God-forsaken place. What have I done?"

Belle, Clare, and even Sonny came down and welcomed Miss Devaine. Gracious and warm—ever the performer—she smiled and thanked them. Vance offered her a sherry, but she declined.

She entered the stage from the back entrance in the kitchen and walked across slowly appraising the saloon. Her gaze fell to the grand piano situated at the foot of the stage. "Bernard, come see this."

He gasped and pressed his long fingers to his throat. "Magnificent!" He swept around and faced Cade. "What is this beautiful creation doing in a place like this? How did you ever get it?"

Cade ignored the insult because he couldn't care less what the pianist thought of him, Brighton, Nevada, or anything else in the world. All he had to do was play, three shows Saturday night and two on Sunday, and he could be on his way.

To Cade's surprise, Sonny sidled up alongside the pianist, just close enough that her breast brushed his arm. "Play it for us, won't you?"

Seventeen, blond, and trouble. Cade had known it when he'd hired her. She hadn't proved him wrong.

With a flourish, Bernard called to Lilly and took his sheet music from the satchel the young maid had carried in.

"Do you mind if we watch?" Cade asked.

Vivian smiled and gave him a wink. "I suppose you ought to get a glimpse of what you're paying for."

With Sonny leaning a hip against the piano, Bernard ran his fingers over the keys, then settled into the first song. Vivian Devaine's voice filled the empty saloon. Cade, Vance, and the girls sat at a front table and listened. After a while Tyler came in and sat by himself in the back corner.

An hour later they went back to the hotel, everyone satisfied that tomorrow's performance would be fine. The saloon opened for business and was packed in no time. Already men were thronging to Brighton from all over in anticipation of seeing Miss Vivian Devaine.

Cade fell asleep that night mentally reviewing future plans. He'd parade an endless number of performers through the Pleasure Palace, unrivaled by anything east of San Francisco. People would come from all over. The West was starved for entertainment. He'd buy a hotel where they'd all stay, and a restaurant too. Maybe a second saloon as well, and book top performers in both, he thought. He'd buy a special passenger car and bring people in just for the performances. Only the beginning, he thought as sleep overtook him. Vivian Devaine was only the beginning.

Belle jarred him awake the next morning as the first gray shafts of morning sifted through his window. He sat up. Something was wrong. Belle never got up before noon.

She pushed a mass of red hair over her shoulder and bit down on her lip. "Cade, something terrible has happened."

He sprang to his bed and grabbed his trousers.

"It's Sonny." Belle sighed miserably. "She's run off."

"Damnit." Cade buttoned up his trousers and paced in front of the window.

"I got up just now because I had to—well, you know. Then I found this note lying on my bedside table." Belle held up a crumpled piece of paper. "I checked her room. It's cleaned out."

"Damnit, she knows how important tonight's show is." He dug his knuckles into his eyes and swore again. "Well, you and Clare can carry it. I'll send over to Carson and get another dancer in here in a few days."

"Well, I wish it were that simple." Belle swallowed hard. "You see, Sonny didn't run off on her own. She took that Bernard fella with her."

The roar of filthy curses woke everyone else in the Pleasure Palace. Belle filled them in on what had happened as they all went downstairs. Cade was at the bar.

"I'd like to tan that girl's hide." Vance, nightshirt stuffed into his trousers, thumped his fist on the bar.

"What is she thinking?" Clare exclaimed. "Hasn't she heard a thing that was going on around here?"

Tyler shoved his hand through the dangling sleeve of his nightshirt and tugged Vance's elbow. "I don't understand."

"Sonny ran off with Miss Devaine's piano player and now there's no one to play for the show tonight," he whispered.

Tyler looked around at the tight, worried faces. "Can't you just get somebody else to play?"

"The other saloons all have piano music," Belle said.

Clare laughed bitterly. "But they all play worse than Billy did."

"Besides," Vance said, "I can't picture any saloon owner letting his piano man help out over here. We're taking business from every other place in town tonight and tomorrow night."

"Can we get somebody in from out of town?" Clare suggested.

Cade paced in front of the piano. "There's not enough time. Besides, finding anybody who can play the piano out here is damn near impossible. I've had ads in every newspaper from here to the coast since Billy left, and not one taker."

"Can Miss Devaine wait until somebody gets here?" Tyler asked.

Belle put her hand on Tyler's shoulder and leaned close. "This is real serious business, honey. Miss Devaine is moving on first thing Monday morning to someplace new. If she doesn't sing at the Pleasure Palace tonight, Cade will be ruined. He's spent every cent he's got on this performance. We might have to shut the place down."

Tyler's eyes widened. "You mean we can't live here anymore?"

"No, honey, we can't. And after this big buildup and then no performance?" Belle rolled her eyes. "We're all liable to get tarred and feathered."

Cade paced and pulled at the muscles of his neck. A long, tense silence stretched nerves tighter.

"Why don't you ask Miss Allison to play?" Vance suggested. "She plays nice."

"Oh, God. . . ." Cade moaned and turned away.

"She might do it," Vance said. "If you explain the circumstances to her, she might."

"Are you crazy?" Clare asked. "A rich, fancy lady like her is not going to come into a place like this and play the piano."

"What if she wore a disguise or something?" Vance suggested. "What if nobody knew it was her?"

"She's got no reason to want to help." Belle paused and looked up at Cade. "Of course, you could always give her a reason."

"Damn . . ." Cade swore softly and turned away. He'd already thought of it. And no matter how hard he tried, he could figure no way to get around it.

Allison Tremaine would be most pleased to play the piano for him, he knew. All he'd have to do is agree to close his saloon on Sundays.

Chapter
Nineteen

"She's a reasonable woman," Belle offered. "She might do it with no strings attached."

Cade's frown deepened to a scowl and he began to pace again.

"If you talk to her, explain everything, there's a chance she'll help," Clare added.

He pulled at his neck. "I can't afford to pay her price."

Belle wrung her hands. "Well, what else can you do?"

"Closing on Sundays might not be too bad," Clare said.

"It's the second biggest day of the week. I need Sundays' receipts to keep my head above water."

"But if you don't agree to close so Allison will play for you, you'll be washed up anyway. Right?" Belle asked.

Cade stopped and glared at her, then began pacing again. "I've got to find somebody else to play tonight. I've got to. I'm not losing everything I've worked for in this town."

A heavy silence descended on the barroom while Cade paced and the others stood by watching, all thinking.

"This is awful," Belle moaned. "Just awful. Finally, the Pleasure Palace was getting where you want it to be and then this happens."

"And all for the want of a piano player." Clare shook her head.

Tyler ventured closer to Cade. He touched his elbow as he paced past him.

Cade didn't stop. "Get on back to bed, son."

"But . . ."

"We'll think of something," Vance declared.

"Cade—"

"Not now, Tyler." Cade took the boy's shoulders and headed him toward the kitchen.

"But I—"

"Maybe you ought to go over and talk to Miss Devaine," Clare suggested. "Maybe she can think of something."

"Do you think a fancy singer like her would perform without a piano player?" Vance asked.

"More likely, she'd head out of town with no performance at all," Belle said.

Tyler tapped Cade's shoulder. "I—"

Belle took his arm and pulled him aside, fearful of the look of strained patience on Cade's face. "Look, sugar, this is real important. This is business. You run along now and give Cade some time to think."

Tyler sighed and turned away.

Vance rapped his fist on the bar again. "We're all in this together, Cade, no matter how it turns out."

"That's right," Clare added. "No matter—"

Piano music suddenly filled the air, rising through the silent room like a chorus of angels singing from on high. Cade whipped around. Tyler sat at the Steinway, his fingers rippling over the keys, coaxing strains from the piano more beautiful than even Bernard had delivered. Cade's jaw fell slack. Belle's eyes bugged out, Clare gasped, and Vance cursed aloud. They gathered around the piano.

Cade pulled Tyler's hand from the keyboard. The boy stopped playing and looked up at him. "Where did you learn to play like that? And don't you tell me you don't know."

Tyler gazed at the four adults towering over him, shifted uncomfortably, and looked at Cade again. "My mama taught me some . . . and my papa too."

A long, tense silence stretched as Cade stared at him. So afraid was he of the answer to his question that he dared not ask it. Finally, he said, "Can you play the music for Vivian Devaine?"

A light sparkled in Tyler's eye, and the lost look Cade had seen in him since the night he'd found him in the kitchen was gone. In its place shone absolute, unequivocal self-confidence.

Tyler nodded slowly. "I can play anything."

Belle let out a whoop and threw her arms around him. "Bless your little heart, you've saved us all!"

Vance slapped him on the back. "Who'd have thought it!"

"Thank goodness," Clare swore.

Bits and pieces fell into place as Cade watched the shy smile tug at Tyler's mouth. No wonder the boy had become hysterical when he'd cut his finger on the broken glass. And now it made perfect sense why he hadn't fought off his attacker in the alley, and why, upon waking, his first concern had been for his hands. Hands that made that kind of music should be protected above all else.

But still, Cade thought, this new knowledge about Tyler raised more questions than it answered.

Belle suddenly flung out her arms and gasped. "Oh, my God! What if that Bernard fella took all the sheet music with him?"

They all tensed again and stared down at Tyler.

He shrugged. "It doesn't matter. I heard the songs when they rehearsed yesterday. I can play them."

Clare's eyes widened. "You mean you can just hear a song once and then you can play it?"

Tyler nodded. "I can read music too."

Cade stepped back from the piano. "Everybody head on back to bed. Try and get a little sleep. We've got a long day ahead of us."

Belle yawned. "Good idea."

"Are you going to talk to Miss Devaine?" Vance asked.

"I'll go over to the hotel at a decent hour."

They all filed past Cade and into the kitchen. Cade caught Tyler by the collar as he went by. "Not you."

Tyler's big brown eyes got bigger as he gazed up at him.

"Sit down. You and I need to have a little talk."

Cade pulled out a chair at a poker table and held it until

Tyler sat down, then took a seat beside him. Cade drummed his fingers on the table.

"Somehow I feel like I'm looking at a ghost. The ghost of Miss Marshall, maybe?" Rupert and Otis had said it sounded like the hand of God across those piano keys; Cade could think of no better description for Tyler's playing.

Tyler shrugged. "I can't stand not playing. It's like the music is in me and it's got to come out."

"How did you get into the church?"

He hesitated, then took a deep breath. "When I first got here I was looking for a safe place to sleep. I found a loose board in the back. I pulled it off and slid through."

"And you played in the pitch-dark?"

Tyler looked up at him. "I don't have to be able to see to play."

Cade smiled. "It must have driven you crazy listening to the way Billy played. Why didn't you tell us before that you could play?"

Tyler shrugged and his gaze dropped to the table. "I don't know."

Cade rubbed his chin and watched Tyler closely. Whatever the boy's past, he'd been content to let it lie. But when he'd heard the first notes rise from the piano, Cade knew for certain Tyler was no dirt farmer's boy.

"Where are you from, Tyler?"

A guarded expression shadowed his face. He didn't answer.

"You probably don't know it, Tyler, but I'm from back East. I've been to the theater and to concerts and symphonies. I know you didn't learn to play like that in your spare time." Cade softened his tone. "What are you hiding from, son?"

Tyler blanched and looked away. "I'll play for you. But please, don't ask me anything else. Please."

Cade read sadness in his expression. Pain, set deep inside and locked in tight. It occurred to Cade that if that pain ever surfaced, it might well tear the boy apart. The fragility he'd always seen in Tyler went hand in hand with the pain, and now with the talent that he possessed as well.

"Fair enough." Cade rose from the chair. "Get up to bed and get some sleep."

Tyler looked relieved as he headed toward the kitchen.

Cade paced the room for a long time, then fixed a pot of coffee and sat at the kitchen table thinking. Finally he went up to his room, washed, dressed, and headed over to the Red Eye Cafe. A waiting crowd spilled out the front door. It annoyed him that he couldn't get his breakfast, then realized that his own saloon had brought those folks into town; that gave him little comfort.

He was hungry and not in the best of moods, dodging the people on the boardwalk at this early hour as he walked toward the hotel. A crowd filed out the door there too. Cade mumbled a curse and turned away.

His gaze fell to rest on the headquarters for the Ladies for the Advancement of Cultural Events. Allison. Unable—and unwilling—to stop himself, Cade crossed the street, cut through the alley, and stopped at her back door. The shades were drawn tight but the window over the sink stood open; he smelled bacon frying. Cade knocked and a determined yipping rose from inside. He smiled.

The shade pulled back, the lock turned, and the door opened before him. There stood Allison. His heart tumbled. Despite the early hour her hair was done up in a neat coif and she wore a deep green dress and all those underthings he wanted to take off her.

She smiled and wiped her hands on her apron. She'd expected to find Jenna or one of the ladies from the club on her doorstep at this hour, but not Cade Jessup. Somewhere deep in her thoughts, it occurred to her that he was a more welcome sight.

Cade pulled off his Stetson. At her feet, the puppy yapped and bounced from front to back paws.

"I see Winchester is on duty."

"He's very good at announcing visitors." Allison scooped up the puppy and he quieted. "And he positively excels at chewing the heels off shoes, shredding linens, and eating everything in sight."

Cade chuckled. "Sounds like he's keeping you busy."

"That he is." Allison petted his furry little head and put

him down. Cade couldn't know what a comfort the tiny puff ball of a dog was to her, especially at night.

A long moment passed while he stood in the doorway gazing at her, content to do no more, his hunger and foul mood forgotten. He could look at her every day for the rest of his life, he knew, and be content in that too.

Allison shifted uncomfortably, unable to decipher the look on his face. She gestured to the cookstove behind her. "I'm fixing breakfast. Would you like to join me?"

"No." He fumbled with his hat and said, "Well, maybe I'll just have some coffee, if it's no trouble. There's something I have to tell you."

She grinned and stepped back from the door. "This certainly sounds mysterious."

Cade hung his hat on the back of a chair and helped himself to a coffee cup in the cupboard.

"How is Tyler?" Allison washed her hands at the sink, then poured hot coffee into his cup.

"Tyler . . ." Cade shook his head slowly.

"What's wrong? He's not feeling worse, is he?"

Cade ran his fingers through his hair and leaned a hip against the sideboard. "He's doing fine. In fact, I found out something about the boy that's pretty hard to believe."

"Did you come over here just to tease me?" She smiled up at him from the stove. "Or are you going to tell me what's going on?"

Cade sniffed and peered over her shoulder. "That smells awful good."

"There's plenty. Are you sure you won't join me?"

"Well, yeah, I guess I could." He glanced around the kitchen. "Have you got any eggs?"

Allison took the bowl of eggs from the cupboard and placed two on the sideboard. He reached around her and lay out four more.

"I guess I'm hungrier than I thought. I usually have biscuits and gravy over at the Red Eye."

She grinned. "You're wasting your money over there, because I make the best biscuits in the state."

"Is that a fact?"

"It is."

He nodded. "Well, maybe I ought to try them out and see
for myself."

Allison pulled an apron from the drawer. "All right. But
you're going to have to work for this meal."

She rose on her tiptoes and dropped the apron over his
head, then slipped behind him and tied it. He didn't move a
muscle. Having her within arm's length was almost more
temptation than he could bear.

They worked together baking biscuits, frying eggs and
bacon, stirring up the gravy. He felt comfortable in her
kitchen, moving around her, feeling the occasional swish of
her skirt against his leg, catching a whiff of her subtle fragrance, more appetizing than any meal he'd ever eaten.

They settled down at the table facing each other over
plates of hot food and steaming cups of coffee. Allison
waited while Cade bit into a biscuit.

"Well?" She leaned forward.

He chewed slowly and his brows drew together, considering. Finally he smiled. "Yes, ma'am. I'd say you've got the
Red Eye beat by a mile."

She smiled and they ate, and Cade knew he never wanted
to eat another meal at the Red Eye Cafe, or any other
restaurant, for that matter. He wanted to sit across the table
from Allison Tremaine. Forever.

"So what's the news about Tyler?" Allison served the last
of the bacon onto Cade's plate. Having him at her table left
her with the oddest desire to feed him. It was his size, so big
and sturdy, she told herself. But buried deep inside her she
knew it was something more, something older and deeper
that touched a primitive part of her she'd never known
existed before. Before now. Before Cade.

They finished their meal and sipped coffee as he filled
her in on Sonny and Bernard's disappearance and how
Tyler had sat down at the piano and played as if the Pleasure Palace were a New York concert stage.

"I should have realized." Allison sat back in her chair,
stunned. "Reading music in large part is doing arithmetic
calculations—that's why he could do them in his head so
well. That explains why he could write with either hand, and
why he thought the alphabet started with the letter C. The

musical scale that every pupil learns first starts on middle
C."

Cade sipped his coffee. "It explains a lot of things. Such
as how the ghost of Miss Marshall got into the church."

"That was Tyler?" Allison shook her head. "Oh, dear.
Rupert and Otis will certainly be disappointed."

He considered it for a moment. "Let's don't tell them.
They're enjoying the ghost stories too much."

Allison smiled and whispered, "It will be our secret."

He wanted to share a hell of a lot more than a secret with
her, but for now it would do.

Allison rose and collected the plates. "You'll never guess
what happened. Aunt Lydia is up and around."

A big grin crept across his face. "Is that right?"

"It's the most amazing thing I've ever seen. One day she
was bedridden, hadn't been on her feet in months. And the
next, she's moving about as if nothing had happened. She's
even planning to come see the ladies' club in a few days."

"Sounds like a miracle," Cade told her as he pumped
water into a pot.

"Something like that." Allison shook her head. "But she
didn't waste a minute's time giving me a speech on being
more careful here in town. How do you suppose she found
out what's going on?"

Cade turned away quickly and set the pot on the stove. "I
couldn't tell you."

"Well, anyway, I'm quite relieved she's better." Allison
scraped the leftovers into Winchester's bowl. He lapped
them up hungrily. "I have to admit that for a while I wondered if something was going on out at the ranch."

He turned to her. "Like what?"

"I wondered if she was being drugged."

"Drugged? By who?" His brows shot up. "By that sweet
little old housekeeper?"

She waved his comment away. "Oh, I know it sounds silly.
But now I realize Aunt Lydia was simply too depressed to
get out of bed. And I think I know why."

Cade poured the warm water into the dishpan. He knew
he'd played a part in Lydia Allbright's recovery, but apparently Allison knew something he didn't.

"I received a letter from my mother yesterday in answer to my questions about Aunt Lydia's will. Mr. Stallworth had told me she'd decided to take someone out of her will, and I thought maybe that was the key to Aunt Lydia's depression."

Allison sat the dirty dishes into the pan. "And, unfortunately, I was right. A young family Aunt Lydia knew quite well in Europe was killed in a riverboat accident last winter just outside of St. Louis. I didn't know them, but apparently Aunt Lydia thought the world of them and was devastated by the news. I suppose it was just too much for her."

"The whole family was killed?" Cade took up a towel and began to dry the dishes. "Kids too?"

"Mother didn't go into much detail in her letter, but I believe there was one child." Allison shook her head. "So sad."

"I can see some comfort in them all going at the same time," Cade said. "It would be tough to be the one left behind."

Allison passed him the last clean plate. "I can't tell you how relieved I am that Aunt Lydia is better. At least now I know the reason behind her problems."

Cade sucked in a deep breath. "Well, I'm afraid that's not the worst of them."

"What do you mean?"

He dried the plate and stacked it with the others. "I found out who has been trying to run you out of town."

Her back stiffened. "Who?"

"Wes Palmer and Rory Stallworth."

She lifted her shoulders. "But why would a lawyer and a ranch foreman care about a ladies' club operating in Brighton?"

Cade tossed the linen towel aside. "It had nothing to do with the ladies' club. That was only a smoke screen."

He took both her hands and felt her grow tense. "I went over your aunt's financial records like you asked. The two of them were bleeding her dry. She probably trusted Stallworth and hadn't kept close eye on what he was doing, especially in the last several months. But as far as I could see, it had been going on for a long time."

Allison shuddered. Anger grew inside her, then dread and fear coiled deep in her stomach.

"The Carriage Works." She whispered the words. "That's why the Carriage Works closed, isn't it?"

He hesitated for a moment. "Yes. Stallworth probably advised her to shut it down. It was bearly eking out a profit, anyway. Losing money, some months."

Allison jerked her hands from his. "The Carriage Works meant more to my aunt than profit. It meant jobs to the people here. Jobs, self-respect, and independence. Her father built this town around that company."

Cade nodded. "I know. But the only thing it meant to Stallworth was that it was losing money. And he wanted the money for himself. I figure Palmer must have found out what Stallworth was doing when he signed on as ranch foreman. He must have wanted a share of the money to keep quiet."

Allison whirled away. Hot tears filled her eyes. Liars and thieves of the worst kind, she thought. Palmer and Stallworth had stolen more than money. They'd taken people's dreams.

"I told Mack what I found out and he confronted Stallworth." Cade spoke to the back of her head. He wanted to hold her, but he didn't think she would allow it. "Stallworth denied everything. He disappeared the next day, and Palmer hasn't been seen since."

Alarm spread through Allison. She turned to face him. "What if they come back? Aunt Lydia's financial records can incriminate them. Is she in danger?"

"No," he assured her. "Palmer knows the books are in my saloon. He has no reason to go out to the ranch."

Allison swallowed hard. "He's a nasty man, isn't he?"

Cade took both her hands. "He is. But don't worry. Mack is keeping an eye out for them. I don't think either will come back to Brighton ever again."

"But they could."

"Yes, they could."

Allison drew in a ragged breath. She pulled herself up to her fullest height and squared her shoulders. "I've thought

about this since I came to Brighton, and now I've made up
my mind. I'm going to reopen the Carriage Works."

With a new sense of pride, Cade eased his way through
the men packed into the Pleasure Palace. Rows of chairs
he'd put in front of the stage had filled up hours ago. Men
stood shoulder to shoulder in the room and three deep at
the bar. Faces crowded in the swinging doors and open
windows.

Latecomers squeezed their way to the bar, turning in the
handbills Cade had passed out at the Lace Ladies' dance in
exchange for free drinks, or buying a round for their
friends. He'd hired two of the Rafferty boys to help out at
the bar and they were busy. The crowd was noisy, and growing anxious. Cade flipped open his pocket watch. First show
in ten minutes, and everything was on schedule.

Vivian Devaine, tucked safely away upstairs, had ex-
pressed reservations about Tyler playing for her tonight
when Cade had suggested it in her hotel room earlier. But
after she'd heard him play this afternoon and they'd rehearsed her numbers, she'd tried to hire him on the spot.

Cade tucked his watch into his vest pocket and sighed
with relief. The girls were in their new costumes waiting
backstage, Miss Devaine was ready to go on, Tyler was
dressed in his new clothes, the Pleasure Palace was full, and
the money was rolling in. What more could a man want?

Cade caught sight of Belle's face peeping through the
kitchen door. She waved him over frantically. His stomach
wrenched into a knot.

"What's wrong?" Cade slipped into the kitchen.

"It's Tyler." Belle hiked up the red lace bodice of her
costume and pointed through the back door. "He's sick as a
dog, out back puking his guts out."

"Jesus. . . ."

He found Tyler crouched on his hands and knees on the
boardwalk, retching into the alley. Clare stood nearby, waving her hands helplessly. Cade knelt beside him and patted
his back.

"What happened, son?"

He sat back on his heels, his face deathly white, and

swayed. Cade scooped him up and sat him on a stack of liquor crates by the back door. Tyler's head fell lifelessly against Cade's chest.

Clare rushed over, frantic. "What are we going to do? If he can't play—"

Cade shushed her. "Get a cold cloth and some water. And go get the doctor."

"No." Tyler moaned and lifted his head. "No, it's . . . all right. I always get like this when I have to play in front of people."

"Oh, my God. . . ." Clare hurried into the saloon.

"Breathe deep." Cade loosed the string tie and opened the top button of the new shirt he'd gotten for Tyler this afternoon. He pulled the boy's head onto his chest again and had him rest there until Clare reappeared. He wiped off his face and let him rinse his mouth.

"Feeling better?"

"I told you, I'll be all right." Tyler sounded weak. "It happens all the time."

Belle stepped through the door. She wrung her hands together. "It's time, Cade. They're getting mighty restless in there. What are we going to do?"

Tyler pushed away from him and slid to the boardwalk. Cade reached to steady him, but without a word, Tyler walked into the Pleasure Palace. Cade, Clare, and Belle all looked at each other, then followed him inside.

The piano introduction brought a hearty cheer from the crowd. Cade said a silent prayer the boy would go through with the performance, gave Belle a wink, and bounded onto the stage from the kitchen entrance.

"Welcome, friends and neighbors, to the Pleasure Palace Saloon!" Cade stole a glance at Tyler as the crowd quieted. The boy sat erect on the piano bench, poised and confident as if he'd done this every day of his young life.

"Tonight, my friends, you are witness to history in the making!" Cade announced. "Not only will you hear the very first Steinway piano west of the Mississippi—"

Tyler played a ripple up the keys and the crowd cheered.

"No only will you see the prettiest dancing girls in the West—"

Whistles and catcalls mingled with the applause.

"But here to entertain you is none other than Miss Vivian Devaine!"

The gathering roared its pleasure.

"And now, without further delay, the Pleasure Palace dancers!"

Cade stepped to the wings as Belle and Clare high-kicked their way across the stage. Tyler never missed a note and the crowd clapped along to the beat. Belle pulled Everette Hawkins onstage and Clare kicked the hat right off his head. Everette blushed and mopped his forehead as the girls danced around him.

The crowd nearly brought the house down when Vivian Devaine stepped on stage, then fell silent when she began to sing. A vision in a low-cut white gown, she floated as if on a cloud, touching the heart of every man in the saloon with her golden voice.

Not one man left the Pleasure Palace until well after the third show. Dawn approached the horizon when Cade finally closed. Every man he knew in Brighton had been in, packed among the new faces in the crowd. Mack had come by to keep an eye out for trouble. Even Rupert and Otis had worked their way inside. He'd seen the Pinkerton agent, Manning, during the evening, but he hadn't stayed long; Cade didn't know the agent was back in town. Will Taylor had been in too, probably having slipped over after Edith was in bed.

Cade turned the lock in the front door and pulled down the shades. Vance and the Rafferty boys were cleaning up in the kitchen; the girls had gone upstairs already. Three shows a night was a tall order for them, especially Belle.

Tyler closed the lid over the keyboard, stood, and stretched. He'd played all night. Not just for Belle and Clare to dance and Miss Devaine to sing, but in between as well. And never the same song twice.

"You did an outstanding job tonight." Cade patted the boy's back.

Tyler grinned and rubbed the seat of his pants. "Thanks."

Charged with the energy of pulling together so successful

a night, Cade did something that rarely occurred to him. "I could use a drink."

"Yeah, me too." Tyler eagerly followed him to the bar.

Cade circled behind and took two shot glasses from the shelf. He poured bourbon in one, and sasaparilla in the other.

"Here's to one hell of a night." Cade lifted his glass in a toast. Their glasses clinked together and Cade drank it straight down.

"I couldn't have pulled this off tonight without you." Cade set his glass aside. "I don't know what I would have done. I'm beholden to you, Tyler."

"No, sir. It's me that owes you more than you'll ever know." Tyler sipped the sarsaparilla. "I wouldn't have played for anybody but you."

"And I do appreciate it." Cade recorked the bottle and returned it to the shelf. He gazed at the empty stage, then turned to Tyler. "I was doing some thinking tonight. Tell me what you think."

Short as he was, Tyler easily rested his elbows on the bar. He leaned forward, pleased at being taken into Cade's confidence.

Cade stroked his chin. "I was thinking about hiring more dancers. Say, ten or twelve."

"Besides Clare and Belle?"

He nodded. "This place would be packed every night. There wouldn't be a man in the state who could stay away. We'd do three shows a night and keep the place full between the big acts coming out from back East. What do you think?"

Tyler considered the idea. "Men seemed to like watching Clare and Belle dance tonight. Almost as much as hearing Miss Devaine sing."

Cade gazed across the barroom, envisioning the notion. "Lots of dancers in fancy costumes."

"The kind with feathers and fans," Tyler added. "With all different colored hair. Men like that, don't they?"

"They sure do."

"But be sure they're all the same"—Tyler leveled his palm at the top of his head—"the same amount of tall."

"Height," Cade corrected.

"Height," Tyler repeated the word. "You can stage big productions, like back East."

Cade nodded and stroked his chin. "Belle could teach them some routines."

"That would be good for your business, wouldn't it?" Tyler asked. "I mean, if you had a big show all the time, we'd never have to worry about leaving here or going hungry, would we?"

"No siree." Cade smiled. "We sure wouldn't."

Tyler chewed his bottom lip. "But you'd have to have somebody play piano for you."

Cade nodded. "That might present a problem. I've had no offers in the newspaper ads I've posted."

Tyler was silent for a long moment, then drew in a deep breath. "I'll play for you."

Regret showed in Cade's face. "No. I don't think so, son. I'm going over to the hotel this afternoon and tell Miss Devaine I'm canceling Sunday's shows. I think everybody in town saw her tonight, anyway."

"Cancel?" Tyler's eyes rounded. "You can't cancel."

"Don't worry about it, son." Cade pulled loose his string tie and opened the top button of his shirt.

"But Belle said you've spent all your money, and people might get mad and make us leave if the show cancels." Panic crept into his voice.

Cade shook his head. "Look, you saved my hide tonight by playing. But I'm not putting you through it again. I made a handsome profit already. I'm not greedy."

"Because I got sick?" Tyler asked.

"That's right."

"But it doesn't matter," Tyler insisted. "I always get sick like that. I'm okay once I start playing. Besides, who else is going to play for you?"

Cade shrugged. "I'll get an answer to my newspaper advertisement sooner or later."

"I'd much rather play the piano than wash the dishes," Tyler told him. "Even if I do get sick."

And he was a whole lot better at it, Cade thought.

"I can even help the girls learn their dance numbers."

The boy could dance too, Cade remembered.

"Please, just give me a chance." Tyler's big brown eyes pleaded. "I don't want anything bad to happen to us."

Cade rapped his knuckles on the bar. "Okay, I'll tell you what. If you can play without throwing up before you go onstage tonight, then I'll think about it."

The boy's shoulders sagged. "I can't help it. I get nervous. I don't want to . . . disappoint anybody if I make a mistake."

"Well, shoot, son, nobody in this crowd would know it if you missed every other note." Cade smiled and chucked him playfully on the shoulder with his fist. "You just play that piano and enjoy it. Don't worry about making mistakes. Relax and have a good time."

Tyler smiled. "I'll try."

"I'm starved," Cade suddenly announced. He rubbed his hands together briskly. "Let's head on over to the Red Eye before the crowd gets there. We'll get some sleep later."

"Okay." Tyler eagerly gulped down the last of his sarsaparilla and wiped his mouth with the back of his hand.

Cade waited beside the kitchen door while Tyler hurried to catch up with him. The boy had grown since coming to the Pleasure Palace, Cade realized. While it was doubtful he'd ever be very tall, he'd filled out considerably, his body transitioning from boy to young man.

Cade remembered himself at that age and thought of his father. He'd been the older man's shadow, listening to every word he'd uttered as if it were gospel. The lessons he'd learned—responsibility, hard work, honesty—had been ingrained in him by example, more often than not.

And now standing in the barroom, waiting for Tyler, Cade suddenly missed his father very much. Sadness overwhelmed him. For himself, and for Tyler, who had no father to dole out punishment or advice, or love.

Cade dropped his hand on Tyler's shoulder. "You did a fine job tonight. I was real proud of you."

A big smile crossed his face. "Thanks."

"Let's go eat. I'm starved."

*   *   *

Allison faced the crowd of angry women at the emergency meeting of the Ladies for the Advancement of Cultural Events, hardly able to contain her own wrath. Monday afternoon, she thought, and a long week lay ahead.

"It's an outrage!" Esther Wade declared over the cacophony of voices.

"Ladies, please, settle down!" Allison waved her hands to quiet the gathering. "I couldn't agree with you more. And something will have to be done."

"It most certainly will." Edith Taylor rose to her feet to address the ladies. "At this very moment, that Cade Jessup is en route to who-knows-where gathering up every floozie he can find to dance in that saloon of his!"

Allison seethed. The news spread through town like wildfire. Cade had made the announcement himself from the platform when he'd boarded the train only hours ago. The most beautiful dancers in the West, he'd said. More dancers than any man in Brighton had seen. Guaranteed to tickle the fancy of every man in the state.

"This will run every decent person out of Brighton, for certain!" Penelope Sage wrung her hands together.

"I have an idea."

The ladies fell silent and turned to Allison. Her hands curled into fists at her sides. "But it will take the support of every woman in Brighton. We must all be in this together, or it won't work."

"We're with you!" Mabel called.

Allison drew in a deep breath and outlined her plan to stop every man in Brighton cold in his tracks.

Afterward, she hurried down the path behind the livery stable and knocked on the back door of Phoebe's place. The ladies had no hope of succeeding without Phoebe's help. A young girl Allison had never seen before opened the door. Polly had left town only a few days ago, and as Phoebe had predicted, another had taken her place.

Phoebe came into the kitchen a few minutes later. Gentlemen were in the parlor, she explained.

Allison came right to the point. "You once said that if there was anything you could do to help, that you'd be willing. Did you mean that?"

Phoebe looked her up and down. "What did you have in mind?"

"I was wondering"—Allison bit down on her lip to keep from smiling—"if you and your . . . employees . . . would like to take a vacation? An extended, all-expense-paid vacation? Courtesy of the Ladies for the Advancement of Cultural Events."

Chapter
Twenty

A dust devil whirled down Main Street, whipping up a small cloud of dirt as it passed down the deserted thoroughfare. The afternoon sun burned hot overhead, and Allison kept to the shade of the Pleasure Palace, thinking the tiny tornado but a preview of things to come. The women of Brighton—nearly every single one of them—surrounded her. She looked at the lines of absolute determination drawn in all their faces, and was pleased.

Noise from the approaching crowd drew their attention to the east end of town. Allison's heart skipped a beat. She wouldn't fail this time. Cade and his bevy of dancers had gone too far. The women of Brighton stood united behind a plan that did not need the endorsement or cooperation of the sheriff, the mayor, or the town council.

The crowd of men advanced down Main Street gazing in awe at the wagon load of beautiful young women, cheering and whistling and waving. They smiled back, throwing kisses, reaching out to touch the hands of the men who jockeyed to get closer to the wagon.

And standing among the women, his back to the saloon, was Cade Jessup.

Allison's stomach coiled into a tight knot. Behind her, she sensed the women close in, blocking the entrance to the Pleasure Palace.

The crowd of men roared when the wagon stopped in front of the saloon. Cade waved his hands for silence.

"Good of all you boys to turn out and welcome these lovely ladies to Brighton! And tomorrow night you're all invited to see them right here onstage!"

Cade gestured grandly toward the saloon, and for the first time saw the women gathered on the boardwalk. The smile fell from his face. With easy grace, he jumped from the wagon.

Allison's resolve faltered. He'd been gone for nearly a week, and seemingly had grown handsomer in that time. She had missed him, but hadn't realized it until now.

A murmur went through the gathering as Cade strode leisurely to the steps of the Pleasure Palace. He hung his thumbs in his vest pockets and gazed pointedly at the ladies assembled on the boardwalk. "It's nice to see that you ladies have turned out to welcome the Pleasure Palace dancers to Brighton. I guess you'll want them to join your ladies' club right away."

The crowd of men laughed.

Allison's back stiffened and anger consumed her. She wished she had her parasol.

"They're welcome to join, of course." Allison stepped away from the crowd of ladies and blocked Cade's path. With the height advantage the steps gave her, she enjoyed looking down at him. "But I don't believe they will be in town long enough."

A murmur spread through the gathering. Cade smirked and looked up at Allison. "And just what are you ladies going to do about it?" he challenged.

Allison's gaze turned icy. "It's what we ladies are *not* going to do that should concern you, Mr. Jessup. You and all the men in town."

The playful grin fell from his face. "What are you talking about?"

"The ladies of Brighton have tried every avenue available to us to bring decency back to our town." Allison spoke loud enough that all the men could hear. "The sheriff, the major, the town council have all ignored our concerns. So, now we've taken matters into our own hands. Until the men

and saloon owners decide to be more agreeable, the women
will be decidedly disagreeable."

Cade's brows rose. His gaze swept the ladies and returned to Allison. "Do you mean you're going to withhold
. . . your favors?"

Her chin went up a notch and she willed herself not to
blush. "That's exactly what we mean."

A chorus of protests rose from the men. The ladies gathered behind Allison stood firmly together.

Cade shook his head. "It won't make much difference.
We'll still take our pleasures. But Phoebe will sure appreciate the gesture."

The men cheered and laughed.

"I believe it will make a difference," Allison declared.

The crowd fell silent. Cade frowned up at her.

"Phoebe and her employees have left town on vacation."
Allison smiled sweetly down at Cade. "Indefinitely."

The men surged forward, surrounding Cade, yelling and
complaining. He pushed himself free of them and climbed
onto the step beside Allison. "You can't hold these women
together. Yeah, maybe for a day or two, but that's it.
Women are obligated to obey their husbands."

"And husbands are obligated to protect their women,"
Allison shot back.

"All right, I'll prove to you that your women won't hold
together." Anger tinged Cade's voice. He gestured to the
men gathered in the street. "We're not going to shave until
your women give up their favors. Then, when you see a
clean-shaven man, you and the whole town will know this
feeble plan of yours isn't working, and will never work, and
that the men are running this town as we see fit!"

Angry cheers rose from the crowd.

A sardonic grin tugged at Cade's lips. "We'll have our
. . . pleasures."

"Fine." Allison arched her brows at Cade. "We'll see if
you men enjoy not shaving as much as you enjoy not doing
. . . other things."

Allison put her nose in the air and walked through the
crowd of men, the ladies following close behind.

*   *   *

"We're running low on whiskey." Vance slammed the crate onto the bar. "I told you, you ought to order more."

Cade tossed the empty crate to the floor. "Like hell you did!"

"I know damn good and well what I said," Vance shouted.

Two gamblers at the corner table turned their way. "Hey! Shut up over there!"

"You don't come in my place of business and tell me what to do!" Cade charged across the room, grabbed each man by the collar, and flung him out the swinging doors. "And stay out!"

The doors swung open immediately and Mack Carson walked in. He raked Cade with a harsh gaze. "What the hell was that all about!"

Cade scratched his seven-day growth of beard. "None of your damn business!"

"Maybe I'll haul your butt off to jail and make it my business!"

The two men squared off. Cade shook his head and looked at Mack. "What are we fighting about?"

Mack dug his fingers into his whiskers. "Hell, I don't know."

They walked over to the bar together. The place was empty now, since Cade had thrown his only two customers into the street, and hot too, though it was barely noon.

"It's those Lace Ladies." Vance wiped down the bar with a linen cloth.

"Hell, every man in town is as jumpy as a frog in a frying pan." Mack scratched his face again. "I broke up five fights yesterday—and three of them I started myself."

Vance set a mug of beer on the bar in front of the sheriff and pulled at the stubble on his cheeks. "I can't believe Phoebe would desert us at a time like this."

"Damn that Phoebe." Cade shook his head. He hadn't been to Phoebe's in a while, anyway, since the girls there held little appeal for him lately, but now it was driving him crazy knowing that he couldn't go if he wanted to.

It was driving every other man in town crazy too. They were all grumpy, irritable, and out of sorts. Not just the husbands who were doing without their wives' comforts, but single men too, and not only because Phoebe and her girls were gone. There was no hand holding, no flirtation, and no swish and swaying of skirts on the streets. Women were rarely seen in public lately, as if they were not allowing men even the simple pleasure of looking.

"Have any of the women weakened yet?" Vance asked hopefully.

"You haven't seen anybody over at Lloyd's this week, have you?" Mack said sourly.

"I wonder what those Lace Ladies are doing?" Vance looked out the window and across the street at the ladies' club. "They've been spending a lot of time over there this week."

"Has Miss Jenna been over there?" Mack asked.

"You ought to marry that woman," Cade told him. "This would be the time for a nice long honeymoon trip."

Mack shrugged. "Too much trouble in town to leave."

Cade nodded. He knew about trouble. He'd already had more trouble than he had counted on, and all of it from the dancers upstairs.

They'd strung clotheslines down the hallway and in the kitchen, and Cade hadn't been able to walk upright anywhere in the building since they'd arrived. The girls fought, they bickered and argued. Or else they were giggling and laughing, whispering and pointing, and talking out loud about things that should be whispered about. Cade had managed to squeeze accommodations for all of them upstairs and the tight quarters were getting on everybody's nerves.

But they were dancing. Three shows a night, every night, to a packed house. Cade had thought Belle would take the girls in hand and oversee rehearsals, but she'd given up after two days. To his surprise, Tyler had taken over. He proved to be a stern taskmaster, and the girls listened to him. There was a command about the boy when he sat before the piano and got up onstage to go through the dance steps. And the men in Brighton who came to watch night after night attested to the fact that Tyler knew what he was doing.

"That old dog Harry Finch has been sniffing around Jenna and I've had about all I'm going to take." Mack drained the last of his beer and dropped the mug onto the bar with a thud. "I'm going to go see if I can't throw his butt in jail for something."

Mack stalked away, scratching his beard.

"Cade, I've got something to tell you." Vance drew in a deep breath. "I'm taking a room over at Mrs. Fulton's boardinghouse. Those girls upstairs are driving me crazy. I can't live here anymore."

"Well, I can't blame you." At that moment Cade wished he could move out too.

Vance shook his head. "It's just not the same around here, with Billy gone and now all those girls."

"It's okay, Vance. I understand."

Cade turned away and gazed out the window at the ladies' club across the street. Nothing was the same as it used to be, he thought, since Miss Allison Augusta Tremaine arrived. Not the town, not the people.

Heat surged through Cade. And certainly not himself.

"You're doing much better." Allison smiled across her kitchen table at Tyler.

He closed the reader. "Cade's been listening to me read every afternoon, except for the last few days. He's been grumpy."

Allison took some comfort in the hope that she was in part responsible for Cade's foul mood. "That's all for today. Keep practicing your letters."

A knock at the back door interrupted them. Allison rose from the chair as Winchester loped in from the bedroom, barking. She opened the door. Cade stood before her. Her breath caught.

His shirt collar lay open and black hair curled out of it. Whiskers covered his face, thick and full. The sight left Allison with the desire to press her palm against his beard. Was it soft? she wondered. Would it tickle if he kissed her? It made him look swarthy and rakish—every mother's nightmare. Every young woman's naughty dream.

"I, uh, I came to see how Tyler is doing with his studies."

It sounded like an excuse more than a reason, but Allison stepped back and opened the door farther. "Come in. We were just finishing up." He stepped inside and the room seemed to shrink in his presence.

"I'll see you again tomorrow, Tyler."

"Yes, ma'am." He gathered his books and looked up at Cade. "I'll get rehearsal started."

"That's fine." Cade nodded as Tyler left the kitchen.

The door closed solidly and Cade knew he'd made a mistake. The internal juices that had simmered within him for these last weeks erupted to a full boil over the preceding days. He'd hardly seen Allison since she'd kept herself holed up in her ladies' club. If he'd have just been able to see her, maybe he would have been all right. Maybe he wouldn't have had to invent some stupid excuse to come over and see her.

Cade blew out a heavy breath and raked his fingers through his hair. "So, how is he doing?"

"Better." Allison put Winchester down and moved to the table.

She leaned forward to gather her tablet from the table and Cade's stomach clenched. Heat seethed inside him as if it were a living thing. He hurried ahead of her and pulled it from her grasp. God help him if she bent over again.

Surprised, Allison moved away. He radiated with a heat she'd never sensed before. "Are you feeling all right?"

No. He felt like a crazy man. And she was what made him crazy. Her and her ladies' club, their demands, the division in the town she'd caused, the sweet fragrance she gave off, the sway of her bustle, the magic that had captured his heart and mind.

Cade scratched his cheek. "I'm fine."

She took the tablet from his hand and gestured to the pitcher on the sideboard. "Will you join me in a glass of lemonade?"

He'd join her in a glass of lemonade, in a full meal, in bed. Cade's knees weakened. He plopped down in the chair, wickedly pleasurable thoughts racing. "Sure."

She filled two glasses and sat down across from him. "When you were over here the other day I mentioned that I planned to open the Carriage Works again. You didn't say what you thought of the idea."

Cade exhaled heavily. The last thing he wanted to discuss was business. But, he thought, maybe it would help keep his mind on safer issues.

"I don't know how much money you've got, but it's going to take every dime of it to get that place going again."

Allison frowned. "I don't see why. It's just a matter of cleaning the place up a bit, rehiring the men, and making carriages."

"It's not that simple." Cade leaned forward and rested his elbows on the table. "Have you been out to the old factory?"

"Well, no," she admitted.

"The place has got to be put back in working order. Men have to be hired, materials purchased. You need a great deal of cash up front to buy what you need. You'll carry the payroll for months before you see a dime in sales. Someone has to run the day-to-day operation, or did you plan to do that yourself?"

"I don't know anything about building carriages."

Cade nodded, acknowledging that she had made his point for him. "You need a market for your product. Who's going to be your front man? Who's going to find buyers? Who's going to negotiate contracts?"

"Lots of men would want jobs like that," she insisted.

"That's true," Cade conceded. "But can you trust them?"

Rory Stallworth and Wes Palmer had given her a valuable lesson in misplaced trust. Allison squared her shoulders. "I'll find some way to get it operating again. The town needs it."

Cade shook his head. "I don't know anybody with enough money or desire to get that place going again. Don't you think I considered it before I decided to open a saloon?"

"You could run it." Allison sat up straighter. "You've had experience in running a business similar to this. Would you take the job?"

"And work for you?" Cade shook his head. "No, thanks. I like being in charge of my own place."

"We could be partners," she suggested.

Cade stroked his bristly chin. "No. I haven't got that kind of money. Besides, I'm not sure about building carriages. The country is going in a different direction."

"I only see the direction Brighton is going." Allison sighed. "Since it was my aunt who closed the Carriage Works, I feel I owe the town something."

"Speaking of owing." Cade sat up straighter. "You still owe me for the piano."

She'd bought his old piano, and the only payment he'd asked was that she play it for him. The music she could produce was not nearly as fascinating as seeing her round little bottom perched on the piano bench. Thoughts of collecting on the debt had been on his mind lately.

"You're not serious about that, are you?" Allison shook her head. "I can't believe that after hearing how beautifully Tyler plays you'd have any interest in me."

He smiled. "Each pianist brings his—or her—own interpretation to the music, I'm told."

"I'm not very accomplished. I don't know what I could bring to the music that Tyler couldn't."

She would be sitting on it. Cade didn't intend to tell her that he was more interested in seeing her play than hearing her.

He leaned forward. "You're not going to welch, are you?"

"I certainly am not."

Cade rose and gestured toward the club room. "After you."

Winchester suddenly ran from beneath the table, barking furiously at the back door.

Allison looked down at the tiny ball of fluff. "What's gotten into him?"

Cade caught her arm. "Get into the other room."

"But—"

He pulled her out of the chair. "Go!"

The back door flew open and Wes Palmer stepped halfway into the opening, gun drawn. Cade pushed Allison behind him. He slapped his hand against his thigh but came up empty. He hadn't worn his gun today. With a curse Cade started toward Palmer.

He pulled back the hammer. "Don't move."

Cade froze. His gaze swept the room, looking for a weapon.

"Try it, and somebody's going to get hurt. Like maybe this little brat." Palmer stepped into the room, pulling Tyler in by the shirt collar.

Cade's fists clenched at his sides. Tyler looked pale, sickly white, but unhurt. Palmer looked desperate.

Winchester growled and bared his teeth. Palmer kicked at him. "Shut that mutt up!"

"Don't hurt him!" Allison dropped to her knees and called to the puppy.

Cade grabbed Allison and yanked her to her feet. He stepped in front of her again. "What do you want, Palmer?"

The gun in his hand held steady, pointed at the two of them. "That bastard Stallworth might be content to live his life in hiding, but I'm not. I want those books."

"All right." Cade nodded. Better to play along, he decided. The odds were against him. He couldn't chance anything with Allison and Tyler both in the way. "Let's go."

"You ain't going no damn where. Tell the boy to bring them." Palmer gave Tyler a shake.

Cade tensed. "Don't you hurt him."

"Tell him!" Palmer cursed and pushed Tyler to the floor. Winchester bounded over and bit into Palmer's trouser leg, snarling and pulling at the fabric.

Cade lunged forward. He pushed Palmer's gun hand upward. A bullet fired into the ceiling.

Allison swallowed the scream that hung in her throat and rushed to Tyler. He scrambled to his feet and they ran into her bedroom together. Winchester trotted in behind them and scooted under the bed.

Another shot rang out. Allison turned and saw Palmer's head snap back as Cade drove his fist into his cheek. Palmer brought the gun down and squeezed off another shot, this one whizzing past Cade's ear.

Allison pushed Tyler deeper into the bedroom and rushed to the bureau. "Hide."

"What are you doing?"

Stockings, corsets, and pantalettes flew across the room

as Allison dug to the bottom of the bureau drawer and pulled a Colt .45 from its hiding place. She raced into the kitchen.

Palmer's gun lay on the floor and the two men were exchanging punches. Blood spurted from Palmer's nose as Cade struck him. He countered with a blow to Cade's stomach.

"Stop!" Allison screamed. She pointed the gun toward the ceiling and pulled the trigger.

Stunned, both men froze, their fists suspended in midair.

Fingers wet with sweat, she tightened her grip on the gun and pointed it at the men. "I said stop."

Palmer grunted and lunged toward Allison. Cade grabbed for him, but missed. Allison squealed, closed her eyes, and squeezed off another shot.

Cade and Palmer both dove for cover as the bullet passed between them. Palmer scrambled across the floor, grabbed his own gun, and dashed out the back door.

Running footsteps sounded on the boardwalk, then a second pair. A shot rang out, then another, and a heavy object thudded against the side of the building.

Cade jumped to his feet and tore the gun from Allison's hand. He raced out the back door.

Her knees buckled. Allison collapsed onto the floor.

Tyler plopped down beside her. "Are you all right? Are you hurt?"

He looked as frightened as she felt. Allison took his hand. "I—I don't know."

He swallowed hard. "I better get Cade."

"No! It's dangerous. Don't go out there."

He didn't stop, but made it no farther than the back door. Tyler gazed down the alley, then turned to Allison, his face pale.

"The sheriff is outside with Cade. That man is lying in the alley." Tyler gulped hard. "I think he's dead."

Allison shuddered. She covered her mouth with her fingers and bit down on her lip.

Cade suddenly appeared in the doorway, her gun shoved into the waistband of his trousers, his face grim. His gaze swept them both, then relaxed marginally. He grabbed Tyler and pulled him hard against him, smothering him in a hug.

"Are you all right?" He held Tyler away from him, his gaze raking him from head to toe.

"I think so." Tyler swallowed hard. "Just scared."

"You and me both, son." Cade hugged him hard again and planted a kiss on top of his head. "You and me both."

Allison forced back tears. Tears of her own fright, and tears of joy at seeing the tender care Cade showered on Tyler. She wanted Cade to hold her too. She wanted to feel his strong arms around her. She wanted to feel the reassurance of his embrace.

Finally, he released Tyler and strode to where she sat on the floor. His brows drew together in a fierce frown.

"What the hell is the matter with you!"

Stunned, she gulped and looked up at him with wide eyes.

"Are you crazy! Have you lost every grain of sense you ever had!" Cade flung out both hands. "Or were you just trying to kill me!"

She choked back tears. "I was trying to help you!"

"By nearly blowing off my head?" He glared down at her. "I told you not to get a gun. I told you something like this would happen. You've got no goddamn business with a gun in your hand! Why did you even bring it out here? Why!"

"Because!" Emotion overwhelmed her.

"Because why?" he demanded.

"Because I didn't want you to get shot. Because I was afraid for you. Because—"

Tears splashed down her cheeks.

"Because—" Allison gulped in a breath of air.

Because she loved him.

Chapter
Twenty-One

"All right now, make a fist."

"A what?"

"A fist." Cade looked down at Tyler and curled his fingers inward. "Like this."

He slid both arms behind him. "You mean with my hand?"

Cade pulled on his beard and exchanged a look with Vance behind the bar. He took a deep breath. "Yes, son, you have to use your hand to make a fist."

"I don't think I want to." He backed away a step.

"Well, you're going to." Cade pried Tyler's hand from behind him and held his wrist. He curled his fingers into shape. "There. Like that. Now, take a swing at me."

Tyler's eyes widened. "You want me to hit you?"

Cade put up his fists. "Come on, give me a good shot. Right on the chin."

"I don't want to." Tyler headed back to the piano.

Cade shook his head slowly. It was early. Only Satch Wilkens occupied a table and he was drinking heavily already. This was the only time of day he'd get Tyler alone. Between the boy's constant piano playing, rehearsing with the dancers, his tutoring with Allison, and the nightly performances, he didn't have much free time. And this was too important to let go.

"You have to learn to defend yourself," Cade said as he followed Tyler across the room.

He stopped at the piano bench. "What for?"

"Did you like getting beat up in the alley? Did you like what Palmer did to you?" Cade softened his tone. "Do you like being afraid?"

"No," Tyler said reluctantly. "But those men were a lot bigger than me. I couldn't have stopped them."

"You're not going to be small forever, so you'd better learn how to take care of yourself." Cade put up his fists again. "Now, come on. Let's see them."

Tyler curled his fingers against his shirt. "My hands. I can't take a chance hurting my hands."

"Better to have a busted hand than to be afraid your whole life. Come on, now—"

"Glory be. . . ." Vance came from behind the bar, staring out the window. "Would you look at who's in town?"

Cade dropped his fists and followed Vance's line of vision to the buggy pulling up in front of the ladies' club across the street. "Isn't that Lydia Allbright?"

"Yep. I believe it is."

Tyler ran to the window and pressed his palms against the glass. "She finally came," he whispered.

"It's been a long while since Miss Allbright's been in town." Vance looked at Cade. "Some special occasion, you think?"

Cade groaned. After the incident yesterday with Palmer when Allison had nearly blown his head off, he could only guess that she was planning now to arm the ladies of Brighton.

"Must be something big," Vance mused.

The bat-winged doors swung open and Mack Carson walked into the barroom. He didn't speak; his face was drawn in a grim expression. Behind him appeared Manning, the Pinkerton agent, followed by a hulking man dressed in somber black with a face that told of a lifetime of differences settled with fists. He held the door as an older gentleman entered the barroom.

White hair fringed a beaver hat. He wore an expensive linen suit with a white silk scarf tucked into the collar of his

overcoat. Brown eyes, sharp and quick, set deep in his lined
face took in the room with the command of authority; he
was a man used to getting his way.

Cade, wary of Mack's expression, stepped forward. He
heard Tyler gasp and from the corner of his eye saw him run
the opposite way. The big man standing between Mack and
the Pinkerton agent ran after him.

With a clatter, Tyler tripped over the piano bench and
sprawled across the floor. The big man bore down on him.
Tyler screamed.

Cade crossed the room in three long strides and shoved
the man as he reached down for Tyler. "Keep your hands
off him!"

Several inches taller than Cade and outweighing him with
sheer bulk, he grabbed Cade's shirtfront with two meaty
hands. "This isn't your concern."

"No! Stop!" Tyler scrambled to his feet and wedged himself between the two men. He leaned around them and
addressed the older man waiting by the door. "Make him
stop! Make him!"

"Enough, Falk."

At the command, the big man released Cade's shirt and
moved back a step. Cade pulled Tyler behind him and
glared up at him. "Get the hell out of my place!"

Falk started forward again, but Tyler pulled at Cade's
arms. "Don't. He'll kill you. It's all right."

"Like hell it is."

Tyler pushed against Cade's chest. "Leave him alone," he
pleaded.

"Nobody comes in my place and—"

"He's my grandfather."

"What?" Cade caught the boy's shoulders.

Tyler's gaze fell to the floor. "He's my grandfather . . .
Devlin Blackwell."

The older man left his station by the door and stepped
farther into the room. "I've come to take my grandson
home."

Tyler broke for the door. Falk grabbed for him, but he
ducked and raced past. Cade started after him but Falk

blocked his path. The bat-winged door banged against the wall as Tyler ran out.

Fear cut through Cade as he saw Tyler dash into the street and heard the thunder of hoofs. "Tyler! Be careful!"

"It's lovely, my dear, simply lovely."

Allison smiled proudly and gazed around the club room, seeing it now through the eyes of her aunt. "Thank you. But I had lots of help, mostly from Jenna."

Lydia turned her smile on Jenna, standing beside the settee holding the tea service. "You're a wizard with needle and thread, my dear. Always have been. And say, where is that lovely little daughter of yours?"

"Holly is playing in the kitchen." Jenna gestured to the curtained doorway. "You should see what Allison has provided for the children in there."

"I intend to see every inch of the place, and get reacquainted with Brighton, as well." Lydia turned again to Allison. "Did I mention to you, dear, how much I've enjoyed those young missionaries staying at the ranch?"

Allison licked her lips nervously. "I'm glad."

Jenna placed the tray on the table. "Missionaries?"

"Yes, the young ladies traveling to Mexico. Allison met them here in town and offered them a few days rest before continuing their journey." Lydia smiled. "Perhaps you've met them, Jenna. Miss Phoebe is the headmistress."

A teacup slipped from Jenna's hand and clattered into the saucer. "Phoebe is at your—"

"Shall we have tea?" Allison slid her arm through Aunt Lydia's and swept her toward the settee.

"Certainly, I'll—"

The door burst open and Tyler ran into the room, breathless, his face flushed. His gaze raked the three women. "Aunt Lydia!"

"Tyler?"

Lydia fainted.

"Somebody better tell me what the hell is going on here." Cade braced his feet wide apart and glared at the other

men. Behind him, Vance held a shotgun on them from behind the bar.

"Take it easy." Mack put up his hand. He looked at Cade.
"He's Tyler's grandfather."

Devlin Blackwell, wealthy industrialist, owner of rail-
roads, shipping lines, and real estate, was Tyler's grandfather? Cade shook his head. "I don't believe it."

"It's true," Mack said. "I saw the papers in my office this
morning. He's got legal rights to the boy."

Cade's gaze bored into Blackwell. "Where have you been
for these last months, when I found him filthy, beaten, and
half starved on my doorstep?"

"Searching for him." Blackwell glared back at Cade. "I
was told he was dead."

Mack stepped forward. "Maybe you'd better explain the
whole thing."

Blackwell looked hard at Cade, then nodded. "Sheriff
Carson told me you took my grandson in and cared for him.
I suppose I owe you some sort of explanation."

The older man moved slowly across the room. "Tyler and
his parents—my beloved daughter, my only child, and that
bastard she married—recently returned from Europe. The
details of the accident aren't clear. Tyler is one of only a
handful of survivors. Those who didn't die in the initial
explosion froze to death in the water. The riverboat burned
to the water line not far from St. Louis, taking my daughter—"

Blackwell's voice broke. Manning spoke.

"Mr. Blackwell hired me to look for the boy. Initial reports indicated he'd gone down with the boat, like his parents, but I found witnesses who saw him rescued. I trailed
him all the way across the country. Nearly caught him in
Kansas City, but he outsmarted me."

"So he was running from you?" It was an accusation
more than a question. Blackwell shot him a scathing look.

"I finally found him here, thanks to the tip I got from
those two old miners here in your saloon," Manning said.

"Rupert and Otis? What do they know about this?"

"Nothing," Manning told him. "But they told me about
the piano-playing ghost in the church. From the way they

talked, I suspected it was the boy. I knew for sure when I saw him playing here for Miss Devaine."

Cade's stomach knotted. "That's how you found him? Because he played piano for me, in my saloon?"

Manning shrugged. "I knew the boy would have to play sometime, with a talent like he's got."

"It's not a talent! It's a gift!" Blackwell turned on Manning. "A God-given gift so rare it should be treasured, protected, and cherished."

"If you think it ought to be treasured and protected," Cade ground out, "then tell me why Tyler was running so hard to get away from you."

"His mind was poisoned!" Blackwell's hands clenched into fists at his sides. "That bastard poisoned him against me. He was nothing but trouble since the day he came into my life. First, wooing my precious Adrian with words of love and pipe dreams that could never come true. Foolish girl. I told her if she left with him she could never come back. He took her away from me, that no-talent, money-grubbing bastard. Took her away to Europe, eking out a living with his pathetic attempts at musical performances."

Overwhelmed, Blackwell sank into a chair. "And then Tyler came along. He was the one with the talent—the gift. A prodigy. He played his first concert at age five, performed before the crowned heads of Europe. People thronged to hear him play. He was the sensation of the Continent."

"They lived in Europe all these years?" Cade asked.

"That bastard kept him there, kept him away from me. I had to sit in the audience to see my own grandson." Anger showed in his face and he rose again. "That bastard lived off of him. He had no talent himself, so he lived off my grandson, parading him across Europe, showing him off, using him. That bastard is dead now. He took my Adrian with him. But Tyler is mine and I'll have him."

Anger welled inside Cade. "He's not a piece of property!"

"You're no better! You used him too!"

"That's a lie!"

"He played for you, didn't he? He kept this place—a saloon—in business." Blackwell's eyes narrowed. "Do you even know what you had in him? He speaks four languages, French and Italian fluently. He's been a guest at the most exclusive castles and chalets in Europe, had tea at Buckingham Palace. Did you think you were doing him a favor by keeping him here?"

"Tyler is here because he wants to be," Cade told him. "And I don't think that high and mighty lifestyle is anything to brag about. The boy couldn't even write his own name when he got here. He can't perform the simplest task. He's scared of his own shadow."

"Bastard. . . ." Blackwell shook his head slowly and dropped his gaze to the floor. "That bastard ruined my grandson."

Silence fell, then Manning spoke.

"Mr. Blackwell intends to be on tomorrow morning's train back to Boston. Let's go get the boy."

Cade's stomach knotted. He didn't want Tyler to leave, and he certainly didn't want to give him over to the likes of Devlin Blackwell. He turned to Mack.

"It's his right." Mack seemed no happier about the situation than Cade. "He's got court papers."

Falk started for the door. "I'll bring him."

"No. You'll scare him." Cade pulled at his neck. It galled him, but he had no other choice. Tyler legally belonged to Blackwell. "I'll get him."

"I'll come with you," Blackwell said.

Cade exchanged a harsh look with him and headed out the door. He crossed the street and knocked on the door of the ladies' club, Blackwell and Mack flanking him. Allison opened the door, her face pale.

"Cade, I'm so glad you came. Aunt Lydia has fainted and Tyler is beside himself with—"

She stopped, seeing the grim expressions of the men on her doorstep. She looked at Cade again. "What's wrong?"

He exhaled heavily. "This is Devlin Blackwell, Tyler's grandfather. He's come to take him home."

"But—" It took a moment for the name to register. Allison turned to the white-haired man. "Devlin Blackwell of Boston? Blackwell Industries?"

He tipped his hat. "Good morning, madame. If you would kindly let me have my grandson?"

Allison hesitated and gazed up at Cade. His expression told her he didn't like it either, but that there was no other choice. Allison opened the door and stepped back.

Jenna knelt beside the settee patting Aunt Lydia's hand as she held a damp handkerchief to her forehead. Tyler stood in the corner, shoulders hunched, his hands shoved deep into his pockets. Fear showed on his face when they walked into the room, and he started to run toward the kitchen.

"Don't move!" Cade pointed a finger at him, holding him in place. "Running is not going to solve this problem."

Tyler shook his head. "I don't want to go with him."

"You're my grandson," Blackwell told him. "You belong with me."

"No! You can't make me go!" He turned to Cade. "Please, don't let him take me."

"He has no say in the matter." Blackwell held himself rigid. "The courts have decided. You're coming with me."

"No!"

Lydia pushed away the handkerchief and rose. "Diplomatic and compassionate as always, I see, Devlin. Why not just throw a rope around the child and drag him back to Boston?"

Blackwell turned to her, seeing her now for the first time. He squinted and frowned as the faded memory blossomed in his mind. "Lydia? Lydia Allbright?"

"Yes, Devlin, it is I, another person whose love you tossed aside like yesterday's news." Lydia folded her hands in front of her and drew herself up straighter. "But you're not going to get away with it again. I'm not going to let you do to Tyler what you did to your own daughter."

Jenna sidled up next to Mack. "What's going on here?" she whispered.

"Blackwell is some wealthy Easterner, come to claim Tyler as his grandson."

She slid her hands around his arm. "But what's that got to do with Lydia Allbright?"

He shook his head. "Damned if I know."

Blackwell glared at Lydia. "What do you know about this?"

"I knew Adrian and James quite well, and Tyler since he was born. I visited them frequently in London and Europe."

Blackwell's gaze raked her. "But you were—"

"A nobody?" Lydia's chin went up a notch. "Yes, when you left I know you considered me no more than that. You drove your daughter away, Devlin, in much the same way."

"No! She left! I told her what would happen if she did, but she left anyway. And all because of that bastard!"

Lydia shook her head. "She was a young girl in love. You made her choose."

"And she chose that bastard over me!"

"There was nothing wrong with James. He was a fine young man who loved your daughter very much."

Sheer hatred shone in his eyes. "He was a bastard. He ruined her!"

"He loved her," Lydia said.

"He took her away from me. He used her. He poisoned her mind. She wanted to come back—I know she did—but he wouldn't let her. He let her die to save his own skin!"

Lydia blanched. "You don't know that."

"I know it for a fact. I've had a Pinkerton man on this since I heard of the accident. He talked to eyewitnesses." Anger, deep and vicious, grew in Blackwell's voice. "The riverboat was burning and he pulled her from the rescue raft. Pulled her out to save himself! Witnesses saw them struggling! Does that sound like love to you? He was a bastard, he used her, he took her away, he let her die—"

"No! Stop it! Don't say that!" Tyler pressed his palms to his ears, screaming. "It was my fault! She died because of me!"

Silence fell, all eyes turned toward Tyler. He was sickly white and trembling.

Cade took a step toward him, but Tyler backed up. The pain he'd sensed buried deep in the boy surfaced. Cade could feel the anguish he suffered.

"It was at night, late. I was supposed to be in bed but I sneaked out to listen to the music in the salon. There was a big loud boom. The whole boat shook. People started running and screaming and jumping into the water." Tyler's breath came in short puffs. He gazed at nothing, seeing nothing but the memories. "Fire was everywhere. I could hardly see for the smoke, but I found Mama and Papa. She had just gotten into a little raft alongside the boat. It was full. There was no room left.

"She got out." Tyler looked up at Cade, his breath now slow and labored. "Mama got out. She climbed back onto the riverboat. Papa grabbed me and dropped me over the side, onto the raft. I screamed for him not to put me in there. I screamed, but he wouldn't stop. They stood there together and the fire came up around them, and—"

Tyler ran to Cade, crying so hard that at first no sound came out. Then, deep raking sobs spilled the anguish that had been held inside for too long. Cade carried his slight, limp body to Allison's bedroom, away from everyone.

Stunned, they all stood together in the club room. No one spoke. Lydia collapsed onto the settee. Allison sat down beside her. Devlin walked to the window and stared into the street.

"I think I should go," Jenna whispered to Mack. "This is too personal. I shouldn't be here."

"Me either."

In the kitchen of Jenna's shop, Mack gave Holly a little hug and set her down. She planted a wet kiss in Mack's beard, giggled, and hurried into her room.

Mack grinned and wiped his beard with the back of his hand. "That's the first kiss I've had in a long time."

Jenna smiled with him. "Everyone in town seems to be taking this ultimatum seriously." Her smile faded. "Somehow, it doesn't seem very important just now."

Mack pulled off his hat. "No, it doesn't. Not after hearing what that boy went through. It makes you stop and take stock in your own life."

"Yes, it does."

"Will you marry me?"

Jenna blinked up at him. "What?"

He frowned and shifted his feet. "I didn't mean to just blurt it out like that, but, doggonit, Jenna, I love you. Do you feel something for me, or are you taken with Harry Finch?"

She shook her head. "No. I have no feelings for Mr. Finch that even vaguely resemble love."

His gaze caressed her, reluctant but hopeful. "Well?"

"I don't know. . . ."

"Is it because of my job? Because I'm the sheriff?"

Jenna nodded. "I lost one husband to violence. I don't think I could bear it if I lost another the same way."

"Ugly as it sounds, losing your husband the way you did just proves it could happen to anybody, anytime. Me being the sheriff only makes me better prepared to handle problems when they come up."

Jenna tried to smile. "Are you sure it's love you feel? Or is it just that Phoebe is gone? I was married for a long while, Mack. I understand how men are."

"No, ma'am," he said quickly. "This has got nothing to do with them whores." He placed his Stetson against his chest. "I love you, Jenna, and that's the simple truth."

She studied him for a long moment. "When this is all over, and the ladies and men of Brighton are back on more favorable terms, if you think you still want to marry me then, come back and we'll talk about it."

His shoulders sagged. "You won't give me your answer until then?"

She shook her head. "I can't be sure until then."

Cade poured the last of the coffee into his cup and set the pot back onto the stove. He looked at the thick, black brew and took a sip. He shuddered. It hadn't tasted the same since Vance left.

"Cade?"

He turned, peered under the dangling stockings that crisscrossed the kitchen, and saw Belle coming down the stairs. She wore her turquoise wrapper. The show would start soon. He'd hired the Rafferty boys to play until he could find a new piano man. They'd had no time to rehearse. He didn't know how it would go tonight, without Tyler there.

He held out his cup. "Want some coffee?"

Belle turned up her nose. "No thanks. I made that coffee myself and I know how awful it tastes."

Cade shrugged and set the cup aside.

"Have you heard anything from Tyler?"

"I was over at Lloyd's place a while ago—"

"The barbershop?" Belle eyed his beard. "What were you doing over there?"

Cade ran his hand over the nape of his neck. "Just getting a trim."

"That's the second trim you've had in a week," Belle pointed out. "Lloyd must be about to go under by now. You trying to keep him in business all by yourself?"

Cade felt guilty for the effect on Lloyd's business he'd caused when he'd committed the men of Brighton to stop shaving, so he'd had his hair cut twice when it wasn't necessary and paid with half eagles both times.

"He's getting by," Cade told her. "The place is still crowded with men discussing business."

"Gossiping, you mean."

Cade shrugged noncommittally. "Anyway, while I was over there Albert Wade came by and said he'd had supper in the hotel dining room while Blackwell and Tyler were there. Tyler threw a fit at the table, knocking dishes to the floor, throwing things, until that Falk bastard hauled him back upstairs, kicking and screaming the whole way."

"That poor boy." Belle pressed her lips together. "He's going to run off again, first chance he gets."

Anger knotted his chest. "Yes, I figure he will."

"He'll be no more than a prisoner, with that big galoot watching over his every movement. I guess he doesn't intend to make it easy for that grandfather of his." Belle sighed. "Maybe I'll go over and visit with him."

"I don't think Blackwell will allow it."

"Like we're not good enough for him." Belle squared her shoulders. "We're the ones who took care of him all this time."

Cade shrugged. "You can try to see him, but you'd better make it soon. I think Blackwell is leaving tomorrow."

Belle took a deep breath and looked up at him. "Cade,

honey, you and me have been together for a long time. We
need to talk."

Cade's stomach knotted. He knew this wasn't good news.

"I don't want you to think I'm kicking you while you're
down, with Billy gone, Vance moved out, and Tyler leaving.
Not to mention the problems you're having with those other
dancers." Belle drew in a deep breath. "But, Cade, I just
can't do this anymore. I'm too damn old."

"No, Belle—"

She held up her hands. "Yes, I am. I can't dance three
shows a night. I'm dragging everybody down."

"You don't have to dance every show, Belle. Do whatever
you feel up to."

She shook her head. "No, I'm not going to be here and
not pull my weight. I've got a chance to move on, and that's
what I'm going to do."

Cade rubbed his forehead. "Where are you going?"

"A cousin of mine has opened a dance studio in San
Francisco and she's willing to give me a job there." Belle
chuckled. "Them rich folks actually pay money to have their
kids learn to dance. Can you believe that?"

"Yes, Belle, I believe it. Are you sure this is what you
want to do?"

She nodded. "It is. You're not mad at me, are you?"

"No, Belle. I'll miss you, though." Cade frowned. "You're
not taking money from those Lace Ladies to leave town, are
you?"

"You know me better than that. I've got enough put away
to see me through. I'll be gone by the end of the week."
Belle gave him a hug and dashed back up the stairs.

Cade batted away two pairs of dangling stockings and
sank down at the kitchen table. He could hear the sounds of
the crowd in the barroom, a full house again, it seemed. But
it didn't matter. Not tonight. Money was rolling in hand
over fist and it seemed of little value to him lately. And
tonight, of no value at all.

He pushed himself to his feet and crossed the room when
a knock sounded at the back door. It swung open before he
got to it and Allison stepped inside. She wore the same pale
green skirt and blouse she'd had on this morning when he'd

left her club, her hair caught up in a simple chignon. She looked drained, as empty as he felt since the incident with Tyler, Lydia, and Blackwell.

Allison handed him a sheaf of paper. "I'd like to redeem this."

Cade unfolded it and saw that it was one of the handbills he'd passed out at her ladies' club dance announcing the performance of Vivian Devaine.

Her chin went up a bit. "I believe that entitles me to a free drink."

Cade shoved the handbill into his pocket and took a bottle of bourbon from the cupboard.

"Your place?" he asked.

Without a word, she nodded.

Cade took her hand and led her out the door.

Chapter
Twenty-Two

Light from the lantern at the center of the table reflected in the amber liquid as Cade set the glass of bourbon in front of her. Allison closed her fingers around it and looked up at him in the soft light.

"I don't know when I've had a worse day," Allison whispered. After the myriad of emotions she'd experienced today, all she felt now was numb.

Cade gripped the glass in his big hand and leaned a hip against the sideboard. "Me either."

"Have you seen Tyler since Devlin took him to the hotel?"

Cade studied the glass in his hand. "No."

"Aunt Lydia went over there."

"What's going on between those two, anyway?"

Allison rolled her eyes and pointed to the chair across from her. "You'd better sit down for this one."

The chair scraped across the wooden floor as Cade pulled it out and sat down. He reared back and folded his arms across his wide chest. "What makes me think this whole thing is more complicated than either of us suspected?"

"Aunt Lydia told me the whole story this afternoon after everyone left. She and Devlin were once lovers."

Cade's eyebrows bobbed and he sat forward. "What?"

"Aunt Lydia's father, Mitchell, was a prospector. Her

mother died when she was a child, so Lydia traveled with Mitchell. He made his fortune in gold in California, and then later in Virginia City's silver mines. That's where they met Devlin Blackwell. He was a young man then, not much older than Aunt Lydia. They fell in love, or at least that's what she thought. But when he'd made his fortune Devlin headed east. He wanted a fine well-bred woman for a wife, not a prospector's daughter."

Cade snorted his disgust. "So Lydia Allbright just wasn't good enough for him. Is that it?"

She nodded. "It seems that way. Devlin Blackwell eventually married into one of Boston's oldest and most prominent families. His wife died only a few years later."

"Lydia didn't let any grass grown under her feet, though. She was part of that society too."

"I suppose it was her way of proving to herself that she wasn't what Devlin thought she was." Allison sat back and smiled. "I have such fond memories of Aunt Lydia as far back as I can remember. She made a place for herself amid Eastern society and made many, many good friends."

"That's how she met you." Cade rolled the glass of bourbon between his palms. "And Tyler's parents too."

Allison drew in a deep breath. "Aunt Lydia didn't say specifically, but I imagine she contacted Adrian as a way to stay close to Devlin, though they never spoke over the years."

Cade's brows drew together. "So Tyler was running away from his grandpa, but he was also running toward Lydia. It wasn't chance that he showed up in Brighton. Lydia was the only other person Tyler knew in this country."

"He had no way of knowing he also had another relative here."

"Who?"

"Rebecca Warwick."

"Christ. . . ." Cade rolled his eyes. "Tyler said she looked like his mama. Where does she fit into all of this?"

Allison rested her arms on the table. "According to Aunt Lydia, Rebecca's mother was also vying for Devlin's attention when they were all in Virginia City."

"That bastard," Cade swore. "He got her pregnant and walked out on her?"

"I don't know that he was aware she was carrying his child. Aunt Lydia didn't say. But she felt bad for her bearing Rebecca all alone, and helped her out over the years with anonymous gifts. She got Rebecca the job as schoolteacher here in Brighton after her mother died."

"Sounds like your aunt has spent a lot of her time cleaning up after Devlin Blackwell."

A sad smile tugged at Allison's lips. "I think she always loved him—and still does."

Cade pushed his fingers through his hair. "Somehow I doubt Rebecca Warwick is going to be happy about meeting her father. Or does Blackwell intend to ignore her still?"

"Aunt Lydia told him about Rebecca this afternoon. I understand he's postponed his return to Boston."

"Well, at least he's trying."

They were silent for a long moment before Allison spoke again.

"I wish I could get the picture of Tyler's parents on that riverboat out of my head." She shuddered. "And think of how Tyler must feel about it."

"I guess that's what his nightmares were about, his pa putting him into the raft." He took a sip of the bourbon. "That's a heavy load for a kid to carry around."

"His parents must have loved him a great deal. They gave up their lives to save him." Allison swallowed the lump of emotion that rose in her throat. "They must have loved each other a great deal as well. They turned their backs on Devlin's money and security to be together. I suppose there's some comfort in them dying together. Don't you think?"

"Hell no." His gaze fell on her. "Comfort comes from living with the woman you love, not dying with her."

An intensity she'd sensed in him only once or twice before caressed her now. She rose from the chair and walked to the sideboard. She heard Cade rise, then felt his presence behind her.

"You didn't drink your bourbon."

She looked down at the glass in her hand and set it aside.

"I didn't want a drink. I suppose what I really wanted was some company."

Cade edged closer. She was trying so hard to be strong. His arms ached to hold her. "I'm glad you came to me."

"Are you?" Allison turned. She reached up and touched his bearded cheek with the tips of her fingers. "We always seem to be at cross-purposes."

He folded her hand in his and pressed it closer against him. She felt soft, fragile. "Your ladies' club, my saloon . . . they don't seem very important right now."

Heat radiated up her arm. His fingers were strong around her hand. "When I think of Tyler who lost his parents, and Aunt Lydia who loved Devlin for all those years, and Rebecca's mother who pined away for a man she could never have, and Devlin who lost his daughter's love—Oh, Cade, it's all so sad, so tragic. I don't want to end up that way."

"I don't either." Cade pressed his lips against the palm of her hand. "We don't have to."

Her flesh tingled, bringing her senses alive. Suddenly she became aware of his strength—every ounce of it—his overwhelming height, his heady masculine scent. Her knees weakened.

Cade stepped closer and slid his arms around her waist, drawing her against him. He touched his lips to hers. She tasted sweet, warm, and inviting. Instinct urged him to plunge inside her and claim her as his own. But he held back. She was no experienced whore. He didn't want one of those. He wanted Allison. And he wanted to make her want him in the same way.

His kiss grew more demanding. She arched her head back. He dug his hand into the hair at her nape, drawing her closer. She responded, her kiss as ardent as his.

He broke off their kiss, his breathing labored. Her lips were wet, her cheeks flushed. Her eyes—those deep brown eyes—mirrored the passion that burned in him. He loved her with all his heart. He wanted to show her that love.

Cade released her and stepped back. No, he couldn't. Not tonight when his love for her burned within him like a firestorm. She was too fine, too gentle. He didn't want to scare her away.

"I'd better go."

She didn't want him to leave, but she was afraid for him to stay. Cade had awakened something in her that she'd never felt before. She didn't understand it. But surely he did. And if he thought he ought to leave, then maybe he should.

Allison tried to smile, but couldn't. "Thanks for the drink. And the company."

Cade headed for the door. If he looked at those big brown eyes of hers another second, he'd never be able to pull himself away. He left without a word.

Allison closed the door and turned the key in the lock. Silence closed in around her. A chill settled over the room. It seemed vastly empty without Cade.

She dragged herself to the bedroom and lit the lantern at her bedside. Too much had happened today. She'd thought that coming to Brighton would be an escape from her problems, but instead she'd encountered more—and they were far worse than anything she'd faced in New York.

Allison kicked off her slippers and removed her skirt and blouse. New York. She trembled at the thought. Now that she was up and around, Aunt Lydia was making plans to travel with her on her return to the city. But Allison wasn't ready to leave.

Would she ever be? She took off her petticoats, bustle, and corset and sat down on the edge of the bed. There were things in New York she didn't want to face. Things, and people. Allison cringed. Well, maybe not people, she admitted to herself. One person. She rolled down her stockings, tucked them in the top drawer of her bureau, and pulled out her night rail.

Allison plucked the pins from her hair and let it fall loose about her shoulders. Through the window she heard the Rafferty boys strike up "Turkey in the Straw." It was a far cry from the beautiful music Tyler had coaxed from the Steinway, even when he played the simple songs the saloon patrons demanded. He'd become a part of her life here in Brighton. She would miss him.

Maybe she could think of a way to keep him here. Allison ran the hairbrush through her dark locks and paced the floor. If only a way could be found to keep Tyler here. And if she could reopen the Carriage Works, the saloons could close. Of course, she'd have to get Jenna to marry Mack, and find employment for Satch Wilkens, since he'd refused to accept passage back East from the ladies' club. Maybe she could make Devlin accept Aunt Lydia—

She plopped down on the bed, her head spinning. So much needed to be done. Tears threatened. She cared deeply for the people and problems in Brighton. She couldn't just walk away.

A knock sounded at the back door and Allison grabbed her wrapper, grateful for the distraction. It was Jenna, she knew. She'd been by earlier, after Aunt Lydia left, and told her that Mack had proposed. Allison knew she'd return tonight after Holly was settled into bed and ask her to come over and discuss it further.

Allison sniffed, threw her wrapper on over her chemise and pantalettes, and crossed the kitchen tying the sash around her waist. She pulled the door open.

Cade stood on the doorstep. Her heart rose in her throat.

The breath went out of him. God, she was the most beautiful sight he'd ever seen. Cade swallowed hard.

She touched her tongue to her lips. "Is something wrong?"

He pushed his fingers through the hair at his temple. "Yes."

He exuded an aura that drew her nearer, bound her to him. Allison felt it. She stepped back from the door. "Come in."

He stood there a moment before entering the kitchen, both sorry and glad that he'd come back. Cade cleared his throat. "It's Tyler," he said. "I realized just now at the saloon that I don't want him to leave, and that got me to thinking."

"About what?"

"You."

He stepped closer. Heat radiated from him. It bathed her as if it were a living thing, touching her like nothing she'd ever experienced before.

"I don't want to lose you either." Cade kicked the door shut. "I'm not going to."

Cade took her in his arms and pulled her against him, her soft breasts molding to the hardness of his chest. He moaned and covered her lips with his.

Problems that seemed overwhelming only moments ago vaporized under the warmth and intensity of Cade's passion. She loved him. She wanted him. And nothing else mattered.

Allison rose to her tiptoes, pressing more intimately against him. She coiled her hands into his hair and parted her lips to receive his kiss.

Cade lifted her into his arms and carried her into the bedroom. Lantern light from the bedside table cast faint shadows as Cade laid her on the quilt and sat down on the edge of the bed beside her. He held her tight against him, his lips seeking the soft flesh of her neck. She moaned softly and he covered her lips with his own, driven by the heat of an ageless, internal fire.

He pulled the sash of her wrapper free and slid his hand inside. His fingers brushed the fabric of her chemise. Delicate female underthings. Cade's stomach quivered. Allison's delicate underthings.

He pressed his hand deeper and cupped the mound of her breast. The exquisite softness caused him to moan deep in his chest. He caressed her carefully and circled the crest with his thumb, causing it to peak at his touch. Allison gasped.

His body burned for her, but he pulled away and broke off their kiss. Cade sat up, his gaze searching her face in the dim light.

"We can stop"—his breath was deep and labored—"if that's what you want."

Cade curled his fist into the pillow beneath her head and gazed down at her. She was beautiful and he loved her with all his heart. If she wanted to stop, he would, though he didn't know how he'd find the strength.

He'd kissed her as no man had ever done. Lying as she was now, he'd touched her as no man had ever dared. Yet she felt no shame, no apprehension. Only love, deep and overwhelming. Allison knew there was no other place she should possibly be than with this man.

She ran her finger down the front of his shirt, feeling the hardness of his chest and the heat that rose from him.

"I don't want to stop," she whispered. "Ever."

Cade wrapped her in his arms and covered her mouth with a deep kiss. She responded, urging him on.

He pressed her back against the pillow and stood beside the bed. Quickly he pulled off his boots and socks, and tossed aside his vest and shirt.

Allison rose on her knees at the edge of the bed and wrapped her arms around him. She stretched up and met his lips.

Cade groaned and eased her to the bed. He blew out the lantern, pulled off his trousers and long johns, and stretched out beside her. He showered kisses across her face and down the sweet recesses of her throat as he worked the buttons of her chemise open and laid back the fabric. She gasped as he closed his hand over the soft mound of her breasts, kneading it gently, lovingly. He dipped his mouth to suckle her. Allison groaned and arched her back, plowing her hands through his hair, holding him close.

Cade pushed the chemise from her shoulders and flung the garment across the room. He pulled loose the draw-string of her pantalettes and pushed them down her hips, tossing them aside. Her silky legs twined intimately with his as he pressed his palm against her stomach. His lips claimed her once more as he inched lower, his fingers seeking and finding the heart of her femininity.

Need and desire grew within her as passion blossomed at his touch. Allison's head spun. She had no will of her own. She was his. And that was all she wanted.

The sweetness of her body was both pleasure and torture. Cade rose above her and eased between her thighs, unable to wait another second. He locked his arms around her and touched himself against her. Cade curled his fists into the pillow beneath her head, nearly overcome by desire. He felt her grow tense beneath him.

Gently he claimed her mouth once more, plying her lips

with kisses as he moved slowly within her. She responded, matching his movements until urgency claimed them both. He thrust deeper into her, lifting her to new heights of passion. Allison clung to him, arching her hips up to meet his as great waves of pleasure claimed her over and over.

When he could wait no longer, assured of her pleasure, Cade buried his face in the sweet recess of her neck and drove himself into her time and again, pouring out his love and passion, claiming her for his own.

Golden shafts of early morning light slanted across the floor, rousing Allison from a deep sleep. She shifted on the bed and opened her eyes. Cade lay on his side, facing her. His beard looked dark against her white linen pillow, his features relaxed as he slept. She'd never noticed before how long his lashes were, or the tiny crinkles at the corner of his eyes. But, she reminded herself, she'd never been this close to him before.

She'd never been in bed with him either. Allison flushed as she recalled their night together. The things he'd done— the things she'd done. She expected she'd feel embarrassed, but didn't.

She studied him a moment longer, seeing him in the daylight. His arms were big and muscular; she remembered them around her during the night. She recalled, too, the feel of his hairy chest pressed against her. She looked at it now and saw the line of hair that arrowed down the center of his taut belly and disappeared below the sheet that was drawn up to his waist.

Her gaze lingered on the spot. Hidden from view was another part of him—an important part—she'd never seen before. Allison glanced up at his face. His eyes were still closed. She heard the steady rhythm of his breathing as he slept. Carefully she lifted the sheet and peeked under.

"Everything to your satisfaction?"

Allison gasped and dropped the sheet. Her cheeks burned as she saw his blue eyes gazing down at her. She covered her face with her hands. "I thought you were asleep."

He chuckled and pried her hands from her cheeks. "I'm

just happy I didn't wake to find you beating me with your parasol or broom, or chasing after me with your gun."

Her chin went up a bit. "You took my gun."

He planted a warm kiss on the back of her hand. "I'm glad now I did."

Allison relaxed. "I could never shoot you. Not on purpose, that is."

"That's a relief." He smiled gently. "Especially now."

A pink blush colored her cheeks and she drew the sheet up tighter against her breasts. She frowned. "I don't remember Mother mentioning it would be so pleasant."

Cade chuckled. With her strong emotions, he knew she'd be a spitfire, if it was all ever channeled in one direction.

"Is it that pleasant every time?"

She looked up at him with those big brown eyes and Cade's heart shuddered. He looped his arm around her waist and drew her nearer. "Oh, yes. I'll see to it."

Cade covered her lips with his and closed his eyes, moaning softly at her delightful taste. An odd movement at the foot of the bed startled him. He pulled away just as a warm, wet tongue slid across his cheek.

"What the hell. . . ."

Cade opened his eyes to see Winchester snuggled between them, his tiny tongue panting excitedly.

"Jesus. . . ." Cade's head fell back on the pillow.

"Good morning, Winchester." Allison pushed herself up on one elbow and patted his fuzzy head. "He always sleeps with me."

"Well, not anymore." Cade threw back the cover and scooped the puppy off the bed. He crossed the room, tossed him into the kitchen, and closed the door firmly behind him.

Allison lay back on the pillow, watching Cade as he approached the bed. Her stomach quivered. He was all hard lines and rippling muscle, strength and raw power countered by the exquisite gentleness he'd shown her during the night.

Cade stopped beside the bed and touched the sheet that covered her. Allison knew what he wanted. She smiled and he pulled the covers away. The warmth of his gaze tingled against her bare skin. She reached out for him.

He covered her body with his. She fit perfectly, her curves molding to his hard, muscular lines. Passion grew between them once more. Allison gave herself willingly to him, for in his arms was where she knew she belonged. He settled himself deep inside her, bringing them together to the height of desire, their union leaving them breathless and spent.

Later, with Allison snuggled close against him, Cade lay staring at the morning light sifting in around the window shade. The town would be stirring soon. Shops would open. People would crowd the streets. And someone would surely see him leaving. He couldn't put Allison through the scandal.

He tucked her head under his chin and sniffed the sweet fragrance of her hair. Every morning, for the rest of his life, he wanted to wake to that scent, he knew. He wanted to sit across the breakfast table from her, and raise a half-dozen children with her. He wanted to sit beside her on the front porch in rockers and wait for their grandchildren to come to visit.

He felt Allison shift, moving against him more intimately. He thought she wanted those same things in her future, though neither of them had said the words. It hadn't seemed necessary. Life seemed to suddenly open up for him, as if anything and everything were possible.

Cade smiled and closed his eyes, contented. But Tyler came into his mind. The boy had no family. They'd all been so busy fighting and bickering that their lives had been wasted. Families were more important than anything, Cade suddenly realized, and the tragedy of Tyler's loss seemed all the more unbearable. Not simply the deaths of his parents, but all the wasted years, as well.

Cade pushed himself up on one elbow and kissed Allison's forehead. "I have to go."

She ran her hand across his chest and grinned. "Granted, I'm not very experienced yet, but I feel sure I can give you a reason to stay."

"You've already given me several." He captured her hand

and pressed a kiss against her palm. "But folks will be on the streets soon. I don't want anyone to see me leaving."

Allison sank back against the pillow. "I suppose it would look bad, the head of the ladies' club being the first one to break the celibacy vow."

Cade pulled the quilt over her and dressed quickly, finding his clothing scattered across the room. He was anxious to go. He had things to take care of.

He dropped a kiss on her forehead and stroked her dark hair for a moment. "Good-bye."

An emptiness clutched her heart as she gazed up at him. She didn't want him to go, but knew he had to. Allison smiled and touched his cheek, and he was gone.

Relieved to find no one in the back alley, Cade closed the door behind him and headed for the Pleasure Palace. He had a lot to do today. He was anxious to begin. For the first time in a very long while, he knew exactly what needed to be done. And nothing would stop him.

Vance stood at the cookstove in the kitchen of the Pleasure Palace pouring himself a cup of coffee. He eyed Cade sharply as he bounded in the back door.

"Where the hell have you been? Missing all last night, without a word. We didn't know what had happened to you."

Cade rubbed his hands together briskly. "Nothing happened. I'm fine."

Vance's eyes narrowed. "You were with somebody, weren't you? A woman."

Was it that obvious? Cade realized then that he was smiling, for no apparent reason.

"Who was it? Where'd you find her?" Vance asked.

Cade pulled on his beard. "Do me a favor, will you? Round up all the saloon owners. I want to have a meeting with them."

"A meeting?" Vance's brows bobbed. "What's going on, Cade?"

Cade reached for a cup from the sideboard. "Just do it, will you?"

Vance shrugged. "All right, I guess. I'll have them over here quick as a wink."

"No." Cade poured coffee into his cup. "Have them meet me over at Lloyd's place."

"The barbershop? Sweet Jesus. . . ." Vance ran out the door.

By the time Cade finished his coffee and headed down the boardwalk toward Lloyd's Barbershop, word had already spread. Men gathered around, until a good-sized crowd had formed. And all of them anxious to know what was up.

"Are you giving in, Cade?"

"You're not closing the Pleasure Palace for good, are you?"

"Them Lace Ladies are nothing but troublemakers—you showed them who was running this town already."

Cade ignored the men, their questions, and the curious looks he received from shopkeepers and pedestrians until he reached the barbershop. Lloyd stood outside with Vance and the other saloon owners. Cade sprang to the top step and looked out over the gathering of bearded men. Mack Carson joined them and stood off to the side, his arms folded across his chest.

Cade raised his hands to silence the gathering. "I appreciate you boys coming over. I wanted you to hear the news directly from me. I've decided to close the Pleasure Palace on Sundays from now on."

Drew Cabbot, owner of the Steer's Horn, broke from the crowd. "You're giving in, Cade? You're letting those Lace Ladies get their way?"

"Damn right." Cade nodded quickly.

"But why?" Hank Minor waved his hands wildly. "Why? We can hold out just as long as they can!"

A disagreeable mutter rose from the crowd.

Cade shook his head. "Yeah, I guess we could. But who wants to?"

A cheer went up from the men.

"I decided that life's too short to spend it arguing and fighting, having the whole town in an uproar. I'm not saying the Lace Ladies are right in what they did, but fact is, none of us will let our women walk the streets alone. I think it's time we made some changes. It's time we get our families together again and stop all this bickering." Cade looked out over the crowd at the other saloon owners. "Who's with me on this?"

The men shuffled and mumbled. Finally, Drew Cabbot scratched his beard. "To tell you the truth, I've about lost my sense of humor over this whole thing. I'm closing down the Steer's Horn on Sundays too."

Jack Short adjusted his spectacles and nodded. "Count on the Crystal Pistol closing too, Cade."

"Do you think you can get Miss Tremaine to bring back Phoebe and her girls soon?" Hank asked.

Cade nodded. "I'll see to it they're back here today."

A roar rose from the crowd of men.

Mack shouldered his way through the gathering, pushing and shoving a path to the steps. He pointed a finger at Cade. "You're closing on Sunday. For sure. Right?"

"Yep. Just like I said."

Mack whirled and grabbed Drew by the shirtfront. "You meant what you said, didn't you?"

Stunned, Drew nodded quickly. "Yes, sir, Sheriff, I meant every word."

Buck Mock ducked behind Lloyd when Mack turned on him. He threw up both hands. "I'm closing the Suds Bucket. I swear."

Mack eyed Jack. "You too?"

"Sure, Mack, just like I said."

"Hot damn. . . ." Mack pushed his way out of the crowd and ran down the street.

Cade stroked his bearded chin and turned to Lloyd. "And now, I'll be needing a shave."

"A shave?" Lloyd blinked up at him.

The gathering of men rumbled with questions.

"A shave? Already?"

"Cade, did you find you a woman last night?"

"By God, I think he did."

"Who was it?"

Cade grinned and walked inside the barbershop.

At three o'clock that afternoon Allison stood in the church holding Holly's hand and choking back tears as

Jenna promised before God to be Mack's lawfully wedded wife. Looking as handsome as the groom—both freshly shaved—Cade passed the wedding band to Mack and gave Allison a wink as Reverend Kent pronounced them man and wife. She and Cade were the only two friends invited to the rushed ceremony. Jenna had begged for time to prepare, but Mack had been adamant. He loved her, he was marrying her immediately, and he didn't care if she showed up at the ceremony in her apron.

Allison dabbed at her eyes as they left the church. She gave Jenna a hug while Mack settled up with the reverend.

"Don't worry about Holly. She'll be fine. Carson isn't that far away. You can be back here in no time, if there's an emergency."

Jenna beamed, radiant as a bride should be. "I'm not worried. I know she'll be in good hands. You'll watch over the shop, won't you?"

"Of course," Allison assured her.

"My next shipment of doll dresses isn't scheduled to go out for three more weeks, but if any of the ladies have problems—"

Allison took Jenna's hands and gave them a squeeze. "I'll take care of everything. Don't worry."

Jenna knelt and gave Holly a hug. "You be a good girl."

Mack picked up the child. "We'll be back before you know it. And we'll even bring you a surprise."

Holly giggled and planted a wet kiss on Mack's cheek. He sat her down, gave Allison a hug, and shook Cade's hand.

"Don't worry about how things are going here in town," Cade said. "Beau will do all right as deputy until you get back."

"Yeah," Mack agreed. "I expect things to be pretty quiet around here for a few days, people staying home. And, of course, Phoebe's back."

Cade gave Jenna a peck on the cheek and wished them both well.

Allison held Holly's tiny hand and waved as Jenna and Mack climbed into the buggy. Cade sidled up next to her and slid his hand around her waist. She smiled dreamily as the buggy headed toward the train depot. "Wasn't that a beautiful ceremony?"

Cade nodded. "I think they've got a lot of happy years ahead of them."

"Thanks to you." Allison looked up at him. "If you hadn't closed your saloon, they wouldn't have gotten married."

"I don't know about that." Cade shrugged modestly. "I believe they would have gotten together sooner or later."

Allison smiled. "But sooner is better."

"I can't disagree with that. And speaking of sooner, all your Lace Ladies know about the closings, don't they? I mean, this thing is over for good. Right?"

"Yes. Phoebe and her employees are back on the job."

"I heard." Cade drew her closer. "I've got no desire to see Phoebe today, or ever again."

Allison smiled and dipped her lashes coyly. "I'm glad."

"In fact," Cade began, "I was thinking maybe later on—"

"I'm keeping Holly at my place until Jenna gets back."

Cade's smile fell. "You are?"

"I couldn't say no." Nor could she tell him that she too felt disappointed that he wouldn't be able to come over. Even with the rushed wedding plans, Allison had thought of little else all day but her night spent with Cade.

Cade gazed down at the tiny child, clutching her doll and holding Allison's hand. He pushed his fingers through his hair. "Well, then, how about if the three of us have supper together over at the hotel?"

"I'd like that," Allison said as Holly hopped up and down.

Cade secured Aunt Mattie under one arm and took Holly's other hand and headed for the Brighton Hotel. They'd just stepped up onto the boardwalk when a second-floor window shattered and a washbowl sailed through the air and broke into pieces in the middle of the street. A second later a matching pitcher followed, then a coat rack.

"What the hell?" Cade pressed Allison and Holly against the hotel, away from the flying debris and splintering glass. "You two stay here, I'm going to find out—"

"It's Tyler." Allison drew in a deep breath. "I saw Esther

Wade this afternoon. She said he's completely destroyed two rooms already. His grandfather won't even bring him down to the dining room anymore because he makes such a scene."

Cade's brows creased. "What the devil has gotten into that boy?"

"He's expressing his unhappiness with the situation." Allison pressed her lips together. "Esther says Devlin has Falk standing over him every second. What else can he do?"

A bed pillow flew through the window, feathers drifting to the ground like snowflakes.

Cade's jaws tightened. "Regardless of the situation, the boy's got no right to tear up the place. I'm going to put a stop to this."

Allison laid a hand on Cade's arms. "Do you really think you should interfere?"

Cade stared up at the window for a long moment, then turned away. "No. I guess I shouldn't."

"How about if we eat at the Red Eye?" Allison suggested.

Cade nodded. He turned to cross the street when a buggy loaded with trunks pulled up in front of the hotel. On board sat a man wearing a bowler and a dapper suit. An expensive suit, Cade realized. An Eastern suit. A feeling of foreboding fell over him. The man glanced at Allison, then openly stared. Cade's hand coiled into a fist.

"Allison?"

Cade's stomach clinched. Beside him he heard Allison gasp. Color drained from her cheeks.

Annoyed now, the man heaved a heavy sigh and carefully climbed from the buggy. "So, Allison, at last I find you. I must say I find this entire escapade of yours quite tiring, but nonetheless here I am. Now, could we please get your things so we can go back to civilization?"

Confused and now angry, Cade stepped forward. "Who the hell are you?"

"Nigel Brisbane." The man gave Cade a critical stare. "Miss Tremaine's fiancé."

Chapter
Twenty-Three

Two days had passed with no word. Nothing. No one had seen her. No one had heard from her.

Cade sat back in his chair and flipped the ledger closed. He was only kidding himself to think he could concentrate on his bookkeeping this morning.

Slowly he rose from behind his desk and walked to the window. He'd spent a good part of the last two days staring across the street at the headquarters of the Ladies for the Advancement of Cultural Events, and the big CLOSED sign on the door. It burned into his memory as had the picture of Allison on the buggy seat with Holly on her lap, riding out of town at Nigel's side two nights ago.

At first he'd been too stunned to question her. Engaged? To some Eastern dandy? While she made love to *him*?

Cade rested one arm against the windowsill and gazed down at the morning traffic on Main Street. He'd been too hurt to do anything after that. Brisbane had shown up and Allison had hightailed it out to her aunt's place with him, no explanation, no nothing. Now, after two days of brooding, Cade was just plain mad.

Cade paused by his desk long enough to pluck a letter from the drawer and went down to the kitchen. Belle sat at the table soaking her feet in a tub of hot water. "Where are you going?" she asked.

"I'm going where I should have gone two days ago."
Cade strapped his gun belt around his hips.

Belle struck the tabletop with her fist. "Well, good for
you."

"Do me a favor, will you?" Cade passed the letter to her.
"This needs to get to the express office today. See to it
personally, will you?"

Belle looked at the address printed on the envelope. Her
eyes widened. "Are you sure about this?"

He nodded. "I wrote it two days ago, but let it keep for a
while. I read it again this morning. I'm sure."

Belle smiled and tucked the letter into the bodice of her
wrapper. "I'm real happy to see this, Cade."

Cade pulled his Stetson low on his forehead and left the
kitchen.

The ride to Lydia Allbright's ranch was longer than he
remembered. Cade tied the stallion at the hitching rail and
bounded up the steps and across the porch. He banged on
the front door with his fist.

After a long moment, Georgia opened the door. "Oh,
my."

"I've come to see Allison."

"Oh, my. . . ." Georgia wrung her apron in her hands
and glanced nervously behind her. "Well. . . ."

Cade's stomach clenched. "She's still here, isn't she?"

"Well, yes. Oh, dear. . . ." Georgia gave herself a little
shake and lowered her voice. "It's high time you got here, if
you don't mind me saying so. Come in, come in."

Cade stepped into the foyer and passed his Stetson to
Georgia. "Where is she?"

"She's not in right now."

He reached for his hat again. "Where did she go? I've got
to see her now."

Devlin Blackwell stepped into the foyer from the hallway.
He eyed Cade sharply. "I thought I heard voices."

"I'm here to see Allison," Cade told him.

From high above them on the second floor a loud thud
sounded, followed by breaking glass. Cade's stomach
churned. The boy was still at it, it seemed. Cade's initial
reaction was to climb the steps and put a stop to this imme-

diately. But Devlin had made it very clear Tyler wasn't any of his business anymore.

Devlin drew in a deep breath. "Come into the study. There's something I need to discuss with you."

Cade didn't move. "Like I said, my business here is with Allison."

Devlin studied him for a moment, then softened his tone. "I would appreciate it if you could spare a few minutes of your time."

The man looked as if he'd aged considerably in the few days since he'd come to the Pleasure Palace to claim Tyler. Things weren't going well, obviously. While Cade would rather get to Allison immediately, he decided it wouldn't hurt him to give Devlin the time he'd requested.

Cade nodded and followed the older man down the hall to the study. Devlin settled into one of the leather wing-backed chairs in front of the fireplace and gestured for Cade to take the other.

"I thought you were still at the hotel in town," Cade said as he sat down.

Devlin uttered a short laugh. "It's the first place I've been thrown out of since I was nineteen years old."

"Tyler made a mess of the hotel, I heard."

"It would have been cheaper if I had bought the place outright." Devlin rolled his eyes toward the ceiling and the commotion going on in the room over his head. "The boy is consistent, I'll say that for him. And determined. Thank God, Lydia is a patient woman."

Cade shook his head. "I wouldn't have been patient this long."

"Yes, I suspected that." Devlin waved his hand, dismissing the subject. "There's a business matter I'd like to discuss with you."

Surprised, Cade's brows went up. "What sort of business?"

Devlin planted his elbows on the armrests and steepled his fingers. "You're Clint Jessup's boy."

Hearing his father's name struck Cade like a physical blow, but he held his composure. Business discussions were

much like poker games, a grimace or smile could tip a hand,
at the cost of a very large profitable pot.

"New Haven Boiler Company," Devlin went on. "Strong,
solid company, sound ethics, reliable products. You ran that
company with your father, then handled it alone while he
was ill."

"Sounds like you've done some checking." Cade tilted his
head. "Why?"

"After my man found Tyler here, I wanted to know what
sort of people he was with. I had to decide if he should be
taken immediately, or if it could wait until I arrived."

Devlin rose from his chair and walked to the window, his
gait slow and measured. He gazed out at the sprawling prairie. "I'm opening a business here in Brighton. I need someone to run it. I want that someone to be you."

Cade shifted in the chair. Devlin Blackwell commanded a
great deal of power and wealth. Being asked to work for
him was flattering, to say the least.

"What sort of business?"

"Trains." Devlin continued to gaze out the window.
"They're crisscrossing this nation like spiderwebs, growing
thicker each day. But replacement components for them
west of the Mississippi are rare. I'm going to convert the
Carriage Works."

Cade blew out a slow breath. "That's a tall order. And an
expensive one. You're going to need—"

"I know what it will take." Devlin turned to Cade, his
eyes narrow. "That's why I want you in charge of it."

Flattered and stunned, Cade sat back in the chair, considering the offer. No doubt, it would be a challenge—a big
one. But the idea took hold. Thoughts, possibilities, and
contingencies flashed through his head. The prospect excited him, as nothing had since he left Connecticut.

"It could be done," Cade said slowly. "But I've got my
own business going. I'm not looking to work for anyone
else."

"The offer is for a partnership."

Cade was taken aback momentarily. "Fifty-fifty."

Devlin shook his head and walked slowly back to his
chair. "No. Can't do it. The idea isn't mine. I was ap-

proached by someone else who is in on it too. The best I can offer is a three-way split."

"Who's the other partner?" Cade wanted to know who he'd be involved with before he agreed to anything.

Devlin shrugged. "An investor from back East. But don't worry. This partner isn't interested in a hands-on involvement. It will be yours to run."

Cade nodded. "It sounds promising. But I'll have to see everything in writing first."

"Of course. My lawyers are already working on it."

The man had built an empire and wasn't the type to start a venture on a whim. Still, Cade had to know if he was serious about seeing the project through. "Why are you doing this?"

Devlin's shoulders sagged and he dropped his hand onto the back of the leather chair to steady himself. "The town is floundering. The business your saloon brought to it is good, but it can't continue without a strong economic base."

"And why do you care about the future of Brighton?"

Devlin slumped down into the chair. "Because I'm leaving my grandson here. I want you to take him."

Cade's heart lurched and he sat up straighter. "Me?"

"I've done a great deal of checking. I know who you are and what you are. I know how you took care of him. You're what he needs now."

"He's your only grandson, your flesh and blood. I can't believe you're just walking away."

Devlin rubbed his forehead wearily. "I've made a mess of a good portion of my life and managed to run off most everyone who cared for me. I don't want to make that mistake with Tyler. Even now, he wants nothing to do with me."

"He needs time to get to know you," Cade pointed out.

Devlin shook his head. "No. That's not all of it. I've done a lot of thinking since I arrived in Brighton and I see things now for what they are. I drove my daughter away. I thought I knew what was best for her. I made her choose. And look what I did to Lydia. She's a fine caring woman. I turned my back on her years ago, thinking I could do better. I didn't. Now I'm all alone."

"I don't think she's given up on you."

"It's a second chance I don't deserve." Devlin gazed at the floor. "Yesterday I went to see Rebecca Warwick. I told her I'd just found out I was her father. She wants nothing to do with me."

"Learning the news must have come as a shock to her. She'll come around."

"No." Devlin looked at Cade, a lifetime of regret etched in the aged lines of his face. "I have no idea who her mother was. I don't even remember the woman."

Silence hung heavy in the room for several long moments, with only the sounds of breaking glass from overhead to keep them company.

Devlin waved his hand toward the ceiling. "I can't handle the boy. I'm not a young man anymore. I don't want to make the same mistakes and drive away my only grandson. He needs you."

Cade rose. "All right. I'll take Tyler. To tell you the truth, I care a lot for him. I didn't like the idea of you taking him away."

Devlin nodded solemnly.

"But I'll raise him my way, with no interference."

"I'll want to see him. Hopefully, I can be part of his life, one day."

"Fair enough." Cade nodded. "I won't have you changing your mind a few months down the road and wanting him back. It's not fair to him. I want legal custody."

He considered it for a moment, then nodded. "I'll have the papers drawn up."

Cade offered his hand. "I'll take good care of him."

Slowly Devlin rose and accepted his hand. "I know you will. Do you want to go up and tell him now?"

"I'd like to see Allison first. She's still here, isn't she?"

Devlin gestured toward the window. "I saw her walking toward the creek a few minutes ago."

Cade gazed out the window. "Was she alone?"

Devlin managed a small smile. "Yes."

Allison sensed his presence a moment before she heard the footsteps in the grass behind her. Shaded by the willows and cottonwoods, she felt a flush of heat as warm as the afternoon sun overhead. A little creek rushed past, shallow and crystal clear, over its bed of rocks, wearing them smooth and round with age-old tenacity. Allison crossed her arms under her breasts, wishing for a course as steady as the stream's.

She turned and Cade stood on the rise, the roof of the ranch house visible behind him. He looked handsome and determined. Her stomach tingled.

He walked forward and stopped in front of her, his face mirroring a thousand questions.

"Where is Brisbane?"

Allison tucked a stray lock of hair behind her ear. "He's gone. I sent him back to New York yesterday."

"Why?"

"I couldn't go through with it, not after—" Allison turned away.

He stepped closer. "Not after, what?"

Emotion swelled inside her, relieved to finally be able to say it aloud, to someone who would understand. She turned to face Cade again.

"You know what it's like. You left the East for the same reason. I couldn't be a decoration in a man's life. Before, when I was there, I thought I could go through with it, that I would be able to do it. But after all that's happened here in Brighton, I knew I would never be the kind of wife Nigel and everyone else expected me to be."

"The wedding is off?"

"Yes." Allison bit down on her lower lip. "And I know now I'll never marry."

His brows furrowed. "Why not?"

"Because of you!" Allison flung out both hands. "I'm going to have to go to work at Phoebe's place because of you!"

"Me!" Cade planted his fists on his waist. "What the hell did I do?"

"I'll never make a good wife because I can't simply stand around and say 'yes' and 'no,' and 'whatever you want, dear.' I can't live that way. You know I can't."

"Well, yeah, that's true," Cade conceded. "But what does that have to do with you working at Phoebe's?"

"Because after you and I—After we . . ."

Cade nodded. "Yes, I know. Go on."

Allison dipped her lashes and wrung her hands together. "I liked it. And if I don't have a husband, what else can I do?"

Cade's chest swelled. He'd known the first moment he laid eyes on her she would be a handful. He hadn't been wrong.

He touched his finger to her chin and raised her face. "May I offer my services?"

Allison felt her cheeks pinken. She pushed his hand aside and turned away.

"As your husband."

She gasped. "My what?"

"Goddamnit, Allison, you've driven me crazy since the first time I saw you. I want to marry you."

Her breath came in short puffs as she gazed up at him. "But you know how I am. No man would want a wife as outspoken and headstrong as I am. Why do you want to marry me?"

He grinned. "Because I love you."

Allison rose on her tiptoes and threw her arms around his neck. "Oh, Cade, I love you too."

He wrapped her with his big arms, holding her close. Then he kissed her, slow and steady, savoring the taste and feel of her.

"So, you'll marry me?"

She smiled up at him. "Yes."

He took both her hands in his. "You should know that Blackwell asked me to take Tyler."

"That's wonderful. We'll be much better for him than his grandfather." Allison pursed her lips. "You should know that Rebecca came by yesterday. She's leaving Brighton. She recommended me to take her place at the school. I told her I would."

"Good," Cade said.

"I'd like to keep the ladies' club too."

He nodded and grinned rakishly. "Just don't spread your-self too thin. I intend to occupy some of your time too."

She smiled. "You'll be plenty busy on your own."

"That's right. Blackwell is opening a factory here in Brighton. We'll be partners."

"Partners?" Allison's eyes widened.

"He wants to be near Tyler."

Allison grinned. "I think he wants to be near Aunt Lydia, as well."

Cade slid his arms around her waist and pulled her against his chest. He muzzled his lips on her neck. "How about you and I go see Preacher Kent tomorrow."

Allison twined his hair around her fingers, savoring his warmth, the strength he possessed. "You'll not get off as easy as Mack. I want a big wedding. I want my mother here."

He chewed playfully on her neck. "That means we'll have to wait to . . . you know."

Her whole body tingled at his touch, and she was tempted to agree to running to the preacher this very minute. But she lifted his head away from her. "Our families should be with us."

Cade groaned, then nodded. "You're right."

"Maybe this would be a good time to contact your fa-ther?" Allison asked hopefully.

He heaved a heavy sigh. "I've already done it. I had Belle mail the letter today. After seeing what Tyler went through because of his family feuding, I knew I had to do some-thing."

Allison rose on her toes and planted a kiss on his cheek. "That's wonderful, Cade. You'll be glad."

Cade suddenly swung her into his arms and whirled her around. She circled his neck and giggled with delight. "I won't be glad of anything again, Miss Allison Augusta Tre-maine, until I have you as my wife."

She met his lips hungrily. "Let's go tell everyone."

They walked into the house through the kitchen door and found Holly perched on a stool, pressing a round cutter into cookie dough. Georgia hovered beside her.

Lydia looked up from the table beside the window and smiled. "Well?"

Allison smiled, a smile that said it all.

Lydia squealed with excitement and hurried to them. She hugged Allison and gave Cade a peck on the cheek. "I'm thrilled!"

"Praise be!" Georgia wiped her hands on her apron. "This calls for a celebration. I'm fixing a special supper for you two tonight."

"Come over here right now, both of you." Lydia guided Allison toward the table. "We've got plans to make."

From upstairs a loud crash sounded. Allison looked at Cade, knowing already what he would do.

"I've had all of this I'm going to take," Cade said. "If you ladies will excuse me?"

He strode through the house and took the steps two at a time. Falk sat outside Tyler's closed bedroom door, his big bulk dwarfing the chair. He rose when Cade approached. Cade glared at him, daring him to interfere. He didn't. Falk stepped aside and Cade went into the bedroom.

Tyler stood in the center of the room, a glass figurine held high over his head, ready to smash it to the floor. He wore a white linen shirt and dark trousers held up with new suspenders, more appropriate clothes for the grandson of a wealthy industrialist, obviously purchased by Devlin. He gasped when he saw Cade in the doorway.

"Cade!" The figurine slipped from his hand as he ran across the room.

Cade pushed the door shut and caught Tyler in a big bear hug, pulling him off the floor. The boy clung to him.

"I missed you, Cade. I didn't think I'd get to see you ever again."

"I didn't think I'd get to see you either, son." Cade patted his back and gave him a final squeeze.

"How are Vance and Clare? Is Belle feeling all right? Who's playing piano for you now? Are the girls doing their routines all right?"

His face was bright and animated, but Cade saw past the eagerness to the dark circles under his eyes, the tired, drawn lines. He looked as he had when he first arrived at the Pleasure Palace. He hadn't been sleeping well, probably having nightmares again.

"Everybody is fine. Everybody misses you."

Tyler smiled, then his bottom lip began to quiver. "I wish I could come back."

Cade squeezed his shoulder. "We need to have a talk."

He looked around the room for a place to sit. The bed linens were heaped in the corner and the mattress lay half off the springs. Every drawer in the bureau was open and pulled completely out, the contents scattered everywhere. Clothing from the armoire littered the floor. All the pictures either hung crooked or were missing. Bits of broken glass glistened in the afternoon sunlight that beamed through the windows, the drapes buried somewhere amid the rubble.

Cade put his hand on Tyler's back, urging him toward the blanket chest that sat against the wall beside the window.

Cade closed the lid and sat down. "First of all, I owe you an apology."

Tyler sat down beside him, his feet dangling. "For what?"

"I misjudged you badly when you came to the Pleasure Palace. I thought you were simpleminded and slow-witted. I didn't realize the reason you didn't understand things was because you didn't speak English very well."

Tyler shrugged. "It's all right."

"I wish you had told me the truth, Tyler, about not understanding things. And about Wes Palmer being after you, and your grandfather hunting you down."

"I was afraid," he said in a small voice.

"I understand now the sacrifice you made in playing the piano in the Pleasure Palace. You knew your grandfather would find you if you played, didn't you? I want you to know I appreciate it."

Tyler grinned. "Well, I was tired of washing dishes anyway."

Cade chuckled and patted the boy's knee. "You've got to promise me, son, you won't keep secrets from me anymore. I can't help you if I don't know what's going on."

He considered it for a moment. "All right. I promise."

"I've got some good news to share. Allison and I are getting married."

"You are?" His brown eyes widened. "She's a nice lady."

"That she is. Probably nicer than I deserve. It makes me feel like the luckiest man in the world."

"I wish I could be here to see you get married."

"Well, I think we can arrange that." Cade looked down at Tyler. "Allison and your grandpa and I have been talking, and we all agreed that we'd like you to come live with us."

Tyler froze. Then slowly he lifted his gaze. "Do you mean you and Miss Allison would be my mama and papa?"

Color had drained from his face and Cade could see that his breathing was slow and labored. He understood Tyler well enough to know where his thoughts were at this moment.

"Nobody will ever take the place of your parents, Tyler," Cade said softly. "You're never going to love anyone the way you loved them. They were two very special people. They deserve that special love you had only for them. Allison and I will never take their places. We know that.

"But I think you and Allison and I would make a fine little family all our own. It sure would make me happy to have you with us. Allison feels the same way."

He swallowed hard. "What about my grandfather?"

"We all agreed this was best."

"I don't have to go to Boston? Ever?"

Cade shook his head. "No, not ever. Your grandfather can't change his mind. I told him I want you legally. Permanently."

A tiny smile tugged at his lips. "I'd belong to you? Not just staying with you, or working for you, but I'd really belong to you?"

Cade smiled. "You'd belong to me forever."

"I'd like that."

The boy leaned close and Cade gave him a hug.

"There's a few more changes going on in Brighton you ought to know about," Cade said. "I'm closing up the Pleasure Palace."

Stunned, Tyler sat up straighter. "Why?"

"Because your grandpa and I are starting a new business here in Brighton."

"But what about Vance and Belle and Clare? What about the dancers?"

"Every saloon in town has been trying to hire Vance away from me since I got here, and Belle is going to San Francisco. If I know Clare, she's about ready to move on anyway." Cade rubbed his forehead. "And those dancers, they can go anywhere they want as long as they're not around me."

"Where are we going to live?" Tyler asked.

"You and I will stay at the Pleasure Palace until the wedding, then I figure Allison will want to live here until we can get a place of our own built."

Tyler frowned. "Is my grandfather going to be here?"

"For a while, but he's got business to attend to in Boston."

"I don't like him. Mama cried when I asked about him once. Papa said not to ask about him anymore."

The bitterness that separated Devlin Blackwell and Tyler's father had caused heartache for so many people, Cade thought, and he wasn't sure who was right. Devlin Blackwell for hating the man who stole his daughter and lived off his grandson's musical gifts even though performing made the boy physically ill, or Tyler's father for keeping his wife and son away from the one man who would crush them with his tyrannical love.

"They had their differences," Cade agreed. "But that doesn't have any bearing on how your grandfather feels about you. He used to sit in the audience just to see you."

"He did?" Tyler frowned, then shook his head. "I still don't like him."

"You don't have to like him," Cade said. "But you do have to be respectful."

Tyler mulled it over for a moment, then nodded. "All right."

"Allison is taking over teaching at the school here. Miss Warwick is leaving."

"Why?"

Cade didn't want to get into the whole story of Devlin

and Rebecca's past. "She was ready to move on. And that means you can go to school again."

Tyler shrugged. "I've never been to a real school before."

"Well, it's time you went."

Tyler drew his legs up and wrapped his arms around his knees. "Can you bring the Steinway out here so I can play?"

Cade shook his head. "No. You don't need to play the piano for a while. You need to go to school, get into a few fights, kiss a couple of girls, and learn a little more about life."

A little blush pinkened his cheeks, then he looked solemn. "But I've got to play."

Cade thought for a moment. "All right. I'll donate the piano to the church. God gave you that gift. You can share it with Him on Sundays, provided you don't get sick."

"I'm doing better," Tyler said proudly. "I only got sick that one time I played for Miss Devaine."

Of course it had taken Belle, Vance, Clare, and Cade to keep him distracted until showtime, but he'd gotten to each performance without throwing up first. Cade smiled at him. "You're doing a lot better."

Tyler was quiet for a moment. "My pa said I would play the piano all my life. He said it's what I was meant to do."

"He may have been right," Cade agreed. "But I think you need to learn a few other things along the way, such as what it takes to run a ranch and a factory. Then you can decide for yourself which you'd rather do when you get older."

Tyler nodded. "Can I go back home with you today?"

"Sure. Right after supper."

He jumped to his feet. "Good. I'm hungry."

Cade rose. "Me too. Get this place cleaned up so we can eat."

Tyler glanced around the room and shrugged. "The housekeeper will clean it."

"Oh, no." Cade shook his head. "You made this mess. You clean it."

"But—"

"Better get started." Cade picked his way across the room.

He looked around at the mess in horror. "But—"

"Think about it the next time you feel like throwing a tantrum."

"But—"

"Hurry. You don't want to miss supper." Cade closed the door behind him, leaving Tyler alone.

Allison waited in the hall. She took a tentative step forward. "Well? Is he happy about us getting married?"

Cade closed his arms around her and muzzled her neck. "The only one happier than Tyler is me."

She giggled and snuggled closer. "Aunt Lydia is making all sort of plans. We're going to have the biggest wedding in the history of the state."

"As long as it's the soonest," Cade mumbled and kissed a hot trail across her throat.

"It will be, I—"

Cade smothered her promise with a long kiss.

"You promised me it wouldn't be this long, dear wife of mine."

Allison smiled up at Cade. "I like the sound of that, husband."

He slid his arm around her waist and pulled her closer, unconcerned now about propriety. Dressed in her mother's wedding dress brought all the way from New York by her family, Allison was his wife, for all the world to see.

"Even with the work at the factory these past two months," he said, "this is all I've had on my mind."

"Our wedding day?"

He leaned down and planted a kiss on her lips. "Our wedding night, actually."

Allison blushed. "Shhh. Not so loud."

He chuckled and hugged her closer. "I don't think people are much interested in us anymore."

Around them, the Pleasure Palace was filled with family and friends, and most everyone in Brighton. The former saloon looked as if it were the finest New York reception hall now, decorated with white linens, silver, and crystal, each detail fussed over by Aunt Lydia and Allison's mother. A lavish buffet had been laid out, punch and liquors flowed steadily, and a musical ensemble commissioned by Allison's father had arrived this morning, only hours before the ceremony in Reverend Kent's church. Everyone was laughing, talking, dancing, or huddled together at the tables, the good folks of Brighton melding easily with the wealthy Easterners in town for the wedding.

"I disagree," Allison pointed out. "I know at least two people who are very interested in every move you make."

Cade followed her line of vision across the room to the table by the door. Devlin and Lydia sat engaged in conversation with Clint and Estel Jessup, Cade's parents.

"I'm so glad they made the trip." Allison glanced up at Cade. She'd been with him when they arrived at the depot, his father clutching a cane, but standing tall and straight. All five of his sisters had come as well, accompanied by husbands, nieces, and nephews, some he'd never met. Everyone had cried.

Cade nodded. "I missed them."

"Aunt Lydia and Devlin have been quite close all day."

"Have they?" Cade grinned. "You're the only thing I've seen today, Mrs. Jessup."

Allison flushed at his bold gaze. She drew in a deep breath. "Now, have we taken care of everything? The train leaves tonight at six. That only gives us a few more hours to handle everything."

"Stop fretting. Esther Wade is taking over at school and Lydia will handle the ladies' club. Tyler is staying with Mack and Jenna. Everything is under control at the factory."

"See? Didn't I tell you Satch Wilkens would make a good foreman?"

Cade rolled his eyes. "What makes me think I'm going to hear that again in the years to come?"

Allison turned into Cade's arms and pressed her palm against the front of his coat. "Because women know things men don't."

He grinned and circled her waist. "Is that so?"

"It most certainly is," Allison said. "Didn't I tell you I'd find a way to reopen the Carriage Works?"

"You didn't have anything to do with it. Devlin got the idea from an Eastern investor who—"

Allison smiled broadly. "An Eastern investor? Really? And whom do you suppose that might have been?"

He regarded her warily, then grinned. "You? You're the silent partner?"

"Yes. I approached Devlin with the idea of doing something with the Carriage Works and he came up with the notion of manufacturing replacement parts for trains." Allison ran her fingers down the front of his shirt. "When he suggested you should run the place, I gave you a hearty recommendation."

Cade grinned and traced the outline of her jaw with his finger. "Are there any other secrets you know?"

"Well, maybe one or two." Allison batted her lashes coyly. "Aunt Lydia is traveling back East with Devlin."

"Is that right?" He chuckled. "Well, good for them."

"Jenna is expecting."

"She is? Already?" Cade looked across the room and spotted Mack standing with Vance. "Well, that old dog, he didn't even tell me."

"Mack doesn't know." She grinned up at him. "See? I told you women know things men don't."

He frowned. "You'll tell me first, won't you? I don't want half the town knowing I'm going to be a papa before I know. Though, at the rate we've been going, I don't know how it will ever be possible."

They'd both been so busy in the last few weeks with Cade getting the factory going and closing down the Pleasure Palace, and Allison taking over the school and keeping the ladies' club going, they'd had little time together. Then their families had arrived and there had been planning, planning, and more planning for the wedding. Nearly everyone in town had them over for supper, they'd had an engagement party at Lydia's, and two months had gone by with no time spent alone.

Cade glanced around the room, then settled his gaze on Allison, his eyes gleaming. "But I can solve that problem now." He swept her through the crowd and into the deserted kitchen.

"What are you doing? Our guests—"

Cade lifted her into his arms. "Hell with the reception.

I've waited two long months and I'm not waiting another twelve hours on the train to San Francisco."

Allison looped her arms around his neck. "Now? But—"

He looked deep into her eyes. "I love you, Allison. You're my wife. I want to make you mine completely. Let's go upstairs."

Love swelled inside her. She brushed her lips against his ear and whispered, "My pleasure."